BRUTAL SECRET

Hot Alphas. Smart Women. Sexy Stories.

BRUTAL SECRET

New York Times Bestselling Author

LAURELIN PAIGE

Cover photography: Anthony Dehodencq

Cover model: Lucas Weslet

This book may contain subjects that are sensitive to some readers.
Please visit www.laurelinpaige.com/brutal-secret for content warnings. May include spoilers.

I am an only child, but my mother came from a big family like the Sebastians. All those members can be confusing.

To help sort that out, you can find a family tree on my website.

To Ann who asked if I'd meant to write a romcom and then was able to convince me that a little humor would not destroy my grumpy cat brand.

And to Kayti and Ryan who provided much inspiration for Lina's quirks. Thank you for living weird lives so I can steal the gold. You better believe there will be a book in the future with a mother cutting her child out of her inappropriate shirt when said child refuses to change and perhaps one with a girl who doesn't respond to questions because she forgets she's there.

CHAPTER ONE

LINA

Denny sets our drinks on the high top and leans close to my ear so I can hear him over the club noise. "The bartender over there wants you to shut up and take his dick like a good girl."

"Ha ha. He does not." I take a sip of my drink and cringe at the initial sour taste. "He does, however, make a mean lemon drop martini."

Denny takes a pull of his beer, his brown eyes cast toward the bar. "Watch. He keeps looking over here at you. He wants between your legs, Lina. I'm telling you."

I refuse even a glance because my best friend is just being an ass by making light of my serious endeavor to get laid by the end of the night. I purse my red-painted lips and scowl in his direction. "You shouldn't be allowed to make sexual jokes if you aren't a sexual person."

"Then you shouldn't be allowed to make dad jokes since you're not a dad."

Hmm. Does he have a point?

No. Fuck that. "That's not fair because dad jokes don't

really have anything to do with being a dad. They're just stupid, silly jokes that—"

Denny cuts me off. "Quick. He's looking at you right now."

I'm a sucker because I look. "Which one? None of them are looking—Oh."

I gasp, not because anyone's staring at me, but because one of the bartenders is Dreamy with a capital D. Completely my type, as far as looks go. Tall with dark hair and broad shoulders and a devil smile that makes me weak in the knees, even in a dark club like Spice and from several yards away.

Or maybe that's the lemon martini. It really does have a kick.

"The one who looks like beardy Superman. You see who I mean?"

I know exactly who he means.

"Yeah, he's hot. Ten out of ten. Would bang. But no way he'd bang me, so maybe keep on the lookout for someone more in the six to seven range, which is probably more my lane." I reluctantly turn away from the eye candy so I don't look like a weirdo gawker. "Also, he's probably a decade older than me."

"First of all, no. You are not lowering your standards just so you can earn the outdated label of no longer being a virgin. Second of all, you look objectively hot tonight. Not even an opinion. You're bangin' right now."

He means I look tame. For me, anyway. I'm wearing a sheer black shirt with a sexy black bra underneath and a tight black skirt that pushes everything in. It's a far cry from the usual colorful graphic tees and craft-fair jewelry I'd wear out for the night.

"Third of all," he continues, "age gap is totally in right

now. But most important of all, Mr. Beardy Superman? Most definitely wants to bang you. Ask me how I know."

"Because he supposedly keeps looking at me."

He shakes his head. Then stops and nods instead. "Yes. He does do that, but also, there's what happened when I went to order our drinks."

Denny can absolutely carry a joke too long, which is absolutely what makes us get along so well, but there's something in his expression that tells me he's being sincere. After ten years of friendship, I'm rarely wrong in the Denny facial interpretation department, and whether it's wise or not, I start to get excited.

"What happened? It was good? It was about me? Tell me right now."

He laughs. "I've been trying to tell you for five whole minutes."

"I'm listening. I'm listening!"

Actually, what I'm doing is clinging onto his shirt with both hands, trying to shake the information out of his mouth like he's a piggy bank.

Though, I'm not sure the coins come out of the piggy's mouth or somewhere else, so maybe that's a bad analogy. Point is, I'm clawing at him, eager for more information.

"All right, so—" He starts to point in the direction of the bar, but realizes he can't with my whole *me* in the way. "Lina, you're going to have to let go of me so I can show you the other guy."

"There's another guy?"

"Yeah, he's—" Again, he starts to raise his arm.

"Don't point! God." I release his shirt, though, and casually sip my drink as I subtly turn until we're both facing the same direction. "Okay, what am I looking for?"

"The suit guy who's fucking around on his phone and chatting up Beardy Superman."

He's impossible to miss. Who wears a suit to a nightclub? Real nice suit, even from this distance. Tailored and shit. Must be the boss or something. One of the Sebastians who owns the place, which is reason alone to not give him a second look.

"What about him?"

"While Superman was making our drinks, Suit Guy noticed he kept looking over at you."

"The bartender? He could not have been looking at me. There had to be somebody—"

Denny puts his finger to my lips to hush me up. "So Suit Guy said, 'Everything you like in a girl, Reid. Hips, lips, and red hair.'"

I swivel to face Denny. "Beardy Superman bartender's name is Reid?"

"Yeah, I guess. Did you hear the part about the hips and lips and red hair? So obviously you."

I nod, and yes, that's me. A curvy big-mouth with unruly red hair. I used to consider it a curse that I got my Dad's Irish coloring when my mother is a gorgeous Italian with thick, dark hair that does what it's told.

Since my father passed away a few years ago, I've grown more into myself. Embraced my mane. Or at least come to terms with it. Tonight it's all blown out and styled, and honestly, this is the best it looks, which is pretty damn good.

I didn't think it was so good that it would attract the hottest guy in the club, but it's my first time in a place like this, so what do I know?

"Then Suit Guy said Superman, er, Reid, should find out if you were a real redhead—ew. But Reid told him to fuck off, so that's a plus in my book 'cause he's obviously not crass. But also, he didn't stop looking at you."

Goosebumps scatter down my arms and the hair at the back of my neck prickles. I swear I can feel Reid's gaze on my profile even before Denny adds, "In fact, he's looking at you again right now."

The hot bartender keeps looking at me, and what he sees is my bestie—who is a man— looking at him.

I grab Denny's face by the chin and steer it toward mine. "Stop staring. He's going to think *you* want him."

He shudders, as if that's the worst thing he can imagine. "*You* stare at him then."

"No, because then he'll think *I* want him."

"You *do* want him."

"I know, but…" I let out a "gah!" that gets quickly swallowed with the swell of the next song.

This is crazy. I dolled myself up and came out to the club hoping I'd find a guy who'd want to take me home and do nasty things to my body, but I didn't actually think it all through. I mean, I thought a lot about the nasty things I wanted done, but I kind of hoped everything before that would just magically happen without any effort on my part.

"What's wrong with you, you goof? Hot guy that's into you is what you wanted."

Denny doesn't get it. Not just because he doesn't get worked up by the opposite sex—or the same sex, for that matter—but because he's charming with all of his social dealings while I'm a trainwreck the minute someone makes eye contact.

"But I don't know how to hot girl back."

I exaggerate my pout, but I really am fussed. It feels like everyone I know is better at this than I am. Better at sex and boys and flirting. They all learned it in high school when I was distracted by my dying father. Then, after he passed away, I was too busy speeding through college and comforting my grieving mother. I spent so much of my free time with her, even agreeing to a trip to her homeland in Italy for *my* graduation present, just to watch *her,* not only jump in bed with the first guy she noticed since Dad's death, but also agree to marry him after a one-week whirlwind romance.

I'm happy for her. Honestly, I am.

By a stroke of luck, her fiancé, aka my future stepfather, lives in New York City so our Brooklyn brownstone—*my* Brooklyn brownstone now, I suppose—isn't far from her new home. So there's that.

Oh, and my soon-to-be stepdaddy is also a Sebastian, the same Sebastians that own Spice and the whole damn block, which means he's as rich as God if not richer.

But now that school's done and Mamma's moved on, I feel aimless. Aimless and behind my peers since I don't have a job and the farthest I've ever gotten with a boy is a very uncomfortable fingering in exchange for jerking him off. Even Denny's had sex, and he would have been happy if he lived his whole life without it. How is that fair?

Not for the first time, I bat my lashes at him and plead. "How about we just go to your place, and we can order hot wings, and you can ravish me, and then we'll watch *Spy X Family* and call it a night?"

"Sounds like heaven minus the part where I ravish you."

I hug his arm and lean my head on his shoulder. "Come on, Denny! It doesn't have to be a big deal."

"If it wasn't a big deal, you wouldn't be this hyper focused on getting a dick between your legs when you can just keep using that dildo my mother bought you for

Christmas last year." For the record, Denny's mom is super cool. "Look, if you really want to forget the whole thing, then fine. But how about you first try a little. You're here. You're hot. You have a hot guy eyeing you, who probably thinks I'm your boyfriend because you can't seem to keep your hands off of me."

I push him away so fast I almost topple over.

"Okay, dork," he goes on. "I'm not sure you can handle a second one, but now's when you go and order another martini. From the hot bartender, in case that needs clarifying."

I feel my face heat at just the thought of it. "Alone? Where will you be?"

"I think the DJ's about to go on break. I'm going to ask him what inspired that last mix of his."

And I'm the dork.

He's already walking away, so I grab his arm again to stop him.

"But what am I supposed to say?"

"Hi, I'd like to order a lemon drop martini?" He shrugs. "I don't know, Leen. Figure it out. Text me a picture of his ID if you decide to leave with him so I can point him out in a lineup if you end up in the Hudson. Otherwise, come find me, and we'll go."

I can tell he's over this—over me and my anxiety.

"Fine," I sigh. "Hate you like I love you."

He's too far away for me to hear if he returns our catch phrase, which means I'm officially on my own. Dammit.

But this time when I peer over at Reid (aka Beardy Superman, aka Hot Bartender), my breath stops because he's one thousand percent looking at me. No questions asked. And as soon as he realizes I'm looking back at him, he lifts his chin in my direction and winks.

Or maybe it's a trick of my vision and he's winking at the man who just ordered, in which case, Denny was way off on his analysis of what was going on when he ordered our drinks, and of course the only way I can know for sure is to pull my panties up and go talk to him like a big girl.

It takes all my nerve and the rest of the lemon drop martini, which I finish off in one large gulp, to force myself to leave the high top and make my way through the crowd, but I do. I get to the bar and take a post at the side opposite of the Suit Guy, who seems intimidating and already too involved in the hookup I'm trying to, uh, hook. I settle in between two stools and straighten up to my full five-foot-nine height so I won't be overlooked. Then I wait for Reid to finish up his current transaction and come take my order.

It's almost hypnotic to watch him, actually. And believe me, I'm watching. There's a rhythm to the way he moves. It's a kind of dance. He leans in to hear the customer on beat one, moves back to grab a glass while simultaneously snatching a liquor bottle on beat two. Beats three and four, he pours. Then—

"What can I get you, honey?"

I'm jolted from my reverie to find the bartender staring at me. A different bartender. Not Reid because, of course, I forgot there were three of them working behind the counter, and I wasn't paying attention to the fact that one of them was closer to me and apparently not busy.

There's probably something suave to say in situations like this. *Oh, thank you, I'm still deciding,* and then mosey my way over to the guy I want to be talking to. Or hell, I know his name. I could just say, *I'm waiting for Reid,* though that might get awkward when *Reid* discovers I know his name and then I'll have to explain everything Denny overheard, which will get *really* awkward.

Or maybe I won't have to explain it *all*, but knowing me, it will come out of my mouth like word vomit anyway, and now that I just thought of the word *vomit*, I feel really stupid and unsexy and completely out of my depth here.

So instead of saying anything at all, I chicken out altogether and run.

With no thought but escape, I dart down a dark hallway beside the bar, hoping it will lead me to the restrooms. Instead, I find something better—a propped open door that leads outside. I slip through and find myself in a courtyard within the Sebastian Center. It's empty, which is surprising for a hot August night, but I can't find the bandwidth to care about that because I'm too busy being mortified.

"What the hell is your problem, Lina?" Yes, I talk to myself. Out loud. Usually when I'm alone. "You can't even talk to a normal looking bartender, and you thought you were going to…what? Sweet talk the hot one?"

As if he'd overlook my complete awkwardness and inelegance and think, *hey, I'd like to take that girl home to fuck.*

"Yeah, fat chance."

Then, as if the universe wanted to prove that I could indeed be more embarrassing to myself than I already am, a deep, gravelly voice chimes in behind me. "I hope I'm the hot one."

One guess who I find standing there when I turn around.

Lord, kill me now.

CHAPTER TWO

LINA

I'm not good on my feet, so I say the first thing that comes to my mind, and it's straight up ridiculous.

"I was practicing for a play," I say as I turn around. "It takes place in a bar, and there's two hot bartenders. Three, actually. It's a whole Why Choose sort of situation. Very complicated."

He stares at me, his eyes narrowed like he doesn't believe me. Which is a little offensive because he doesn't even know me. What if I really am an actress who's struggling with her lines and decides the best time to rehearse them is on Friday night at the club? Maybe I'm a method actor. He should give strangers the benefit of the doubt and not immediately decide they're lying, even when they very clearly are.

I don't double down on the deceit—something I am very prone to do—because just then he steps forward into the light. The man was heaven to look at when we were in a darkly lit space, but now? The lamp lands on his face just right and he might as well have been hit with a spotlight.

His thick black hair is tousled, his jaw square, and his shoulders broad. He wears a simple white short-sleeve Henley, and with his arms crossed it's evident he does some lifting.

The thing that makes my breath catch, though—or rather, *things*—are his eyes. They twinkle with a devilish glint, like he came out here looking specifically for trouble, and he's pretty sure he found it.

"Oh, Jesus, Mary and Joseph, I am not prepared for this." Have I mentioned that I have no filter?

The glint brightens. "Another line from your play?"

"No," I say, as if it's obvious. "Plainly, I'm not prepared for my play."

"Hence why you're rehearsing."

"Exactly."

It should feel like a win, but the creases near his eyes look like they're fighting a smile. Really, what do I expect? I'd be laughing at me, too. I sort of wish he'd just be more transparent about it so I can hang my head in shame and run off in mortification, this time to somewhere he won't follow me. Like the women's restroom. Or the Hudson River.

I don't know what to do with this in-between thing he's giving me—this humorous sort of scowl. Not knowing what else to do with them, I swing my arms back and forth, then realize I probably look like even more than an idiot, or at least, like a kid, so I stop suddenly, clasp them behind my back, and try to stare at his forehead so I don't get consumed by the weight of his gaze. "So…"

"You aren't supposed to be out here."

Oh. Fuck. I glance around, noting the bench and the outdoor ashtray, and the propped door behind him. This time I see the clearly painted *Employees Only* on the glass and realize it's a break area of sorts. It makes more sense now why I'm the only one out here.

"Well, shit. I didn't—" I point to the sign. "I should have because it's written right there. I was just." I wave my arms in a way that probably looks more like I'm trying to throw up rather than what I'm going for, which is a sense of drama. "Lost in character."

"It happens." He leans his shoulder against the lamp post, and I literally bobble because the sight is so hot it makes me dizzy.

"More than you would think. Like, so…much…more." *Oh my God, I'm unhinged.*

And the thing is, I made a specific vow—this morning, actually—to try to be less unhinged. In general, but with men specifically. It's one of the reasons I want to shed my virginity label so badly, because the anxiety of not knowing what it's like, or how it will happen, or *if it ever will* is this enormous, looming…thing…that influences way too much of everything I am. With it out of the way, surely I'll be more grounded.

Or less desperate, anyway.

Less uncertain, certainly.

But I'm never going to get a guy to want to take me to his bed if I can't have a normal conversation with him first. And fuck it. This guy already thinks I'm batshit, so might as well take the opportunity to practice what I should have said to him in the first place, so that it's not so hard the next time I'm faced with a guy way out of my league.

I mean, if I ever decide to go looking for a hookup again after this. Right now, it's looking pretty unlikely.

"Hold on," I say.

I put my finger up as if he isn't already waiting for me to do something—leave, probably—then turn around to face the direction I was in when he came out, preparing for my do-over. I catch myself before saying the word *rewind* out loud, but a stupid little whirring noise comes out of my mouth instead, which is infinitely worse, so when I turn back around toward him, I know my cheeks are flaming.

"What are you do—?"

I cut him off, without meaning to, the do-over speech already spilling from my lips.

"Actually, Reid. I'm not practicing for a play. I was really coming to talk to you, and then when you heard me call you hot, I panicked. I don't know why I chose to say I was rehearsing because I'm not an actress or into theater at all. Not since the time I tried out for *Noises Off*, anyway, and flubbed my British accent so bad that it sounded French and, which—I know. They sound nothing alike. And then I knocked over this set piece and spilled this bucket of paint, and I had to swear never to step foot on a stage again, and all of it was super mortifying, which maybe that's why I thought of it because this moment is also…"

It occurs to me suddenly that I said his name when he never told me.

"I only know your name because of my friend. I'm not, like, stalking you. He overheard it. When he was getting us drinks. He wasn't stalking you, either. He also overheard you might be into me maybe, which is really—" I let out a short laugh "—when I think about it. But he was fairly certain about it, and he insisted you were throwing me looks. The good kind of looks. Not like you were snake-eyeing me from a distance. And I was skeptical, because look at you. But I'm working on being more confident and put together, though it probably doesn't seem like it right now. Far from, I'm sure. The point is I'm trying. And this is me trying."

Another short laugh slips out—this time it's more of a horrifying snort, which seems about right—because did I really just quote Taylor Swift lyrics to the hot AF zaddy standing in front of me?

And as much as I want to sneak away into the background and let the darkness envelop me, I realize that dammit, I missed a crucial point.

"I'm into *you*, if that wasn't obvious," I add. "In the let's hook up sense, I mean. Across the room, I thought I would be interested, anyway. And now that I've seen you up close, I'm…still. Or more, even. No *or*. Just more."

I'm officially never leaving my house again.

He speaks up before I have a chance to do or say something even more unhinged. "You have your ID?"

Yep. He thinks I'm a child. I'd thought I couldn't be any more humiliated. Always learning new things about myself. So fun.

"I'm legal. I swear it." I dig for my ID in my bra—because that's where I keep it and my phone since clothes manufacturers still aren't making women's clubwear with pockets—and cringe when it comes out damp from boob sweat.

He steps forward to take it from my hand, and I manage to not apologize for the said boob sweat by focusing on a thought that hadn't occurred to me.

"Unless…There's not, like, a waiting period, is there? Twenty-one on the day counts. Right?"

Reid studies the card in his palm, and I try not to think about how dorky I look in the picture that only arrived in the mail yesterday. "Today's your twenty-first birthday?"

I nod, then stop nodding. "It's not midnight yet, is it?"

He gives a slight shake of his head. "Happy Birthday. Emmalina."

The way he adds my name to the end puts emphasis on it. Makes the choice to speak it sound purposeful and deliberate, and the sound of it on his tongue is so good, I don't even mind that it's my real Christian name, which I've always hated. It sounds so good, in fact, that it sends a stupid shiver through my body and makes me audibly sigh.

I scramble to cover it with a clearing of my throat. "See. Old enough. I'm a trainwreck, but I'm old enough."

"Can't be too cautious, these days." He hands my card back and starts walking toward me. Swaggering, really. The kind of stride that only a self-assured man can pull off.

I tuck my ID in my bra again and walk backward as he approaches. Impulsively. Until my thighs hit something metal, and I fall on my ass.

Fortunately, what I hit is the bench, and my ass hits the seat instead of the ground. Reid doesn't pause at all. Just keeps coming until he's standing right in front of me.

Then he leans over, and braces his hands on the back of the bench so that he's hovering over me. So close that when I tilt my head up, his lips are mere inches from mine.

"Serving someone underage is bad enough. It's another thing altogether when you fuck them."

"Oh." I'm pretty sure I've forgotten how to breathe. "So…that's a yes, right? That came about quicker than…" My words trail away when his scent hits my nose. Woodsy with a touch of citrus that I imagine is from working the bar or the lingering of my martini on my own breath. And is that a hint of spice?

Maybe if I just raise my head…

"Are you…sniffing me?"

I shake my head. "Nose tickle. I'm fine." Fine is now the word I use for freaking out. It's all good.

His lip curves up on one side, a half-smile that makes

my stomach somersault. His eyes, on the other hand, turn dark, and I'm half sure he would eat me up if I let him.

So, do I let him?

"Here's how this is going to happen." He nods toward his left without moving his gaze from mine. "That door over there leads to the parking garage. It's the quickest way to the street. There's a hotel on the next block over. A five minute walk. I'll get us a room, order some birthday champagne, and then I'll fuck you so hard you won't be able to walk for a week. You'll stay all night in case I wake up and want to do it again, which I will. In the morning, we'll part. No last names exchanged. No phone numbers. That's it. One night and that's all. Sound agreeable?"

The rumble of his voice is hypnotic, and I have to blink a few times to try to process everything he's said. A hotel. Okay. A hotel is safe. Hotel is safe. There will be cameras everywhere, and his name will be on the room. Probably won't get murdered.

"Okay." I swallow.

His grin spreads.

"Except…" It flies out of my mouth.

"Except?" He raises a brow, which is so incredibly cool that I almost forget my objection.

Then I remember. "You already saw my ID. Which means you know my last name. Emmalina Quinn is a unique enough name. Easy to find me again, if you wanted to."

The grin turns smug. "I won't."

"Well, thank you very much for being so certain."

"It's not personal—"

I'm not interested in hearing all the reasons he doesn't do repeat business. Whatever. That's not the point. "I'm sure it's not personal. And maybe I don't want to find you again either."

He looks skeptical. Honestly, I am too.

"But the playing field isn't even. You saw my address, too."

"You think I memorized it?" Leaving one arm on the back of the bench, he drops the other one to his side as he draws back slightly.

"You could have. I don't know you. You might have some super talent, or you're just really good at mnemonics and figured out a trick to remember it."

"You give me a lot of credit."

"And are we tied to your agenda just because you're the guy and you're older—I'm assuming—or do I get a say? Not that your whole this-is-how-it's-gonna-happen speech wasn't panty-melting." *Like really panty-melting.* "Because it was, but it seems sort of presumptuous."

"We're tied to my agenda because I'm paying for the room."

"Because you think I can't go halfsies on it? I mean, it sort of depends on the quality of the hotel. I could chip in, at least. A hundred, anyway. Though, I should save enough for a car ride back to Brooklyn, since I won't want to take the train if I can't walk. Fifty. I could put in fifty. Or you can just pay, that's fine. That really doesn't bother me, I'm just saying what if *I* want to wake up in the middle of the night and do it again? Or what if I want to in the morning? Or what if I don't want to sleep at all?"

He moves in so quickly, I don't realize what he's doing until his mouth is pressed against mine. My lips part to let out an, "Oh," and then his tongue slips in, and then oh my God.

Oh. My. God.

Is this what kissing is really supposed to be like? Rough and possessive and all-consuming? He's bossy, and my mouth follows his lead without question. It's as though he wants to take the air from my lungs and make it his own before he gives it back to me, and I'm not mad about it because I feel the same. I grab onto his shirt to bring him closer. Or maybe for support since, even though I'm sitting, I feel like I'm about to fall.

But it's the best kind of falling. The kind of falling that I wish could go on and on. The kind of falling that feels euphoric and somehow also primal. As though this is what I was made for. As though my body is capable of secret pleasures that I'm just becoming aware of. Dirty secret pleasures. The filthiest.

When he pulls away several breathless seconds later, it's much too soon. My core is buzzing, my thighs vibrating. My mouth follows him, and my back arches, until he puts a firm hand on the side of my neck, settling me back in place.

When I open my eyes, he's smirking at me. "This is going to work out just fine, Emmalina."

I bite my lip, and try to get my bearings.

Honestly, I'm used to a little more warning before being kissed. The few boys who've bothered have been the polite, ask-for-consent type, which I've always appreciated. Their kisses were gentle before they grew into more. They were courteous on all counts.

But a kiss has never been as hot as this one. My skin feels charged, and my thighs are slick, and I think Reid's take charge approach probably has a little to do with it. Or a lot to do with it.

Or *all* to do with it.

Point is. "Yeah. I think this is going to work out just fine."

CHAPTER THREE

LINA

Reid takes a step back, which might be my cue to stand up, but I'm not sure my knees will hold after that bananas kiss so I stay sitting. Honestly, I'm a little unsure what the protocol is with one night stand situations. Movies and books tend to skip the in between parts. They go from the couple flirting at the bar to them getting it on in a bedroom, their clothing already discarded, and that leaves for a lot of practical questions.

Like, who takes off the clothes? Do we undress each other or strip on our own?

And do I hang around the bar until he's done working or do we set a time to meet up later?

The intense way Reid is looking at me, it seems he's waiting for something on my part, so stand up it is.

"So when are you thinking all this should happen?" I hear my uncertainty and decide there should be clarification. "I mean, I know tonight. But like in an hour or…?"

"Are you ready now?"

My insides tremble with the force of a small earthquake.

"Now? You can just leave when you want? Or did your shift just finish or something?" I go to pull my phone from my bra to see what time it is and remember that I had to check it in at Spice's front door since it's a no phone kind of club.

"Or something." He has that amused twinkle in his eye that I can't quite read. "Let's do it."

"Awesome. Yeah. I just need to get my phone first." And freak out for a minute because of how fast things are happening.

"Change of plans then. We'll grab your phone and sneak out the side door."

Reid puts his hand at the small of my back and leads me inside. He steers us clear of the bar, perhaps because there's a line now, and he doesn't want to get caught in the crowd.

When Reid realizes the phone check has a line too, he leads me to a door beyond it that says *Staff Only*. He pulls a key card from a chain around his neck and presses it against the sensor. It opens into an empty hallway.

Reid asks for my claim ticket, then disappears behind another door that I think must be the employee entrance for the phone check room. My guess is confirmed when he returns a minute later with my cell in his hand.

"Benefit of leaving with an employee," I say, turning my phone on.

"Benefit of leaving with *me,*" he corrects. "One of many."

Just like that, I'm blushing. It doesn't take much, unfortunately. Pale skin saga.

I bend my head over my phone, hoping he doesn't notice. "I just need to text my friend real quick so he doesn't think I disappeared."

"The guy you were with earlier? He's not your boyfriend, is he?"

Explaining our relationship is complicated, and I don't think it's my business to share Denny's personal details. Besides, it's hard to hold a conversation while also texting someone else, so I keep my answer short. "Does it matter?"

"The benefit of anonymous hookups is no baggage. If you're using me to make him jealous or get back at him for something—"

"I'm not using you." It takes effort not to roll my eyes. "Well, not for that, anyway."

I finish up my message and turn on my find a friend app. We used to use the app to find each other on campus. I'm proud of myself for remembering it.

Then I tuck my phone into my bra, with my ID.

When I look at him, Reid is staring at me with amusement. "Have you ever thought of carrying a purse?"

"A purse? Oh. My bra? Is that why you're laughing at me?"

"Trust me. I'm not laughing at you."

"Purses are so…" I make an expression that I hope conveys that I think they're a pain in the ass. "You know, to dance with. And…" I gesture as though I'm stuffing something in my bra. "So much more convenient."

"Convenient for you, perhaps." He adjusts himself, and it's only now that I realize the man is hard.

"Shit. Is that from…?" Again I make the stuffing bra gesture. "Or from…?" I nod my head in what I think is the direction of the courtyard, and the memory of our kiss pushes another blush onto my cheeks.

Or maybe it's the idea that I made a man hard that has my face heating. Without doing much of anything. Like, whoa. That's not a power I knew I possessed.

"From before. But I'm not going to lie—you have nice tits. Bringing emphasis to them doesn't help."

"I'm sorry."

He lets out a deep chuckle that sends tingles to my core. Tingles that magnify in intensity when he caresses the side of my face with his thumb. "You are going to be so much fun."

He kisses me, softer this time, but still with promise, and now I'm hoping I'm the one who will be undressing myself, because the status of my panties is embarrassingly wet, and that's not shit anyone needs to know about.

"Ready?" he asks when he pulls away.

Am I? I have to think about it a second. "Yes?"

"That sounded like you aren't so sure."

"No, I'm definitely, definitely sure. I just..." While I feel safe enough with him, he said it himself earlier—you can't be too careful these days. "Can I borrow your phone real quick?"

"Yours not working?"

"Precautions, is all."

He does that cool one brow raised thing that I've tried to master (and failed) since I was seven, but unlocks it and hands it over.

For a moment, I revel in the power that he's given me. Phones are everything these days. Photo albums and security centers and wallets and journals. I have access to all of it, right here at my fingertips.

Not that I know what to do with it or where to begin. Especially since he's staring at me. So I stick to my plan, open the keypad, and enter Denny's number, the only one I know by heart besides my own.

In case I'm never seen again, this is the number of the last person I was seen with.

I send it and hand the phone back to its owner.

"Texting yourself." He shoves the phone into his back pocket. "You know I'm going to have to block that number after tonight."

I should be annoyed. He clearly is concerned that I'm going to latch onto him after this evening, which I'm so very not. Probably. Maybe. What do I know? I've never had sex, so.

Point being, he has some real trust issues. Considering that I'm the one who is really proving my trust—agreeing to leave with him and all—I don't bother to tell him that it was really Denny who I texted.

"Guess you'll never know whether I have the strength to resist you or not then."

It doesn't even take one breath before he's got his hand wrapped in my hair and braced at the back of my nape. He pulls me close and leans down to my ear. "You don't. Want to know why I'm so sure?"

"Why?" My voice is practically a squeak.

"Because I can smell your pussy, and I've barely even touched you."

"Oh." Like seriously. *Ohhhh.* I'm half embarrassed and half even more turned on.

I'm also not about to miss pointing out the flaw in his thought process. "That doesn't mean anything about the future, though. That's just about now. I mean, you have an erection right now. Does that mean you won't have the strength to resist me? Maybe I'm the one who should be blocking *your* number."

"Maybe." He seems to be fighting a grin as he peers down at me, studying my face.

His pupils are large in the dim hall light. The rims of his eyes, green, though when I look harder, I see there are brown flecks in them as well. They're the kind of eyes a person could spend a lot of time looking into. More than one night. Is it bad that I could see that person being me?

Almost as if he's read my mind, his expression goes serious. "Twenty-one, huh? Are we sure this is a good idea?"

I feel like he's really asking himself, but a sudden desperation clamps around my ribs. "Are you worried you can't keep up?"

"No. Definitely not."

"I don't know. I think you might have to prove it."

"I'll prove it all right." He slides his hand from my neck down my arm to wrap it with mine. Then he pulls me with him down the hallway to another door.

Like the one he'd pointed out before, this one also leads to the parking garage. It's (thankfully) well lit, but it's not a public lot so it's quiet and mostly empty.

Since we're walking, I'm pretty sure his moment of doubt has passed, but I'm nervous he might change his mind again.

Actually, I'm just nervous, period. I'm letting a stranger take me someplace very secluded, and if we make it out of here without him murdering me, then he's going to see me naked. It's weird that my concerns are those two very different things, but both are valid reasons to be nervous, in my opinion.

And when I'm nervous? I say things. Anything that comes to mind. Without thinking.

"It must be cool working at a nightclub. Especially one as elite as Spice. It's like the hottest place in town right now.

I didn't even think we'd get in, but Denny is in this DJ forum—not because he's a DJ, but because he's really into watching and knowing people who DJ. Kinda like a special interest, though I don't know if that term is appropriate because Denny's never actually been officially labeled as neurodivergent by a specialist or anything, but do you have to have a specialist tell you that? It seems if a person thinks of themself as neurodivergent, that should count.

"But anyway, someone in his forum had a friends-of-the-DJ password we could use to cut the line, even though we don't actually know the DJ playing tonight. We still had to pay, of course. And I just realized that maybe I shouldn't have admitted that to a Spice staff member because it's probably breaking a rule or something. So forget I said all that. Not all of it. The first part is still good. The part where I was saying it must be cool to work for Spice. How long have you been there?"

"You know, you're making it hard to keep this anonymous sex anonymous."

"Fuck. Sorry. I wasn't thinking."

He pushes open another door, and when we walk through, we're on the street.

And I haven't been murdered.

Which is a relief. But now that means this guy will definitely see me naked, and also he probably thinks I'm an idiot.

With my hand still linked in his, he tugs me down the street toward the corner traffic light.

"Is it the age gap thing?" I ask, because the nerves make it impossible for me to be quiet. "Is that why you're into this all being anonymous? Does that reveal too much to answer?"

He fights a laugh. "No, it's not too revealing to answer."

When he doesn't give me more—admittedly, I don't wait long—I launch into reassuring him I'm not bothered.

"I'm into it, too, actually. The anonymous thing. One night only. Then walk away. Nothing else. Not for any real specific reason, but because my mom is getting married, and that means…" I stop myself just before I start spilling my family history. "I don't need any complications. Which I guess is probably the same for you. I just wondered if you were stuck on the twenty-one thing. 'Cause isn't banging a younger girl supposed to be a conquest for men your age?"

"How old exactly do you think I am?"

I examine his profile, as though that might be helpful, when in reality, I'm terrible at guessing ages. "You're not… forty, are you?"

He jerks his head toward me. "Forty? You think I look forty?"

"I don't know! I'm not good at ages. Everyone over twenty looks the same to me."

"Then you guess low. So that you don't offend anyone."

"Are you offended?" I can't tell if he is or if he's just making a point.

"Yes, so offended." His tone is dripping with sarcasm.

But I don't think he could admit it if he is, because he seems to want me to think he's sure of himself, which is admittedly part of the hot factor.

"I only guessed high because you seemed freaked out that we might be too far in age, and I thought, 'What would be considered a large age gap,' and I don't know. Someone old enough to be my father, probably, and I thought if I guessed something in that range, you would see I don't have a problem with you being old enough to be my father, and then maybe you'd be comfortable with it too. So in this case, guessing high was supposed to alleviate any possible offense."

"A dozen years is definitely not old enough to be your father."

Thirty-three, then. I clutch onto that little tidbit of information, and tuck it away, like it's a prize. "Not old enough to be my father. So not too big of an age gap. See? Are you really offended?"

"I'm not offended." He pauses. "Twenty-one is just impressionable. I don't want this to mean more to you than it should."

"It's sex, Reid." I look away from him so he doesn't realize I have no idea what I'm talking about. "Most people I know were banging at the age of fifteen. Twenty-one is not impressionable. Perhaps thirty-three is just egotistical."

He laughs. "Point taken." A beat passes. "I really don't look forty, though."

"I'm sure you don't."

"I mean, really."

"I believe you." My grin is wide. *He's sensitive about aging.* Any tidbit from someone who isn't keen on sharing feels significant.

Even though none of this is supposed to be significant. And it's not. It's an item on my To Do list that needs crossing off, that's all.

The light's red when we reach the corner. A handful of other people are already waiting when we join them. Even though it shouldn't be, my curiosity still itches with reasons Reid is so set on a no-strings hookup. "Did you get your heart brok—"

Without warning, Reid wraps an arm around my waist and pulls me against him, his mouth landing near my ear.

"I am really, really looking forward to preoccupying that mouth of yours."

"Just how do you plan on doing that?" I'm not insulted. I talk a lot. I can joke about it.

"I can think of plenty of ways. Really. Naughty. Ways." And then he presses his hips forward, and I'm once again aware that I have, um, affected him.

Or that he's still affected. I don't know enough about how that all works.

What I do know is that his package is intimidating, and that he has plans for said package—really naughty plans—and suddenly I'm hit with how close I am to this thing—this *act*, this possibly overhyped and under-explained experience—that I've worried and wondered about for years.

And for the first time in my life, I get so nervous it actually shuts me up.

CHAPTER **FOUR**

LINA

We cross the street in silence, which makes my mind extra loud. Pretty much the reason I'm always chattering away is so that I don't hear the constant stream of voices in my head.

Turns out, the quiet also makes my body extra loud. In the metaphoric sense. I've never been so aware of my heart-beat. Never noticed the sweat gathering at the back of my neck on a hot summer night. Never realized how tight my chest gets in the presence of a hot guy. My palm is damp wrapped in Reid's. The hotel is only half a block away, and by the time we get there, I'm relieved that I have to drop his hand to enter through the revolving door so that I can subtly wipe the sweat on my skirt.

Well, I attempt to wipe the sweat off. The fake leather of my skirt mostly just moves the moisture around, and since I'm self-conscious about it, I preoccupy myself with finger-combing my hair so that he doesn't reach for my hand again once we're inside. It's disappointing because I really like holding his hand, but it turns out that hair can also be a good absorbent.

When we reach the elevator, my hands are no longer clammy, and I feel a whole lot less gross. But since I've been distracted with the whole am-I-too-sweaty-to-be-fuckable dilemma, I don't realize we didn't stop at the front desk until we're in the elevator and Reid is swiping a hotel card and pressing the button for the fortieth floor.

In other words—he already has a room.

A lot of things get blurry in my head then, and my voice returns to sort them out. "You're a player!"

"What?" He seems unsure whether or not my accusation will interfere with our tête-à-tête, and frankly at this point, I'm not quite sure either.

Hence why I need to do some sorting. "We didn't check in. You already have a key, which means you were already planning to stay here tonight. Logical reasons for that might be that your own apartment is unavailable—maybe you had a pipe burst or the a/c is out—or you just like staying in hotels for fun, which is, I guess, something people might do."

The doors open on our floor. I step out, and continue as I wait for Reid.

"But the most likely reason for already having a key is that you were planning to bring someone here tonight."

He walks out of the elevator after me, then puts his hand at my back and ushers me down the hall.

The warmth of his palm through my sheer shirt is distracting, but I manage to keep my train-of-thought. "Either I'm a fill-in for someone who didn't show up. Or you were planning to pick someone up. Anyone. The first person who looked interested, maybe. Considering how early it is in the night, and that you were still on your shift right before we met, it seems unlikely that you were stood up. Also, I can't imagine you being stood up, so I'm going to go with the notion that you were planning on a random hookup, and who gets a room beforehand unless it's something they do often? I think, by definition, that person is a player."

He stops in front of a door, unlocks it, and motions for me to walk in.

I step past him into the suite. "And if you're a player, this is your fuckpad. But that's kind of dumb to keep the same room if you're trying to keep things anonymous. A girl could just remember the number and come back—."

Reid walks in, and before the door has even closed behind him, he pushes me against the wall, pinning me in place with his hips. This seems to be his tactic—shut me up with his dominance, which should maybe have me grumbling about equality and what not, but it appears I like to be manhandled. I raise my chin because I think he's going to kiss me, or maybe because I'm not really that good at being bossed and I *want* him to kiss me.

He smirks, as if he knows exactly what I want, yet his mouth hovers inches above mine. Teasing. "I have the room so I can be close to the club when I work late." This close, his breath is hot against my skin. "It's practical. But I like sex. A lot. So I bring women here, too. Usually they don't notice we skip check-in, and if they do, I'm not generally worried since a special key is required to get to the residential floors."

My heart is fluttering like a hummingbird, but I play it like I'm unaffected. "This is a residential floor? In a luxury hotel. On a bartender's salary."

Come to think of it, his watch looks a lot like the fancy kind my soon-to-be stepdad wears, and I'd bet money

Reid's shoes are designer. Either bartenders make more than I realize or he has a side gig.

He's not expecting me to *pay* for his services…is he? "I know I offered to help with the room, but I really don't have much on me."

God, that grin. "Room's charged to the club."

"The Sebastians pay for your fuckpad? Sweet deal you got going there."

Honestly, I shouldn't knock it since I'm hoping to get preferential treatment from the Sebastians soon myself.

Fortunately, Reid doesn't seem interested in discussing it. He lifts a curl from my shoulder. "Sweet deal I have going *here*."

I remember what Denny said he'd overheard at the bar —the suit guy teasing him that I was his type. "You gotta thing for red hair?"

"I gotta thing for you, at the moment."

At the moment.

His need to remind me this is temporary at every opportunity is almost comical.

"And those curves of yours…" He pulls back so he can scan my body, and hisses. "Those curves are dangerous."

"Thank you?" My size sixteen hips are not used to adoration. "It is a compliment, right?"

"They're making me crazy. Do you consider that complimentary?"

I bite my lip and nod.

His eyes zero in on my mouth. "I need to know now, Emmalina, if any of this is going to be a problem or if you're going to stop teasing me and let me peel you out of this skirt so I can drive these curves with my tongue."

It's a player line if I ever heard one. Not that I've heard many, but it works. My skin is vibrating with want. Burning up with the need for his touch, in whatever form he'll give. The fact that he has experience only makes me more sure he's the right person to guide me through this transition, from caterpillar to butterfly. From virgin to whore. From desperate to sated.

Dramatic, maybe, but I've been waiting for this moment for a long time.

Still attempting to play cool, I give a one-shoulder shrug. "I suppose this fuckpad comes stocked with condoms? Because I only have one."

He's already figured out I don't have pockets or a purse. His gaze flicks to my chest. "Kept in your bra? Jesus, woman, I need you naked."

I've never been so motivated to strip down in my life.

But when Reid pushes off the wall, he takes my hand and pulls me further into the suite. He leaves me in front of a dining table—*the room's so big it has a dining table*—and slips into the kitchenette. "I believe I promised champagne."

I actually don't have a lot of experience with bubbly. Wine, yes. My Italian mother let me start drinking it at the dinner table in my early teens. Perhaps that exposure is why I've never cared too much about alcohol.

But watching a tall, dark hottie expertly pop a cork, I find I'm suddenly a champagne enthusiast.

Bottle in hand, he grabs a flute from a cupboard and saunters toward me. Actually *saunters*. It's a word I've never seen in motion before. Reid, with his swagger and his relaxed confidence, is the very definition.

He stops directly in front of me. "Happy birthday."

"Thank you." Of course I blush, because awkward is the very definition of me.

He pours some bubbly into the single glass and sets the

bottle on the table. Then instead of handing the glass to me, he takes a swallow himself. Then he kisses me, pushing the liquid from his mouth to mine.

"I prefer champagne with a little tongue," he says afterward.

"That's, uh, really good champagne." I don't give a shit about the champagne. But he can give me alcohol kisses all night long. Can a person get drunk like that?

I might be drunk already. Drunk off his taste and his vibe and the influx of hormones surging in my blood.

He lifts the glass to my lips, and this time when he kisses me, he doesn't stop when the champagne has been swallowed. This kiss grows and grows until I'm grabbing onto him with an urgent need. Every part of me is fire. Every part of me is begging for a relief that I'm certain only he can give, and when his hands find their way to my skin beneath my sheer top, I practically tear the thing trying to get it off of me.

Reid is decidedly more chill than I am. "Easy, there."

As though I don't weigh more than a feather, he picks me up and sits me on the edge of the table. Then he gestures for me to lift my arms, and when I do, he patiently pulls the item off of me and tosses it to the floor.

Which is when I remember the plethora of shit I have stashed in my bra cups. Figuring that's coming off next, I pull items out like I'm unloading a clown car. My phone. My ID. My subway pass. A sweaty and bent business card from a tattoo artist I met earlier in the night. The single square foil packet I swiped from my mother's medicine cabinet.

Reid watches, mesmerized. Not the amusement kind of mesmerized, either. More like I-can't-take-my-eyes-off-this-glorious-sight sort of mesmerized.

It's a nice surprise. I'd thought the see-through top had left little to the imagination. And while I'm a D cup, I always assumed the significance of the curves I have at hip level overshadowed my top side.

Guess I was wrong.

Reid draws a trail between my tits with his finger. "I'm going to want to fuck these later on."

"Okay." Pretty sure he wasn't actually asking permission.

He picks up the abandoned flute, and I think he's bringing it up for me to take another swallow. Instead, he pours it on my chest.

I gasp as chilled champagne drips down the same path he'd traced with his finger and gathers in my bra band.

"Whoops." As if he hadn't spilled on purpose. "Guess I'm going to have to clean that up."

He bends to flick his tongue over the damp skin at the top of my breasts. Then repeats the action a little lower. Then a little lower still, until he's licking up the liquid pooled in my band.

"Did you just make slurping sexy?" *Did I just say the least sexy thing imaginable?*

"Did I?"

I've never been big into soulmates or the idea of a one-true-love, but I might now be convinced that there might be some higher power behind our pairing. Truly, the perfect match for awkward, bumbling, inexperienced me? A cool as shit Daddy who doesn't get distracted by the dumb shit that comes out of my mouth and isn't turned off by the taste of champagne laced with boob sweat.

High praise to the cupids in charge of fucking. Well done.

There's more kissing. Then more teasing of my breasts. Teasing I say, because the man isn't in any rush to remove my bra. Instead, he tugs on first one nipple then the other through the fabric, making them stand at attention like soldiers under Reid's command. Then more kissing before his hands slide down my torso and find the zipper at the side of my skirt.

He tugs the zipper down, then places a hand on my belly and pushes me so that I fall back onto my elbows. It's not a gentle push, but his aggressiveness mirrors my own need. When he pulls my skirt over my hips, I lift them without prompting, more than ready to be stripped down to nothing.

"You're so fucking beautiful." He mutters it under his breath, reverently almost. As though he also recognizes the fates who brought us together for this one night stand, and this is his prayer.

A shiver runs through me, and for a brief second, my eyes prick like I might cry. Compliments can do that to me, which is embarrassing under normal circumstances. If it happens during foreplay, I will never let myself live it down.

Fortunately, I'm distracted from sentimentality when Reid brings out the bottle and pours champagne on my stomach. More specifically, my belly button.

Surprisingly, it doesn't feel as cold as I expect it to, considering all the nerve endings located there. Also surprising is how erogenous that zone is. One dip of his tongue into that hole, and my body practically comes off the table.

On another note, I'm writing to every "first time" article that I read in planning for tonight to demand they add *clean belly button* to the prep list. I can't think of the last time I specifically addressed the area, and I'm absolutely mortified.

Until I spot the bulge pressing against the fly of Reid's pants. Dress pants, I realize now that I'm paying more attention. Nicer than the kind of slacks I'd expect a bartender to be wearing on his shift.

More fascinating is the *size* of the bulge. It's grown since I last looked. Or since I last felt. And it had felt pretty decent in size to begin with. What the fuck kind of gun is this guy packing?

"I can't tell you how much I like the way you're looking at my cock right now." Reid's voice sounds as strained as his fly looks. "Like a greedy little girl. Is that what you are?"

"I am. That. Exactly." Right now, I'm anything he wants me to be. Especially if greedy means really turned on and a skosh scared.

More than a skosh, possibly. I need to get a real handle on the dimensions of his pants monster before I decide for sure.

As if he can read my mind, Reid pronounces, "Rule of the room—you have to come before I bring it out."

I'm about to ask, *come where?* Thankfully, I put the meaning together before making a fool of myself.

"Oh. Really?"

And considering the way his mouth is inching down my belly, it's clear just how he means to make me come.

"Yes. Really." He lifts my foot and removes my shoe before propping it on the table. Then repeats the process with my other foot. The sight of his face framed between my thighs turns me molten.

Sheesh, all he'd have to do is blow across my clit, and I might fall apart right then.

So now I have another dilemma. I was prepared to get through this experience with little to no pleasure on my part. My research says it's quite typical for women not to achieve an orgasm during intercourse, like, ever. I practiced faking it, obviously. But I hadn't expected there would be a spotlight on me at the time.

"I don't mind if we skip that part."

I attempt to sit up, but Reid splays his hands across my stomach and urges me back down. "It's a law, really. I can't break it."

"That's too." *Intimate.* "We can." *Just get to the main event.* "Oh, holy night, what are you doing?"

What he's doing is burying his face in the cotton panel of my panties, which is embarrassing enough, and then he goes ahead and inhales. Deeply.

I want to die.

"You smell fantastic. Soaking wet already. I can't wait to make you come."

"Okay that's nice." Really, nice, actually. I've heard lots of selfish lover stories, so I hadn't really intended to have to admit this. "But I don't orgasm well."

"I'm listening." He wraps his fingers around the elastic waistband of my panties. "Lift your hips, baby girl."

My body does what he commands. Just like that. My hips lift, and he pulls my panties down. Call me a generic pet name, I guess, and all of a sudden, I have no free will. Or maybe there's some setting somewhere that I wasn't aware of—a switch inside my belly button or a lever behind my neck. Something he triggered inside me that gave him charge of my actions.

It's not like I don't want him to take my panties off. I really do. I just expected it would require more coaxing and possibly more alcohol in my system. I mean, I'm practically naked. In front of a man. A hot, hot, hot man. I was not informed of how vulnerable this would make me feel.

Though the way he's looking at me may be all the persuasion I need to do any filthy thing he requires. His eyes are pools of dark. Hungry. Possessive.

Does he want me to deep throat? I gag on just my toothbrush, but for that look, I'll figure it out.

Rather flip me over and do anal? *Please, Reid, make me your slut.*

I'm at his mercy, and that's the most dizzying realization I've had all night.

My only recourse is to stare just as intently back.

He breaks contact first, when he runs a finger over the patch of hair that I asked the esthetician to leave at my wax appointment. "A true redhead."

His voice is barely restrained. Like he's on a leash, tugging at the collar.

"You have a thing for redheads." I grin, convinced now. There's validation in knowing that I have weapons of my own when this guy makes me feel so powerless. My hair color, my curves. Superman's kryptonite is basically just me.

That should help me regain some footing, but mostly it just goes to my head.

Instead of confirming or denying, he presses his thumb between my folds, easily finding my clit. "What were you saying about orgasms? You have trouble getting to the finish line? I'm not afraid of a challenge."

"Uh." Thinking is hard enough under his piercing gaze. Add what he's doing with his thumb, and I'm nearly mindless.

But he breaks eye contact when he bends down, giving me a reprieve, and I take the opportunity to try to explain. "Not necessarily trouble. It hasn't really been a problem, but I actually don't know if—" I catch myself before admitting I've never had an orgasm from another person before and thus don't know if I have trouble when not self-administered. Alone, I'm fine, but I'm definitely more relaxed in those situations.

And while I'm eager to find out what I'm like with someone else, I do have concerns. "What I mean is that when it happens, I'm not very…attractive?" I pause. "That's not a question. It's a statement of fact."

Yes, I've taken videos of myself. Not to give to anyone, but to know. It feels like an important bit of information to have before getting intimate with someone. Fight me.

"I make funny sounds and my face scrunches up and my body does this seize-like thing and—" I'm cut off by the swipe of his tongue across my clit. "Oh."

Oh, as in I'm already halfway to orgasm. Oh, as in I don't think there's any way to stop this. Oh, as in *to hell with vanity, this is going to happen.*

"You taste incredible." This time he licks the entire length of my seam before returning his attention to my very swollen, very sensitive clit.

And here's where hormones do funny things to a head, because even though I know they're just sex-words—standardized statements for particular moments like *great to meet you* and *have a nice day*—my head reacts like it's a real and true compliment, and my face gets so hot that I'm convinced a thermometer would say I had a fever.

No, wait. The heat isn't just coming from the sex-words. The heat is building lower, from what he's doing with his tongue. And his mouth. And his teeth, and oh my, oh my, oh my, I must be a statistical anomaly because it shouldn't be this easy to orgasm the first time it's not self-administered, but that is indeed what is happening and yep, my face is scrunched up tight, and my body is convulsing, and the noise that is coming out of my mouth sounds like someone just stepped on a dog's tail, recorded the sound, and slowed it way down.

Oh, and an incredible joyous heat spreads through every nerve. Pure energy like I've never felt before. Like the sun exploded inside my vagina and now, as my limbs start to settle and my breath returns, I'm nothing but happy, floating stardust.

"So fucking beautiful when you come."

I jolt to awareness. It's not like I forgot Reid was here, but I forgot Reid was here. "Oh, God, I'm so embarrassed."

I cover my face with my hands, only to have them easily removed when Reid plies them off and pins them over my head.

"Most beautiful thing I've ever seen." More sex-words that I'm trying my best not to believe. "Swear on my life."

He stretches his body over mine, and I recognize my scent on his mouth only a second before his lips take mine, and my taste is on my tongue. Which is astonishingly not gross. Or maybe *I'm* gross because not only do I think it's not gross, but I also think it might be one of the hottest things that anyone has ever done to me.

But then thought leaves all together, and all I am is desperation. Desperation so wild and raw that I no longer feel civilized. I tug on Reid's shirt, wanting things I can't put into words. My hips buck, demanding things they don't understand.

He grinds his pelvis against mine, the hard shape of his cock so close and so far away. "I know, baby. You need me inside you."

Yes, that. That is what I need.

With heroic clarity, I remember the condom. I glance toward the items discarded from my bra, eyeing the foil, hoping that's enough for Reid to understand what I'm saying. Praying that there won't be any argument about it.

"That's not going to cut it. I'll go grab a larger size. But first…" He seizes my mouth with another aggressive kiss. A kiss so nasty, I nearly come again. I probably would if I wasn't so preoccupied with his last words.

Because here's the thing—I've practiced putting condoms on my dildo so I wouldn't fumble like an idiot when it came time to put it on. I never really got the hang of it—turns out there's a right way and a wrong way to unroll them—so I planned on leaving that job to my partner. Point is, I know what size that particular piece of latex is. What size it fits. My dildo has decent girth.

And Reid is saying he needs something *larger*?

I was already intimidated. Now I'm verging on alarmed.

It's what he says next, though, that really gets me terrified. When he releases my lips, drags his tongue along my jawline, then settles his mouth at my ear. "You better like it rough, Red, because I don't have the restraint right now to be nice."

It pops out then, like half the things I say do. Without warning. Without permission. Without forethought. Despite having no intention to ever tell.

"I'm a virgin!"

CHAPTER FIVE

LINA

Time stands still.

I've heard people say that before and never understood quite what it meant until now. Reid is frozen above me, his eyebrow arched in that extremely cool way of his. My heart thuds in my chest, but my breath is trapped in my lungs, unable to escape while my head screams that I'm the biggest fucking idiot on the planet.

"Forget I said that," I say. When I get over my horror enough to try to erase my slip.

Reid speaks, practically on top of me. "A virgin?"

I swallow. Then nod because I'm a terrible liar, as noted in my earlier attempt to convince him I was rehearsing for a play.

He places his hands on the table, one at each side of my head, and straightens his arms so he can look down on me. Or at least it feels like that's his intention. "If you're saying that because you think that's what I'm into—"

I cut him off. "I'm not. I don't." Actually, I hadn't thought about it. Isn't the whole antiquated pure-as-snow bride concept based around the idea that men kind of do want untouched women? "I guess you could be into virgins."

He pushes off the table to a stand, leaving me feeling very naked and on display.

Probably because I am practically naked and on display.

Sitting up, I reach for him, trying to recapture the earlier mood. "It's not a big deal. At all." I rub my hands up and down his torso. "Like, I don't think there will be blood or anything. I'm into self-care, if you know what I mean, and I'm sure I broke my hymen years ago, but you said you were going to be rough, and I just worried that might not work out exactly so I thought I should mention it. Especially if you're, um, a big boy, so to say, and whoa those are some serious pecs you're packing under there. Lots of hard things on your body it seems."

For the love of everything holy, Lina, stop talking.

He looks at me with that same confused/enchanted way he did in the courtyard. Not confused *and* enchanted, necessarily. I just can't tell which of the two it is.

"You're not twenty-one?"

Confused it is, then. "No, I'm twenty-one."

He grabs my hands and lifts them from his chest. "You're twenty-one and still a *virgin*?"

"Well, that's sort of judgy." More than sort of, but I'm still hoping to get laid here so I minimize my chastisement. "Look, the important points are that I'm legal and naked and would like to have your cock inside me, please."

I pull out of his grip, intending to place my palm on said cock. Except I'm literally cock blocked when he swipes my hand away and takes a step back. "No."

Sometimes—okay, more like a lot of times—I assume the worst of situations. Birthdays are like New Year's, though.

A good time to make resolutions and try to better oneself, and so I hereby resolve to assume the best about Reid's denial. "You still need to get the condom! Right. Do you want to go get that? Should I come with you? Maybe move this to the bedroom?"

"Only place this is moving is out the door." He bends to pick up my shirt. And my skirt. And my panties. Then tosses them at me.

…and this is why I don't make resolutions.

But also…"Seriously?"

He points at the floor. "Your shoes are down here."

There is not an ounce of humor in his expression. The man is fuck-ass sober.

"And don't forget all your shit." He gestures to the items I discarded from my bra.

I blink several times. "You're seriously stopping this because I'm inexperienced?" It's kind of funny how easily *turned on* can turn into *pissed off*. "Are you *virgin* shaming me?"

"I told you this wasn't supposed to mean anything." Strangely, he sounds as fired up as I am.

"It won't. It doesn't." I pull my shirt over my head, suddenly in as much of a hurry to dress as I'd just been to be undressed.

"I said I didn't want impressionable. Your age is bad enough—"

"*Youth* shaming now."

"Add that you're a virgin? No. I'm not doing it. I refuse to be that important in your life."

"Oh, you're a narcissist. I see." I pry my sweaty, sticky thighs off the table and hop to the ground. "Convinced I'll never get over my one night with you."

"You remember losing your virginity. It's a remarkable moment."

"Says an archaic societal tradition that valued women only for their ability to bear children." My panties on, I start working the skirt over my hips.

Reid stares as I dress, with as much heat in his eyes as when he'd put his mouth on my pussy. In complete opposition to his annoyed tone. "You've kept it for this long. Must mean something to you."

Of course he's too privileged to understand a lack of opportunity.

Before I throw any other comebacks, I turn away from him and take a breath as I stuff my bra with my phone and stuff (minus the unused condom). How did we get from a spine-tingling orgasm and promises of a night filled with sex to this ridiculous conversation? Am I reading him wrong? Can any of this be salvaged?

When I turn back, I'm calmer. Honest. Vulnerable. "It means nothing. Which is why I was trying to get rid of it. It's baggage. I don't want to remember it. I don't want to think about it ever again."

"And maybe you'll go on to have tons of meaningless sex with partners that you never think of again, but the first time comes up in conversation. The first time gets shared with friends over drinks and with lovers, years after the fact. The first time becomes an anecdote. That's not my idea of meaningless or forgettable."

Nope. Not salvageable. He's too big of an ass and obviously needs therapy for his paranoia. "Well, congratulations, Reid with-no-last-name. You have successfully embedded this moment into my memory forever. And I'm still a virgin."

"I'd rather be remembered as an asshole."

"Then you shouldn't have been so insistent on giving me an incredible orgasm before you even had your pants down." I'm not keen on complimenting him at the moment, but I'm more interested in scoring the point. "That's not how you do forgettable one night stand."

"If you weren't a virgin, you wouldn't have thought it was so incredible."

"You're admitting you're only a mediocre lover?"

He takes a step toward me, his expression mocking. "No, I'm suggesting that you're too ignorant to know the difference."

Ouch. Like real ouch.

Because that's the whole drive behind my desire to get rid of this virgin burden. Because I feel left behind by my peers and left out of a very large community of people who aren't ignorant. People who know the difference between a great orgasm and a meh one. People who know what it feels like to be a "good kind" of sore and understand the internal bliss that comes with a freshly fucked glow.

Then, of course, there's the fear that I will always be ignorant. That I'll never be part of the *in* crowd. That I'm not the kind of girl who gets invited into that club.

I can be hurt about it.

Or I can make sure he remembers me too. As an asshole, since that's what he prefers.

"You're right. Absolutely right." I unzip my skirt again and shimmy out of it.

"What are you doing?"

"Admitting the truth. I'm totally obsessed with you already." Grabbing the bottle of champagne off the table, I take it with me to the bedroom. "Memorized your room number, swiped your key card while you weren't looking.

So impressionable that one little orgasm thrust me into my *Fatal Attraction* era, and you called it. Bravo."

The king size bed has been turned down with a mint on the pillow, which I swipe, before plopping down on top of the covers. "Might as well fuck me now since your worst fear has already happened."

Reid, having followed after me, looks at me incredulously from the doorway. "I am absolutely not fucking you."

"Like I'd fuck you now, you arrogant pussy tease!" I take a swig of the champagne and set it on the nightstand. "But I'm also not leaving until you apologize for being such an impertinent turd."

"You want me to apologize?"

"Have you ever done that before? Do you know what an apology is?" Honestly, I just want him to be annoyed.

Also, now that we're not creating our own heat, the room is kind of chilly.

I jump off the bed, head to the closet, and open the door.

"Now what are you—get your hands off my stuff."

His *stuff* is a few more pairs of dress trousers and a single dress shirt. Behind them, I find what I'm looking for—a hotel monogrammed bathrobe. "Perfect."

I pull the robe off the hanger and put it on. "Holy shit, this is high quality." I'm thinking of changing my social media status to *in a relationship with a bathrobe*. "Oh, maybe that's my ignorance talking again. Is this actually poor fabric? Maybe you can tell me."

Objective achieved—the man is definitely annoyed.

"You know what? Fine. Stay. *I'll* leave." He disappears from the bedroom threshold.

Surely it's a ploy.

I trail after, though, because I'm curious.

He stops midway to the door and pulls a keycard from his back pocket—because I didn't actually swipe it—and tosses it at me. "Here, have it. I'm obviously switching to a new suite after this, anyway."

"You still think I'm going to come chasing after you. Amazing."

"Room's paid up until ten am."

"Awesome. I'll order breakfast. Twice."

He ignores my threat, which isn't really just a threat because I wholeheartedly intend to do it. "And, uh, come back to the club, and I'll have you kicked out."

"Like to see you try." I don't think I'm the kind of girl who will use the privilege of the Sebastian name to my benefit, but I might make an exception if my soon-to-be stepdaddy can get a certain bartender fired.

He points his finger at me and opens his mouth to say something, then seems to change his mind and lowers it again. After opening the door to the hallway, he pauses to glare at me. "Enjoy your lonely night dreaming of the cock you'll never have."

"Now that's just low." The door shuts halfway through the sentence, so I'm pretty sure he didn't hear me. Which is just as well, since it wasn't the best comeback.

A second later, a better one comes to mind, though, so I rush to the door, open it, and call after him. "*Dream* about your cock or *forget* about your cock? Make up your mind."

I don't realize there's an older couple walking down the hall in the opposite direction until after I've finished shouting obscene and inappropriate things.

Ugh. What if I get kicked out of a room that's not even mine?

"Inside joke." I fake a laugh, as if everything is fine, and

I'm not on the verge of mad tears. "A different kind of cock. The…never mind."

With a sigh, I shut the door, lean my back against it and slide to the floor.

I'm not going to cry.

I'm not.

It's my birthday, and I won't cry if I don't want to.

Except…

I squint at the microwave clock in the kitchenette. It's past midnight. Not even my birthday anymore. That makes things marginally better. The good part was my twenty-first birthday. This fucked up fallout is just regular old life.

I'm not going to cry.

But if I'm sincere about that, I'm going to need to call in reinforcement.

An hour later, Denny is filling his knapsack with miniature liquor from the suite's fridge while I sit on the couch and mindlessly scroll TikTok. "I can't believe he just left you with free rein of his room."

"His mistake."

I've told Denny the whole story now, minus the X-rated parts, and proving his best friend status, he immediately added Bartender Reid to the Dead to Us Google sheet he created that is literally a list of people we currently hate. Then he recanted his earlier statement about age gaps being in and reminded me that old people don't really understand sex-positivity.

"The front desk didn't even question me when I called them to add you to the room. Saved you the embarrassment of having to walk through the lobby with me in this robe because I wouldn't have changed if I'd had to go down to meet you."

"The streaks on your face are more concerning than the robe. There would have been questions."

Turns out my mascara ran everywhere during my maybe-not-so-incredible-after-all orgasm.

Okay, and I fucking cried. Not a lot, but enough.

"I packed up all the liquor I could fit in my bag. Want me to bring you something? Bourbon? Tequila?"

"No, thank you. But I wouldn't mind some ice cream." I point my phone at the QR code displayed on the side table. "Want anything from room service?"

He pops open a beer can and joins me on the sofa. "What do they have?"

I scroll through the late night menu. "The regular stuff. Margherita flatbread. Quesadillas. Oh, steak. Expensive steak. Wine. No ice cream, but they have chocolate cake."

"Let's order all of it."

"All of it?" Actually, that's not a bad idea. "Everything on the menu. Would they do that?"

"Place like this? Their motto is that they'll take care of all your needs. They'll probably bring you another robe if you ask."

It feels good to laugh, but it fades fast.

"Come here," Denny says, holding up his arm and offering a cuddle spot on his chest.

I scoot over, relishing the warmth of another human body. Trying not to remember the heat that there had been earlier with Reid.

He props his chin on the top of my head. "Did I tell you about that time I tried to read a book about glue?"

"No."

"I couldn't put it down."

I moan. "Did you just tell a dad joke? That's my job."

"I thought you might like someone else carrying the burden for once."

It's the smallest gesture, but it feels so big and nice and unexpected, and I'm half afraid I'm about to start crying again, for real this time, all over Denny's shirt. "I'm so humiliated."

"Why?"

"Uh, were you listening earlier?"

"But who knows about it? Me. You. That asshole prick who is dead to us. We never have to think about it again."

"Wouldn't that be karma? To never think of him again." I chew my bottom lip, still swollen from Reid's bruising kisses. "I guess I can't get him fired then."

"Do you really want to be that girl?"

I shake my head. "We're never going to Spice again."

"We'll never say the fucker's name."

"It will be our secret."

Denny runs a hand over my hair. "We can try another club next week, if you want."

"No. I'm done with this mission. For the time being, anyway. I want to focus on getting Mamma settled in her new life, and figuring out what's next in mine. When it happens—*if* it ever happens—I want it to happen naturally."

"It will happen."

I shrug, not so sure.

Denny squeezes me in a hug. "Don't give up. The right guy will come along. I feel like this is my fault, since I'm the one who pointed this fuckface out to you."

I sit up and stare down at him. "That's right. Which means you get to be the one who calls room service."

"Fine." He reaches over me to grab the room phone. "One of everything?"

"One of everything." It's petty revenge, but it's the Sebastians paying for the room. It will be covered, and hell, maybe Reid will be fired all on his own when he has to explain the bill to his employers.

"Actually," I say, liking the idea the more I think about it, "make it two."

CHAPTER SIX

LINA

I walk into Panache's private dining room ahead of my mother to be sure the blinds are drawn. "All good."

Unable to help myself, I set down the garment bags I'm carrying and pull a window covering back so I can peek outside.

Wow.

The view from the fifty-seventh floor is as crazy unbelievable as I was told. All of Manhattan is visible from this height. Past the Empire, I spot the One World Tower and beyond that, the Statue of Liberty in the harbor with the iconic Brooklyn Bridge on the other side.

"Put that down. Do you want to be seen?" The chastisement comes with a smack on the back of my head from my aunt. Since she was a surprise sibling, born eleven years after my mom, Angela is actually closer to my age and therefore treats me as if I'm her sister rather than her niece.

It's annoying.

"No one's going to see us. Sheesh."

Actually, someone might see us, hence the reason the

blinds have all been lowered. It's apparently quite common for paparazzi to rent out rooms across the way and use long range zoom lenses to try to capture prestigious events held in the Sebastian building. They have even used drones on occasion.

It's still incredible to me that my mother is marrying a man who has to fight for his privacy, and I suspect it will take time getting used to. But seriously. If someone gets a shot of me in my maid of honor dress before the wedding, I don't think I'm going to feel like it's a big intrusion.

If they snapped pics of my mother, though. That's another thing entirely.

I drop the blinds, and turn to find her seated at a vanity station, putting on the fifty-thousand dollar diamond drop earrings that her groom bought her for an engagement present.

With her rich dark hair and classic beauty, she looks like she was meant to wear things that fine.

"The weather is fantastic, Mamma. You couldn't have lucked out better."

Especially, since it's not unheard of to have snow this time of year. Instead, the sky is clear and the current outside temperature is sixty degrees. Incredible for November.

"Isn't it? I think Samuel paid extra for that."

We laugh, but I'm not certain it's a joke. That's how much money the guy has.

Case in point, a survey of the room includes three full hair and makeup stations, five full length mirrors, several food trays, and enough flutes of champagne to get the entire bridal party drunk before the service, all of which might be appropriate provisions if we hadn't gotten ready at a hotel down the block beforehand.

That hotel, to be specific.

It's convenient to the Sebastian Center, so a logical choice, and since I'm never speaking of what happened there that night three months ago—excuse me, what didn't happen—I couldn't come up with any reason to object. Even safely tucked away in a suite several floors down from The (Non)Occurrence, I was a wreck the whole time, hurrying my mother and Angela to get ready faster so that we could get out of there and over here.

Needless to say, my nerves have settled significantly since we got in the limo.

Yes, we drove a block and a half in a limo. Couldn't have a Sebastian family member-to-be seen walking down the street. What would people think?

Also, I suppose there's the tradition of keeping the bride out of view until she walks down the aisle, but there have been a lot of unconventional choices for this event already. Mamma's wearing a pantsuit, for one. With a train, but still a pantsuit. The pantsuit is cream instead of white, for another. I'm giving her away, for yet a third.

She wasn't going to have anyone give her away at all since it's a second marriage for both of them. Samuel had been the one to suggest it be me. Not only was the idea "incredibly thoughtful"—Mamma's words, not mine—but it also felt right, considering it's been just the two of us for a while now.

After today, it will be the two of *them*. I'll be on my own, I guess. I've yet to figure out what that looks like. Thinking about it makes my chest pinch. I grab a champagne flute to help loosen it.

Along with a piece of shrimp because food might not actually relieve pain, but it certainly distracts.

My head is once again smacked before I can dip the shrimp in cocktail sauce.

"What are you doing? You can't eat in your dress. You'll make a mess."

"If you keep smacking me in the head while I'm dealing with dark sauces, yeah. Seems likely." What I hate most is, Angela's right. I'm not abnormally clumsy, but I'm human, and that's enough.

Then why did they bring all this yummy food out here in the first place?

"Stop doing things that deserve smacking, then."

As often happens when Angela and I are together, Mamma steps in to subtly break us up. "Which one of you has my jacket?"

"That's me." I cross to where I dropped off the garment bag, and together with Angela, we spend the next several minutes helping my mother into the overcoat.

Almost on cue, the photographers show up in time to photograph the last bits of prep. They'd been in the hotel suite as well, so they could capture every minute of today's event. On top of their arrival is the return of the makeup artist, stopping by to retouch my mother's look.

Then there's a long stream of people in and out, all with different intentions and agendas: Samuel's assistant with a last minute note about the evening's schedule (the toast will come after dinner now, but before the cake). Denny and his mom with well wishes and the offer of Xanax. The minister, to be sure Mamma's entering this marriage of her own free will. People I've never met before come by. People I haven't seen in ages. Almost everyone snacks on the food and drinks a celebratory glass of champagne, and it's not long before I understand that whoever set the room up knew exactly what they were doing.

With most of the attention on my mother, and Angela at her side like a loyal puppy, I'm starting to feel like lost baggage when my soon-to-be stepsister shows up and seeks me out. "I've been looking for you."

Wearing a satin slip dress that matches mine, Adly and I still look hardly alike. Her brown hair and slim figure could make strangers believe she's my mother's biological daughter if their ages weren't only separated by eight years.

I know. It's kind of gross, but my mother doesn't seem to think the age difference is a big deal. Only time will tell, I suppose, and as Denny likes to remind me, if there's divorce in Mamma's future, the pre-nup assures it will come with a hefty alimony payment.

"So that's how this dress is supposed to look," I say, hoping it sounds complimentary rather than pitiful. "You're gorgeous."

She shakes her head in dismissal. "Fuck that. Slip dresses are meant for curves. Your mom obviously chose her bridal party design with you in mind. Especially the color. I'd wondered if champagne pink would clash with your hair, but damn, Giulia knew what she was doing."

As I am with any compliment, I'm flustered. "The wedding planner helped."

Adly waves off the comment. "I saw what the wedding planner chose. Giulia was right to stand her ground. Anyway, I know there's a million things going on right now and our world can be chaotic and overwhelming, so I wanted to be sure you're good and drop off a little gift."

"A gift?" I take the small blue Tiffany box from her hand, afraid I fucked up some rule of wedding etiquette that I wasn't aware of. Was I supposed to get presents for people? She's already told me she's trying to find a job for me at SNC, which is more than I would have expected. "I don't know what to say."

"It's not that big a deal. I promise."

"Should I—?"

She seems to know what I'm asking. "Open it. Yes. If that's okay?"

Honestly, I'd rather open it in private so I don't have to worry about reacting correctly, but I'm just as bad at no's as I am at reactions. "Oh. Yeah. Of course."

I pull the ribbon from the box and open it to find a double row, hinged rose gold bangle with diamonds. "Oh, Adly. This is…"

It's the most beautiful thing I've ever been given, is what it is. The most expensive thing anyone's given me, too, probably, and that's counting my college tuition, which my mother paid for.

Adly holds up her own wrist. "It's identical to mine."

"Like a friendship bracelet or something?" I'm well aware that most things that come out of my mouth are not in the slightest eloquent.

"I was thinking more like a sister bracelet? If that's all right."

I swallow past the lump in my throat. A lump that has been forming all morning, if I'm honest, what with all the nerves and emotions brimming. "I know I said this before, but I really don't know what to say."

Wait. There's a phrase for situations like this.

I rush to add it. "Thank you. And yes. That's all right. Sister bracelet is all right." I stare at the bauble as I try to wrap my head around the offering. I'm pretty certain Angela would give me away before she would consider getting me a gift, and we're blood related. And Adly already has two real siblings. "I mean, are you sure?"

"Sure that I want to give it to you or sure that I want you to be my sister?" She laughs, but even though she's classy and put together and a dozen years older than me, I don't feel like she's mocking me in any way. "Yes, to both. I'm very sure. I've always wanted a sister. Here, let me…"

She reaches over to take the bangle out of the box and shows me the mechanism to open it. Then she puts it around my wrist and snaps it shut.

Just like that, we're family.

Her hand remains on my wrist. "I know Holt and Steele haven't been as welcoming. That's not about you, I promise. Or Giulia. It's complicated Dad dynamics with Holt. And Steele is just…Steele. He's a little bit of a strange one, so. Men. Am I right? Which is one reason I feel so lucky to have you, and I truly hope you'll let me dote on you the way I've always wanted to dote, and also thank you for making it so I'm not the baby of the family anymore."

I giggle. It was either that or start tearing up, and I'd hoped to make it down the aisle before having to redo my mascara.

…and that's why the makeup artist returned. Yep. Real good wedding planner.

"Thank you," I say again, twisting my arm so the light hits the diamond. "It's beautiful. You're beautiful. I'm lucky too. And excited and overwhelmed, and yeah. Dote on me all you want." Does that make me sound spoiled? "Or don't want. I'm here for, you know. Whatever. Gah. I'm nervous. Ignore everything I say. Not that I'm not sincere. I'm just babbling."

"I understand you perfectly." She hugs me.

Just in time for a photographer to snap a pic.

"Let's get a few more like this," she says, gesturing to her assistant to move the light umbrella. "Adly, could you put the bracelet on her again? That would have made a good shot."

We spend the next quarter of an hour posing for

pictures. My new sister is a pro at it, always standing at exactly the right angle while the photographer adjusts me for almost every frame. I remind myself that she's had a lifetime of being in the spotlight. She probably knew how to do this shit by the time she was out of diapers.

So instead of berating myself for my awkwardness, I follow Adly's lead, and emulate her as much as I can. By the time I think I'm getting the hang of it, the wedding planner bursts into the room. "Thirty minutes until line-up!"

"Oh, shit." Adly turns to me while everyone else scrambles to their last minute readying. "I almost forgot. Um." She pauses. "Don't let this scare you."

The absolute number one way to scare someone is to lead with a phrase telling them to do the opposite. I brace myself. *It can't be that bad, can it?*

"Dad wants to see you before the ceremony."

It's worse than I could have imagined.

"Samuel wants to see *me*? Right now?"

"If it makes you feel any better, he scares everyone. Even his kids. Especially his kids. But he's really not that bad. Usually." Her tone doesn't sound promising.

"Am I in trouble?"

"No, no." She reconsiders. "I don't think so. What could you be in trouble for?"

Nothing that I can think of specifically. But on most days, I'm convinced I might be in trouble for just how I breathe. Especially when I'm around the Sebastians. Their personalities are as big as their bank accounts, all of them poised and self-assured while I'm typically standing in the corner trying to pull a wedgie from my crack.

But this is my life now. Or Mamma's life, at least. I just

have to get through today's spotlight, and then I can go back to hiding in the darkness. "Sure. Uh, where is he?"

"I'll take you to him."

"Okay." I start to follow her to the door but then realize this might be my last chance with my mother before the procession. "Just a second, Adly."

I navigate the throng of mostly strangers to find my mother and steal her away for a not-so-private moment.

Before I get the chance to interrupt whoever currently has her ear, she spots me. "Excuse me. I need a minute with my daughter." She reaches her hand out, and I clasp it as tightly as I did when I was a five-year-old, afraid I might be separated from her in a crowd. "Are you all good? I'd thought this would be just us and low-key, but I guess I misjudged. Are you okay? Nervous? Do you need anything?"

The funny thing is that I've felt more like *I* was the mom since my father passed away. Now she's about to leave me for a new life, and she's suddenly trying to mother me like it's the way back days.

Or maybe she's projecting.

"I'm good, Mamma. And I think this is as low-key as it gets going forward. Can you handle it?"

Terror flashes in her eyes. "I don't know. Can I?"

This is more like our typical dynamic.

I take a deep breath. Part of me wants to tell her that we should run away right now. We were okay on our own, weren't we? Just the two of us. Do things really need to change?

Problem is that I think she really wasn't okay. She was lonely and lost, and if I'm honest, it would be healthier if I had other things in my life too. Like a job. And a boy. Or a dozen. Or at least sex.

"You absolutely can handle it," I tell her. "Not only handle it—Mamma, you're going to thrive. I've never seen you look so beautiful. This is what you want, right? You aren't just marrying him for the money? There are other forms of stability that don't come with million dollar jets."

She curls a finger around a lock of red hair that has fallen loose from its knot. "When did you get so grown-up?"

"Oh my God, don't. Don't be sentimental right now. Just tell me it's what you want, because if it's not, I can have an Uber waiting downstairs in fifteen minutes."

She grins. "It must seem really odd for me to go from cloistered widow to blushing bride as fast as I did." In fact, it has been only five months since she met Samuel at an art fair in Italy. "And Sam is a much different man than your father was."

"Yeah, like, twenty years older."

"Twenty-five years older," she corrects. If she weren't my mother, I'd still be grossing out about whatever that looks like in the bedroom. Age gaps are definitely very, very out. "But when it's just the two of us, I barely notice the age difference."

"So you really do like him? And not just his money?"

"I don't think you can separate the two, to be honest. He's self-possessed and self-reliant. Powerful. Dominant. A lot of those traits are probably tied to his wealth. And it's true that we don't know each other very well yet. But I like him. I like talking to him. He's a good lover—"

"No, Mamma." I scrunch my face up in disgust that's only partially mocking. "I don't need to know that."

"Well, he is. And what's the risk of marrying him? If it doesn't work out, I'm not trapped. Meanwhile, what a fun adventure this is. I'm having a blast, and I hope that even if you're miserable, you don't resent me for it."

"Oh, geez Mamma, no. Never." I pull her in for a hug, careful not to wrinkle her coat. "I could never resent you." I ignore for the moment that she thinks I might be miserable. "I want you to be happy. If you are, then I am, and this is the best day we've had in a long time."

"One of the best," she agrees. "There were plenty of best days when it was just the two of us, too."

I have a feeling that we could both go on like this for another hour—her reassuring me, me reassuring her—but the wedding planner makes another round with her military-like pronouncement. "Fifteen minutes, people. Fifteen minutes!"

Another hug, a few whispered I love you's, and a comment that the next time I see her, we'll be walking down the aisle together. Then I'm scurrying behind Adly as she takes me out of the private dining room, through the Panache front lobby to a second private dining room on the other side of the restaurant. Though she hasn't said it out loud, her quick steps make it clear we're in a hurry, and I suspect that Samuel might not be too keen about having been kept waiting.

Regardless, my thoughts are on my mother. Have I been wrong about our relationship this whole time? I thought I'd been taking care of her, giving up a life of my own to make sure she wasn't alone. Did she think she was doing the same for me?

One thing's for certain—going forward, I intend to live. Mistakes and embarrassments behind me. Starting tonight, it's time for me to have a blast, too.

CHAPTER SEVEN

LINA

Adly accompanies me into the private dining room. The layout is identical to the one that I've been camped out in with Mamma, except no windows since this part of the restaurant is on the inside of the Sebastian Center building.

Beyond that, the setting is completely different than the one I just left. Mamma's "dressing room" was filled with hustle and bustle and a frenzied energy. Though there are almost as many people here, the mood is laid back and casual. Instead of champagne flutes, there are bottles of expensive whiskey and tumblers in many a hand. I recognize some of the men from events I've been dragged to over the last couple of months, but most are strangers.

My eyes easily find the people I know. Holt and Steele, my soon-to-be stepbrothers, are shooting the shit in the corner. Some other Sebastians who I don't know yet by name. Samuel, who has yet to put on his jacket, is on the other side of the room, one leg perched on a chair, his hands animated as he tells some story to faces that don't look familiar.

Apparently, it's a funny story, because they burst into simultaneous laughter.

I also have a feeling it's a dirty story because of one particular gesture that Samuel makes, which I frantically try to unsee while trying to decide if it's better or worse if the story is about my mother.

Thankfully he notices us before the anecdote gets too filthy.

"Ah, there they are." He takes his foot off the chair and slaps the back of one of the men. "Remind me to tell you the rest later. My girls have arrived."

A warm worm of a feeling wriggles in my belly at being called *his*. It's weird because I'm not opposed to having a good relationship with him. Adly's welcome to the family threw me off guard, but I'm into it. I've always wondered what it would be like to have siblings. I have room in my heart for that.

On the other hand, he may be dead, but I already have a father. A father that I loved desperately, and missing him is a chronic pain in my chest. I don't need another man filling that role. Especially one I haven't had enough time to get to know. And Samuel is the reason my entire life feels upside down at the moment, so there is that.

But my mother seems happy so I'm keeping an open mind.

"Adly, Lina." Samuel beckons us with a wave of his hand with the kind of confidence that suggests people usually jump when he snaps. "Don't they both look beautiful."

We cross the room together. Adly is better at keeping her head held high when complimented. Meanwhile, I'm low-key dying under the weight of so many eyes. This isn't even a fraction of how many people will be watching me when I escort my mother down the aisle, but I'm planning on everyone being focused on her.

"Brains on both of them as well," Samuel adds as an afterthought. He leans toward the same man he'd slapped. "It's important to praise girls for other traits these days. They like to be known for more than just being nice to look at."

Adly moves in to hug her father. "*They* also like to be referred to as *women* and the sentiment of praising other traits doesn't work so well when it seems like you're only adjusting your behavior because your daughter is in the room and you know she's going to scold you when you're alone."

To his credit, he takes it in stride. "Seems you scolded me in public, actually."

She pulls back from the embrace. "Did I do that? Wonder who taught me my manners."

I definitely have a girl crush on Adly. Or at least I want to be her when I grow up, which maybe is the same thing. Or maybe this is what having an older sister feels like.

"Mea culpa. I try, but I can't keep up with the latest rules of society. I'm an old man." He flaps his elbow toward the man who might be a close friend. "Not that old, though."

The crowd around him laughs and claps him on the back. The "close friend" guffaws loudest, and so now I'm wondering if he's maybe just a good audience.

"Dad." It's Holt this time with the reprimanding tone. "This isn't a locker room." He gives me an apologetic look that makes my heart flutter incrementally less than usual, which is progress. Soon-to-be brother or not, the man is fine and my lady bits respond accordingly, but I am working on it.

I raise a single shoulder in a shrug, hoping I come off more chill than I feel. While I know that Samuel is a typical man for his generation, I haven't been around a lot of men like him. My father was a softer and gentler kind of guy. Not to mention twenty years younger.

Again, Samuel takes the correction in stride. "Good call, son. Got carried away with the celebratory mood, but it's inappropriate when there are girls—wait. *Women* present." He glances toward Adly. "See? He can be taught."

She toggles her head back and forth, as if weighing her response. "I think it's more performance than transformation, but I do have faith in your trainability."

Definitely my hero.

Samuel grumbles. "Fair, fair." He stretches out his arm to look at his watch. "Christ, is that the time? I've got to hustle so I can meet my bride."

The room casually kicks into motion. Chairs move. Men stand. Drinks are quickly consumed. Samuel strides to a nearby clothes rack and removes a jacket from the hanger, and I'm pretty sure he's forgotten why he summoned me—which I'm totally okay with—until he clears his throat.

"Thank you, gentlemen, for your company today. If you could kindly leave us, now, I'd like to have a word with my dear Lina."

Like that, the room clears. There's no lingering, no last minute words exchanged. Just, poof. Everyone's gone.

My stomach roils. If my palms weren't so sweaty, I'd reach for Adly's hand. It's silly, really. I don't know why he makes me so nervous except that everyone makes me nervous. And there's something about Samuel's assumption of authority that makes me feel extra small in his presence. Like I've been sent to the principal's office or stopped by a TSA officer at the airport. As if he might give me detention or make me get back in line without my shoes this time.

As if I wasn't anxious enough, Samuel's eyes find Adly's. "You, too, sweetheart."

Without hesitating, she turns to leave, but pauses to squeeze my hand. "All bark, I swear," she whispers. "You'll be fine. I'll see you at the line-up."

Okay, great. Dogs' barks can be pretty terrifying, even without the bite, but sure. No biggie. I'm fine.

The click of the door behind me sounds like the slam of a jail cell.

"Lina. Beautiful Lina."

Yeah, he's not a quick learner, it seems.

He crosses to me and settles his hands on my upper arms, and under my generalized anxiety, I worry that he might be about to creep on me because I'm a woman and that's the kind of thing we have to worry about.

But I don't note any sexual subtext to the gesture, which feels more grandpa-ly than pervy, so I take my breath and try to relax under his touch.

"It's been a whirlwind getting to today, and so I haven't had a chance to connect with you as deeply as I'd like to."

"It's all—"

He speaks over me. "But I wanted to make sure I took a minute before the ceremony."

This time when he pauses, I don't rush to fill the silence because I *am* a quick learner, and apparently this is a monologue type of situation.

"Your mother brings me absolute joy, and I'm committed to making her happy in return. As a parent, I recognize that you are the single most important person in her life, and thus you are an important person in mine."

"Thank you, I—"

"I also know you don't need me to be your father." *Whoops. Still not my turn.* "Hell, I have one, and he's more trouble than he's worth sometimes. He's here, somewhere, I think. He hasn't stopped by yet, which is probably his idea of a wedding gift."

I chuckle because I think there was supposed to be a joke there.

"It's appreciated. Trust me. Point being—though I have no intention of replacing your father, I hope that you don't mind if I think of you as a daughter."

My throat tightens, unexpectedly. It's just words, I know, and the man is a bit of a buffoon—Denny's words, not mine—but I do think Samuel genuinely cares for my mother. And even though we don't yet know each other very well, I believe the branch he's offering comes from a place of sincerity.

Turns out I might also be more in need of a family than I realized, because I'm sincere when I reply. "I'd like that. Thank you."

Surprisingly, he doesn't interrupt. "Good. That makes me happy." He drops his hands from my arms. "Then to more practical matters, we need to talk about your future."

Oh. Well. That took a turn.

I mean, it's on my mind a lot as well. Perhaps not so much ten minutes before he's supposed to get married, but I nod in agreement since trying to get words in edgewise seems to be futile.

"My children work for my company," he continues. Not exactly true since he and the board fired Holt from the CEO position at the Sebastian News Corp just a month ago, but sure. Steele and Adly still work there, anyway. "You majored at CUNY. Entrepreneurial Management, I hear. Fast tracked your master's. Decent grades. I've seen your transcript. Hull seems to think you could have applied yourself more—I spoke to him about you a couple of weeks ago—but we can work on that. I'm sure you would have had a different attitude at an Ivy League school. No worries."

It's a good thing I'm not expected to talk because there are too many thoughts going through my head to sort through them quickly enough to respond in real time. Like, he's seen my transcript? He talked to Mr. Hull, my advisor? And did he just praise me and berate my education all at the same time?

"It's a fine enough background. Definitely something we can work with. I'm semi-retired at the moment, as you know. I've been helping August out a bit since he stepped in as interim CEO, which is temporary. Neither of us are interested in being there full time anymore, and of course I'm taking off with your mother for the next month to the Galapagos Islands. Anyway, point is I won't be there, but Adly will find a good position for you at the company. A notable position, obviously. Nepotism isn't as big of a problem when the company is privately owned."

He winks, and I take that as my cue to laugh again. None of this is news, but he seems to think it is, so I let him deliver it as though it is.

"We're all set with that then. Adly'll be expecting you bright and early Monday morning. You can get all the information from her, where to be, what to bring, how to dress. Sound good?"

Oh, wait. I'd been under the impression this was only a maybe-thing. "Be there *Monday*?"

"Monday. Yes. Typical workweek starts then. Goes through Friday." He smiles like he's waiting for me to acknowledge the joke.

"Ha. Right. Yeah. I'd heard that." My giggle is nervous. "I just didn't realize it was a done deal."

Another smile. "Like I said, my children work for me."

I nod, trying to process.

In sentiment only? Or is he expecting me to change my name from Quinn to Sebastian?

But also, wow. In the family. In the will. A secure job at a billion-dollar company.

It's a lot to sort through and not much time to do it.

I'm grateful, of course. Extremely. Might have liked the job to be more of an offer instead of an expectation. Like hell he's all bark—this feels an awful lot like a bite. Like teeth snagging into my skin and locking down around bone, trapping me on a career path I've never considered. Trapping me in this world that is out of my league.

My mind flicks to my mother. This decree of her husband-to-be's is as much for her as for me. For her happiness that also means everything to me.

Then there's the fact that I not only have no other job prospects, but I honestly have no idea what I want to do with my life. I've toyed with "lying flat" as the Chinese do-only-the-bare-minimum movement terms it. Get a generic job and lay low for a while. It seems that's off the table now. Which is a bit of a mind adjustment.

But maybe I do want to work for one of the biggest media corporations in the world. Maybe I want to be an important executive type who wears tailored suits and has ruly hair. How many people would kill for an opportunity like this? I'll get to work with Adly. I'll have a name badge that gets me onto the restricted floors in the Sebastian

Center. Onto the tourist favorite rooftop without waiting in line. I know without asking that the pay will be beyond what I can get anywhere else. Much higher than I'm worth.

I bet I could even wave that Sebastian name badge around and get into Spice, despite Bartender Reid's declaration to keep me out.

Not that I care anymore, but it's nice to think I could do it. If I'm ever feeling down on myself, it might be a nice way to spend an evening.

And if I don't end up liking it, I can just quit.

Which would probably be terrible and complicated, but that's a problem for another day. Today, I'm living, and having a cush job and the support of one of America's richest men means a better quality of life.

"Lina, I take care of my family." Samuel's tone is serious now. "I'll take care of your mother. If something happens between us, God forbid, and things don't work out, she'll be taken care of. You, as well. I've already revised my will to include you both. You're a Sebastian now."

I understand it now—why so many try so hard to earn this man's attention. Why Holt is standing with the wedding party today when his relationship with his Dad is supposedly strained. Why Adly knew I'd want to be in here, alone, under his gaze. He exudes power like he's the sun. It's warm in his presence. It's his light, but he makes me feel like I shine.

This is why my mother loves him. This is why I know I'll grow to love him too.

I open my mouth to say something—try to express how grateful I am, how moved. Then I realize that Samuel is already halfway out the door. Guess a response wasn't needed, but I shout after him anyway. "Thank you!"

He's a presumptuous, bossy sort of man, but he's going to be good for us.

"Oh, shit." It occurs to me suddenly that if Samuel has left the room, he's probably headed to get in place for the ceremony. Meaning I need to get in place as well.

With a new sense of purpose, I scurry out of the room and back toward where I came from, passing by the restaurant lobby as I do. Most guests are already seated, but a couple of stragglers are making their way to the main room. I keep my head down so I won't have to make uncomfortable eye contact with strangers, then notice there's a woman wearing the most incredible shoes. The stiletto kind with red soles and strappy metallic leather. Too high of a heel for my flat feet and my uncoordinated body, so clearly that makes me wish I could wear them even more.

After she's gone by, I lift my head to catch a glimpse of what kind of woman can pull off such a beautiful shoe and see she's the thin, athletic type. Blonde with a dress that shows off a perky ass to go with it. Lucky bitch.

When I turn back to look where I'm going, I run smack into a firm, tux-clad body. Super firm. Her date, presumably. Also athletic, because don't they seem to come in pairs?

Sorry, starts to form on my lips. But when I look up, the face that goes with the super firm tux-clad body is not only blindingly hot, but also the very familiar face of Bartender Reid.

"You," I snarl. Yes, *snarl*. A very unattractive sound to go with a very unattractive person.

Clarification—unattractive *personality*. He's still as panty-melting gorgeous as ever because that's how the devil likes to package the worst ones.

"You," he snarls back. Probably a reflex, honestly, since I

don't really deserve his ire. Receive a snarl, give a snarl in return. It's not something you even think about. "You cost me over two thousand dollars in room service charges."

Oh, right. That.

Okay, maybe I do deserve the ire.

With a punch to my gut, I suddenly remember everything I've tried to forget about Bartender Reid. How he humiliated me. How he made me feel no taller than the four inch heels on his blonde companion. How he gave me the most incredible orgasm I've ever experienced and made me physically hurt with how badly I wanted his cock between my legs.

Nope, nope. Not allowing that last thought to remain in cognition.

"Only two thousand? It was the least I could do to pay back your hospitality." My words are laced with another ugly sound. More of a hiss this time because I like variety.

The infuriatingly hot jerk points a finger at me. "You know, I have your number. I almost tracked you down and turned you in to the cops. Decided you weren't worth the trouble, but here you are. Maybe I should summon security."

"Yeah, do that. Just watch how fast I get you thrown out of this wedding."

"You'll throw *me* out?"

Daddy Samuel's job offer—er, job demand—seems to have already emboldened me with confidence. I don't even have a Sebastian name badge to wave around and yet I'm gleeful with newly appointed power.

"Should I wait?" The blonde doesn't seem bothered by our heated exchange. Perhaps she witnesses these exchanges with him often. There seems to be a familiarity between them.

I ignore the stupid pang of jealousy tightening my chest. Sure, he's probably fucked *her*. Whatever. I don't care.

Just then, Adly appears. "Lina. Perfect. It's time to line up." But she maybe realizes I don't have the happiest look on my face because she frowns. "What's wrong?"

Before I can answer, the worst thing imaginable happens. She glances at Reid. And smiles.

"Hey you." She gives him a quick hug. "I didn't know you were coming. It's good to—" Her smile disappears when she sees the blonde. The scowl that replaces it more closely mirrors my own emotions. "Reid Oliver Sebastian. Are you fucking kidding me? It's his wedding, for God's sake. Have you no moral fiber?"

The blonde waves all cute and innocent like. "Good to see you too, Adly."

Reid sort of cringes. Sort of shrugs. "My Dad. You know how it goes. I have to—"

She punches him on the shoulder. Not as hard as I would have preferred, but not gentle either. "Shame on you. Grow a fucking backbone."

She returns her attention to me. "We don't have time for this. Let's go." She grabs my hand and tugs me with her across the lobby, toward the hall where I already see my mother and the wedding planner lined up and waiting for us.

I am thoroughly confused.

A bunch of other emotions on top of that. The ones Reid rekindled, for starters. Disappointed, for another, since it doesn't seem I'm going to get to kick the asshole out of the wedding after all. Then I'm anxious about getting in place and being there for my mother, who I can tell is already tearing up. And frazzled because a lot of shit has gone down in the last two minutes. Last twenty minutes, actually. Last several months, if we're going to really put things into perspective.

Oh, and resentful. Toward Adly, which is a little surprising. But come on. Why is my sister—as I shall forever refer to her from now on—hugging the enemy? Obviously, she doesn't *know* he's the enemy, but aren't siblings supposed to have a sort of psychic connection?

And did I mention I'm absolutely out of my mind confused about what just went down, particularly about the part where she tagged Sebastian onto his name.

Oblivious to any sort of fuss that isn't the ceremony, the wedding planner points to the spot next to my mother, glares at me, and loudly whispers. "You. Here. Adly." She points to the spot in front of her. "Here."

Adly tries to drop my hand so she can get into place, and I know it's not the right time, and that this should all wait until later, but I'm impulsive sometimes, and I cling to her hand like it's a lifeline.

She peers back at me, her brow raised in question.

There are so many places I could start. My mouth decides for me. "Who is that bartender?"

Confusion flashes across her features. "Reid?"

"Yeah. The bartender. From that Spice club. Why is he here?"

"Oh, he's not a bartender. He owns the club. He's my cousin." Her grin returns. "*Our* cousin. Welcome to the family!"

And suddenly I don't know what's worse—that I almost fucked my "cousin," or that I still very much wish I could.

CHAPTER EIGHT

REID

"You know who she looks like?" Alex slides into the chair next to me. Two hours late for the wedding, but he doesn't have the same obligations I do. I'm surprised he showed up at all.

As for who he's talking about, I don't have to ask. He probably followed my line of sight. I haven't been able to stop staring at Emmalina since I realized she was here. Since I realized who she was.

Cousins. We're fucking cousins.

I throw back the last of my scotch, having ditched the champagne as soon as the bar opened. "She's one and the same."

"The redhead who ordered everything on the menu?" My brother's a dick so he laughs. "Shit."

He doesn't know the whole story. I don't generally fuck and tell. Fuck and hint, maybe. Fuck and imply.

I would never have said a word about Emmalina if Alex hadn't been at the club that night, too. He pointed her out to me, after all. Not before I spotted her myself, but the point is he knew who I left with, and the next day when he razzed me, I had to give him something.

So I *implied* that shit went down the way it should have gone down. The way it *could* have gone. Told him I left her in the morning and that she ordered the shit out of room service, which was possibly more than he needed to know, but I was pissed and needed to vent.

Impressed, too.

But mostly pissed. It isn't like I couldn't afford the bill. It was the principle of it. The fact that she'd wanted to punish me, like I was some sort of villain. I wasn't the bad guy. I'd been fucking noble. It wasn't my problem that she couldn't see that.

"What are the odds?" Alex strokes his beard. It's as dark as mine, but fuller where mine's just scruff. He likes to say that means he's more of a man. I think it makes him more of an ape. "Think Samuel set you up on purpose?"

"Not sure."

It's the question of the day. I can't make sense of how or why that would be the case, though. My uncle doesn't know I have a thing for redheads. What was there for him to gain if he did set me up? He doesn't have personal beef with me. Not yet, anyway. It's my father who usually stirs the shit, or sends people to stir the shit.

People like me. Today, I'm the shit-stirrer.

"She's a hot one, though. I get it."

I glance at Alex to find he's still staring at her, much like I have been all day. While I'm not too worried about him making a move—Hunter's the brother who thinks it's cool to gobble up leftovers—I still have a strong urge to cut his eyes out with my dessert fork.

He chortles again, moving his attention back to me. "You fucked our cousin. You're a cousin fucker."

"Two years older than me and you're still about twelve years less mature."

He shrugs off the insult. "I'm not the one tied to Daddy like a toddler on a leash."

In case I don't know what he's referring to, he nods to the woman sitting on the other side of me. He smiles at her when she looks up from her phone. "Hi, Francesca."

"Hi, Alex." It's a salty return that has me wondering what their history is. I didn't even know they knew each other.

When she turns to me, her tone is more well-mannered. "I'm going to freshen up. You don't have to stick around on my account."

"Nice try." She's not getting rid of me that easily. She's the main reason I'm still here. Otherwise, I would have stayed for the ceremony, teased Holt about being in the lineup for a father he detests, and been out of here over an hour ago.

That's the excuse I'm giving myself, anyway. There's a real good possibility the reason I'm still here is because of a certain curvy redhead.

My gaze travels back to her of its own accord, just like it's done over and over the whole day. Doesn't matter that she's off-limits—more now than ever. Doesn't matter that I don't need that kind of drama in my life. Doesn't matter that she's a vulnerable, naive child—granted, there is nothing childlike about that body of hers or the very adult reactions it elicits from my own—I can't. Stop. Looking.

"What's her plan, anyway?"

It takes me a beat to realize Alex isn't looking at the same woman I am and instead is watching Francesca as she crosses toward the restrooms.

Fuck, I meant to keep an eye on her. "Not sure. Watch her for me, will you?"

Before Alex can answer, a firm hand claps on my shoulder.

I look up to see Holt. I'd not only forgotten to stay focused on my date, I also hadn't noticed Holt had left the bridal party, let alone that he'd come over to our side of the room.

"Hey." I stand up to embrace him, which he lets me do before he tears into me.

"What the fuck, man?" He nods toward Francesca's empty seat.

It hits me that *he's* been watching *me* this whole time, waiting for an opportunity to come lay it on me. With my luck, he saw me creeping on his stepsister and is planning to chew me out for that as well.

Can't say I don't deserve it on both accounts.

Before I can decide how best to respond, Alex—who is not as cool with Holt as I am—stands up and steps in. "Your father isn't the only one who can hook up with a Bunny. That's the thing about those girls. They tend to make their way around."

So that's how Alex knows her.

When my father informed me I'd be taking Francesca to the wedding today, he'd only told me that she'd been Samuel's ex. I hadn't realized she was a groupie. 'Bastian Bunnies, as they're sometimes called—most often by my father's generation—are only after the money and status that a relationship with a Sebastian offers. They don't tend to be the ones any of us marry. They're the ones we fuck on the side.

It's not like I'm unaware of the Bunnies. Plenty of them hit me up at the club, but most have learned that I'm not good for more than a night, which is not the kind of grab they tend to be looking for.

And I can respect that. Nothing wrong with women—or men for that matter—knowing what they want and using any means to get it. I would and have given away parts of myself for my club. Parts of my soul, which arguably is far worse than trading a physical act for benefit.

"I don't care who Reid hooks up with. He can fuck all the Bunnies he wants, just as long as he doesn't bring one that my father hooked up with to my father's wedding." Holt cringes, as if he didn't like what he just said. "And don't fucking call them Bunnies. That's degrading, even for you."

"Look at you—out of the Bunny circle yourself for, what? A handful of months, and you're suddenly above everyone else." Alex nudges me, as if he thinks I'll join him in the ridicule.

But though I was sent to be a source of drama, I'm not interested in actually starting it. "Hey." I put my hand up like a stop sign between them. "Holt's right—we shouldn't call them Bunnies. And it's tacky that I came with her today. Especially because we all know I'm not hooking up with her."

Alex rolls his eyes. Usually we're on the same side when it comes to our father, but I can't help wondering if Dad's going to hear about this.

Ignoring him, I address Holt. "But we've been here two hours and nothing's happened. Do you really think I'm going to let her cause a scene?"

He looks like he wants to stand his ground, but he can't argue. "I'm guessing Reynard put you up to this? Are you ever going to stop being his errand boy and—?"

I cut him off, not in the mood for more criticism about

my relationship with my dad. "You already have your trust fund, free and clear, and you already had access to it when you finally dumped your dad, so maybe you should put a pipe in whatever lecture you're about to give."

He holds his expression a beat then lets out a sigh. "I'm just looking out for you, man. I'm on the other side now. Freedom is freedom."

"Freedom with a hundred million dollar bank account is freedom." I raise my hand again because I don't really want to talk about what cutting the family strings must feel like. I can already imagine it clearly, and it's not an option for me at the moment.

"You're right, you're right. I have financial security. It's not the same." He wants to say more about it, I can tell. Like a sinner who's just found religion, but he seems to recognize this isn't the time. "I'm just a bit pissy that you have to babysit Dad's fucktoy. If Reynard wanted her to be here, he should have brought her himself."

"What a decent suggestion," Alex says sarcastically. "Considering Dad's invite seems to have been lost in the mail."

I glare at my brother. No one on God's green earth expected Samuel to invite his brother today. They already have to share a lot of space publicly because of their name. Neither of them do it on purpose.

Holt opens his arms in a halfhearted shrug. "Point is, it's not our feud."

"Then why are you here dissing on Reid about it?" Sometimes Alex misses the nail, but when he hits it, he hits it hard.

Holt has no comeback for a good span of seconds. "Where is she right now? The bathroom?"

Since I'm not a hundred percent sure, I wait for Alex to nod before I say, "Yes."

"Any idea what she might do? The dessert's already been served. Pictures have been taken. What would she even gain from making a scene?" Holt's eyes narrow as he imagines the worst-case scenarios.

I try to imagine what he's imagining—a destroyed wedding cake, red paint thrown on the bridal outfit. We already had to go through a metal detector on the way in, so she's not hiding a knife in that tiny purse of hers.

"Does it matter?"

I'm not sure if Alex is trying to help de-escalate the situation or if he's trying to wind it back up. Sometimes I think he'd make a better pawn for my father than me.

But then he continues. "You just said this isn't our feud. Why are we policing what happens? They're both adults. Giulia's an adult. She has to know Uncle Sammy fucked before her. If he didn't handle the breakup in a dignified manner, that's on him. If he wants Francesca gone, he can have her escorted out by his security team. He obviously doesn't find her a threat. She probably just wants him to know a wedding ring doesn't deter her. Her presence alone gives that message. A thousand dollars says that's her entire plan."

Holt and I exchange glances. I wonder if he's as annoyed as I am that Alex is being the reasonable one.

"So we let what happens happen?" I ask.

Holt reluctantly nods. "You're off the hook for babysitting, I guess."

"And you can stop playing concerned son," I say. "It's not a good look for you."

Holt tips his head to the side, as though he's thought of a reason to back off from the truce. "It's Giulia who I'm concerned about. She shouldn't have to deal with my father's shit on her wedding day."

It's an interesting change of attitude. The last time I'd talked to Holt about his father's engagement, Holt hadn't been too happy about it. He also hadn't been as consumed with it as I imagined he would be, likely due to the presence of Brystin Shaw in his life, who was currently charming Grandpa Irving, the last I checked. Then Holt fucked up his position as CEO at SNC, and Samuel didn't do anything to protect him from getting ousted. I guess it's not surprising his opinions about his father's life in general have gone through the wringer.

"Your father's shit is now her shit. She signed up for it when she said yes," Alex says, and for once, I think he's actually trying for reassurance.

Surprisingly, it seems to do the trick. "She did. I, on the other hand, did not."

"So nothing to be worried about." I'm not actually sure that Francesca isn't going to be trouble, but it doesn't need to be Holt's problem.

More accurately, *I* don't want to be Holt's problem.

"Fine. Sure." He doesn't sound certain, but he sounds resigned. "But I'll take that thousand dollars from Alex if she stirs shit."

Good. So that's settled. I'm free to leave if I want.

Which means I'm also free to stay and devote my attention to where it keeps wandering anyway. "So you like her then? Giulia?"

I'll be honest—I don't really give a fuck about what he thinks or feels about his new family situation. At least not where his stepmom is concerned. I'm too preoccupied with my *curiosity*—yeah, that's what I'm calling it—about his stepmom's daughter.

"I actually do. She's got backbone."

"Backbone. That's good." As casually as I can, I make my segue. "And it appears you got a new sister in the deal, too."

"Yes, tell us about the sister."

Fucking Alex. I forgot he was still here.

"Lina?" Holt raises an eyebrow. "That's *my* sister now, you fuckhead. Don't get any ideas."

"Not like we're blood related." Alex being Alex looks in her direction and lets out a hiss of appreciation. "I don't know a Sebastian woman that has a booty hot as that. "

Holt looks like he wants to slam Alex's head into the table, and not only do I understand him, I kind of feel like I might beat him to it.

I settle for smacking his arm with the back of my hand. "Shut up, asshole."

He winces, and I turn to Holt. "Ignore him. He's fucking with you. No one's making a move on your sister. Stepsister," I clarify, because even though I haven't fucked her and have no intention of fucking her, it seems important to establish that clarity.

Then, because I can't help myself… "Did you say her name's Lina?" It fits better than Emmalina. Less pretentious.

"Short for something, but that's what she goes by. She's a good kid. Young. Still figuring herself out."

I somehow manage not to point out that she isn't *too* young since that doesn't seem helpful to the conversation.

But like I said, Alex is a dick. "She's legal, though, right?"

Once again, Holt's eyes flash. "She's off-limits, Alex. No matter what the law says. Touch her and you deal with me."

Finally, Alex gives up the ruse. "I'm just screwing with you, assface. I don't want to fuck my cousin. Your dad would have my balls if I even looked in her direction."

There's no doubt his last sentence is for me. A brotherly warning that I don't need. Even before she was family, she was off-limits. Otherwise, I would have fucked her that night. It's not like I didn't want to. I *really* fucking wanted to.

I still want to.

But I know how to keep myself in line. I've ignored thoughts of her for the past three months. Never used her number, even though I kept it saved in my phone. I can keep her out of my head now, too. No matter how many times my eyes seek her out. I am the definition of will power.

So I don't need the warning about Lina.

Holt seems to still doubt Alex's denial of interest. "I'd castrate you before Dad got there. Like I said, she's a decent person. Not like any of us."

A decent person and now she's a member of the Sebastian family. I wonder how long that will last.

And why do I suddenly have the impulse to be the one to ruin her first?

No, no. No. I'm focused on the club. I'm single-minded about my goals. No attachments. No distractions. No room in my life for ruining.

This time when I look over at her, she's already looking at me. Our eyes lock and her cheeks pink, and I'm suddenly transported back to that night in August. When she was near naked, writhing under my tongue. The way her whole body flushed with pleasure…

Damn, it was the hottest fucking thing I'd ever seen.

But memory fucks with you. It changes and morphs and

leaves a bigger impression than the reality of the situation. Before today, I was convinced I'd made her up to be more than she was because every time I thought of that night, my cock got stiff and my insides twisted with regret, and I'm not the kind of guy who jerks off to memory porn let alone to missed opportunities. I am not the kind of guy who gives enough fucks to have regrets. It had to be a trick of the mind. No woman could possibly be as sexy as the one who had been living rent-free in my head.

Then she shows up today, in a champagne dress that clings to every curve, and red lipstick that makes her hair pop, and all I can think is that my memory didn't do her justice. She's not just hot—she's arresting. So breathtakingly stunning that my heart forgets to beat. My head forgets she's nothing but baggage. My eyes forget to look someplace else. My so-called iron will wavers.

Then Lina moves her gaze from mine first.

I follow her sight line and land on a younger version of Giulia who slinks past Alex and drapes herself on my cousin's arm. "Holt, why haven't you introduced me to this delicious looking thing?" she asks.

"We were just talking about your niece, actually." His gaze darts to her hand on his shoulder, but he's a good sport about it and lets it be. "This is my cousin Reid. Angela is my step aunt, now, I suppose."

"Nice to meet you," I say, wondering if Lina's still watching. Knowing I shouldn't care.

"A pleasure." Angela practically purrs as she extends her hand out to mine. While Giulia never gave me the impression that she was shopping for a rich husband, her sister seems to be on the hunt for a Sebastian of her own. "What were you saying about my sweet Lina?"

"Just that I haven't had a chance to meet her yet." The

lie falls smoothly off my lips, and without thought of consequence.

Alex lowers his head, apparently fighting to keep a straight face.

"Haven't met Giulia either, for that matter."

"Is that so?" She lets go of Holt and moves to slip her arm around mine. Even though I'm sure she's one of the types of women I like to stay clear of—the kind only interested in my status and my money—I let her cozy up next to me, pretty confident I know what she's planning to say next. "Isn't it fortunate that you just met the perfect person to make introductions? I could take you over right now."

It's a bad idea. The worst. The kind of idea that could land me in a whole heap of trouble.

On the other hand, Lina owes me. Explanations at least. For charging up my credit card. For wanting to give her V-card to a total stranger. For why she chose me to be the one.

And there's still the possibility that it was all a con job. If she's close with Samuel, then maybe she was sent to fuck with me the same way I was sent here with Francesca to fuck with him.

In which case, this isn't about failed willpower. It's about delivering a message.

"I'd love that, Angela. Thank you."

No, I don't need any warnings about Lina Quinn.

But maybe someone needs to warn Lina Quinn about me.

CHAPTER NINE

REID

Angela takes me the long way around the reception space, giving me a quick rundown on the backstory of the Romano family as we go. Giulia and Angela are apparently the two only children, born eleven years apart with several miscarriages in between. They are dual citizens of Italy and the United States, primarily living in Brooklyn but spent all their summers in Florence, Italy with their Nonna until her death in…

Words, words, words. Blah, blah, blah.

I get bored and stop listening when I realize that Lina is shooting daggers at—me? Angela? Perhaps the two of us together? Whichever, it's more interesting than the history lesson.

Until Angela gets to talking about Lina, at which point I listen quite attentively. "She's going to work for the family now, it seems. Adly's arranging a position at SNC, but Lina's not suited for the corporate world, if you ask me. Her minor was in art—Lina was always making silly crafty things. Nothing that could sustain a living, which I know is why she went the business route with her major, but now that Giulia can support her..."

She leaves the sentence open ended, letting me fill it in on my own. The freeloader life is not exactly the Sebastian way. All the grandchildren are expected to work in one of the Sebastian divisions, either for the Industrial Corp or the News. At least until the hundred million trust fund we each are entitled to becomes available once we turn thirty-six, which we are encouraged to invest back into the family business in some way or another if we want to see shares left to us at Grandpa Irving's death. Holt is the first grandchild who has hit the requisite age and walked away. How that plays out will be of interest to us all.

Sure, there are some stay-at-home spouse types, but it's not all sitting on couches and eating bonbons while the twenty-thousand-square-foot living space is cleaned by paid staff. There are social functions and charities and philanthropy work. It's an actual job. There's no room for passion projects.

Which is why I had to get creative when I decided I wanted to open a nightclub at the age of thirty-one. Deals were made. I sold my soul. Been open now for two years—successfully, I might add—and it's my entire life.

All this to say, the kind of life that Angela is describing doesn't exist for Sebastians. We're rich as fuck, yes, but we're American royalty. Our paths are laid out for us at birth. If Lina wants to be supported—or Angela, for that matter, since I'm positive she's gunning for the same future she's painting for her niece—she'd be better off becoming a Bunny.

I wince at the thought. Picturing Lina as a groupie, passed around to anyone willing to pay her bills, makes me inexplicably uncomfortable. It's the whole virgin aspect, probably, if she still is. If she ever was. Or the fact that she's "just a kid," maybe, though there are plenty of eighteen-year-old Bunnies. Whatever. I'm not examining why I feel the way I feel about it. I just do.

Angela, on the other hand…

I truly look at her for the first time, noting her features and thin form. She's attractive. I'd fuck her. She's not doing it for me right at the moment, but in other circumstances. If every glance at her full lips didn't make me think of someone else with almost an identical pouty mouth.

"...the brownstone since Giulia isn't going to be living there anymore," the copycat mouth says, though I guess technically, Angela had it before her niece, "so Lina and Denny will be living there together, and I'm just a block over."

I realize I must have spaced out again only when I hear Lina's name paired with someone else's. *Denny?* The name is familiar. *Who the fuck is he?*

The question is on the tip of my tongue—minus the *fuck* because cursing about it makes me sound like I care, which I don't—but before I can get it out, we're standing in front of the newlyweds who have taken to mingling with guests in the same spot where they were officially married earlier in the night.

Angela shifts to drape on my shoulder the way she draped on Holt's. "I found one of the Sebastians who says he hasn't met you yet."

I don't think I imagine the *dibs* in her subtext. It's funny to think she has any say in who I belong to. I'm not sure I even get a say myself. "Reid," I say, extending my hand toward Giulia. "Congratulations and welcome to the club."

Samuel wraps a guarded arm around his wife and leans toward her. "Reynard's youngest." The detest in his voice is hard to miss. He doesn't even attempt a whisper. "I didn't expect to see you today. And with a date, it seems. Are you solo now?"

I take back when I said I didn't want to cause drama. I meant it when I was addressing Holt. Not so much when I'm staring into my uncle's beady eyes.

"I believe I'm with Angela now, actually." Might as well make use of the woman. "Would you say…?"

"I'd definitely say." She practically glows.

Lina, on the other hand, glares.

She's three feet to the right of us, a couple feet back, with the same guy she'd been with that night at the club. The one she'd called just a friend. This must be Denny.

My cousin Steele is telling them an inappropriate story, which Lina appears to be only pretending to listen to, that seems to be about a time that his girlfriend was hidden under his desk during a business meeting or something? It's difficult to catch all the details and still remain present in my own conversation, but I can't help but be aware of Lina.

Can't help but recognize that she's aware of me too.

A slap on my back jerks my full attention back to my current situation. "This boy understands family bonds. Unlike your brothers or your ass of a father."

"Hey, Grandpa."

Angela relinquishes me so I can give the old man a hug.

"It's why you're currently my favorite," he continues.

He says that to everyone. Impossibly, I also think it's always true.

"Alex is here, too." I glance around, wondering if he's still keeping watch on Francesca, despite our conversation about washing our hands clean of her. "As for Dad—" I side-eye my uncle. "I'm not sure he was invited."

"Nonsense. Family events are open invitation to everyone with my name."

Grandpa Irving is the smartest man I know. He's soft in his old age, particularly with his grandkids, who all receive their inheritance in the form of trust funds. To his sons, however, he's an iron hand who could not only change his will at any moment but also threatens to do so quite often.

So when he says family events are open to everyone, he's not playing dumb to the feud between his sons—he's scolding Samuel for it.

"You make sure your father knows that." Okay, scolding Dad as well. Lucky me who gets to be the messenger.

"He did send a gift, at least. And his regards." Alex, coming out of nowhere, approaches Grandpa's other side. "Hey, Gramps."

Alex meets my eyes as they hug.

I frown. Calling Francesca a gift is an inciting statement, even from him. Once again I wonder why he isn't Dad's lackey instead of me.

"Gifts are not substitutions for a man's time," Grandpa Irving says. "You're all spoiled beyond nature's intention with what money can buy. Time is the only thing you can possibly give each other that's of value."

My brother and I nod at Grandpa's lecture in unison. "We'll be sure to tell Dad," Alex says.

Fine. Sure. *We'll* do that.

Honestly, the only thing I can think about at the moment is how Lina is impossibly even more stunning at this distance than she was from across the room.

It's only when a strange hush falls upon the men in my group that I realize Dad's "gift" has joined us. Should have expected she was nearby when Alex popped up.

"I'd thought you'd left." Francesca sidles up to me,

never mind that Angela is still hanging on my opposite shoulder like she's a coat and I'm the rack. "Samuel," she says with a nod of her head.

My uncle's lips draw tight, his jaw clenched.

To her credit, Francesca remains poised when he doesn't respond. Without blinking an eye, she reaches out a hand to Giulia. "So glad to meet you. Francesca. Your outfit is gorgeous, by the way. Not many women can pull off a pantsuit."

"Thank you. I appreciate that." With Francesca's hand still in hers, Giulia draws attention to the men with her eyes. "What's up with all their awkward shifting about? I'm guessing you're a former flame?"

Francesca nods her head. "Men think we can never get over them, don't they?"

"Or that we'll feel threatened by each other's presence."

"You're wearing the gold band. Why should you feel threatened?"

"Platinum, actually, but exactly."

Shade? I'm not quite sure. A glance at Alex says he isn't either.

Giulia turns an eye toward her husband. "He looks frightened to death by your appearance here, doesn't he?"

"Won't even acknowledge my existence."

The personal attack breaks Samuel from the stunned silence. "Taken by surprise, is all. Yes, Giulia, Francesca and I dated in the past."

"*Recent* past," Francesca clarifies.

"Seems fairly obvious it was recent," Angela chimes in.

Giulia finally lets go of her rival-not-rival's hand and pats her husband on the arm. "Take Francesca for a spin on the dance floor, darling. For old time's sake."

Samuel looks as though he's afraid this might be a test. I'm not certain it isn't.

"That's not really necessary, is it? Francesca and I have already had closure." He looks to his ex to back him up.

She quirks her lip up. "Did we, though?"

The three women exchange glances.

"Go," Giulia insists, lightly pushing at her husband. "For my sake. Show everyone how secure in her relationship your new wife is."

Damn. She's good. Meant to be a Sebastian kind of good. Maybe even too good.

"And since the bride is free…" Grandpa offers his arm to his new daughter-in-law. "Would you mind a dance with an old man?"

In awe, Alex and I watch as the two couples make their way to the floor. "I guess that takes care of that," he says.

Yes, and strangely, satisfyingly so.

"Wrapped around her finger. She's a mastermind." Apparently, Steele's joined us now too.

If he's here, then…

My eyes race toward Lina. Or toward the spot she'd just been standing in, because it's now empty. Scanning the room, I find her with her "friend" on the dance floor as well.

Why does that piss me off so much?

Only a minute later, Angela is pressed against me as we sway to whatever big band era slow song is playing.

"You brought your uncle's ex to my sister's wedding?" she asks, in a tone that says she's not as cool with it as Giulia may—or may have pretended to—be.

"In my defense…" Except I don't have one. I also have no interest in trying to make one up. Especially not while trying to tactfully move us closer to a particular couple. "It's complicated."

"I'm sure you think it is."

The woman presents like the superficial type, but I'm starting to get the feeling she's got as much going on underneath the facade as her older sis. "Touché. If you don't mind, I'd—"

I don't have to finish the statement, because that's when I "accidentally" whirl us into Lina and her dance companion.

"My pardon," I exclaim, as though that's a word I use on a regular basis. "I wasn't watching where we were going. So sorry."

Angela laughs. Lina narrows her eyes until they're shooting laser weapons.

"Gives me a chance to introduce you to your cousin. Lina, this is—"

I cut her off. "Actually, we *have* met before. Just realized it. Mind if we swap partners?" I don't allow the man with whom Lina is dancing a chance to interject. Or for anyone to interject, for that matter. "Thank you. So kind."

"I don't. But I'm. This is." Lina's protests are ignored.

And then she's the one in my arms instead of her aunt. Full-body curves and warmth pressed against me. Soft orange spice in my nose. Devil red lips curled into a scowl.

Fuck. Why does her mouth look so kissable when she's blatantly annoyed?

"Have you heard of a thing called consent?" She doesn't pull away, though, as I spin her away from the two we've left behind.

I throw a glance toward them. They're talking as they dance, seemingly content with the switch. "He would have said yes. Men understand each other."

"*My* consent." She steps on my shoe. Purposely, I'm guessing. "You didn't even ask me."

"Ah, no I did not. Too much of a risk you'd say no."

"That's exactly the point." But she settles into my rhythm, her form melding with mine. "I would have. Said no. To be clear. If you had asked, like a decent person. I don't want to cause a scene, is all."

"Uh hm." My fingers feel like fire where they meet the soft skin of her exposed back. How did she not entirely consume me that night with her? How did I find the strength to do the right thing and walk away?

Her eyes meet mine, and immediately her cheeks flush. Like she's thinking about the same things I am. About the last time we were this close, and the things I did to her. The things I didn't.

She's the first to pull her gaze away. "Samuel is watching us, by the way. Guess we're cousins now, aren't we?"

My uncle's name reminds me why I needed to talk to her, though I didn't fully realize I needed to until right this moment. "Was it all an act?"

Her eyes fly back to mine, her head pulling back in surprise. "All an act? That night? Why would it...what would I even...?" The reaction is so entirely confused and genuine, I'm convinced she wasn't sent to pull something on me.

The knots in my shoulders melt away.

But then her expression changes. As though an idea has struck her. "Yes. Actually. It was."

"It was, was it?"

"All an act. The whole thing. I had a fight with my boyfriend, see. I was trying to make him jealous."

I nod back toward the dork I stole her from. "That guy him? Your boyfriend?"

"Denny. Yep."

"Doesn't seem bothered that I'm with you now."

"Well, I never told him in the end. Nothing happened. So what would I tell him? You probably don't remember since you insist on forgettable interactions. But nothing did. Nothing at all."

"Mm. Right. Nothing at all." I cock my head. "Strange how distinctly I remember the taste of your pussy on my tongue."

"That's. You can't. No one says things like…" Even the tip of her nose gets red when she's flustered.

"Still a virgin then, I'm sensing." It's a low blow, but I can't help myself. The need to know is deep and primal in my gut.

Her lips purse. "Never was. That was part of the act." She pauses. "I mean, of course I was a virgin. At one point. But not that night, is what I mean. I only said that because I was feeling guilty, and I knew it would make you stop."

"Ah. Because just saying 'stop' wouldn't work."

"You've proven today you don't care about consent."

A dance is not the same as sex, not to mention the fact that she had zero reason to think I wouldn't respect her before she blurted out her virginity status. But there's no point getting into all that. "See, the thing is, *Lina*, you tried to tell me you were rehearsing for a play when we first met, if I recall. So you don't exactly have a track record for telling the truth."

"And you don't exactly have a track record for…for… being a decent person." She rolls her eyes a little, as though annoyed with herself over the weak insult she managed, but she tries to hold her head high. Succeeds a bit. "Anyway. We're fine now. Me and Denny. It was a minor blip. Happy as can be. As a real couple. So real that…he moved in, actually."

"Yes. I heard that."

"You did?" She shoots a glance toward her aunt, her eyes darkening. Now, that look on her face—that's what I'd call jealousy.

Am I imagining that?

But when I follow her gaze and see that her "boyfriend" is watching her intently, like he might cut in and tear me apart if she gave the cue, I start to wonder if I'm wrong. If she's telling the truth about all of it, that it was an act—just not for the reasons I thought, but that this nobody who probably doesn't deserve her really is her boyfriend.

When our eyes return to each other, my confusion must show on my face because she asks, "What?"

I shake my head. "Can't remember ever caring if a girl had a boyfriend or not."

Whoa. Hadn't planned to say that out loud.

She swallows, and my gaze drops to her lips. I swear I can still feel them on mine. The heat of them. The fullness of them between the nip of my teeth. Want drowns out my sensibility. "Can't remember ever wanting to keep dancing with one either."

A flicker of…something…flashes across her face. I'm not sure what the *something* is. Surprise? Annoyance?

Then she stops in her tracks, refusing to move, her expression suddenly hard. "Best we stop this now, then. Before it becomes meaningful. Wouldn't want to make an impression or anything, would I?"

Without waiting for me to respond, she turns on her heel and leaves me alone on the dance floor.

I stare after her, watching the hypnotic sway of her hips

as she walks away, a smile playing on my lips. Not sure what I find amusing because I'm eighty percent convinced my uncle's watching, reminding me that she's a hundred percent off-limits, even if I had room in my life for more than a one night thing.

And I'm a thousand percent intrigued all the same.

CHAPTER
TEN
LINA

"Did you hear about the king that went to the dentist?" Looking around the room, I'm met with a few faces trying to puzzle it out, but no guesses. "He needed to get crowns."

"Groan." Amani actually says the word out loud instead of making the sound.

Joe shakes their head. "Should have gotten that one."

"I've heard it before, and I didn't get it." Poor Denny has heard all my jokes, many of them countless times. He could probably do a full set of them himself because I've made him listen to all of mine.

After years of being awkward in social gatherings, I discovered bad puns were a way to break the ice and have been collecting them ever since.

Now it's my one party trick, and since this is technically a party…

Really, it's more of a get together. A few friends of mine and Denny, over to celebrate the fact that the family brownstone is now mine. Not technically, since my mother's name is still on the title, and most of the furniture is still the same pieces she picked out years ago, but for all intents and purposes, it's now mine, completely rent free.

Mine and Denny's. He's taken the garden level, which used to be my father's accounting office back in the day, and though he keeps on insisting he's going to pay rent, I've yet to accept the offer.

Currently, we're all spread out in the living room chit-chatting and listening to Mother Mother while drinking beer and eating pizza from the corner Italian restaurant. Denny is playing DJ. Jamal and Shiv are staked out front and center on the sofa, playing the latest Zelda. Eric, Amani, and Joe are playing keep the cherry, which is some game that involves not letting the flame go out as they pass their joint around. Which means they're already pretty stoned, and the perfect audience for my stupid jokes.

"Give us another one," Eric says, on an herbal scented exhale.

"Hm." I clear the smoke with my hand as I sort through my repertoire. "What happens when doctors get frustrated?"

"They lose their patients," Jade answers as she comes into the room from the kitchen, carrying two glasses filled with some red punch alcohol concoction. She hands me one before sitting on the armchair.

"Dammit, I had that." Eric pouts like he's sincerely bummed.

"Speed up your answer next time then." Jade raises her glass and reaches toward me to clink with mine.

"What's in it?" I sniff, trying to sort out the ingredients, as if I know anything about distinguishing one liquor from another.

"Best not to ask." She kicks her feet over the side of the

chair and takes a swallow. "I practically drank a whole glass trying to get the mix right, though, so drink up. You're behind."

Since I'm not big on beer—which is all we've had until now—this is my first alcohol of the night. I take a gulp and wince. "Oh my God, Jade. What did you use? Rubbing alcohol?" I down half of it quickly, hoping that will be enough to "catch up."

"Like I said. Best not to know." She grins. "I have a joke for your collection, by the way. What's the best air to breathe if you want to be rich?"

It's one I already know. Truthfully, it's hard to stump me. "Millionaire."

Jamal takes a break from Zelda to chime in. "Don't you mean *billion*aire? We practically have one in our midst."

"She's billionaire adjacent," Joe quips.

"Something like that." My laugh is weak because I don't know how else to react. I follow it up with another sip of my drink so I don't have to keep talking about it. It's as weird for them as it is for me that I'm suddenly connected to unimaginable wealth. I'm still figuring out how to navigate it all.

Shiv pauses the game and sets down her controller. "Do you interact with them at all?"

"Not really." Mamma's been on her honeymoon since the wedding, so I haven't had any leisure time with the Sebastians, but I do see Adly almost every day at the office. "At work, but that's all."

"Oh, right. You've got a job at SNC now. How's that going?" Jamal's attention is now completely on me, and I wriggle a little under the intensity of his stare.

He's a newer friend of Denny's, so I don't know him that well, but I have the impression that Denny thinks he'd be a good candidate to take care of the virginity thing. Jamal certainly is attractive. He makes me feel all glowy when he looks at me because that's how I always feel under the weight of a confident gaze, but he doesn't give me the butterflies in my panties feeling that I got from Reid.

Fucking Reid.

It's been almost two weeks since he took me in his arms on the dance floor, and my skin still vibrates every time I think about it. My heart skitters and the things happening between my thighs don't need to be mentioned. I hate to say it, but maybe he was right. What would have happened if we'd actually banged?

Or maybe it's because we *didn't* bang that I keep obsessing over him.

And what was with what he told me that night? *Can't remember ever wanting to keep dancing.* Was that just to fuck with my head? Because of the credit card bill, or the rivalry that Adly has alluded to between his father and my step-dad, or just because he's a bully? I can't find any logical reason for the comment to have been sincere, because he's made it very clear he isn't interested in being my first. Unless…

Is he trying to get in line to be my second?

I kinda hope that's the case.

Except, even if it is his game plan, it's not happening. We're cousins now. Sorta kinda not really. But it's best if I keep the mindset that we are, because when Taylor Swift wrote that song about trouble, she was talking about Reid Sebastian. Maybe even literally.

I should do some Googling to see if they ever dated…

"That good, huh?" Jamal asks, reminding me we were talking about something.

I tug on my braid and frown, trying to remember what it was.

Oh, yes. Work. God, was that alcohol that strong or did I get a second-hand high? Probably it's neither, and Reid Sebastian is to blame. It's not the first time I've spiraled into thoughts about him out of the blue, but it's embarrassing when it happens in front of a hot guy.

"No, work's good. I mean, I still don't know where I'm going to end up. So far it's been a lot of aptitude tests and training courses and tours of different departments. Adly has a rigorous onboarding process for new employees, which I think I'm failing, and she's just too nice to tell me."

More likely, she's overlooking my flaws since her father is insistent that I be part of the company. Even though I know nothing about news or media. My business degree was focused on entrepreneurship, which I'd thought I'd use to start my own small business, not be part of a billion dollar corporation.

"Whatever. Aren't there like a million branches of the Sebastian empire? They'll find something for you." Jade's given me this speech already.

"I'm sure you're right." It's more complicated than that, with the rivalry between the brothers. There's family politics and all, which I explained to her before. There's also the fact that I'm not sure I actually want to do anything I've been introduced to so far. But then I'd just sound ungrateful, so I don't attempt to explain further.

"You didn't invite any of them tonight?" Amani asks.

"Invite one of the Sebastians? To this place?" I practically laugh.

The place is nice, don't get me wrong. My parents bought the four-floor brownstone decades ago, and even though it needs some maintenance, I'm sure it would go for over ten million in today's market. It's a literal dream house, and yet, next to the luxury that the Sebastians are used to, it's a dump.

I shudder thinking of Holt in his crisp suits or Adly with her designer shoes standing in the room. The thought is so jarring, it feels wrong to try to imagine. "No, no. No siree. This whole place is like the size of my mom's closet at her new place."

"She's not joking. I've seen it." Denny fades the current song into something from Japanese Breakfast.

"But…family." Amani is a hearts and rainbows kind of girl, which is why we get along so well, but even I'm not that innocent.

"Some families aren't as family as we are," I say. Speaking of which… "Angela should be here any min—"

I'm cut off by a knock on the door.

"That's probably her now." Denny looks at me, though, because we both know that I'm not the type to lock the door until bedtime, and Angela isn't the type to knock. But there isn't anyone else we're expecting.

"Maybe I locked it." I shrug and hop to my feet, realizing that I'm definitely starting to feel a buzz. Perfect timing since I've discovered in the last few months that I've been legal that inebriation makes Angela easier to be around.

The door turns out to be unlocked when I get there, but a quick glance through my peephole shows her on the doorstep. I start talking as I open the door. "You made me get up when—"

The rest of my sentence is lost—lost like when a computer file isn't saved before shutting down and it's gone forever, never to be seen again. Because my brain does just that—shuts down entirely when I see that it's not just Angela on my doorstep. When I see that she's with Reid.

Reid Oliver Sebastian.

My hot as fuck cousin.

Who I almost had sex with.

On my doorstep.

"I would have walked in like usual, but this guy says it's rude not to knock," Angela says in explanation. She steps inside, handing me a bottle of champagne as she passes by. A bottle she couldn't afford on her own, which I only know because it's the same champagne Reid brought out to celebrate my birthday.

The champagne I drank directly from his mouth.

The champagne that he licked off my body.

The champagne that will never not make me feel like a filthy wicked vixen.

I feel my entire body go red as I stand frozen, my jaw dropped, my stomach landsliding to the floor.

"Hello, Lina." Reid's tone suggests not only that he knows the effect he has on me, but also that it was an effect he intended. He taps on the bottle with a single finger. "A little housewarming gift. A brand you like, I think."

The fucker has the audacity to wink.

Then he walks on by. Just strolls in, his spicy, woodsy scent trailing after as he follows my aunt to the living room, as though he was a guest on the invite list. As though he's been here a hundred times before.

Did Jade spike my drink with some hallucinogenic? Either that or the pot those guys are smoking is laced with PCP.

"That has to be it," I say to the now empty doorway.

Or I'm having a psychotic breakdown.

Or a very frightening dream.

But then Angela is introducing Reid to Jade, and Joe's offering him the joint, and Denny's looking at me with both worry and like his eyeballs are about to pop from his head, and for some reason I don't think he'd be so horrified for me if this wasn't real as fucking fuck.

Denny mouths something that I can't understand, but since he's pointing in the direction of the kitchen, I assume that's where he wants me to go, especially when he heads there himself.

Yes. Good idea. Kitchen.

I start in that direction, keeping my head low.

"Lina, you should bring out—"

Holding up the champagne bottle like it's a shield, I cut Angela off before she can finish her request. "Putting this on ice. Be right back."

I push through the swinging door to the kitchen and immediately lean against the nearest supporting wall.

Denny is immediately at my side, whisper-yelling at me, since the room isn't exactly soundproof. "Holy shit. Did you know he was coming?"

"Oh yeah, totally," I whisper-yell back, unable to pause to let the joke settle in before going on. "Of course I didn't know he was fucking coming. You think I would have fucking forgotten to mention it? I am fucking mortified right now. What the hell is he doing here? He brought us the champagne, Denny. *The* champagne." Not that he has any idea about the champagne because I didn't get into details with him before. "And oh my God, I told him you were my boyfriend. You have to pretend you're my boyfriend. I know that's totally unfair and all but—"

Suddenly an even more horrid thought occurs to me. A thought that makes my stomach turn. "Is he…is he on a *date* with Angela?" Fuck. Have they banged? "I need to sit down."

He catches me before my knees give out, then walks me over to the kitchen island so I have something to lean on. "You told him I'm your boyfriend?"

"Was that really the most important thing I just said?" Actually, for him—probably yes. I bend over and knock my head lightly against the counter. "I made you my beard without consent. I'm the worst friend."

His expression says he's about to disagree when the door swings open, and Jade slides in. "Hi, hi, hi." She sidles up next to me at the island. "Why is an old guy at our party? He's hot and age gaps are very in, so I'm guessing there's a story here. What's the story? Tell me the story. I need the story."

Jade is a good friend. Not like Denny good, but right up there. The kind of friend I trust with my secrets but don't always go out of my way to keep up-to-date. Particularly when I've vowed to never speak of the incident again.

But now Reid is my cousin and he's in my living room and he's fucking my aunt… I groan and hide my face in my hands.

Denny takes that as his cue to fill in some of the major gaps. "There was a Night."

"Oh. A Night!" Her eyes light up.

"Before I knew we were cousins," I say, without lifting my head.

Jade prods. "An Unforgettable Night?"

Denny rubs my back in soothing circles. "Unforgettable for the wrong reasons."

"Oooo." She drags the sound out. "And now he's your cousin."

"And he's here with Angela," Denny points out.

I pull the neck of my sweatshirt up to cover my face like a turtle nestled in his shell, wishing I could hide my memories from my mind as easily as I can hide my face. "And he's seen me naked."

It comes out muffled though because of the fabric covering my mouth.

"What did you say?" Jade asks.

I bring my face back out to reply. "He's seen me naked."

At the same time, Denny answers as well. "He's seen her naked."

"Not completely naked," a voice behind me clarifies. "But I suppose little was left to the imagination."

Yep. That happened. This is happening.

I don't have to look in the mirror to know that my face is fifty shades of red, and there is no way in hell I'm turning around. Or like ever leaving my turtle shell again. Can I just go back inside my shirt and die now? If some magic force in the universe ever decided to Groundhog Day my life, this would be the day I'd like to repeat. I would never speak those words. I'd never answer the door. Or invite Angela. Hell, I wouldn't even have a housewarming party.

Across from me, Jade lifts her head in a nod and smiles. "Hi."

If I survive this night, I'm going to need to remember to give her some tips on not acknowledging the literal elephant in the room.

"Just came to see if I could be of help opening the champagne," Reid says, all cool and suave. Like he didn't just walk in on me airing our sex drama to my two besties. "But perhaps this isn't the best time."

"Uh…" Jade pauses, meeting my petrified gaze.

Don't engage. Don't engage. Don't engage. I will her to hear my thoughts, and for half a second I think she might get what I'm putting out there.

But then she says, "Not quite the level of alcohol needed at the moment?" her voice lifting up at the end of the statement to make it a question. "Yeah. I think we're going to need to stick with the punch."

"By all means." He pauses, and I pray with all my soul that he just leaves. Not only my kitchen, but my house. My life.

But I hear no sounds of movement and Jade's eyes are still pinned in the same place, as though he's still standing in the exact spot he's been standing in for the last thirty terrible seconds.

And then he says, "I should add—I regret not seeing more."

Yep. That's it. I'm dead. Officially. Dead.

And now I have to hide away in my bedroom and never be seen again.

I lift my hand up to the side of my face, a shield of sorts so that I don't catch sight of Reid in my periphery when I turn. Then walking as casually as I can, I cross the kitchen and bolt up the stairs to my room, where I slam the door behind me, fling myself on my bed, and pull the covers over my head.

It's not more than a minute later before the door creaks open because Denny is the best friend on the planet, and he never leaves me alone in a crisis.

"Tell everyone I've died. It's not even a lie. I'm literally dead. Literally, literally. Lit.er.al.ly. Dead."

"Mm. To die a virgin. Such a shame."

That's been entirely my point about wanting to ditch the label. It's a waste of a willing vagina, but that is the lowest of my concerns at the moment because that rough as sandpaper voice does not belong to Denny.

I close my eyes and pretend I'm not here.

Never worked as a child or when I tried it in college, but I'm twenty-one now. Maybe it's a skill that comes with age. Maybe I've never wanted it enough. I can't imagine wanting it more than I do at this moment.

But then I realize that pretending I'm not here has not made him go away, and my silence just gives him permission to go through my stuff.

Since I'm still in the process of moving things from my old room upstairs to this room—the room that my mother used to occupy—a lot of that stuff is in open crates and boxes, easy to peruse.

I know that's exactly what Reid is doing without looking.

Which pisses me off enough to fling the covers off and face my monster. "What happened to 'it isn't polite not to knock?'"

He's to the side of me, no longer wearing his coat, which is problematic because his form is now visible, and I suddenly remember how cut the man is. As if I needed reminding.

He shrugs, and his taut muscles strain against his tight shirt as he flips through a desk drawer that I haven't bothered to put back into the desk since me and Denny dragged it down here. "You already think I'm not a decent person. There's no one else in the room to impress."

I scowl. Extra hard.

Not that it's productive, especially since he isn't looking at me. It's hard to think of something else to do when I'm doing a quick catalog of what might be in the drawer he's looking through. *Sketches of works in progress, pens, pencils, batteries*...fuck.

Too late, he raises his hand, a small remote control gripped between his fingers. "Does this go to what I think it goes to?"

Goddammit.

I jump off the bed and swipe the device from his hand. Surprisingly, he relinquishes it without a fight.

"Vibrators are more fun controlled manually, anyway," he says.

I'm instantly livid at my mind for going where that statement takes me. And at my nipples for perking up like they're interested. Oh, and at Reid for being in my goddamn room in the first place. "Why are you here?"

"In your room or in your house?" He turns toward me, and I have to hand it to him—he knows how to use his assets as weapons. His face, being the weaponized asset in this particular situation. His perfect, beautiful face with the green rimmed brown and rust flaked eyes and his wickedly assertive mouth that has my body in full sense memory mode. "And don't try to convince me you share this room with Denny. This is one hundred percent your room."

"Uh..." I blink.

"I'm at your house," he offers when I can't seem to give him an answer of my own, "because Angela invited me." His eyes narrow as if he spots something of interest on the floor. "Your room," he says, crossing to inspect whatever has caught his attention, "because that's where you are."

I want very badly to take a moment to let myself react to what he's just said. There's a lot to unpack there. A lot to examine in terms of how those words make my heart trip and my pussy vibrate and my head buzz.

But I can't. Because I have to rush across the room to

grab the panties that he's taken from my laundry basket—dirty laundry basket—out of his hand before he…

He brings them to his nose and sniffs before I make it there, his eyes darkening with the inhale. "I thought I imagined how good your pussy smells."

"Oh my God." I bring my hands to cover my face. This is really next level mortification. I had no idea it was possible to feel this embarrassed and still keep a heartbeat.

"It's confusing, I agree," Reid says, as though that's what's at the top of my mind.

I mean, it's on the list. But I'm more focused on the depth of my humiliation. Priorities and all.

"I didn't forget this," he says after a beat. "This shade of red you turn when you're turned on."

"This shade of red is not arousal." All right, maybe ten percent arousal. Twenty-two percent tops.

"Hard to get the whole effect with your hands over your face." Without any pause, he changes the subject. "You did these?"

I don't need to see to know what he's looking at, but I drop my hands because what's even the point.

Sure enough, he's rifling through the crate filled with my paintings. The unfinished ones, to be precise, which is especially annoying since they aren't ready to be seen by anyone, let alone him.

"For fuck's sake. Would you stop getting into my things?" I jump out of my bed, grab them from his hands, and stuff them back into the crate. "Why did you come tonight, Reid?" To torment me? Was that his entire agenda?

"I told you. Your aunt—"

"Angela invited you. Right." A sharp stab of jealousy hits me in my chest. "Like…is this a date? Why did you say yes?"

He shoves my dirty panties into the pocket of his jeans along with both his hands and leans his back on my dresser. "I haven't fucked her yet."

My thoughts and emotions are complex and contradictory. It feels like I'm being pulled in several directions at once. Like, he has my panties. And why does he look so unbearably sexy standing in that position? Does he *want* me to try to climb him like a tree?

Then there's the relief that he hasn't slept with Angela. As well as the *yet* that means he still might.

It's the twisting knife of jealousy that wins my focus. "She's using you, you know." It occurs to me that there are reasons it might be hard for him to believe me. "I mean it this time. She's trying to compete with my mother. That's her only interest."

"Maybe." He pins me with his intense gaze. "Or maybe I'm using her."

His words sit in the air. Tangible, almost. Heavy and present. Using her…for what? To get to me? He *had* me. He didn't *want* me.

"Lina?" Denny's voice travels up the stairs. "Everything…okay?"

He cannot seriously be asking me that. He has to know Reid followed me up here, which by the way, didn't Denny think to stop him? It's irritating that he didn't.

And also I'm ashamed that I'm irritated because it's not his responsibility to deal with my tormentor, and I'm sure he feels bad about it already.

But what am I supposed to do with the not okayness? Stay locked up here in my room? The only person I was hiding from is already here.

"Look, I don't know why you're here, but if you're going to be here, you're not going to be *here*. In my room, I mean. Party's downstairs. This space is off-limits." It's not the most authoritative tone, but it's pretty strong for me. Admirable, even. Denny will be proud when he hears about it later, even without me building it up in the retelling.

That is, if Reid actually listens to me and leaves.

Because he doesn't, at first. Instead, he scans the room again, studying it. As though putting everything to memory.

Then he opens my door. "Let's get going then."

It feels like a win.

And also a trap.

One thing I know for sure—if I'm going to survive this night, then Jade's right. I'm going to need more punch.

CHAPTER ELEVEN

REID

"You doing all right?" Denny asks, rubbing Lina's shoulder. They're sitting on the floor, a few feet away. Far enough that I shouldn't necessarily be able to make out his quiet words since there is plenty of other noise around us, but I seem to be tuned in to every word that passes between the two of them so I hear it clear as day.

For some reason it makes me want to break his fingers.

Really, he should be admired for his concern. She's had way too much to drink in way too short of a time, and no one else has bothered to try to put a stop to her. And it's not about trying to police a woman's drinking. If I were her bartender, I would have cut her off an hour ago, no matter her gender.

If I were her boyfriend, I would have kicked everyone out of the house by now and taken her upstairs to be tucked into bed.

So Denny's gentle check-in with her now feels far below

what should be expected from him—if he is, in fact, her boyfriend, though I'm still not sure what to believe.

This is only one of a list of many boyfriend failures that I have silently noted over the course of the evening. He steps on her stories—not a cute couple thing; it's annoying and upstaging. He doesn't offer to refill her glass—meaning he also doesn't slip her any much needed water—or get her something to eat to help absorb the alcohol. He doesn't react when the Jamal dude openly leers at Lina's tits or stares at her ass.

It's made it hard for me to get a real handle on their relationship. They're close, yes. Irritatingly close. And also, they're…not. I haven't been able to put my finger on what's missing between them, besides the obvious fact that he's a shit boyfriend.

If I have to be fair, he is quick to defend her.

And gives her credit when due.

And glares at me like I'm a predator whenever I even glance in her direction. Which means he's been glaring at me all night because, as always when she's in the room, I can't seem to take my eyes off her.

Lina doesn't answer him, seeming too engrossed in a conversation about cats that has spanned at least thirty minutes to hear him. Not for the first time, she turns to him eagerly. "We should get a cat."

He gives the same response he has every other time. "Not happening."

Her responding sigh grows bigger each time, perhaps because of the increased level of alcohol in her blood. Even so, it's obvious she's pining for one.

Get the girl a fucking cat, man. Another one for the boyfriend failure list. Thousand bucks says they break up by Thanksgiving.

If I don't try to break them up before that.

Why the fuck do I care?

"Are you about ready to leave?" Angela's been antsy for the past I-don't-know-how-long. It feels like she's been prodding since we got here, but my annoyance might be more about how often she interrupts my focus on Lina.

My fingers grip the arms of the chair.

Well, one hand grips the arm. The other grips my knee, having been relegated to my lap since the arm of the chair is occupied. I took this seat thinking she would find a spot somewhere else in the room. Instead, she perched at my side and remained there, draped on my shoulder for most of the evening.

"We could give it a few more minutes." I think I said that the last time she asked.

She leans in to whisper in my ear. "Did I tell you I'm not wearing underwear?"

"Mm." My dick doesn't even twitch.

"I'm going to use the bathroom and get our things." She disappears into the kitchen where our coats have been stored, thrown on the dining room table along with everyone else's.

My Cucinelli spread out on a fucking dining room table. Where people eat.

Another reminder that this is not my scene.

I'm a shitty date.

Truth is, I never intended this to be more than a hookup. When Angela first reached out, I hesitated. She's too close to family to get involved. There's a chance I'd see her again. There's a chance fucking her would hurt Lina.

That last reason gnawed at me. Since when have I cared about a girl's feelings? That's the whole point of my MO—to *not* care. To not *have* to care. So then I decided I should fuck Angela just to make sure I had my head on straight. I gave her the address of my hotel room and said I'd meet her there sometime after midnight since I like to be at the club until things get swinging.

But when she said that worked out perfectly because she wanted to stop by Lina's housewarming thing first, my plans instantly changed.

It was almost an out-of-body experience—my mouth telling her I'd like to accompany her, that I'd pick up a bottle of something as a gift, and pick her up at seven. Those aren't words I would ever say in my right mind. My assistant Kaya felt my forehead when I told her she was in charge of the club for the night. I can't remember the last time I took a day off, let alone a Friday.

What the fuck is wrong with me? I can't begin to answer that question.

"We could play *Mafia,*" someone says. I don't know who. It doesn't matter.

Lina tilts her head, her pretty mouth parted as she considers. "Do we have enough people?"

"We could play *Never Have I Eve*r instead," one of them counters.

Someone else—"Or Never Have I Instagrammed."

This suggestion makes Lina laugh. "Oh my God, you're such a nerd."

Is this the first time I've seen her laugh or just the first time I've noticed? Her whole face lights up and her eyes crease. But it's that adorable little nose wrinkle that makes my cock stir. She makes the same face right before she comes.

I shouldn't know that. I shouldn't remember.

I should get myself to stand the fuck up and leave right

now. Take Angela to my suite, fuck her until I'm not seeing red hair and pouty lips every time I close my eyes. It's been since before the wedding since I've gotten laid. That's probably all I need to get this out of my system.

It's a natural time to depart, too, since a lull has hit the party—and I use that term loosely. It's kid shit, especially if they move into drinking game territory. No thirty-three-year-old man should be sitting around on a Friday night playing *Never Have I Ever* with a bunch of twenty-one year olds.

Angela returns, coats in hand. "Ready?"

At the same time, the dark-haired stoner girl prods Lina with her toe. "You should tell another joke, Lina."

"No tell another joke, Lina." She shakes her head, talking about herself in third person.

It occurs to me that I might be responsible for her level of intoxication, since she filled her glass the minute we returned from her room. One sniff of that punch practically had me drunk myself. It's a good old fashioned jungle juice concoction that I haven't encountered since my early high school days.

It's just another reason I should get my ass up and leave.

I don't move. "Another joke?"

"Lina tells jokes," Jamal says. He's the only name I remember besides Jade and Lina's dick boyfriend's.

"Jokes?" It's so on brand, and so unexpected all at once, and I'm warm inside with this bit of knowledge about her that I didn't have before tonight. I tuck it inside my chest with the titles of the books that were on her desk (*Skinny Legs and All* by Tom Robbins and *A Little Life* by Hanya Yanagihara) and the name of her body spray (Orange Sky) in the box by her bed and the sketches she'd drawn (raw, unpretentious pieces ranging from landscapes to portraits to abstract, all remarkable and captivating). And her whimsical paintings of imagined worlds…

"Lina does not tell jokes right now." She frowns at Jamal, a warning of sorts, before she sweeps her gaze across the room, letting it collide with mine.

She seemed to try to look anywhere but at me earlier, but the last little while, she's met my eyes more and more. That's one benefit of her increased blood-alcohol level, I suppose.

Or a detriment, considering the way her gaze makes me feel impulsive and tight-strung.

"Reid?" Angela moves in front of me, blocking my Lina view, and for the first time in an hour, I can think clearly.

"Right. We should go." I manage to get to my feet.

Honestly, I don't belong here. Not just because I'm too old for this scene, but because of how everyone here interacts. Their connections are raw and authentic and meaningful. One day I'll have to learn how to do that again—how to *be* that. How to hold conversations that lead to something more.

Am I even capable of that anymore? Or have I left my life too long on pause?

The question is knocked out of my head when Angela hands me her coat. I'm helping her put it on when a notification dings from her pocket.

"You're leaving?" It's the first time Lina has spoken directly to me since we returned from her room.

I swear there's a hint of disappointment in her tone.

Why do I feel equally disappointed when I reply? "It appears so."

"Actually," Angela says, looking at her phone, "can you give me a few minutes? My work is texting. They're having an issue with closing the system. I have to call and walk someone through it. It might be a while. Sorry! New employee."

It occurs to me that I have no idea what she does for a living or what her position is. At the same time, I realize I haven't thought about Spice all night. Haven't once thought about checking in.

Maybe I should do that while Angela's on her call.

But then Jamal says, "*Spin the Bottle*."

Fucking Jamal. It's the kind of game a guy suggests when he wants to get lip locked with someone in particular, and I know exactly who he's aiming for.

I shouldn't be surprised when almost everyone agrees. Everyone except Lina. Now that Angela is gone again, she's back within my sight lines. This time, when she turns her stare on me, I see a flash of defiance in her eyes. "Or *Seven Minutes in Heaven*."

Oh, hell no. She's not ending up in the closet with that ogling asshole.

I wait for Denny to protest, as a good boyfriend should. "You guys play. I think I'm just going to call it a night."

A bunch of goodnights are called out to him as he stands up. Once on his feet, he lifts his chin toward me. "Careful on the steps when you go. It gets icy at night."

It's a goodbye and don't-let-the-door-hit-you-on-the-ass statement if I ever heard one.

"We'll do that." I watch him as he heads to the stairs that lead to the basement.

And somehow I know without a doubt that he only feels comfortable going to bed because he thinks I'm leaving. Just like I'm absolutely certain that Lina only made the suggestion to piss me off.

Me, not her supposed boyfriend who is sleeping in the

basement instead of in her room. I'm the one she wants to get a rise out of. The one she's taunting with sex games and other men.

"Truth or Dare," I say before thinking it through.

Yeses murmur throughout the room.

"Except the dares are always dumb." This from Jade, who makes a fair point.

I amend my suggestion. *"Truth or Strip."* Better anyway, because it leaves all the kinky shit in view of the entire room. No sneaking away to get up to who knows what.

Lina's face pales. "Uh, I don't know…"

"Nah, it will be fun." Of course Jamal is on board.

Fucking prick.

"But you were leaving." The defiance isn't entirely gone from her eyes, but now there's more there as well. Pleading. Excitement. Terror.

"Angela's on her call. I can play a few rounds." I sit on the floor at her side, in Denny's place. Never mind that my date for the evening is about to return, ready to go. Never mind that this is the worst idea I've ever had in my entire life. I'm committed.

She pivots toward me, her voice low. "That's ridiculous. This is not your thing. You don't want to game play with us."

"How do you know what I want?"

"I know what you *don't* want. And I know what I don't want. Which is to play this game with you."

"Why not?" My eyes coast to her lips, so close I could kiss her.

"It's not a good idea. You know why."

Everyone else has vanished from the room, and it's just the two of us. Somewhere in my head, I know they're still there, but it doesn't matter. It's me and her, nobody else.

And fuck, I feel mean.

For a myriad of reasons. Because I can't fuck her. Because she won't get out of my head. Because she's dangling what should have been mine over other people instead. "What are you afraid of, Lina? People knowing you're a virgin or being naked with me again?"

Her face goes red, but she holds her head high. "Definitely not the latter because you nope out."

"After giving you an earth-shattering orgasm, so don't know why you're complaining."

"All right, you want to play?" Her voice is spiteful and back at normal volume. "Truth or strip? You go first." She doesn't give me a chance to speak before choosing for me. "Truth? Oh, good. Why are you still here?"

That's a fucking fantastic question.

In the beat I take to reflect on the answer, I feel the eyes of all her friends on us. A couple of them whisper back and forth. Jade looks delighted, metaphorically eating popcorn and intrigued with the show.

Oh, right. We're not alone.

What the fuck am I even doing? Why am I pushing this game? I don't want her naked, not in front of all these people.

But I can't back down now. "That's not how truth or strip works. I get to choose whether I want to tell a truth or take off a piece of clothing. Then you get to ask a question or tell me what item you want me to lose."

Her jaw tightens. "Thank you for the mansplanation. I don't know how we could play the game without you."

I've never wanted to put someone over my knee and spank them this badly in my life. "You're welcome. And I choose strip."

Coward's way out of replying to a question I don't

know the answer to, but it's better than reflecting on things I haven't yet been able to figure out.

"Well, I'm not picking you anymore." She's so salty, I can almost taste it on my tongue. "Jamal. Struth or trip?" She shakes her head. "I mean. You know what I mean."

He chooses strip and loses his shoes because Lina doesn't demand he lose anything risqué, which makes me happier than it should. Jamal chooses Shiv, who also strips, then it's Joe who goes for truth, then Amani who again chooses truth, and by now I'm twitching in my seat, anxious for my turn, though I have to say, the game makes it a hell of a lot easier to learn names I have no interest in learning.

Finally, Jade chooses me, and I lose my pants. My shoes too, since I have to take them off to get my jeans down, and there isn't much point putting them back on afterward.

"Now this is a game," Jade says, clapping her hands when I'm only in my boxer briefs and shirt. "Your turn."

Her name is out of my mouth before I can even think it. "Lina."

Her answer comes just as quickly. "Strip."

She holds my gaze, as though we're playing some sort of chicken on top of the other game, and maybe that's exactly what we're doing because I don't want her stripping, and I'm pretty sure she doesn't want to strip, but here we are, pushing each other in exactly that direction, trying to see who will back off first.

It's not going to be me. "Bra."

She swallows. Then chugs the rest of the punch in her cup—as if she needs more alcohol—before unclasping her bra through her clothes, then pulls the straps down her arm and off without removing her shirt in some sort of ninja move that is both impressive and infuriating.

It's surprising, though, how easy it is to see the shape of her breasts through the thin material of her light shirt. They're full and heavy, sagging with the weight of natural tits, one drooping more than the other. Her nipples are noticeably taut, and as tempting as they'd been when I saw her wearing nothing but her bra, they're even more tempting now. It's all I can do not to lean over and tug at one with my teeth.

And yes, I see Jamal staring at them with the same hunger in his gaze that I feel, and I think I should get a medal for not punching him in the teeth. He fills me with just enough rage to keep my boner at bay, but just barely.

So now it's Lina's turn, and the spite in her eyes spells my name before she says it out loud. "Reid."

"Strip."

"Socks."

"Boring." It's poor sportsmanship to keep the game just between us, but she started it, so after pulling off my socks, I swing it back to her. "Lina, truth or—"

"Strip," we say in unison.

"Pants."

She stands and undoes the drawstring on her sweats. They drop to her ankles and I zero in on the triangle between her legs because I'm a man obsessed, but her shirt is long and falls to cover that sacred spot. *Touched by how many? Who else besides me?*

Why can't I get the wonder out of my head?

She's still on her feet when she says my name this time.

"Strip." As if she even has to ask. As if I'll choose anything else.

"Shirt." It's bold on her tongue, like she's finally found her nerve.

I stand to meet her stance, pulling the Henley over my

head quickly. So quick that I catch the flash of lust in her eyes before she can hide it. See her teeth graze over her bottom lip.

And fuck, my dick definitely just went hard.

"Damn," Jade says.

"You said it." Amani's tone echoes Jade's appreciation.

Of course I throw my turn right back at Lina, and now it's a choice between getting another pair of panties to take home or finally seeing those gorgeous tits exposed. I'm greedy because I want both. "Panties," I say, my voice raw.

She peels them off and, as if she knows they already belong to me, she drops them in my hand.

It takes everything in my body not to bring them up and sniff. I need to know if she's as turned on as I am. If the scent of her arousal is stained on the cotton lining.

That confirmation will have to wait for later, when I'm alone. I shove them inside the waistband of my boxer briefs for exactly that. For now, it's just the two of us again, the rest of the world zoned out as we're eye to eye, toe to toe in a battle that I want to win so bad I can taste it as clearly as the memory of her pussy on my tongue. "Your turn."

I have nothing left to lose except my briefs. Unless she chickens out and goes for my watch. Panic flits along her face as she realizes her choices are slim.

Dare you. I only mouth the words, but I know she understands.

Without batting an eye, her lips part. "Jamal."

Did she…*Did she just win?*

She's still on her feet, but she turns to him, putting her back to me. Cutting me out. She gets him out of his pants, and because he's a hungry little pervert, he tosses it back to her.

"Strip."

"Lose the shirt," he says, and no fucking way. No fucking way is this *his* prize.

So when she crosses her arms in front of her and wraps her fingers in the hem of her blouse, I have no choice but to intervene.

"Okay, that's it." I pull at her arm, forcing her to let go of the material. "Game stops now. This has gone too far."

She spins to face me. "You're the one who started it."

"Which is why I get to finish it."

"On what grounds?"

"On the grounds that you are not sober enough to make good decisions."

"Really? Feels more like on the grounds of you're a stupid jealous human confused holedick." She thinks about what she's said. "Confusing dickhole, I mean..." She pauses to think again, her nose crinkling in that delicious way it does when she's frustrated.

"Point made."

"You are not the boss of me." She tries to pull her arm away from me, but she isn't strong enough to free herself from my grip. "Why are you even?"

I'm not sure if it's another wording mistake due to alcohol or a purposeful statement. It would probably have me biting back a smile if I wasn't so goddamned pissed.

"Look, uh...maybe you should back off." Jamal to the rescue. Go Jamal.

Go fuck off, that is.

"We're fine," I say.

At the same time she says, "I can handle myself, myself."

Then she stumbles. We aren't even moving, and she fucking stumbles.

"Okay, we're talking about this in private." She protests

as I tug her toward the kitchen, only remembering Angela is in there at the last minute and redirecting to the darkened hall.

Once there, she tries to yank her arm free again. Unnecessarily because I release her as soon as we're alone. The force causes her to stumble again.

When I catch her, my hand accidentally lands at the side of her breast. She slaps it away as though I've burned her.

Barely a beat passes before she reaches out for my hand and guides it back, placing her palm over it to keep me from moving it away.

As if I want to move it away.

God, the weight of it in my hand… She's all curves and flesh and woman. I brush my thumb across her nipple, wanting to do so much more. Knowing I shouldn't be doing any of this. I feel stretched, like a man on a rack being pulled and pulled and pulled toward destruction.

"Why are you doing this?" she asks, stepping closer so she's pressing against my palm.

"It seems you're the one—"

She cuts me off, quick despite the alcohol. "You know what I'm asking."

I don't know.

It's the right answer. The honest answer. *I don't know why I can't stop. I don't know why I'm drawn to you when you're the worst idea that's ever crossed my mind.*

I. Don't. Know.

But I chicken out again. "Lina, you've been drinking." As though this is all her fault. As though she's the one out of her mind.

The accusation doesn't seem to register because she moves a hand down to my crotch and finds my cock, thick and hard. Should have been playing *Stiff as a Board* instead. I would have won hands down.

And fuck.

Her small palm wrapped around my dick feels like fucking heaven. If I were in a closet with her, I don't think I could make it seven minutes, even just with a hand job. Her stroke is tentative, but it's killing me.

"Lina," I groan, wanting to buck my hips forward. Wanting to push her to the ground so I can find warmth in her mouth. My hand squeezes around her breast, and the moan she lets out almost does me in.

Her thumb brushes against my crown. It's too dark to see the spot of pre-cum on my black boxer briefs that I know is there. "You want me," she says. "You can't say you don't."

"I never said I didn't. That was never—" My words are cut off with an involuntary hiss as she explores lower. Cups my balls in her palm.

I want her. God, I fucking want her.

But all the reasons I couldn't have her before still exist, and now there are even more to add to the list. She's Samuel's stepdaughter. She maybe has a (terrible) boyfriend. Her aunt is in the next room. Her aunt is my supposed date.

Most importantly, she's drunk and, as far as I believe, still a virgin who deserves more than a quick fuck. So I absolutely cannot press her against that wall and explore every part of her body that I've yet to explore. I cannot pull out my cock, lift up her shirt and bury myself inside her, but every second that passes, it becomes more and more unlikely that I'll be able to resist.

I cannot.

Somehow, I muster up the strength to be the decent guy she insists that I'm not and shove her hand away from my crotch, letting go of her breast at the same time. "Lina, you think you want this, but you're drunk."

Even in the dim light, I can make out the severity of her pout. "I don't care. I want this. I want—"

"When you're sober, baby girl."

"No, now." She steps forward, her lips reaching for mine. "Please, touch me."

The *please* is almost more than I can resist. "When you can think straight. I'll owe you. I promise." I have no right to be making promises that I can't keep, but here I am, saying it like I mean it. Almost convincing myself as well. "But not tonight. Not like this."

A kiss though. Just one taste of her. I could give her that. Give us both that.

I take a step forward.

...and then immediately step back when light spills into the hallway and Angela stands in the kitchen doorway.

"I thought I heard voices. I'm ready to go when—" Her gaze takes note of our attire. Or rather, lack of. "Uh...where are your pants?"

It's unclear which of us she's addressing, but I know I should one thousand percent take responsibility. I'm the sober one. I have no excuse.

But then I'd be admitting there is something between us, and that's exactly the thing I've been trying to avoid.

So I play the asshole instead. "Strip game that got out of hand. Your niece here has had way past her drinking limit. She let herself get carried away."

"Me? You're going to blame—"

I raise my voice to talk over Lina. "She needs an escort

to her room. I think it would be more appropriate if you take over from here."

Angela takes a beat to assess, her eyes lingering on my near-naked form. Not in the hungry I-want-to-bang-you-later way, either. More like the okay-but-why-are-you-also-undressed way, furthermore-why-are-there-women's-panties-sticking-out-of-the-waistband-of-your-shorts. She's not an idiot.

"Yeah, I can do that." She steps out of the kitchen, sending the hallway back into the dark with the close of the door behind her. "Lina, honey?" She puts her arm around her niece.

Lina throws Angela's arm off. "I don't need a fucking escort to my room."

But Lina's eyes are on me. The sting of betrayal is written all over her face.

It's maybe the cruelest thing I've done to her—treating her like a child when she is by far more of an adult than I am. If I've learned anything from my father it's to control others when you can't control yourself. First time I've put that lesson into action.

Shouldn't I feel more of a sense of satisfaction?

"Fine, then, take yourself up," Angela says with a familial cheeky tone. "And for God's sake, drink some water. You smell like a distillery. Your mother would be—"

Lina rolls her eyes, and it's the first time I've seen her behave in a way that reflects her youth. "Oh, fuck off, Angela. I'm not your responsibility. You want to take care of someone? Get your date his clothes and suck him off in the car, or whatever it is you're hoping to do with him. Just make sure he leaves."

She storms off, back to the party, which is the opposite

direction she should be heading, but something about the look on Angela's face says I'm not allowed to be concerned about it. "You better not think you're getting laid tonight."

Like I said, she's not an idiot.

No, that's definitely me.

CHAPTER TWELVE

LINA

My heart thuds as Adly flips through the gallery on my phone. I don't make art for anyone but myself, which is why I don't typically show it to others. My pieces are private and informal and mine.

I'm not sure how I decided to invite Adly into that space —maybe it's the whole sister thing she's been pushing on me—but here we are.

She studies one in particular, sending my pulse rate up a notch. "And they each represent a different book?"

"Mm hm."

The manicurist taps on my arm, kindly suggesting I quit biting on the thumbnail that she's just painted.

"Sorry," I say, dropping my hand to my lap.

Needless to say, I woke up with my head pounding along with a phone full of texts. Two from Angela that I ignored. One from Denny who was too lazy to walk upstairs and check on me. And one from Adly inviting me to mani-pedis at the Sebastian Center spa.

Hers was the only one I replied to, declining the invite due to said headache. Then of course she needled me into admitting the headache was brought on by alcohol, and suddenly the invitation for mani-pedis turned into her on my doorstep with a car waiting to take me to get the full hangover treatment.

Four hours later, I've been detoxified with mud, wrapped in tea leaves, and massaged Thai style. Currently, along with getting both my fingers and toes prettied up, I'm hooked up to an IV to replace my fluids, and I feel so much better that I might have to mark this as one of the best days of my life.

I mean, obviously, I'd rather not have a hangover at all, but if it has to be, there is officially no better way to deal with it than Sebastian style.

Appropriate since this hangover was caused by the most maddening Sebastian of them all.

"Which book is this one for?" Adly stretches her robe clad arm toward me, my phone in her hand.

I squint at the screen. It's a loose sketch of a blonde little girl and a big black dog. "*Vicious* by V.E. Schwab. It's like… a villain origin story? Two books total. Mostly it's about Victor Vale and Eli Cardale. The girl can bring people back from the dead. She resurrected the dog, and, yeah. It sounds sort of young adult, but it's really fantasy."

Immediately I'm judging my answer. I spoke too fast. Sounded too excited. Should have been more sparse.

"One of my favorites," I add a beat later, which is unnecessary because I have a million favorites, and I wouldn't have done a piece for it if I didn't love it a lot.

And now I'm worried she thinks I only read super nerdy books—though, I suppose reading at all can be considered nerdy, and what's wrong with nerdy?—so I rush to clarify. "They aren't all fantasy books. I love all sorts of genres. Donna Tartt and some Gillian Flynn and Fatimah Ashgar and Erin Morgenstern. Well, she's fantasy too, but you know. Do you read much?"

God, I'm so awkward.

"Smut," she says proudly.

I lower my head so she doesn't see my cheeks go red. "I read a bunch of that too."

"All day, every day." She hands me back my phone. "Your art is really good. You could sell them."

I open my mouth to protest, but she beats me to speaking. "Or you could if Dad didn't have you on the Sebastian Career Track. Not a lot of room for outside entrepreneurship in this family. That's the price for being American royalty."

Her tone is apologetic and also morose in a way that makes me think she isn't just saying it for me. One day when I feel more comfortable with her, I'll ask her about it.

Maybe.

We'll see.

"Anyway." She taps a newly scarlet painted finger against her chin. "You have more of a creative mind than I realized. What do you think about training you for management in the art department? You'd have to work your way up, but you'll be fast-tracked as a family member. Sound good?"

"Um…yeah." *Hell, yeah.* Finally, an area I know something about.

"Awesome. It's settled."

The manicurist finishes cleaning the edges of my nails and then, after ensuring we don't need anything else, leaves the relaxation room.

Which means that Adly and I are alone together for the

first time, and I can finally ask her the question that has been squirming inside me since it popped into my head last night while falling asleep.

"So…what's the deal between your dad and Reid's dad? They're in some sort of fight or…?"

I've only caught whiffs of their feud. Reid's date to the wedding, apparently, was Samuel's ex, which should confirm every worst suspicion that I've had about Reid's indecency. I mean, it does—who would do something so shitty to a family member on such an important day?—but also, was that the only reason he brought Francesca? To stir trouble and not because he likes her?

It's terrible that that's all I care about.

Or it was all I cared about until my drunk brain had a moment of clarity—what if Reid's interest in me is only more of the same?

Adly's long sigh tells me I'm stirring up a can of worms that she probably thinks should be well left alone.

"I'm sorry. I shouldn't have asked."

"No, you have a right to know. It's just complicated because I don't really know the answer. None of our generation does because it happened before we were born, and no one really talks about it. From what Holt and I have figured out, we think it has to do with our mom. Both Reynard and my Dad were in love with her.

"But I also think it has something to do with the division of jobs. When Grandpa's company was split back in the nineties, Reynard was given the co-CEO position at the Industrial Corp and Dad was given the CEO position at the News Corp, and I guess Reynard always thought it should have been the other way around. Hunter, Reynard's oldest—if you haven't met him yet, beware; he's a piece of work

—has been after SNC since Dad retired, which I think is in honor of his father. Like he thinks it should have been his birthright, and that tracks with other snippets I've heard over the years."

I nod my head as though I'm following all of it. I kind of am, but it's a lot and Adly speaks fast, and really the only part I'm interested in is whether or not I've accidentally become part of their feud.

"So really all of that just means that Uncle Rey and Dad don't ever see each other unless they have to and also that they're always on the lookout for ways to aggravate the other like they're still teenagers. If you ask me, they're both spoiled, entitled brats, but I'm probably just more of the same, so who am I to talk?"

"No, no. No. I don't get that impression of you at all." It's not lip service either. Adly is genuinely a kind and generous person, and also really strong and confident, and seems to know exactly who she is and has no shame. In other words, everything that I hope to be someday. The kind of person who wouldn't obsess over a guy who is possibly using her to piss off her stepfather.

My stomach twists realizing that's the most likely reason Reid showed up at my house last night. Well, and also because it might finally be calm enough for food, but that's not foremost on my mind at the moment. "Do you think that…?" I pause, not sure how to frame the question. "Would, you know, one of Reynard's kids try to…?" Fuck, this is hard. "Reid brought that woman to the wedding. Would he try other things to rile up your dad? With other people?"

I'm talking nonsense, but Adly's suddenly on high alert. "What happened? What did Reid say? What did he do?"

"Uh..." I hadn't quite thought out this conversation as much as I should have, because it's only now that I see that telling on Reid means telling on me. While I'm into developing the sister relationship, I'm not quite ready to admit how far I let things go last night. How far I wanted them to go. "He showed up at my house last night? Without an invitation? And was sort of a dick?"

I shake my head at my timidity. "Without the question mark inflection. He did all of that. And I was just wondering why he'd want to come to my housewarming party unless, you know, I was an agenda of some sort."

Adly's out of her lounge chair in a flash. "I saw him in the gym earlier. I'll talk to him."

Shit. I did not see that coming.

"No!" Impulsively, I start to follow after her, remembering just before the needle is yanked out of my arm that I'm still hooked to an IV. "Adly, wait! That's not necessary!"

She spins around, walking backward as she talks. "No, he needs to know you're off-limits. Don't worry about it. Gives me a chance to play Big Sister." She turns forward again, but calls over her shoulder. "When I get back, you can explain why I didn't get an invite to your party. Don't think I didn't pick up on that."

I have a feeling I would have appreciated this type of Big Sister energy much more at eleven than I do at twenty-one.

And also—Reid's here? Like, in the building? Right now? My stupid heart starts racing, which I'm blaming solely on the fact that whatever Adly plans to say to him, it's sure to be as embarrassing as hell. Is there a spa treatment that can make me unrecognizable since I'll never be able to show my face again after this?

Then again, maybe this is exactly what the situation calls for, because even after everything that's gone down between us—even knowing that I'm just a pawn in his game—I'm not so sure I wouldn't once again try to jump him given the chance.

CHAPTER **THIRTEEN**

LINA

It's a long ass seventeen minutes before I hear from Adly again, and it's via text.

It's taken care of. 

While I'm down here, I'm going to hit the pool. Want to join?

Thankfully, I have a good excuse, which at least gets me off from having to explain why I didn't invite her to my boring house party that she would never have been interested in attending.

I don't swim. But thnx for the offer.

The spa attendant frowns at me for typing while she's trying to unhook me from the IV, so I wait impatiently until she's finished before following my last message with another.

I think I'll just hit the shower and go home. Thank you so much for the best day!

Since it feels like I should say something more and don't know what to add, I include an embarrassing amount of emojis before shoving my phone in the pocket of my robe and heading to the dressing room.

As to be expected, there is a separate, secret dressing room for anyone who bears the Sebastian name. I'm still a little surprised to have been granted the entry code. There are top execs at the company who don't have one, according to Adly, since they're not family. It's a strange entitlement that feels over-the-top and unearned, but I have no complaints when I walk in and find I'm, as expected, alone. Body positive though I try to be, I've never enjoyed getting naked in public.

The one downside to a silent space is that there's nothing to muffle the noise in my head. Adly's constant chatter kept my thoughts from going too far astray, but now that I'm alone and my brain is clear, I find myself thinking back to last night as I grab two towels from the linen shelf and head toward the shower. I was drunk, yes, and not in my right mind, but his voice was raw with want, wasn't it? His cock was hard in my hand.

Maybe that's just what happens to men when they're being touched like that, no matter the girl. Because he still said no. So many times that I feel my cheeks flush just remembering. Did I really beg him like that?

I cringe as I drop the towels on the counter and reach into the stall to turn on the water. "Not one of your finer moments, Emmalina Quinn."

"You seem to have plenty of those," someone says from behind me.

I swear I jump a mile high. My heart lodges in my throat, where I can feel it pounding in rapid sixteenth notes, and if I thought I felt flush before, that was nothing compared to the heat rushing through my body now, because I know exactly who I'll find when I turn around.

Reid continues, apparently unaware that I'm currently having a mini heart attack. "Do you want to explain what the hell you think you were doing getting Adly involved in places she doesn't belong?"

"Do you want to explain why you're in the women's locker room?" I spin to face him.

Big mistake.

Huge.

Because the man standing in the doorway is once again shirtless, and either because the bathroom fluorescent lights hide nothing or because my fuzzy brain didn't accurately catalog the sight, I find I'm unprepared for exactly how goddamn good he looks. He's nothing but definition and hard lines. With beads of sweat enunciating several prominent ridges. My eyes follow the creases at his waist that cut down below his gym shorts, and a little whimper escapes before I bite my lip to suppress the sound.

But then I realize he doesn't just look annoyed—he looks pissed. "Wait—are you *mad* at me?"

Sure enough, malice flashes across his features. "Adly. Of all people. You have no idea what shit you may have stirred up."

"First of all, I didn't send Adly anywhere. She's a grown adult who thinks for herself, and whatever she said to you, that was her. Second of all, if you're going to treat me like a child, maybe you should expect that I'll act like one."

"You know what I got when I was a bratty kid? Spanked."

Despite my irritation, I can't help the shiver that runs through me, and with all the steam filling up the room, I can guarantee it's not because I'm cold.

Folding my arms over my chest so he can't possibly see the peaks of my nipples through the robe, I lift my chin defiantly. "You wouldn't dare."

"Wouldn't I?" He looks like he wants to eat me up, which I might be into if he didn't also look like he wants to murder me.

It's the murder look that has me most concerned. "Adly's still in the building." I kick myself as soon as the words are out. How childish do I sound now?

"Good job. You just reinforced every suspicion I had about your lack of maturity."

I have the tiniest urge to cry, but thankfully, it's overwhelmed by anger. "Oh, fuck you. I'm not going to be gaslit into believing that my reactions to your bad behavior are the problem."

"Me with the bad behavior? You were the one who was drunk and begging me to touch you. Do you know how many ways I could have taken advantage of you?"

"So what, now, you're a saint for being a tease?" This guy is so back and forth, I have whiplash. "You crashed my party then spent the whole night acting like a jealous pervert. You and your stupid mixed signals. You can't blame me for being confused about what's going on between us."

"Us?" He takes two large steps toward me. "There is no *us*, Lina. There was no us that night we met and there is no us now."

The statement would have more power if his eyes didn't keep dropping to my lips. If they didn't keep dipping lower

—to the open cleavage of my robe. That stare alone makes my pussy feel all sorts of funny.

But fuck him for all the showboating.

And fuck him for acting like it's me who's pursuing him.

And especially fuck him for being so…so…mean. "You're a bully."

"You're naïve."

I don't even blink at the insult. "But I know what you're about, so you can knock it off. Using me as a pawn in your father's feud—honestly, the fact that you think I mean that much to Samuel is flattering. But it's way off base. I barely know him. Whatever you think you'll gain from messing with me, you're wrong."

"My father and Samuel?" He seems truly taken aback. "You think this is about their feud?"

"Stop acting like I'm ignorant. I *know*, Reid. So go ahead and act pissed about Adly, but you're really just mad because I caught you out. Because I figured it out. Game's over now. We're done."

His mouth is tight as he nods his head. "Yes. We are definitely done. You made sure of that."

"*I* did?" Again with the gaslighting. "God, you're such a prick. Whatever. If we're done then leave already."

"I'm leaving."

"Awesome."

"Good." He doesn't move. His eyes are so dark I can barely see the green rims.

I swallow, feeling an awful lot like prey in the sight lines of a predator.

"I suppose, if we're done," he says after a beat, "that means I'm off the hook for last night's promise."

"Last night's promise?" My brain rewinds and replays

our drunken encounter, this time skipping past the humiliating part where I beg for him to touch me and suddenly recalls his response. *When you can think straight. I'll owe you. I promise.* "Wait…what?"

"You don't even remember."

"No! I do!" I don't know why I'm so excited. If we're done and everything.

Except, he *is* still standing here.

And the tension between us feels as sexually charged as ever. "Anyway, I never believed you meant it."

Am I seriously trying to taunt-lose-my-virginity here?

It's fine. Totally fine.

"I was never going to fuck you, Lina."

In my whole life, I've never known anyone who could ratchet up my hopes and then completely dash them in a matter of seconds.

"Just like I said—a bully. Add a liar and a coward to the list." I turn back toward the shower so he doesn't see the tears pricking at my eyes. How he can manage to hurt me after all this is beyond me. "Leave already. I'm wasting hot water."

Barely two seconds have passed before I feel him behind me, his breath at my ear. "The reasons I wouldn't fuck you before haven't changed, baby girl, but there are other ways I can take care of you. Other ways to fulfill that promise."

Tingles spread throughout my body.

Stupid body, because pushing him on this is a bad idea, whether he promised it or not.

"Like…what kind of ways?" My mouth appears to be just as stupid as the rest of me. *The ways don't matter, Lina. Tell him to go.*

"I could show you. Show you and then be done." His

hand comes around my waist and grabs the belt of my robe. He doesn't tug, though. "Is that what you want?"

The fact that he asks my permission almost ends this. Because he's making me own it. Making me declare that this is not just him messing with me this time—it's me allowing it. It's me accepting it.

I think he might be a mastermind.

With a shuddering breath, I answer. "Only because you owe me, and you promised. And then we're done." As if I'm offering him something rather than the other way around.

"And then we're done. Swear on Grandma Adeline's grave."

My response is barely above a whisper. "Okay."

As quiet as my consent is, he must be tuned in to me because as soon as the word leaves my tongue, he yanks on the belt, and pulls my robe open. I hear his breath grow heavy as he stares over my shoulder and down my body. My nipples were already standing at attention, but now they're tight and thick beads, and the heat from my face has traveled down my neck and torso to my pussy.

"Fuck, so beautiful." He says it so quietly, I'm not sure I was meant to hear.

I'm greedy and want to hear it again. "Hmm?"

Reid ignores me, pulling the robe off my shoulders and letting it fall to the floor so now I'm standing completely naked in front of him. It's easier than I expected, maybe because it's my backside that's facing him.

Still, he's tall, and I know he can see everything, and the ragged draw of his breaths gives me the confidence to look him eye-to-eye.

"No," he says when I start to turn around. He puts an arm around my waist, keeping me in place. "Stay like this."

There's a dozen other reasons he might not want to look at my face besides the obvious. Reasons I'll be able to come up with when I'm not so in-the-moment distracted by the throb between my legs.

With his arm still around me, he guides me forward, into the stall until my toes hit the bench and the spray lands on my breasts. "Put your hands on the wall," he commands. "And your foot on the ledge."

It's funny how fast I respond, without thought. As though my body belongs to him as much as to me. With my arms up, my torso pitches forward and the water sluices down my backside. Reid hasn't undressed, so he has to be soaking wet, too. I want to turn my head to look, but somehow I know without asking that it's against the rules, whatever those are.

Somewhere in a far corner of my head, a voice of reason shouts at me for thinking there are any rules at all. For believing that I'm under his reign. For submitting to his bid.

Fuck that voice.

That voice is the reason I'm still a virgin. She'll die with her hymen intact, if she has her way.

It's the voice of want that speaks now. "Reid…I need…"

The thwack across my ass comes quick and sudden. "Don't tell me what you need. Whatever you think it is, you're wrong."

I tense, suddenly afraid I've walked into some elaborate trap. He'd hinted that he wanted to spank me, and I basically just offered up my backside for him to do just that.

But also, *damn, it felt good.* And the truth is that, trap or not, I'm five seconds from begging for him to do it again.

There's another thwack, then a third, followed by his palm rubbing away the ache before another two quick thwacks. "Your ass looks good when it's red from my hand."

"This isn't what you promised."

"I promised to take care of you. Now shut up and let me." He's massaging my tender skin with his palm when the water moves from my backside. At first I think he's just redirected the spray but then the whole shower head is in his hand and he's holding it in front of my belly.

Oh.

Ohhhhhh.

Okay, maybe I jumped the gun a little with the criticism.

Reid stretches his body over mine, standing so close that I feel his erection against my backside at the same time that I feel his breath in my ear. "Have you ever gotten yourself off with the shower nozzle?"

No, sir, I have not.

I give a quick shake of my head. Spoken words tend to be hard to manage when I'm super turned on, and I am so super turned on that I've become mute.

"Lucky me. I get to be your first."

If I could talk, I'd point out that he could be my first in other ways, but as noted, I can't, and he did just tell me to shut up.

And if I weren't speechless before, it's at that moment that he brings the nozzle head to my pussy, and holy-fuckarama, my clit lights up like the Sebastian Center Christmas tree. Instantly, I'm on the verge of orgasm. The sensation is almost too much, and the noise that comes from my body is barely human.

"Now see? Bet you didn't know you needed that."

Somehow his smugness is more irritating when it's deserved.

Still, I want more, which I try to say but it comes out in

the form of a prolonged moan. An unattractive moan. If anyone overheard me, they'd probably think I was in labor and call an ambulance.

Please, God, don't let anyone overhear me.

Reid just chuckles. I think. The sound is buried in my skin as he trails kisses along my shoulder and up my neck. "You're so easy to play with. Fun. So responsive."

"Yeah, I got an A in responsibility last semester." I know I'm not making sense. I'm surprised I tried to word at all, let alone managed to speak.

He chuckles again as he rubs his nose along my upper back. "Figures you're the responsible type. I was, too. Before you."

"Hm?"

"Spread for me, baby." He kicks my standing leg so there's now space between my thighs. With his free hand, he reaches down from behind to draw a circle around my entrance.

It's so much sensation. All coming from one place, and I can barely concentrate on anything but the tornado of pleasure stirring over my pussy.

His words come as a distant murmur. "You're forbidden fruit, Lina Quinn. The least responsible choice to make. Absolutely off-limits, and still I can't stop myself from taking one tiny taste."

He swipes his tongue along the lobe of my ear and adjusts the shower head at the same time so I'm not sure which action it is that does it—a combo of both, probably—but tumbling into ecstasy I go, crying out in some made-up-on-the-spot language as I do.

He pulls up his arm, giving me relief from the intensity of the spray while still his arm remains wrapped around my waist. Somewhere through the blissful haze I hear him whispering. "I got you."

And I feel *got.*

Like I haven't in a long time.

Like I'm not alone. Like if I fall, I'll have help with the land. Like I'll be held until I feel sturdy enough to stand on my own.

It's a fleeting feeling. Gone almost as soon as I register it, because as soon as I've recovered, Reid is on his knees behind me, spreading my ass cheeks with one hand.

My *ass* cheeks.

I might not be able to see what happens back there without mirrors and lots of creative angling, but I know that whatever goes on, it should remain behind closed cheeks. In other words, private. "Hey, that's—"

But that's as far as I get in protest before the wand is once again directed on my clit, sending my thoughts into a spin, and as if it wasn't already enough to befuddle me, Reid's mouth is suddenly on my cunt.

His tongue, to be precise.

He circles it around my entrance and then licks up—up, like to my asshole, up. Which should be the grossest thing I can possibly think of, or at the very least off-putting, but it's exactly the opposite. Like it might be the most not gross thing that has ever been done to me, and when he sticks his tongue *inside* that should-be-gross hole, sparks literally fly. My entire vision is filled with fireworks, in fact.

That's when my body starts trembling. I'm a brand new baby doe trying to stand on wobbly legs, and I cling to the stall wall for support, not just with my hands, but with my face. The position just happens to push my ass out like I'm asking for more, and so no wonder Reid keeps giving exactly that.

Keeps tracing and retracing that pathway from one virgin hole to the other, occasionally pausing to eat one out before moving to eat the other. And I swear to God that if I wasn't so fucking blissed out, I would be appropriately ashamed.

Maybe.

Okay, probably not.

What is even happening right now?

All this time I've been concerned about what I was missing out on by keeping hold of my V-card, and no one bothered to tell me about butt stuff? That butt stuff was AH-mazing? Like, is it even possible that regular stuff is better than this, and if so, am I prepared?

No, ma'am, I am not.

Then all lucidity is lost to the biggest surge of pleasure I have ever felt in my life. Tears stream as I let out a long cry. The fireworks become one solid screen of light. Reid pulls away and lets my climax rush over me like one of those giant tidal waves that wipes out anything and anyone standing in its wake, and I've always been terrified of the ocean because of that immense power. Because I imagined it would take me over just like this. That it would own me. That I'd be wrecked. That I'd be swept away.

But I never imagined that force would come with such euphoric peace.

Every single cell in my body is ignited with blissful calm. Every knot of tension is gone. I'm loose and limp and boneless.

And when I can breathe—when I can open my eyes and process that I'm still upright in the world, that I'm still who I was, who I am—I see that I'm also alone.

The shower nozzle hangs slack and there's no one else in the stall.

Hurriedly, I grab a towel and wrap it around myself then run toward the lockers, hoping I'll catch him there.

Relief hits me when I hear stirring ahead of me, but when I turn the corner, it's Adly in a designer bikini that looks like it was tailored specifically for her.

"You're still here." Her bright smile makes me feel guilty for wishing she were someone else. "I thought you'd be gone by now."

"Yeah, I'm…" How long was I with Reid? And thank God, she seems to have missed him. "I guess I really got into my shower."

"State of the art shower head, am I right?"

"Uh…" *She doesn't mean* that. "Totally. Best shower head I've ever encountered." I hope she thinks my flushed skin is from the hot water and not from a life altering orgasm and stupid tongue-in-cheek references to the source of said orgasm.

"Anyway." She peels off her bikini top as though she's alone, without any shame, and I try hard to find something else to focus on without looking like I'm as awkward as I feel. "Like I said in my text—talked to Reid. Told him you're not into the feuding game, and if you were, you'd be one hundred percent Team Samuel. In case he was trying to use you to get to Dad, or whatever. He probably wasn't, but better to be safe. Not that you weren't ever safe, but he won't bother you again."

"Okay." I know she's right.

The worst part is that I wish with all my being that she wasn't.

CHAPTER FOURTEEN

REID

I step out of the car and stretch as I look out over the horizon. Sun is high, the water's blue. Nothing but ocean for miles and miles.

Alex gets out of the car and comes up beside me. "I suppose if we're forced to spend time together, this isn't the worst place to be."

"Three days," I remind him. "We can be out of here first thing on the morning of the twenty-sixth. The flight plan has already been submitted."

"Just three days." He looks as unconvinced as I feel.

I'm sure we sound ungrateful and spoiled. Every year, Grandpa Irving assigns each of his sons a holiday to spend with him. I'm not sure Grandpa has ever said the rest of us have to come as well, but as the sons are all still fighting over who will be left what position in his will, they all bend over backward to make the holiday Norman Rockwell picture perfect. In other words, Grandpa might not expect us to come, but Dad sure does.

And what Dad expects, I have to deliver. At least for the

next few years. Alex is still a year away from his trust fund and is working at SIC, so he's sort of indebted as well. Hunter is the lucky one out of the three of us. Since he's already collected his inheritance, it's harder for Dad to keep him under his thumb, which is why I was surprised when he got on the private jet this morning with the rest of us. Though, I suppose I might choose to come too, if I had the choice, for Grandpa's sake.

This year, our family was assigned Christmas on Grandpa's private island in the Caribbean, which is one of the better days to have to miss work. It's the only time the club is dead. Most other holidays are big business occasions, and I hate leaving the place in the hands of my assistants when I know it's going to be packed, so it's a relief not to have that worry this year.

And Alex is right—Pier Point Island (named after Grandma Adeline's maiden name) is not the worst place to be when temperatures back in New York City are averaging only thirty-five degrees Fahrenheit. If Dad's going to be in my face anyway, it's a whole lot easier to tolerate it behind a pair of sunglasses.

Another car pulls into the beach house drive and parks behind the other two. Dad and Nelani—his wife of the week—were in the car before us, so this has to be Hunter and his "guest."

Nonchalantly, I peer over my shoulder and watch as they climb out. "Which girlfriend is this?" I quietly ask Alex. "East Coast girl or West Coast?"

"Actually, they're exclusive." Alex doesn't sound too thrilled about it. Or maybe he's just as skeptical as I am about Hunter having a meaningful relationship since he's typically into transactional situations.

Casually, so I don't look too obvious, I turn to get a

better look at Hunter's plus one. He'd ushered her to the bedroom on the jet too quickly for me to see her earlier, and they'd stayed there the entire four hour flight. When we landed, Alex and I bolted off the plane, but Hunter and his girl had hung back. Probably took a minute to find all their clothes, if I had to guess.

Now that I have a better look, the brunette seems familiar. "Where do I know her from?" Victoria's Secret, most likely, since Hunter is very Leo DiCaprio in his choice of female companions.

"It's Zyah."

"The singer?" I squint over the edge of my Aviators. Sure enough, it's her. Her latest single is one of the most requested songs at Spice this month. "Hunter's not usually so trendy."

"He thinks he'll have a better chance at getting the CEO spot at SNC if he's more audience friendly."

That doesn't sound like how the board typically chooses CEOs. "He said that?"

Alex glances at them before answering. "No, that's my impression. Do you really think Hunter knows how to have anything real?"

I'm not sure I want to think too hard about the answer. The truth is, I'm pretty sure none of us know how to have anything real, and for some reason that makes me think of the person I have tried my hardest not to think about for the last thirty-four days—Lina fucking Quinn. Every day it's a struggle. Every day, I wake up with her taste on my tongue. Every night, I fall asleep imagining her in the bed next to me. I feel like I'm always two seconds away from using the number she programmed in my phone, constantly having to talk myself out of it.

I was pissed as hell when Adly got herself involved, but

it was honestly the best thing that could have happened. Her suggestion that I would play Lina like a pawn made me sick to my stomach, but it was also a big fat reminder that I'm not the one who decides my life these days. I would never use her, but if Dad thought I could, there's no telling what he'd ask me to do.

It's the only way I've managed to stay away from her—to keep her off his radar.

It's a stupid little obsession, anyway. A symbol of all that I can't allow myself to have. One day, when my deal with Dad is done—maybe then I'll be able to live a more fulfilling life. In the meantime, I have to keep my head down and my blinders on.

I let too much time pass after Alex's question without an answer.

"Exactly," he says, as though my silence is affirmation. "She might think it's genuine, but there's no way Hunter treats her right. Have you heard the way he talks to her?"

This is the first time I've seen them together at all, so no. Alex, on the other hand, has always been closer to Hunter than I am, but it's only been the last few months that he's been particularly critical of our older brother. "You invested in this girl too, or what?"

He glares at me like I've crossed some sort of line that I was unaware existed. "She's a human being, dumbass. I don't have to have an investment in her to think she deserves to be treated like one."

I raise my hands in surrender. "My bad. You're right. No need to get worked up."

His features immediately relax. "Sorry, it's just… Hunter…" He looks toward the front door and watches as Hunter and Zyah disappear into the house. "He can be a fucking tool, you know?"

"Everyone knows. Why do you think we all avoid him?"

"Yeah, well…" He shrugs. "Three days."

"Just three days."

A beat passes, and I'm sure he's thinking the same thing I am. We should probably go find Grandpa and greet him, but going in the house means possibly interacting with Dad and Hunter as well. There's plenty to do here at Pier Point, though. A lot of ways to avoid them…

Alex is the first to break the silence. "Three wheeling on the beach?"

"Give me twenty to get changed, and I'll meet you at the shed."

With avoidance decided as our plan, we both skip the front door and head down the sloped yard to sneak in the lower level walkout. We split up once inside, each of us heading to our usual rooms. I pass the rec room and the gym, then turn down the hallway toward my suite. The door is closed, which means there's a good chance my luggage hasn't been brought down yet since the staff usually leave rooms open after they drop off belongings.

If I have to go track it down, I will, but that will mean putting myself at risk of being pulled into whatever Dad and Grandpa are currently arguing about, so I say a little wordless prayer as I push through the doorway.

Right away, I see luggage.

Only, it's not *my* luggage.

Also, there's someone asleep on top of the bed covers. Someone red-haired and full-lipped, and while I know I'm prone to visions of Lina Quinn, they're generally not this lifelike.

And she's typically naked, while this version is (unfortunately) dressed.

I stare at her for long seconds, trying to make sense of her presence. Her mouth is slightly parted, her brow creased from a dream, her breaths deep and even, and fuck, she's more beautiful than I remembered her.

More beautiful and just as forbidden.

Why the hell is she here? Is this some kind of test? Did Dad decide to use her to fuck with Samuel on his own? Or did Santa decide I'd been a good boy this year and deliver my Christmas present early?

It's ridiculous how I'm already semi-hard, just from watching her.

I'm still frozen in place, fighting a full out erection, when Alex comes rushing into the room. "Dude, you'll never guess who else was invit—?" He cuts himself off when he sees what I'm seeing. When he speaks again, his voice is closer to a whisper. "Oh, shit. Maybe you will."

"Samuel's family's here?" It's not how the rotation works, but it feels like the most logical assumption.

He nods. "At least you didn't walk in on Adly changing into her swimsuit."

I cringe.

"Yeah, awkward as fuck."

Barely registers on the scale compared to how awkward it will be if I have to spend any of this holiday around Lina. I haven't just seen her naked, I've seen her come. I've *made* her come. The sounds she made are etched in my mind. I've beat myself raw several times replaying the memories.

Not that Alex suspects any of that.

"Where do you think they moved—"

This time I cut him off. "It's a mistake. Obviously. Samuel fucked up the schedule."

I pivot and head out of the suite, Alex on my heels, leaving Lina still asleep—God, she's a deep sleeper. I'm both thrilled and pissed to know this about her. It's information I shouldn't have, but I tuck it into a corner of my mind like it's precious treasure, and try not to think about it—try not to think about her—as I climb the stairs up to the main floor.

It's easy to track down Dad and Grandpa because as soon as we open the basement door, heated voices are heard coming from the front room.

"—our year for Christmas," Dad says. "It's been five years since the last time we had this holiday."

"Our name is clear as day on the email invitation we received in January. We're here and unpacked. They can just get back on the plane and turn around."

I look to Alex to be sure I recognize who's speaking. "Samuel?"

"Samuel," he confirms.

We wind around the butler's pantry and stop when the arguers are in sight. Dad and my uncle are positioned at either side of Grandpa, who's sitting back in his armchair like it's his throne, his legs stretched out on the ottoman in front of him.

Dad has his phone in hand, scrolling as he talks. "I always knew you were an idiot, but I didn't realize you were blind as well." He holds his screen out toward his brother then swings it for Grandpa to see. "It's our name on the schedule." He brings the phone back to his own gaze, as if to confirm he hasn't gone insane. He taps the screen. "Right there—Reynard. Not Samuel."

"Fuck you, you think that's proof? You probably tinkered with that just for kicks, like how you had your mini-you bring my ex to my own wedding."

"I think that's you he's referring to. Sorry, bro." Alex doesn't seem that sorry.

Someone else appears on the other side of me, and I turn to find Holt. "Who do you think fucked up?" he asks.

I shrug then nod at his girlfriend as she sidles up to Holt. "Hey, Brystin."

"Welcome to holidays with the Sebastians," Alex says to her, then directs his attention to me and Holt. "Should we start bets?"

"Thousand says it was my Dad." This from Adly. She pulls her cover-up tighter around her body when she addresses Alex. "Don't even look at me in your periphery, you perv."

Holt raises an eyebrow and looks at me.

This I know the answer to. "Apparently, there was an accidental walk-in-while-changing incident."

"Accidental, he *claims*." She then turns her sneer on me, as though she's just remembered the last time we had a tête-à-tête. "Don't think you're off my list."

"What did you—?"

I shush Alex, not only to prevent this conversation from taking a terrible turn to Lina, but also because Grandpa stands up and appears about to speak.

"I sent out two different invite lists, you fuckwads," he says. "A different one to each of you." He raises his finger toward my father. "And before you dare and try to call me an idiot—it was on purpose."

Alex stifles a laugh. I get it—it's usually fun to see Dad get in trouble, but I'm too concerned about the implications of us all being here on purpose. "You wanted us all here?" I ask, loud enough to make our presence known.

Holt piggybacks off my question. "Are Henry, August, and Arthur coming too?"

"The house is big, but not that big," Adly mutters.

"Thank you for asking, boys, but no," Grandpa says. "It's just all of you."

My anxiety overshadows the pride I'd normally feel from a Grandpa Irving compliment.

"But why would you…?" My stepmother, Nelani, starts to ask, and it's only now that I notice her sitting on the loveseat. She seems to think better of her question—either that or Dad gave her a glare that I can't see from where I'm positioned—because she lets it trail off.

Giulia gives her a sympathetic look from where she's perched on the arm of the sofa.

Grandpa answers anyway. "Because I'm getting closer to death. And I want to spend time with the people that I want to be with, and I'm not interested in letting a thirty-eight-year-old feud stand in the way of that. I paid for all your extravagant lives, don't you forget, so I think I get a say."

"Thirty-eight years," Holt mouths to his brother, Steele, who wandered in sometime between Nelani's comment and Grandpa's answer.

"Hunter," Alex mutters. Thirty-eight years ago would have been when he was conceived. This is the closest anyone has gotten to admitting that the argument between our fathers is about Hunter's mother, who also happens to be Holt, Steele, and Adly's mother.

Adly beams like she's won on Jeopardy. "We knew it."

Surprisingly, Dad is shut up by Grandpa's declaration. Or maybe more surprising is that Samuel is not. "I appreciate that you're confronting your mortality, Dad, but this is not just some silly little feud. You know as well as I do that your son deserves to be in jail."

"For fuck's sake—jail? Whatever you think you know about—"

Samuel speaks over my father's interruption. "I cannot, and will not, forgive that man."

"I don't fucking care if you ever forgive him," Grandpa says. "Hate him until he dies. That's your right. My right is to be able to ask my family to suck it up and be in the same room if I want them to be. If it's too much for you to handle, then by all means, you can go. But then remember it's also my right to remember that when I'm making out my final will and testament."

"Just our families?" Adly asks quietly.

Holt scratches his neck, his head turned toward us. "He's fucking with them."

"They sort of deserve it," Alex says.

Adly chuckles, and I can't tell if she thinks this arrangement is terrifying or humorous as hell.

I'm going with both.

Across the room, Hunter walks in from the opposite wing, his cell phone pressed to his ear. "I've already contacted the flight team," he says, moving the receiver from his mouth. "Anyone else wants to head back, they'll be refueled and ready to go in ninety minutes."

Zyah trails out behind him, and I swear it feels like Alex is trying his damndest not to look at them.

"Wish Simone wasn't with her sister," Steele says. "She'd love this."

Alex finally has someone else to look at. "Your girlfriend's so weird. But yeah. I can see the entertainment value."

"I'm not giving up my beach time," Adly says.

Holt looks to Brystin.

"Whatever you want to do," she says.

It's quiet, but I hear his response. "If Hunter's not going to be here, no reason to leave."

Samuel seems to be the only other one considering the offer, though there's no way he'll leave on the same plane Hunter's on. "We're staying," he says after a tense beat. "But Reynard can take the guest house. Giulia and I are already settled in the right wing suite."

"With pleasure," Dad says. "Think I want to see you more than I have to? The guest house has the better view, anyway."

Hunter stares directly at me from across the room. "What about you? You staying? I'd love to chat with you about some things if you want to ride back together."

"I...I'm...uh...I..." Shit, I sound like a dimwit. I swear everyone's staring, waiting for my response.

On all counts, it shouldn't be a difficult question, but it's maybe the most difficult one I've ever had to answer on the spot. For one thing, Hunter rarely gives me the time of day, let alone invites me to "chat". My curiosity is definitely piqued. And the three-day prison sentence on a tiny island with my father was bad enough—add in a rival brother, and I'll need to be drunk the whole time to get through it.

Problem is that intoxication is absolutely not an option. Not if I stay. Not with Lina here. With my wits gone, I don't stand a chance of resisting her, as has been proven in the past. I'm not even sure I can resist the draw if I'm completely sober.

Which is why I shouldn't be here. Why I should take Hunter up on his offer and deal with Dad's wrath later. Whatever the consequences, at least I won't be in danger of involving Lina in all of this.

But there's always a chance Dad could try to pull shit with her on his own. Adly acts like she can protect her, but she doesn't know my father. Doesn't realize how good he is at manipulating people.

And as much as I hate to say this about my own flesh and blood, Samuel's statement about Dad deserving jail only confirms my deep rooted suspicions that my father might be a really bad man. The facts are that Sebastian money means that none of us have to play by the rules. How many rules has my father broken? Does he have any morals at all?

Maybe I'm being paranoid, but I couldn't live with myself if Dad tried to approach Lina, and I wasn't here.

Or maybe that's just an excuse because I'm a greedy fucking asshole that knows this is the only way I'll ever get to be around her, and secretly, it's the only thing I want at all.

"I'm staying," I say finally. "Grandpa wants us here, I'm here." I don't even feel guilty pretending my grandfather is the reason. Like I said, I'm an asshole.

"Suit yourself," Hunter says with disgust. "Daddy's boy."

"Fuck him," Alex whispers.

Whatever.

Grandpa claps his hands together as though closing the book on a case. "Now that that's all settled, Elias will get you in your proper rooms. Some of you won't be where you normally are. Anyone has complaints, you can suck it up, buttercups."

"Fun times," Adly says, under her breath.

"I brought weed," Steele offers.

"And I have Xanax." Brystin has apparently quickly learned how to fit in. Good for her. I wonder how the other newest Sebastians are faring.

As though I've summoned her by the thought, her voice comes from behind me. "I fell asleep. What did I miss?"

We all turn to address her, and I wonder if anyone else

notices her wide eyes when she sees me. If they notice the way her skin instantly pinks up like she's just remembered something filthy.

Is she remembering the same filthy things I am?

Fuck. I can't think about that. I shouldn't even be looking at her.

Right now, though, my gaze is stuck to her like glue.

It's Steele who answers her. "Family time just got 100% more family. Buckle up for the ride, Little Sis."

"Oh," she says, seeming to understand the situation quicker than I'd expected. "Ohhhh." Am I imagining the terror in her expression?

Am I imagining the excitement?

"We're supposed to talk to Grandpa's assistant to be sure we have the right sleeping assignments." Holt points out Elias to Lina. "I'll introduce you."

"Okay." She lets him escort her across the room, only glancing back once, but when she does, it's to look directly at me.

Not too hard to miss since I was already staring after her.

Unfortunately, Adly notices too. "Don't think I'm not watching you, Reid."

Yep. No doubt about it.

This is definitely going to be a holiday to remember.

CHAPTER FIFTEEN

LINA

"...And Grandpa Irving made us get up before six for some sort of family activity on the beach, but he and half of the others are late, and it's already sunny, and the water is noisy, and it doesn't feel like Christmas Eve, and I miss my bed, and everything's the worst."

Denny is literally a hero for listening to me complain about a vacation that most people would die for. I'm such an ingrate.

"Yeah, yeah, everything's terrible. But can we go back to the part where you said Reid is there?"

Of course that's what he wants to focus on.

Honestly, it's why I called, but I'm trying to play like it's no big deal, as if pretending will make it reality. "What about it?"

"Come on, Lina. Spill."

"Well..." I pull my feet out from the sun into the shade of the umbrella I'm currently perched underneath and lower my voice, even though I'm yards away from the pier where the rest of the group is gathered.

Groups, actually, since Samuel's family is distinctly separated from Reynard's, but that isn't the tea that Denny's interested in. "We're ignoring each other."

"Ignoring each other? At a family get-together?"

"Yeah. It's cake."

The two family faction thing makes it easy because everyone's ignoring someone. At lunch and dinner the day before, Reynard and his bunch sat on one side of the table while Samuel and our bunch sat on the other. Both meals were tense as all get out with the two brothers scowling at each other every time they accidentally made eye contact. It might have been the most awkward experience of my life if, A. I didn't have a whole portfolio of awkward experiences to compare it to, and B. Grandpa Irving didn't seem to find the whole thing entertaining.

"Right. How long is that going to last?"

"I feel there's an implication there that I resent. I just don't know what it is."

He laughs. "So you're saying that if he weren't ignoring you, you'd be perfectly cool with still ignoring him?"

Oh.

"Uh…" I want to say yes and mean it. There are a dozen reasons to never give him the time of day again, but my body hums every time he's near, and when our eyes meet, it feels like there's still a connection. Not a connection I'm proud of, necessarily, but chemistry is chemistry. It's not my fault that his pheromones mix well with mine.

Denny seems to make assumptions from my silence. "Tell me this—how close is his room to yours?"

I allow myself a second to fantasize about sneaking into

his bed and despite my ankle-length maxi dress and sweater, goosebumps parade down my arms.

Stupid goosebumps.

"Look, nothing's happening. My mom is here. Adly is hovering over me, playing protector…"

"That's not what I asked."

I hate that I know the answer. It's not like I have any idea where Alex is sleeping. Or Holt, even. "His bedroom is upstairs on a whole other wing. Like I said, nothing's happening."

"You think the simple matter of bedroom location would stop me if I wanted to get to you?"

I glance up at the body looming above me and drop my cell in the sand. "Fuck. Reid. Fuck."

"It was me you were talking about, I assume?"

I don't answer. I'm too mortified to even look at him as I scramble to pick up my phone. "Uh, gotta go, Den. Talk soon."

Call ended, I put my hands in my lap and don't move because who knows? Maybe this trick will work out for me one day. Why not today? Christmas miracles and all that junk.

"I'm still here."

"I realize that," I say through gritted teeth, my gaze focused hard on the horizon. "I'm pretending that *I'm* not here."

He laughs in a way that says his amusement is as surprising to him as it is to me. "Come on." He offers a hand—the one that isn't holding a travel mug and now I'm wishing I'd known that taking my coffee with me from the breakfast table had been an option. "Grandpa's already on the boat. Let's go."

I'm so startled by his hand, then distracted by the warm

strength of it around mine as he pulls me to my feet, that it takes me a minute to register the rest of what he said. "Boat?" Sure enough, family members are boarding the large yacht docked at the end of the pier. "I can't get on a boat."

"None of us *want* to, but it isn't really our choice," Steele says, coming up from behind us.

Reid drops my hand like it's a hot potato. "I was just helping her up."

I'm the worst at social cues, and even I realize that Reid's comment only brought attention to something that my stepbrother had been previously oblivious to.

Steele's brow pinches behind his sunglasses. "That's… cool." He points to the yacht. "We going?"

"Yes," says Reid.

At the same time, I say, "No, I mean, I really can't."

"Can't get on the boat?" Steele looks at me like I'm speaking a foreign language. "That's the thing we're doing, though. Grandpa is driving us out past the waves so we can swim in the reef."

"I definitely can't do that." It's seventy degrees out, and I break into a cold sweat.

"Are you not an ocean swimmer? Once we're away from the undertow, it's really not any different from a pool." Steele is trying to be comforting, but I'm five seconds from a full blown panic attack.

"I don't swim. Period. Or boat. I get super sick. In fact, I might puke right now just looking at that boat."

"You don't swim?" Steele sounds almost disgusted.

"Do you not know how or…?" Unlike his cousin, Reid's tone is more curious than judgmental.

"I don't know…how?" Why does that feel like admitting an enormous secret? I've never been ashamed of my lack of aquatic skills before today, but then again, I've never felt like I was a weirdo for it.

I'm so wrapped up in the shame and the panic and memorizing the fading warmth from Reid's hand in mine that I don't see my mother running up the pier until she's upon us. "Lina, I just heard. I thought we were just having breakfast on the yacht. I didn't realize we were going out on the water. Samuel's going to explain to his father—"

"Explain what to me?" Grandpa Irving does not run up to us like my mother. He arrives on a golf cart, and after watching the way he drives this tiny vehicle, I'm not sure I'd get on a boat that he was driving even if I wasn't afraid of boats.

"She doesn't swim," Mamma and Steele say in unison, which makes me feel just like an eight-year-old child again, unable to communicate my own needs.

"I'm sure Lina can speak for herself," Reid says. He sneers at Steele, so it looks like just another mini battle between the two families rather than a move to defend me.

I mean, maybe that's exactly what it is. I try not to let it mean anything, but my heart does a little flip thingy all the same.

Fortunately, Grandpa turns his attention to me.

"I never learned. Boats make me sick, and I was always scared of swimming pools." For good reason since a boy I knew in elementary school nearly drowned. Then, when I got older and was curvier than most other girls, I avoided pools so I wouldn't have to don a bathing suit. I'm less self-conscious now, but I live in Brooklyn—it's not like the opportunity to learn has been knocking down my door.

Grandpa looks almost as confused as Steele did. "But all Sebastians can swim."

"She's only recently become family, Grandpa."

I might be imagining Reid's subtext, but I swear what I hear is, *we're not really related*. Not that anyone's concerned about that for any reason or anything.

"I know that, son. You think I don't know that? What I meant is that this won't do at all." He moves his lips together as though he's chewing a thought or adjusting his dentures. "Obviously, you're going to have to be taught."

"Throw her in the ocean and see if she makes it back to the boat like my dad did with us." Steele's suggestion sends my heart racing.

Mamma must notice the fear in my expression because she casually puts her arm around me. "We're not doing that."

Grandpa nods his head back and forth, as though he's considering.

Once again, Reid stands up for me. "Grandpa, we're not doing that."

"No, no. We're not," the old man finally agrees. "Not if she's going to be throwing up just from the boat ride. But we're not going to leave you back here alone, either."

"I'm fine. Really. I have a book—"

"Reid," Grandpa says, ignoring me. "You stay back with her."

"Uh…" I can't quite read his eyes through his sunglasses, but I'm pretty sure Reid is now as panicked as I was just seconds ago.

I'm panicking now too, just for different reasons. Very different reasons.

"I'll stay," Mamma says, and I love her so much, but I kind of want to punch her in the tit for making me feel like I need a babysitter.

"I'm really fine on my own."

"Nonsense," Grandpa says, addressing my mother, as

though I haven't spoken. "You're practically still on your honeymoon. Reid's the best swimmer of the kids. He'll be an excellent teacher for her."

"Teacher?" Reid and I say in unison.

Which is not a sign that we're in sync or that the universe wants us together.

Definitely not.

"While we're out on the boat. Teach her the foundations. At least get her comfortable in the deep end." Grandpa is already turning the wheel of the golf cart, as though the matter's been settled.

Ha ha, Steele mouths to Reid, as though being stuck with me is a punishment, which it probably is, and everyone knows it, and God I'm so embarrassed.

I try again to voice my protest. "This really isn't necessary, Grandpa Irving."

"Hop on, Giulia," he says, because obviously he can't hear anything I say. "I'll give you a lift back to the boat."

My mother hesitates for the briefest of moments before climbing in beside him. "You'll be fine," she says to me. "Have fun."

Have fun? She expects me to get into a deep body of water with a man who likes to torment me and she wants me to *have fun*?

"Can I jump in the back—"

Steele is halfway on the vehicle when Grandpa shoos him off. "Your legs ain't broke."

Ha ha, Reid mouths to Steele, who responds with the middle finger before jogging off toward the boat.

It would all be a whole lot funnier if I wasn't freaking the fuck out. As it is…

"I can get a class at the Y when we're back home," I shout after the golf cart. "It will be my New Year's resolution. It's just a couple of weeks away. I really don't think I'm going to need to know how to...." They're long gone now. "Oh, fuck a nugget."

I turn toward Reid, hoping he might be more reasonable than his grandfather. It's not like he has to do everything Grandpa says...right?

But I swear the man is fighting a smirk, and after scanning me up and down, all he says is, "Better get your swimsuit."

There are still eighteen hours until the day is over, but I'm calling it now:

Worst. Christmas Eve. Ever.

CHAPTER SIXTEEN
LINA

Somehow, I manage to convince Reid to put off the lessons until a more reasonable hour, so it's just after nine am when I wander out to the pool deck for the first time since we've arrived on Pier Point.

To be fair, it has one of the most beautiful views I've ever seen in my life. It's located on the cliff side of the island, and the water cascades over the side, eternity pool style. It's a dream reading location. I would gladly pull up a deck chair and an umbrella and lounge all day with one of the many books on my TBR.

I do not, however, have any interest in getting in that pool.

Especially now that the sun is higher in the sky. I'm wearing an oversized hat and a long-sleeve swimsuit coverup that goes to my shins, and I swear I can feel my hands and ankles start to crisp up the second I step outside. My skin is not made for tropical islands.

Reid's skin, on the other hand…

He's doing laps when I approach, and even though we've only been here one full day, he's already turned a shade of bronze that makes me sure that he's never had to deal with the aftermath of peeling skin let alone a wicked burn. The way he moves in the water, too, is insane. It's like he was born to use his body like this. Each stroke seems effortless. Each tilt of his head to catch a breath of air, completely natural. It's hypnotic.

And beautiful.

And really fucking sexy.

And goddammit, I hate him.

Thank the Lord for sunglasses so he can't see the stew of admiration/lust/hate in my eyes when he breaks from his laps and drapes his gorgeous, buff swimmer arms over the side of the pool. "You can't swim in a coverup."

"Thank you, Oh Wise One. I had no idea." I watch the rivulets run down his face and wipe my own cheeks, as though that will remove the water on his. "There's no way I can take this thing off, though, without half a bottle of SPF 50, and oops. I didn't bring any since I had expected to spend the entire trip in the shade."

He nods to a basket with towels rolled up inside. "There should be some in there."

I shuffle to where he's indicated, praying that he's wrong, but sure enough, there are several bottles buried in between the rolls.

As expected.

It was a longshot to try to hope otherwise. The Sebastians are freaking billionaires. Of course they have sunscreen.

Which means I have to ask for the favor that I very much didn't want to have to ask. "Well then, if you're finished showing off, could you, maybe, like…help me with my back?"

It has always been my impression that asking a man for help applying sunscreen is code for *I want you to touch me.* Even though I very much need sunscreen on every inch of my body if I expect to not be suffering tomorrow, and I know full well that I can't reach everywhere I need to reach.

Ideally, there would be someone else to ask, and maybe there is someone. A house employee who isn't currently making beds or preparing lunch or raking the beach—yes, there are people who rake the freaking beach like it's a five star resort.

But I'm not about to go look for them because, as much as I hate to admit it to myself, I actually really do want Reid to touch me.

I know. I've got problems.

"All you had to do is ask."

He smirks as he pulls himself up and out of the water in this hot athletic move that makes me very aware of my own lack of coordination, flexibility, and strength. It's incredibly hard not to stare as he crosses over to me. The whole water dripping down his gorgeous body thing is real life porn, and my lady bits have fond memories of his ability to please. It's all super distracting.

"Can you hand me a bottle?" he asks, as though it's not the first time.

"Can you not have six-pack abs?"

He looks down at his torso, like he doesn't know what he'll find. "This bothers you?"

Yes. Very much so.

But more importantly…why did I say it out loud?

I bring my fist up and bonk it lightly on my forehead a

few times. "I have a real problem with blurting out everything that crosses my mind."

"I've noticed. But you don't need to apologize. It's… uh…kind of adorable."

"I wasn't apologizing. I was stating a fact." I slap a tube of sunscreen into his waiting palm. "And you can't say things like that about your cousin."

"First of all, I can and do. Not about Adly, because she's just a pain in the ass, but my cousin Sydney is the definition of adorable. A very different kind of adorable than you, but the point remains." He squirts a blob of lotion into his hand, and I bite my lip so I won't ask what kind of adorable I am without meaning to. "Second of all—you are *not* my cousin."

There is no mistaking the purpose of the statement. His tone is full of raw want that would be wholly inappropriate if we were blood relatives. Heat spreads low in my belly, and I suddenly feel like my knees might give way.

"But I'm still off-limits," I say, a reminder for him as well as for me.

His response comes reluctantly. "You're still off-limits."

I nod.

Then ask anyway, "But…why, exactly?"

"You know why. Drop the coverup and turn around."

I start to turn, then stop. Because I'm actually not sure that I do know why. "The feud?"

"Mainly."

"But that's not all it is."

He sighs, impatient. "The feud, the difference in our age, the fact that we can't just anonymously hook up, that we'd see each other again—"

"That didn't stop you last time."

He goes on like I didn't interrupt him. "The difference in our experience level."

"Because you think that it would mean too much to me because of the whole virginity thing." Right. How could I forget?

"Yes. That. Turn around."

"What if I wasn't a virgin anymore?"

"You're not?" Jealousy flashes across his features. "Denny?"

"No! Not…grr." I actually say grr. I'd forgotten I'd led him to believe I was with Denny, but also, who in their right mind could spend any time with us and think we were anything more than friends? And also, also, why wasn't me having a boyfriend on his list of reasons I was off-limits?

But mostly grr because I am still a virgin, and I haven't bothered to try to lose it since that night with Reid because there's just no one else I can imagine offering it to.

Then he goes and reminds me that's never going to happen.

I turn around, undo my cover up, and let it drop to the ground. "Do my back, please."

"Not…grr?" There's confusion in his tone, and he's yet to start rubbing me.

"I'm not with Denny. I'm still a virgin. I don't want to talk about it anymore. Just…do me, please." Before he can think I mean it another way, I correct myself. "My *back*! Do my back. God, you're like twelve years old. Your mind is always in the gutter."

He lets out a short laugh. But a beat passes before his hands meet my skin. I inhale at the contact, not just because the lotion is surprisingly cold for having been outside, but because Reid is touching me. Really touching me. Working the sunscreen across my back and up my neck and down my arms.

Then he gets another blob from the tube and bends to do my legs.

"I can do th—"

"I'm already doing it." His hands come on either side of my thigh. Then all the way up—to where my leg meets my pelvis. The top side of his finger repeatedly hits the crotch panel of my bikini, and I'm half afraid it might be considered assault except that I'm not at all mad about it, oh, and the fact I spread my legs further apart before he did it might have been an invitation.

Like I said, I have a problem.

When my legs, arms, and backside are thoroughly greased up (and my bottoms are damp, though I've yet to get in the water), Reid tells me to turn around like he's planning to slather up my front as well.

"I got it," I say, trying to take the tube from him.

But he lifts it out of reach. "You might miss a spot."

I consider fighting harder for it, but it's a fleeting thought, and I drop my arms. "Don't forget my ears."

"I won't forget anything." He squeezes another ball of lotion onto his hand, then freezes when he actually looks at me. "Could you not wear something so revealing?"

"Are we going to run out of sunscreen?" I do have more landscape to cover than some, and considering how fair I am, I can easily go through a whole tube.

"That wasn't my concern."

He starts at my belly, but his eyes are glued to my tits, and though I'm not dumb, I'm also not the best at social cues, so of course I have to ask. "Is all that I'm revealing… bothering you?"

"I wouldn't say bother."

"But it's distracting? You've seen it before. More, actually. You've seen it all."

"Just because I've seen it before doesn't mean I'm not going to react when I see it again."

I'm dying to look down that washboard stomach to see what kind of reaction he's having, but Reid's hands land on the tops of my breasts, and then I forget my intentions as all the breath leaves me in a whoosh.

"Especially when you react like you do to my reaction," he says.

"I don't know what you're talking about. I'm completely unaffected."

"Sure you are." His touch is firm as he rubs the lotion with just his thumbs so that his palms accidentally graze my breasts.

And then not-so-accidentally. When he spreads his fingers and cups my tits outright. My nipples are hard knots under the thin material. They tighten as he squeezes them between his knuckles. "Still unaffected?"

It feels like some game of chicken, just like when he had us playing strip games at my house party. I lost big time that night, and I'm wary of making the same mistakes. It's the only reason I don't reach down to feel what he's packing in those swim trunks. The only reason I don't beg him to forget about the lessons and fuck me right now on the patio.

So obviously, I lie. "Dry as a bone."

I see it in his eyes—how he wants to check for himself. My shades give me the upper hand, since he's not wearing any, and his hazel eyes say a lot more than he probably wants them to say. Like how much he wants me, despite all his insistence that anything between us is impossible.

I'm so sure of it, I hold my breath waiting for him to make another move.

When he doesn't, I get bold. "Why don't you find out?"

It's *too* bold, and he immediately retreats, dropping his hands to his sides and stepping back. "When you're finished putting on your sunscreen, you can meet me in the water."

He hands me the tube, and before I can squirt some out, I hear him splash into the pool behind me.

"Sure hope that water's cold," I mutter to myself. "For your sake."

"Did you say something?"

Playing innocent, I rub the lotion onto my face and swing my head toward him. "Hm?"

He treads water, his eyes narrowed, as though he doesn't trust me. Which is fair, but also annoying.

Equally annoying is when he says, "Don't forget your ears."

After flipping him off, I cover the rest of my body with SPF (including my ears) until there's no possible way the sun can break through to my sensitive skin.

Then I turn toward the pool, and my heart starts jack-hammering inside my chest. With all the flirting—was that what we were doing? I'm not experienced enough with the activity to be sure—I forgot about the whole learning how to swim thing. Including the part where I'm afraid of any body of water that's higher than my shins when I'm standing in it.

I approach the shallow end and consider best how I can get out of this.

"Maybe I should just sit here awhile and get used to the temperature?" Except when I plop down on the edge and stick my feet in the water, I discover it isn't cold at all. "Oh. That's very…temperate."

"The pool is kept at eighty-two."

"That's too bad." So much for the cold water helping with whatever situation he may have been having in his trunks.

"Quit dawdling. Take off your sunglasses and get in."

"Take off my sunglasses?"

"So you can put your face in the water."

"So I can put my face in the water? No way am I putting my face in the water. Isn't that, like, lesson four or five? At least? Shouldn't we start with…I don't know…walking in past my knees?"

His expression serious, he stalks up the slope, stopping when he's hovering above me. "First lesson is usually learning to hold your breath under water. Which definitely means putting your face in. But if you'd rather, we can start with floating."

"If floating means we can get out one of those inflatable raft things…"

Ignoring me, he snatches the sunglasses off my face and tosses them onto a nearby deck tray before pulling me up to my feet.

"If I'm not going to put my face in the water, then why can't I have my sunnies?"

"Because I said so."

"Perfect old person answer. Good job using the official language."

He tugs me with him down the slope, which is much steeper than it appears from the outside, because I'm in above my knees after only a few feet. "Okay, this is good. We're good. Let's do the floating thing now."

"Not deep enough. We should at least get in past your torso."

"My torso? Oh my God, you want to drown me, don't you? Was that your plan all along? Is this your father's way of pissing off Samuel? I really, really don't want to be a feud casualty. You don't have to do this. There has to be another way."

Yes, I use dramatics as a coping method, but since he drags me in deeper with each word that I say, we are now in water that is higher than my breasts, and I am no longer feigning freak out—I'm freaking out for real.

"Holy shit! Holy shit. Reid!" I could reach the ground just fine a second ago, but I start to panic and flail, and I guess I pull my legs up or propel myself deeper because suddenly I'm no longer touching, and then something screamlike comes out of my mouth, and I claw at Reid in a desperate attempt to save myself, until finally, I get my fingernails firmly in his skin, pull myself closer, and wrap my legs around him so tightly, I'm not going anywhere.

"Um…" But he doesn't push me off. Instead, he circles his arms around me.

Several silent seconds pass like this, the two of us bobbing in the water as little by little my pulse returns to normal.

Or at least, it's not high anymore because of the threat of drowning.

Now it's racing because the way we're tangled around each other is very un-cousin-like. Our mouths are inches from each other. Our breaths mingle. His gaze darts from my eyes to my lips, and I swear he might kiss me.

"Look, I'm floating," I say, nervously.

"This isn't floating."

"Speak for yourself." My tummy feels like it did that

time I went up in a hot air balloon. It was still tethered to the ground—I wasn't brave enough to go on an actual flight —but that butterflysy feeling was the closest I'd ever felt to floating until this.

More seconds pass, and soon I realize that the bobbing is just Reid walking around, and in fact he's walked us into shallower water because now he can slightly bend his knees and still keep us immersed up to our shoulders.

The knee bend is an important development, since now the way his pelvis is positioned, it's more like I'm sitting in his lap. Which means I can feel that definitive, hard ridge against the very part of my body that wants to feel that ridge the most.

Of course I buck my hips so my pussy drags across his cock.

His breathing shallows, and I swear that the next time I buck, he does too, increasing the pressure against my clit.

I bite my lip so I won't moan.

Reid's hands move lower to settle on my ass, and the next time I grind against him, he tilts me closer at the same time.

"Really still a virgin?"

"Really still a virgin."

This time when he slides me along his cock, I do moan.

"Why?"

I shake my head as if I don't know, but of course I know. Of course I say it. "Haven't found anyone else I want to do it with."

"I like that," he says. Quiet and heavy-like. As if it's a serious confession.

Now I'm really floating.

A grin fights to take over my lips, and it feels like such a mood breaker, for so many reasons. Like the reason that I want him to keep rubbing his cock against my clit and the reason that I don't want him to start overthinking shit. So I fight it by sucking in my cheeks and making fish lips.

"What are you doing?"

"Not smiling." I manage to keep the fish lips while talking.

"Why don't you want to smile?"

"Because I don't want you to know that things you say make me happy."

The side of his mouth lifts, and that does it—I'm grinning despite myself.

"Whoops." I try to reclaim the fish lips, but now I'm giggling.

"Why don't you want me to know that things I say make you happy?"

I shake my head again, knowing I shouldn't say it. Knowing I can't keep it in. "Because I don't want you to think I'll make too much of the time we spend together." My voice is barely above a whisper. "Even though I can't stop thinking about every moment. Every single one."

"Lina..."

It's full of pity. The way someone says your name right before they explain to you why you're so off base. So delusional. So mistaken.

I'm such a fool.

Not because I've misinterpreted anything that's happened between us. I know what's going on better than he does, it seems. There is *something*. I'm not off base.

But I'm a fool for thinking he'll ever be bold enough to do anything but dance around it.

Before he can continue with whatever patronizing speech he's about to give, I push out of his arms, and thankfully find that I can stand just fine in the depth we're in. "Thanks for the lesson. I'm done now."

Then I march out of the pool.

"But you didn't learn anything," he calls after me.

"Yeah, I did," I say without turning around. "I learned to avoid the deep end."

Next time, I'll stay where it's shallow.

Better yet—I won't let there be a next time at all.

CHAPTER SEVENTEEN

LINA

Pretending I had a headache and skipping dinner so I wouldn't have to face Reid was a much better idea when I still had a trail mix hidden in my suitcase.

But at three in the morning, the snacks are long gone and my stomach has gone from a little bit rumbly to full out hunger-panged.

Thankfully, there are so many windows on every floor that the moonlight streams in, and moving about the house is easy, even without turning on any overheads.

The problem comes when I'm standing in front of the open stainless steel refrigerator. There is plenty of food to choose from, as expected from the family who wants for nothing, but everything that happens at Pier Point—as in any Sebastian house, no matter the location—is carefully planned, and I have no idea if the bowl of potato salad (or the deli meat or the sliced watermelon or the fruit yogurt) is up for grabs or is part of tomorrow's menu.

And where's the stuff they served tonight? Surely the

family didn't devour everything from dinner. "Do they not know about leftovers?"

"Grandpa doesn't believe in keeping them."

Startled to find I'm not alone, I jump so high, I bang my knee on the open fridge drawer, and am about to scream when a firm hand covers my mouth from behind.

"He says they're wasteful to keep for ourselves," Reid continues, because of course it's fucking Reid, his voice soft at my ear. "So he lets Yasiel take them home with her to the main island for the shelter. If I remove my hand now are you going to scream?"

I shake my head, and as soon as he releases me, I put a yard of distance between us. "Are you kidding me?"

He raises his hands like he's innocent. "I thought you knew I was here. Who were you talking to?"

"Myself!" How does he not know I am a chronic talk-to-myself person by now? Surprisingly, my wits are together, and I remember to whisper my yelling. "Of all people… how many other people are in this house? And it had to be you who shows up. And you couldn't put a goddamned shirt on?"

"I didn't realize I'd be seeing you." He glances down my body, taking in my sleeping shorts and spaghetti-strapped tank. "If I'd known, I wouldn't have bothered to put on sweatpants."

I refuse to wonder if that means he isn't wearing underwear.

Which of course means that's exactly what I'm wondering, and also, did he really just say that? "Okay, stop. No more of that rile-me-up talk."

"Rile you up?"

"You ever heard the term 'cunt tease'? 'Cause you are the very definition. And no, it's not a compliment." I bend to rub my knee which is throbbing. It's definitely going to be bruised tomorrow.

"*Cunt tease*." He shakes his head. "You're right. It's definitely not one of my better traits. Let me look at it." He points to my injury.

"No. I don't need you to doctor me."

"You don't need me to, but it's my fault. So just let me—"

I let out a literal growl.

But I'm too hangry to fight about it. "Fine. Fine. Go ahead and—"

Before I've finished speaking, his hands are around my waist and he's lifting me up on the counter. "Oh for fuck… okay. Sure. He can lift me like I weigh nothing. Why am I surprised?"

He chuckles as he leans past me to flick a switch that turns on the under cabinet lights. They're dim, but helpful, and sure enough when he lifts my knee to examine it, I can see the startings of a bruise.

"Does this hurt?" he asks, running his finger along the tender spot.

"Not any more than when you weren't touching it." The pressure actually helps, but I'm not giving him that satisfaction.

"Then it's okay if I keep touching it?"

I nod, but then I remember that I'm not letting him fuck with me anymore, or rile me up, and that means absolutely no sensual petting. "No."

"That's…probably a good answer." He smiles, his fingers lingering on my skin for a handful of seconds before removing them and taking a step back.

"Self-preservation," I say, even though I'm fully aware I don't have to explain myself.

"I admire it. I could learn something from you." I think he might go on, but my stomach takes that moment to let out an embarrassingly long and loud growl. "You're hungry."

"It's kind of why a person raids the kitchen in the middle of the night."

"Shouldn't have missed dinner."

"Shouldn't have made me want to miss dinner."

His features soften. "I'd hoped it wasn't because of me."

Don't you dare feel bad about it, Lina.

Sometimes it's hard to remember that my feelings are valid too. That I don't need to minimize my emotions to make someone else feel better. Look where it gets me. I've done it for years with my mother, and now I'm a twenty-one-year-old virgin. I refuse to keep doing it.

"Well, so…do better," I say.

He considers, as if it's a revolutionary idea I've given him. Or as if he doesn't think that doing better is an actual option.

Instead of responding to it, though, he just runs a hand through his bed hair, which is tousled but sexy, unlike the unruly knots in mine, and then points a single finger in my direction. "Let me fix you something to eat."

"No…you don't need…" Except, I still don't know what food is off-limits and also, it's the least he can do after all the shit he's pulled on me.

Side note, I really do have a thing for men who serve me. I'm an Acts of Service love language girl, all the way. Which is not at all why I'll let him do this. It's about practicality, is all. And only if he isn't going out of his way. "I mean, if you're making something for yourself… Were you?"

"It's kind of why people raid the kitchen in the middle of the night," he says, throwing my own words back at me.

"You are such a dick."

"As established." That grin is killer, when he allows it.

I lower my eyes quickly so that it doesn't penetrate the barrier I've erected, which I must admit is a fairly thin barrier, and also comes down all together without much effort. In other words, I'm pretty vulnerable, so the best I can do is pretend that I'm not, and maybe he won't know the difference.

"I was going to make a sandwich." I can tell from his tone that his smile dropped, probably when my gaze did. "Just as easy to make two. I'm sure I owe that to you. Though…you did charge up my card with all those room service items…"

"You can't keep bringing that up. You get why, right?"

"Why?" Without giving me a chance to answer, he continues. "Turkey, bacon, tomato, lettuce, cream cheese?"

"Cream cheese?" I lift my head and see all the items he's mentioned lined up on the counter. Sure enough, there's cream cheese. "Okay. I'll try it."

I watch as he makes the sandwiches, and even though it's a simple task, he's as hypnotic at this as he is at bartending and swimming. His every move is graceful. Like he understands how to exist in his own skin instead of like me, who always feels like my body is something separate from me that isn't fond of cooperating.

It's enchanting.

And unfair. Is it because he's a man? Because he has money? Because he has a dozen years more experience being human? Or just because he's a different person than I am?

I'm jealous and intrigued. And aroused. I can imagine

him moving over me with the same confident energy. He'd command my pussy like he does that knife. He'd open me up like I was that tomato. He'd lick my juice from his finger like—

"Lina?"

"...hm, what?" I blink my eyes. "Sorry, I was…" What I was thinking about shouldn't be said out loud, and I can't come up with something else so I just shake my head. "Did you say something?"

"I asked why." He gives me a second to get the context. "Why I can't keep bringing up the room service?"

"Oh. Oh, right. It's because that was getting even with what you owed me before. You were really terrible that night. Cutting me off like you did? Such an ass, and—"

"An ass? You had an orgasm."

"I can give myself an orgasm. I can't give myself real live dick."

His eye twitches. "I was being noble."

"Noble? You were being *noble*?" I can't believe what I'm hearing. "For deciding that you knew what was best for me, even though we'd just met, and didn't know what I needed at all, plus I'm a full grown adult who can make her own decisions about her body and what she wants to do with it, and who she wants to do it with, and—"

"Okay, okay. It wasn't noble. But I was trying to look out for your—"

"It wasn't about me at all. It was about you and your… whatever drama you made up in your head that puts an overemphasis on a woman's virginity—whatever virginity even means, these days—and ignores the fact that sometimes we just want to bang, same as men do, and for every thing there is a first time. The only one who was bothered about that was you."

He stares at me, which is only slightly intimidating, considering he still has a knife in his hand. "Okay. It was about me," he says, eventually.

"It was selfish."

"Sure. Selfish."

"And demeaning."

"Okay."

"And hurtful." As long as he's being agreeable, I'm going for it all. "Imagine how it made me feel to be rejected like that."

"It was not a rejection, Lina. I never said I didn't want you."

Cunt tease. "Well. Actions speak louder than words."

"Okay, okay. I get it." He sounds remorseful, anyway.

Which is something?

I watch as he cuts one of the two sandwiches he's made in half—triangle-wise—and slides it over to me on a napkin. "Thank you. Now do you get why I charged up your card?"

"It was retaliation. I deserved it."

"Exactly. It made us even."

"So I can't bring it up like it's still outstanding."

"Yes. That's right." I take a bite and put my hand up to cover my mouth, because I don't want to wait until I'm done chewing to say what I have to say. "Now you owe me for your bad behavior after that." I swallow, just as he hands me a bottle of water, which I immediately take a swig of. "Thanks. This is really good. Cream cheese. Who knew?"

"You're welcome." He leans a hip against the counter and ignores his own sandwich, choosing to watch me eat instead. Like a creeper.

"Stop looking at me. It's weird."

He doesn't move his gaze. "It's been pretty bad behavior, hasn't it?"

"Well..." I take a second to clear my mouth, the seriousness of this conversation finally hitting me. I'd told myself I wasn't going to engage with him like this ever again, but I hadn't thought we might have an opportunity for real talk.

Maybe I'm opening myself for more disappointment, but we're only stuck here together for another day. It might be my only chance to say the things I've wanted to say. "Yes. It has been pretty bad. And not the bad behavior I wanted. Some of it was, I guess. The shower."

"The shower." The gravel in his tone says it was as hot for him as it was for me.

It's validating, somewhat. Knowing that it hadn't just been a pity...shower stimulation situation.

But then that begs the question..."Why did you disappear that day?"

He takes a deep breath in and lets it out before answering. "I shouldn't have been there in the first place."

"Then why were you there in the first place? And don't say because you owed me. I'm not stupid, contrary to whatever you might think—"

"I don't think you're stupid."

I continue as though he hasn't spoken. "You wanted to be there."

"I did. I wanted to be there. But—"

I'm tired of his buts. I've heard them already. "I'm off-limits. I've got it. But if that's really so important to you, again I'll ask, why were you there?"

"Because..." He moves to stand in front of me and places a hand on the counter on either side of me, caging me in. "With you, I can't stop..." It sounds like there's going to be more to the sentence, but then he just leaves it there and shrugs. "I don't know why."

Uh…wow.

I try to ignore the flip my heart does. "If that was an apology, it was real lame-ass."

"It wasn't an apology. It was a statement of fact."

"Well, thank you for pointing it out, Captain Obvious."

"I just wanted you to know I realize I'm an asshole."

"Okay." I don't know what else to say. Maybe that's all there is to say.

Except that he's still standing over me. Still caging me in. Still staring at me with those intense hazel eyes.

"Okay," I say again.

"Have you ever sucked a cock?"

"What…!" It's a good thing I don't currently have food in my mouth because I would spit it out. "Where the hell did that come from?"

"I can't stop wondering."

I pretend not to notice his eyes darken as he stares at my lips. "You can't just say, 'oh, I know I'm an asshole,' and then think that gives you permission to keep being an asshole."

"I don't think that at all. I'm out of control around you. I just said that. There is no premeditation to my assholery. It just happens."

"That sounds like a real good reason to be sure that you're never around me then." My words hang in the air, and I wish I could take them back.

Not that he hasn't already come to the same conclusion. "I actually think I did a pretty good job until Grandpa Irving stepped in and fucked up my track record."

He did an excellent job. We went a whole month without seeing each other, and it was fine. Life was drama free. No one turned me on and excited me in that time period, but also nobody stomped on my heart. I thought it was a good compromise.

Until I saw him again and realized I really like feeling alive.

"Fucking Grandpa Irving," I say.

"Fucking Grandpa Irving," he says, and I'm pretty sure we both mean just the opposite.

Another tense beat passes, and I wonder if he'll try to kiss me. I wonder if I'll let him.

He leans in closer. "Have you ever sucked a cock?"

"Oh my God!" I suppose it's a form of kissing?

"Have you?"

"I don't know if I should talk to you about this."

"Have you sucked Denny's cock?"

I'm blushing and tingling in all my sensitive places. I take a second to be sure I'm not uncomfortable with the situation, because I don't have to stand for this. I'm not alone in the house. I can excuse myself and scream for help if he tries to take this anywhere.

But I'm not uncomfortable.

And I'm glad we're as alone as we are.

And I want him to take this somewhere.

"No, I haven't sucked Denny's cock." I brave up and reach out to trace along the firm plane of his pecs. "I told you—I'm not with him."

"You've never been with him at all?" His thumbs start drawing lazy circles on the outsides of my thighs.

"I mean…" The warmth of his touch is dizzying. "I had a crush on him for a minute in high school, but when I realized he wasn't into me, and that we make better friends, I got over it."

"Is he gay? How could he not be into you?"

"That's a fucked up assumption, and no. He likes women."

"And he doesn't want to fuck you?"

It's not my place to say it, but I know Denny won't mind. "He doesn't want to fuck anyone. He's not into sex."

"I don't understand that."

I laugh. "Yeah, I'm sure you don't."

A beat passes and the tension between us thickens.

"So…" He reaches beyond me and brings back a banana from the fruit bowl and holds it up. "Have you…ever… sucked cock?"

I open my mouth to answer—not sure what I'll say since I don't want to scare him off by telling him I'm as virgin in this area as I am in the other—but before I can speak, he sticks the unpeeled banana past my lips.

"What are you doing?" I say around the fruit.

"Imagining." He pulls it out only to stick it in again, further this time, and I start to choke.

He withdraws the banana, just far enough that I can speak again. "I gag easily."

"That's hot."

"You're…sick."

"You had to think about it because you think it might be hot too." He doesn't let me respond, pushing the banana in again. This time, I manage not to gag. "...Fuck. I want to break your mouth in so fucking bad."

"These are really mixed messages, Reid." It's possible he doesn't understand what I said, what with my mouth being occupied. I put my hand over his and pull the banana all the way out. "Tell me straight—are you a groomer? Are you grooming me?"

"No, I'm not a groomer." He says it like he's offended. "Why would this be grooming? Maybe you're the groomer.

Because, I'll tell you, months ago I would not have been this..."

"This...what?"

"Stupid. I wouldn't have been this stupid. I wouldn't have allowed myself to think such stupid thoughts. Want such stupid things."

He shakes his head, and for a second, I think this might be where he chickens out and runs away. Like always.

So with my hand still on his, I direct the banana back into my mouth, and push it in as far as I can stand, helping him with that imagination of his.

His breath intakes sharply. "I should..." Then he pulls the banana from my mouth and removes his hand from under mine. "I should go."

Faster than I've ever moved in my life, I jump down from the counter, onto my knees, and tug at the drawstring of his sweatpants. "This isn't stupid, Reid."

"This is very stupid."

"Why?"

"Lina..."

"Don't do that. Don't treat me like I'm naïve or too inexperienced or too young to know what I want. From my viewpoint, you're too old not to know what you want."

He peers down at me. "I know what I want."

"Okay, well I do too." I loosen the drawstring more, and when his pants slip down, he lets them fall to the ground.

My eyes immediately go wide.

First of all—he's commando. As speculated. So boom. It's right there. In my face. Long and proud and very erect.

Second of all—I've been dying to see this monster since the night I met him, and wow. I had no idea a cock could be so...beautiful. Not too veiny or dark, with a perfect mushroom cap head that I immediately want to put in my mouth.

Third of all—and the reason I haven't put him in my mouth already—he's huge. Just like he'd advertised. Thick and fat, and I'm pretty sure it grows even bigger the longer I stare.

"That is..." Words are hard when I'm this stunned. "That is a lot of cock."

"You aren't responsible for taking care of it." He brushes a strand of hair from my face, and I can already sense that he's going to play the martyr and say something shitty again about how I'm not ready, and this is bad, and blah blah blah.

So before he can, I lean forward and lick the salty bead of liquid off his crown. "Teach me how to take it."

He groans, and just like that, I'm soaked between my legs.

I lick him again, all the way down his length this time, and then back up the other side. "I don't know what I'm doing, Reid." I swirl my tongue quickly around his head. "Tell me what to do." Then I open my mouth and suck.

"What you're doing is incredible."

"Mhm," I say, the sound vibrating around his cock, and then I pull back. "Give me direction. Tell me what you like. Teach me what to do for you."

"*Fuck,*" he mutters. "Okay. Um...You don't have to deep throat. Use your hand." He shows me where to circle him at the base. "Then just...love it with your mouth."

I look at him, questioning.

"It's all nerve endings from top to bottom. Rub me, massage me, suck me, lick me—watch to see what I like. It's best for me when you're having a good time."

A good time? On the one hand, I'm on my knees on the

hard stone kitchen floor, and my impression from friends has always been that giving a blow job is just that—a job. I've always assumed they were only fun to receive, not the other way around.

But I want this.

I'm the one who got on my knees. I'm the one who undid his pants. I want his cock down my throat. I want to make him feel good. I want to see him come and hear his sounds the same way he's seen me come and heard mine.

So despite my prior notions, I quickly find that I love sucking him off. It's new and interesting and not like anything else I've ever done, but not too hard to figure out when I watch his reactions. He likes it when I hum, I discover. And when I move my hand at the same time as I move my mouth down his shaft. And though I know better than to bite down, he moans with pleasure when I accidentally scrape him lightly with my teeth.

He lets me play and experiment at whim, which is probably a form of torture considering how easily I lose my rhythm. Several times, I have him worked up, only to drop him down when I pull back too far, and he accidentally pops out of my mouth. Then it's like starting over, finding the right tempo again, getting back into the groove.

Then a couple of times, I work him up and bring him down on purpose, and the frustration on his face is as delightful as the pleasure.

Finally, his patience wanes. "Your mouth feels so fucking amazing, baby girl. Do you mind if I help out a bit?"

I shake my head, ready to get to the ending myself.

He braces his hands on either side of my face. "Keep your hand around the base, okay? Then keep your lips tight around me, and hold your head still. Got it?"

"Mm-hmm."

As soon as I give the word, he starts pounding into me at a frenetic speed. Faster than any tempo I've given him so far, and I can't help but imagine him pounding like that into my pussy. Using me for his pleasure. Taking me rough like he'd said he'd do that night in the hotel.

I'm so turned on from the thought. I feel like a powder keg that will take only one tiny spark to go off.

And that's just from giving him head. What would it be like if he was inside me in other ways?

As frenzied as he is, he still seems somewhat in control. He aims his crown into my cheek, so I never gag. I help him by tightening my hand and my lips around him, and pretty soon, I can tell from his breathing that he's close.

"I'm going to come in your mouth." His voice is strained. "If that's not okay, drop your hand now."

I don't drop my hand. I want to taste him, the same way he's tasted me.

"Good girl. Then you're going to take it, okay? I want you to swallow every drop." He barely gets the words out before his body seizes. His control is lost. His thigh muscles go rigid and his thrusts slow and the sound that comes from his throat is low and guttural, and his facial expression, all screwed up and tense, is the sexiest thing I've ever seen in my life.

At the same time, hot liquid streams into my mouth. The taste leaves something to be desired, but I swallow it quickly, and think about that amazing half a sandwich waiting on the counter, and it's not so bad.

And it's worth the look in his eyes when Reid sticks his finger in my mouth, and gently pries it open to find my tongue empty. "You took it all? You're so fucking perfect."

He continues to stare down at me, and I want to say

something meaningful or profound or, I don't know, sexy at least. My pussy is aching, and I can't say that I'm not hoping that he'll push me on to my back, spread me wide, and eat me out on the kitchen floor. The way he's looking at me seems to suggest he's thinking the same thing.

But suddenly a creak comes from the hallway.

As fast as I got down to my knees, now I scramble to my feet. Just as quick, Reid pulls his sweatpants up and rushes to the counter. He's casually putting the food items away while I'm nibbling on my sandwich with a focus that's probably too intent when my mother walks into the kitchen.

She smiles when she sees me. "Did you find something? I woke up worrying about you." Then she notices Reid. "Oh, hi. You're here too." She tightens the robe of her belt. Then looks at my sleep clothes.

I press my thighs together, worried there's a wet spot. It's pretty dark, but if anyone can scope out something like that, it's a mother.

Which is probably why I feel the need to overexplain. "Hi, yeah! I found something. I woke up hungry and came up to look, and I didn't know what was free to eat, but then Reid showed up, and he was making sandwiches anyway so he was nice enough to make one for me, and it's really good, with cream cheese and turkey and you should try it sometime. You want one right now? I bet Reid can make you one. Or I can make you one. I'm sure. It's easy ingredients. Not hard at all. Or you can have the other half of mine. Oh, and I have a banana, too."

I hold up the banana as though it's an innocent piece of fruit and not a phallic instrument of foreplay. As though all I've been doing in this kitchen has been nourishment related. As though my pussy isn't vibrating with want, and I can't still remember the taste of Reid's cum.

Reid closes the fridge and turns toward my mother. He gestures toward his untouched sandwich. "You can have that one."

Of course he's composed and cool as a cucumber. The man can play unaffected like he's got a master's in theater. There's no sign that less than three minutes ago, he was out of control and coming apart. No runaway awkward monologue from him.

"That's not yours?" Mamma asks.

I should let him answer, but the adrenaline is so high in my system that I can't stop myself from stepping in. "It's extra. It's fine. He already had his. Right? Right. It's all good. Yeah. Thanks for making them, Reid. I owe you."

Then I do finger guns in his direction because I'm the most ridiculous person on the planet.

Mamma looks at me for a long blink. Then at Reid. "If you're sure…"

He doesn't look in my direction. "Take it. I'm sure. My middle of the night craving has been satisfied. Goodnight, ladies."

"Goodnight! Sleep well! See you tomorrow! Merry Christmas!" For fuck's sake, there's no helping me.

It's no wonder that, as soon as Reid's gone, Mamma crosses her arms over her chest and bores her eyes into me. "Emmalina Alessia Quinn."

I cringe. She doesn't bust out my full name unless I'm really in trouble.

My only hope is to play ignorant. "What? What did I—?"

She cuts me off. "Not him. Do you understand?"

"I don't know what—"

She isn't having it. "Anyone but him. Or his brothers. Another Sebastian, even. Fine. But not Reynard's kids, Lina. Not them."

My mother is compassionate and reasonable. She never asked me to put my life on hold for her—that was all me. She will move the earth for me. I'm half convinced she married for my sake. So that she'd have someone to take care of her. Someone who would also take care of me. I'm the most important person in her world—I know that.

She wouldn't ask me to give up anything unless it really mattered.

So when she says, *Not him,* I know there's no arguing.

"Okay," I say quietly.

"Promise me, Lina."

"Not him, Mamma. I promise." It shouldn't be the hardest thing to give him up when he hasn't ever been mine to begin with.

So why does it physically hurt to give her those words? Like she's picked up the dirty knife from the counter and ran it straight through me.

Her expression softens, and she crosses to embrace me. It's hard to accept, because the last thing I want is her touch. The last thing I want is to mean my promises.

"*Grazie, mi bambina,*" she says. "You know I love you."

"I do."

It's just the first time that I've realized her love for me might have limitations.

And that my love for her might have limitations, too.

CHAPTER **EIGHTEEN**

REID

There is no Xmas present better than your mouth.

I read over the text several times, trying to decide if I'm going to send it.

I shouldn't.

She's still off limits, no matter what happened in the kitchen last night. We were seconds from being caught by her mother, too. What if it had been Samuel in the kitchen, instead? Or Dad?

But I can't stop thinking about Lina Quinn.

And this is the last day we have on the island. Is it really the worst thing to indulge for one fucking day?

The truth is I don't know that I can resist, no matter what I decide.

Before I can change my mind again, I hit send and then try to keep myself from staring down the table in order to see Lina's response.

Fortunately, she's easily within sight lines. All I've had

to do is turn my body toward Adly, who is next to me, and pretend to be wildly engrossed in everything she says.

Boom. Lina's directly in my vision.

Which means I can see her phone turned upside down next to her plate. Full minutes after I've sent my text, she still hasn't picked it up. Are her notifications off? Leave it to her to be politely off-phone during Grandpa's mandatory Christmas brunch. No one else is that courteous, though Steele is the only one not bothering to hide his cell in his lap while he exchanges dirty texts with his girlfriend.

At least, that's what I suspect he's doing, based on the look on his face. I know that look. I experienced it last night with Lina's blue-gray eyes staring up at me, cream cheese dotting the corner of her mouth looking like cum on her lips, her hand frantic to keep up with my speed.

Fuck. I'm hard again.

"Next, in Nelani's name, I've donated to Every Mother Counts, a non-profit that works to make pregnancy safe for every mother, everywhere." Grandpa raises his mimosa, and we all clink our glasses with our butter knives in response.

It's the annual tradition. Instead of exchanging gifts—because Grandpa Irving rightly says we're all too spoiled as it is—he donates a hundred thousand dollars to a charity in each of our names. The expectation is that we'll each go home and donate or promote the same charity as our gift to him, so he's very thoughtful about his choices, going out of his way to research what we're into and picking foundations that mean something to each of us.

So of course that begs the question—why is his gift to my stepmother about pregnancy?

"I suppose we should take this opportunity to make our

announcement." Dad puts his hand over his wife's, and I have to suppress a shiver.

When he married Nelani a few years back—a Bastian Bunny two years younger than me who, I suspect, needed a green card—no one was under the illusion that it was a love match. The situation reads trophy wife all the way, and every time I come anywhere close to confronting the fact that they have sex (probably a lot of sex, considering the reputation of my father), I want to throw up.

It's just not right for a child to think about their parents in those situations. Especially when one is pushing seventy and the other could be my sibling. It's grossly inappropriate.

Is that what people would think about me and Lina?

If there could ever *be* a "me and Lina" outside of this secret…thing…we have going on.

"Oh my gosh, you're pregnant!" Giulia legitimately gushes, suggesting she hasn't quite learned the silent rules about non-fraternization between the Samuels and the Reynards. "Congratulations!"

Sure enough, Samuel throws a discreet glare in her direction.

Alex and I exchange glances. "You'll no longer be the baby," he says.

"I was never the fucking baby." I was the youngest, though, and it is strange to think that after thirty-three years, that will no longer be true. "Congrats, Dad. Nelani."

More congratulatory remarks are passed, except from Samuel, and for a second, I actually think he might be able to keep his mouth shut.

But as soon as the comments die down, he mutters, "Might want to be sure there isn't a Me Too hashtag attached before determining well wishes are in order."

"Samuel," Grandpa warns.

Dad, being Dad, isn't about to let his brother get the last word. "You can't let me have one goddamned thing, can you? Anything that's mine, you have to steal."

"I've never had to steal. That's the difference between me and you—I don't have to force—"

Grandpa stands to cut them off. "Shut the fuck up. Both of you. I won't have this today, of all days. Your poor mother is probably rolling in her grave."

Everyone at the table quiets.

Lina still hasn't picked up her damn phone.

"Now." Grandpa sits back down. "Moving on. In Hunter's name—"

I hope he gets shit from Dad when we get home for not being here, but since he's not, I'm really not interested in what his gift is.

I tune out and send another text to Lina.

That cinnamon roll frosting on your lips is obscene. I want to lick it off.

Again, I wait for her to turn her phone over.

Again, nothing.

She just keeps eating, as if I'm not halfway down the table, silently begging for her to glance in my direction. Just once.

Adly leans toward me and whispers, "Is it true that Nelani was pregnant before and your dad made her get rid of it because it was a girl?"

"What?" I'm so surprised, I forget to whisper back.

Fortunately, no one seems to have heard.

"What the fuck kind of sick rumor is that?" I ask, hushed this time.

She shrugs. "It's not even the worst thing that's been said about any of them."

The disgusting part is that a lot of the worst things are true. This one has to be a lie, but if it's not, I pray I never find out.

Grandpa finishes with Hunter.

He toasts.

We clink.

He moves on to Alex.

Finally, Lina picks up her phone, looking at it as though it just vibrated. Surely cellular isn't lagging that much? Or did she ignore the other notifications?

I watch her expression to try to gauge what she's reading. First her eyebrows go up. Then her cheeks go red. Then redder. She glances in my direction, too quickly for me to capture her eyes and keep them before she begins typing furiously.

I sit with my phone in hand and wait for it to buzz.

And wait.

And wait.

When almost a minute has passed, I start to wonder if it isn't me that Lina is texting. Then she sets her phone down, and I'm sure it's not me.

I stare hard at her, as if I can will her reply to me with just my eyes, even as I clink on my glass following Grandpa's toast.

And that's when my phone buzzes.

"In Reid's name…"

Goddammit.

Listening to Grandpa's toast when I want to be checking my texts is an exercise in willpower that I'm not sure I can endure. My knee starts bouncing under the table. I force myself to concentrate on Grandpa's every word.

"...charity: water, founded by a former nightclub owner and promoter who spent two years on a hospital ship off Liberia and realized the effects of dirty water firsthand. This charity aims to bring clean water to the 1.1 billion people living without it."

The toast.

The clinks.

Alex leans over just as I click on my phone. "Is this Grandpa's way of saying you should be doing something more meaningful with your life?"

"Fuck you." My attention is on my phone screen.

Hey, so, this isn't actually Lina's number.

Is she playing with me? It's the number she herself entered into my phone. If she mistyped when she put it in, the responder wouldn't know her name.

"You're texting Lina?" Alex asks, over my shoulder.

I pull my phone to my chest. "Mind your business much?"

And the answer, apparently, is no. I'm not texting Lina. Who the fuck have I been texting?

Another buzz comes in, but Alex's face is all up in mine. "You know what a bad idea that is, right?"

An even worse idea would be punching his face in at Christmas brunch, so I take a deep breath before I answer. "We're trapped here for three days. Just a little fun to pass the time."

I feel like shit minimizing my attraction to her, and I ignore the way my chest tightens at the thought of a clock running out on whatever it is we're doing.

But I managed to stay away from her before, and we still

have twenty-four hours before we part. It's literally a problem for another day.

"I guess it's not the stupidest thing anyone in this family has done. Speaking of the minx…"

I tune in just in time to hear Grandpa announce Lina's charity. "...the Eaton Fund, which gives aid to women in need. It was named after Ellen Eaton, who was an eccentric artist who lived an independent life and never married."

Of course Alex has to share his thoughts. "Doesn't look like Grandpa thinks she should be coupling with anyone."

"That's not what he's saying." *Is it?*

Whatever he's fucking saying, it doesn't matter. He doesn't get to decide if or when she…couples.

The toast. The clinks. I don't bother to lift up my glass when I tap my knife this time since my cell is still clasped in my other hand, which is itching to turn the phone over so I can look at that unread text.

"At least be careful," Alex whispers over the clatter. "She's young."

"You think I don't know that?" *Believe me, I know.* It should be enough guilt to make me put my phone away.

It's not.

She texted me once from ur phone so Id know who she was with.

Denny. It has to be. He's who she was with that night.

OK. Give me her number then.

I'm not giving that to you.

Also, fuck with her, I come after u. I dont care who you are or how much money u have. She doesnt deserve ur drama.

Now I've been warned away from Lina by Adly, Alex, Angela (sort of), and if my suspicions are correct, Denny. Not to mention there's the strong possibility that her mother knows there's something up after she walked in on us last night. I swear she looked at me like I had devil horns on my head.

Deservedly, since I'd just violated her baby girl's mouth like it was my right.

Problem is that it's one thing to know that I shouldn't be doing something. It's quite another to be told. I don't take well to it. It makes me want to say *fuck you all*.

I type out a reply to Denny.

She's a big girl. She can take care of herself.

Then I block his number before he can reply and tell me more shit I already know and don't need to hear. I get it already. I'm a predator. She's barely old enough to not be called a kid. I understand what it means to be Reynard's offspring. She's only just dipping her toes in what it means to be Samuel's. I'm the one who knows better.

Last night shouldn't have happened.

But given the chance again, I wouldn't just have her on her knees—I'd spread her out on the counter and make her mine once and for all.

Did I miss that opportunity, or would she still let me?

I need to be the kind of man who will let that possibility go.

I'm not that kind of man, though, so an hour after brunch is over, I find myself in Lina's hallway, knocking on her door.

It would have been sooner, if I hadn't spent thirty minutes explaining to Dad that Adly didn't say anything to me worth sharing with him and another twenty-five minutes listening to a lecture about the importance of sucking up to Grandpa that was really meant for Hunter.

I have to knock again before I get Lina's reply.

"Uh…who is it?"

"It's me. I'm coming in." Her suite is not near any other rooms, but to be safe, I make sure no one is around before opening her door and slipping in.

"Um. Hi. Okay. Yeah. Come in. What's up?" She's in her bed, her hair and blouse ruffled, and I have the suspicion I must have woken her up.

If her night was anything like mine, she had a hard time falling asleep after our kitchen rendezvous. I feel a little guilty for disturbing her nap.

But I'm already here, so…"I thought we should talk."

"Yeah. Right. Sure. Uh…" She tugs her hair over one shoulder. "You go first?"

That was actually as much as I'd had planned.

So I'm winging it, it seems. "You gave me Denny's number?"

"Not to fool you or anything. Just so someone knew where I was. You were the one who assumed it was my number."

"Ah."

"I can give you my real number, if you want. It's not a secret. I'm just not sure it's the best idea? I don't know."

"Probably doesn't matter if you give it or not. I could find it out if I wanted to."

"Oh." She nods. "That makes sense."

Her eyes are everywhere but on me, and I can't decide what that means. Is she embarrassed about last night? Is she worried I didn't enjoy it? Does she not get that I'm fucking out of my head about her?

I clear my throat. "I sort of thought," *hoped,* "that you'd come to my room."

"After breakfast?"

"No, uh…" Feeling stupid and awkward standing over her like this, I sit next to her on the bed. "Last night."

"Really?" She finally looks at me. Hope tinges her tone.

"Yeah, really. It was—" There aren't words to describe what last night was for me, but also there's something solid under my left ass cheek. "What am I sitting on?"

I move the covers to look, and she shrieks. "No, no. Don't!"

Too late. I've already found the offending object—a hard, purple, silicone dildo.

Oh.

I didn't disturb her sleep. I disturbed her "playing."

Fuck. The tip is even wet.

"I can explain," she says, her face red as a beet.

"I'm not sure this needs explanation." Vile and shameless, I bring it to my nose to sniff. The scent of plastic is strong but doesn't quite overwhelm the delicious scent of Lina's cunt.

"Oh my God." She covers her face with her hands. "This can't be happening. It's a dream. It has to be a dream."

"How far did you get before I came in?"

"I was tired, so I must have fallen asleep."

She's adorable and so fucking sexy when she's flustered like this.

Gently, I tug at her forearm, forcing her hand down so she'll look at me. "Did you come yet?"

She shakes her head, quickly.

"Let me see." I lift the corner of her blankets and pause, giving her a chance to stop me before pulling them all of the way off her.

The skirt she was wearing at breakfast is gone. No panties either. She's completely naked from the waist down. The short red hair glistens with moisture, and I'm so fucking hard, it hurts. "Did you use lube or is this all you?"

"Just me." Her laugh is short and nervous.

"What were you thinking about?"

She bites her lip. Then shakes her head.

I know the answer. Know it as sure as I know that I beat myself raw last night after I returned to my bed, and again this morning in the shower. "Say it, Lina."

"You. I was thinking about you." I see a flicker of hesitation in her eyes, and then she spreads her legs, and reclines against the headboard, which is an invitation, if I've ever seen one.

Thank fuck.

I lean over one of her legs and prop my elbow between her thighs. With my other hand, I bring the dildo to circle her pussy opening. "Were you pretending this was my cock?"

She nods; then, as if knowing I'll want to hear the word, she says it. "Yes."

"It's not quite big enough, baby girl. Close, but not quite." Her breathing speeds up as I stick the tip inside her pussy lips. "Can you take all of it?"

"Yes."

"I want to see."

"Reid." She sits up again quickly.

It's the first indication that she might not want this, and as much as it pains me to do so, I pull back.

"My mother…she thinks…" She shakes her head. "She says there can't be anything…" She trails off, but I don't need to hear more. The rest is evident.

"This has always been off-limits. Now you know it as well as I do."

She's quiet, her brow furrowed as she considers.

Then suddenly, though I've given no indication that I'm about to leave, she says, "Don't go."

"I won't go." I bend down to kiss the inside of her thigh. "But I'm going to need to watch your pussy take this dildo."

I'd like to say I'm restrained enough to wait for her consent, but I'm already pushing the toy inside her when she says, "Please."

Please.

Fuuuuuck.

I stop when I hit resistance. I haven't forgotten she's a virgin, but I'm not sure I've actually hit an unbroken hymen. She's already said she thinks she got rid of that long ago, and if she's been fucking toys like this on a regular basis, I suspect that's true.

This resistance feels familiar—like a woman who needs a little more attention.

Gives me the excuse to lean forward and suck her clit into my mouth. At the same time, I ease the toy out. Then work it in again. Slowly.

This time I feel her body relax, and I'm able to nudge all the way in. She's so wet now I can see fresh pussy juice when I pull out. The next time I push in, the dildo goes easily the whole way, and she lets out the filthiest whimper I've ever heard.

I sit back so I can watch her.

"Fuck, Lina. You're incredible." Gently, I saw in and out of her with the toy. "Is this how you imagine I'd fuck you with my cock?"

"Mm hmm." Her eyes close, and her top lip comes out over the bottom one.

"Open your eyes, baby girl. I want you to see who's fucking you."

She does as I ask, locking her eyes on me. My own gaze can't stay still. I look from her face to her cunt to her face to the toy dripping with her juice.

It's the most erotic sight I've ever seen, and I'm not anywhere new to sex. My catalog is rich and full. But something about her enthusiasm, her trust, the obscene way her greedy pussy swallows the toy—it's beautiful and depraved, and when her thighs start to tremble and her expression contorts and she stutters out a guttural moan, I desperately try to memorize every single detail.

This is moving.

Which is never a word I thought I'd use about someone else's orgasm, but that's exactly how I feel—moved. Like I'm no longer in the space that I was in before. That my being has been, not just transported, but transformed.

With her breaths still uneven, I toss the dildo to the bed, climb up her body, and do the thing I haven't done since the night I met her—I kiss her.

Limp and spent as she is, it only takes her a fraction of a second before she's kissing me back. Her arm comes around my neck, and my hand cradles her face. My tongue is eager and demanding, and I have to force myself not to get carried away.

Whatever the fuck that means anymore.

She's the one who puts voice to the elephant in the room. "Whatever reasons you've had for not taking this further..."

"I know."

She continues anyway. "They don't make sense anymore."

"You're right. I know." I kiss down her cheek then take her lips again.

She pulls away. "Reid. Are you listening? We basically have—"

"One more night." I lean back and brush a strand of hair from her face. "You're sure you want this? With me?"

"Yes, I'm sure. I've been telling you that since...forever. I know what I want."

I fucking want her too. So bad that I'm in physical pain every second that goes by not having her.

But I'm trying so hard to be noble. "There's no future here, Lina. That's all it can be, is one night."

"I know." She runs a finger over the scruff on my jaw. "That's all it was ever supposed to be. Remember?"

That almost one-night-stand seems so long ago. The excuse of not wanting to mean anything to her is so moot now, it's laughable. The situation is completely different now. "We'll have to live with this secret. When we run into each other at family functions, when we see each other with other people..."

"Now who's making this into something more than just sex?"

She's wiser than I am in very many ways.

Also, still naïve. She doesn't understand how she'll feel after. How we'll have to pretend for the rest of our lives. How keeping those kinds of secrets can be brutal.

But those are lessons that can only be learned by living them.

And I can't stand the idea, anymore, of anyone else being the one who lives them with her.

Besides, in all honesty, it's myself I'm protecting. Not her.

"At midnight," I tell her because this isn't the right time. Any minute, someone could be looking for us. I don't want us to feel rushed. "Meet me on the pool deck. If you're not there, I'll know you changed your mind."

"Midnight," she agrees.

I kiss her once more—for longer than I intend—then push away before I can't stop. "Midnight," I say again.

I'm almost to the door when she calls after me. "And Reid…I'm not going to change my mind."

CHAPTER
NINETEEN
LINA

At four minutes to midnight I step onto the pool deck to find it's empty. "Probably the only time in my life I'm early and no one's here to give me credit."

I half expect Reid to be hiding nearby—because isn't he always—so when he steps out from the shadows, I'm not jolted out of my skin for once. I mean, I'm jolted in a good way—he's again only wearing pajama pants, this time with sandals, and the way the moonlight hits his bare chest is absolutely obscene. I want to lick him. Every part of his exposed skin.

Parts that aren't exposed, too, for that matter.

It seems he's also learned that I'm always startled by his presence since he approaches cautiously, and he doesn't talk until after we've made eye contact. "I'm here. And you get full credit."

I beam.

Silly because all I've established is that I'm eager. But I've always liked gold stars, and more to the point, I am one thousand percent focused on the fact that I'm about to (finally) get laid, and how can I not glow about it?

"While we're giving credit," he whispers, moving so close I can smell his woodsy scent on the salty air, "I'd like to point out that I was here even earlier."

Now I'm giddy as well as glowy.

"That…um…really…" *Turns me on and makes me feel validated and not like I pushed you into this so thank you and also take me now.*

But my mouth isn't cooperating with my brain, and the words are stuck on my tongue.

Reid puts a hand on my hip and brushes his lips on the lobe of my ear. "Yeah, me too." Then he gently nudges my attention toward a narrow path off the side of the deck that I hadn't noticed before. "We're going that way. Stay close behind me. It's steep in places and dark."

It's light enough to see that the route he's pointed out requires shoes.

"Uh…" I look down at my bare feet. Perhaps I should have realized that we weren't staying on the pool deck. The fact is that I wasn't thinking much about the details. The intention of our rendezvous has loomed so brightly over the rest of my day that I haven't been able to think past *Sex, Sex, Sex. Sex.* "There goes my gold star."

"Gold star?"

"Never mind." It's not worth explaining. "Stay here. I'll be fast."

He stops me before I can sneak back in the house in pursuit of shoes. "Here." He kicks off his sandals. "Wear mine."

"I'm not wearing yours. What will you—?" But he's already on his knees with a shoe in hand, and I'm such a sucker for a Cinderella trope that I lift my foot and let him slip it on. Then again with the other foot. "What about you?"

"My feet are tough. Come on."

He takes my hand and guides me into the darkness, which seems poetic. I almost make a joke about him being the villain who leads me astray, but the finding words thing is still a problem, and anyway, I'm starting to feel like maybe not everything I think is best said aloud, and maybe speechlessness is an inconvenience that I should hope for more often.

So it's in silence that we walk away from the house toward the ocean. The path is narrow and steep, as Reid had suggested, but not too rough, and I stop worrying his feet will be torn up by the time we get to our destination, and instead put all my focus into staying close behind him.

Short minutes later, we arrive at a private cove away from the main beach. The sand here is undisturbed, and driftwood and ocean debris litter the water's edge. The whole place would seem undiscovered if not for the deliberate stone path and the wooden cabana tucked against the rocky cliffs.

"Come on," Reid whispers, taking my hand and leading me inside. It's identical to the ones on the main beach. Small but cozy, with a thatched roof and white linens draped down the sides. The soft queen-size bed takes up the entire space. There's an alluring sense of isolation here, away from everything and everyone. Hidden from prying eyes.

It's perfect.

"Is this like…a love shack?" It seems pretty obvious that's exactly what it is.

"When the grandkids were younger, this was the grownup beach. The other was the family beach." Reid finds a lighter tucked into one of the hidden pockets on the back wall and lights the tiki torches outside the cabana as he talks. "When we got older, this one became unnecessary. Now it's…" He looks at me. "Yeah. A love shack."

"Have you ever used it?" I casually finger one of the drapes, hoping it doesn't look like I care about his answer.

"No."

I'm more relieved than I should be, and also really curious. I know he's got a lot of notches in his belt, but his sexual history hasn't been something I've thought too much about until just now.

As interested as I am, though, I have more pressing things on my mind. "Is there a chance someone will come down tonight?"

He takes the question seriously. "My father and Nelani won't. Alex, Steele, and Adly aren't going to. Even if there was an eligible member of the house staff, they all had the day off. Your mother and Samuel…?"

I shake my head. "I went by their room. They were both snoring when I pressed my ear to the door."

"And Holt told me earlier he was taking Brystin out on the yacht for a night alone."

That's all I need to know.

Go time, Lina.

The thing is I'm excited, but I'm also really nervous, and when I'm nervous, I get weird and awkward, and the only cure that I've discovered in my years of being a weird and awkward girl is to just woman up and be bold.

So after kicking off his shoes, I lift the hem of my white nightgown, pull it over my head, and let it fall to the sand. I'm wearing nothing underneath. No bra to have to fight with. No panties to lose in the sand. The flickering torches illuminate the room, and I'm completely exposed. I've never felt so vulnerable.

Then I see the look in Reid's eyes as he drinks me in, and realize I feel pretty powerful too.

"God, you're stunning," he breathes, his expression dark with need. His gaze roams over every inch of my skin, as though he's never seen me like this before. Which he has. As though maybe he's never allowed himself to really take me in.

The intensity of his stare sends shivers down my spine.

He reaches out to touch me. Tentative fingers trace slow circles on my hip, and I can sense the end of his restraint fighting for his attention. "Last chance to walk away."

"Not a chance." It takes all my willpower to offer him the same out in return. "What about you? I'm aware we're playing with fire."

He nods once. "You know what I say to that?"

"What?"

"Let it burn." His lips brush against mine once before claiming them hungrily.

Then the world outside disappears as our bodies collide. His hands are everywhere on me, exploring my skin the same way his tongue explores my mouth. It's reminiscent of those first kisses, that night in the hotel. The same greedy desire sets the tone. My reactions are just as potent. The butterflies in my stomach vibrate their wings at the same frenzied speed.

But there's something else here this time too—a trust that hadn't yet been established. I'm nervous, but less in my head and more in my skin, which only magnifies the fierceness of my want.

"Reid… I'm… Need…" In between kisses, I try to articulate my desperation, and fail miserably. I tug at the drawstring of his pjs instead.

But his hand comes up to stop me. "Let me get you ready first."

I'm so fucking ready for his dick that I'm about to argue. The whole time we've spent on this island together has felt like me getting ready for his dick. The entirety of the weeks since we first met has been me getting ready for his dick.

But I remember the rule of the room at the hotel—that I had to come before he'd bring it out—and I have a feeling I'll have as much power to protest now as I did then if I try to skip to the good part.

Besides, I've had his tongue on my pussy before—it's by no means a bad part. And if we only have this one night, why the hell would I turn down any Reid-induced orgasms? Particularly since I'm well aware that the chance of an O my first time having sex is slim.

So I let him guide me over to the bed.

"Hold on, before you get on…" Reid lifts the lid from a tall basket and pulls out a fresh sheet, which he spreads out on the mattress.

Then he spreads *me* out.

The linens are cool, in direct contrast to Reid's touch. His eyes never leave mine as he slowly makes his way down my body, kissing and caressing every inch of me. He gives extra attention to my belly button—thankfully, I remembered to clean there this time—which sends electric sparks to my pussy, so that by the time he kneels between my legs, every last nerve is already awake and on fire.

Which makes it extra maddening when, instead of putting his mouth where I want it, he teases me with feather-light kisses along my inner thighs instead.

"I'm going to make you feel so good." His warm breath

brushes against my exposed skin, making me shiver with anticipation.

"Like...soon? Because I feel like you're maybe dawdling..."

That earns me a smack on my pussy.

Pussy smacking is not something I knew was a thing. Definitely wasn't something I would ever have thought would feel so...good? If the feeling of intense, overwhelming sensation can be described as *good*. I'm of the opinion it needs a contradictory adjective to properly do it justice. Cruelly pleasant, perhaps. Or fiercely delightful.

Especially when he pets the sting away with his fingers. "Your pussy is so beautiful. Let me enjoy myself."

It's impossible to argue with such a fervent request.

Pushing myself up to my elbows, I peer down at him. His gaze is intense and raw, as though he's as turned on as I am. Despite my thick thighs and baby fat that has become just regular old fat, he looks at me as though I'm the most beautiful woman he's ever seen.

That look alone sends jolts of pleasure through my veins.

Then there's what he's doing with his tongue. He traces intricate patterns along my skin with the tip, and when he parts my folds and finds my clit, I can't help but let out a soft involuntary moan.

"Fuck, Lina." He groans, the vibration of his voice only adding to the incredible sensations. "I could eat you for every meal."

His words, so filthy and unapologetic, only heighten my arousal.

"Reid, I'm—I'm going to—" I gasp, my fingers clutching at the sheets beneath me, unable to form a coherent sentence. My body trembles uncontrollably as I near the precipice, my breath coming in short, desperate pants.

"Do it," he urges, his voice laced with need. "Come on my tongue."

With his command, I fall over the edge, my orgasm washing over me in powerful waves. He laps up every drop, continuing to tease and coax me through the aftershocks. The intensity leaves me breathless, my body trembling from head to toe.

As soon as I calm, Reid jumps from the bed. He pulls a condom from his pocket, then unties the drawstring of his pants and lets them fall to the ground. He studies me with a heavy gaze as he tears the condom open, and I don't know what's sexier—the way he's looking at me or the fact he remembered a condom.

Then he starts rolling it on and oh my God, I'm done for. His erection is big and proud and the way he touches himself, with dominance and authority, makes my insides spasm. "I legitimately might come again watching you do that."

"Hold that thought." He crawls up the bed, lies at my side, and kisses me. "Because next time you come, I want it to be around my cock."

"I'm not expecting miracles. If I don't come again, I've already been served. Don't worry about me."

"Uh-uh. Fuck that. That's not how this is going down."

Rather than argue, I kiss him again. "You taste like pussy."

"Really? Wonder whose…" He grins when I smack him lightly on his chest.

His firmly sculpted, too-gorgeous-to-believe-I'm-touching chest.

Then we're kissing again. His hands roam my body with

more intention than earlier. As though before was for him, an eager exploration of my skin. This time, each caress feels purposeful and meant to elicit a response from me. He rubs a nipple between his finger and his thumb, and I whimper. He strokes his fingers down my back, and goosebumps sprout on my limbs.

It's torture, all this foreplay. Drawing it out. Some people might say the waiting is worth it.

Me?

I'm not meant for torture. I'm the type that would give up my country's secrets the second someone tickled me. I'm a big ass baby and not above begging.

"Reid, please," I say, between agonizing caresses.

"Please…what, baby girl?"

"I'm ready to be fucked now."

He pulls back to gaze down on me. "Are you?"

"Come on, Reid."

With his eyes locked on mine, he reaches down to my pussy, trails his hand past my clit, and circles the rim of my opening with a single finger. "Let me just see."

He slips his finger inside me, all the way, then pulls it out. The next thrust, it feels like two fingers. Then three.

I squirm when it's four, unused to being stretched so far.

Afraid he'll take that as evidence to prolong the act yet again, I plead my case. "I need *you*. Your *cock* is the only thing that's going to break me in. Not a dildo. Not your fingers. Your cock."

His eyes close briefly. "You drive me fucking insane when you say shit like that. Makes it hard to be a gentleman."

"You've never been a gentleman. Why start now?"

Instead of answering, he brings his fingers from my pussy to his mouth and sucks them off one by one.

"Oh, Lord... I'm already horny, Reid. I can't be any more turned on. It's impossible. So for the love of Go—"

He cuts me off by sticking his single unsucked finger in my mouth. I close around it instantly, and lick him clean. It's a little not the most delightful taste in the world, but worth it when he lets out a groan.

"All right, Lina Quinn. Even if you're not ready, I can't wait any longer."

But then instead of climbing on top of me, he moves up the bed and leans against the headboard. "Come here."

Curious, I crawl up to him, only to be pulled into his lap so that I'm straddling him.

"Oh, hi." His cock is hard and thick underneath my cooch. As hard and thick as my toy dildo. Thicker, actually —no exaggeration on Reid's part there. The biggest difference, though, is the heat of his flesh, which is so much different than the cold plastic toy. There isn't any comparison. Nothing is like the real thing.

And it's not even inside me yet.

"You're so sexy right now." He cups my breasts with his hands and kneads them, pushing the ample flesh together as he does.

My hips roll back and forth over him of their own will. "I thought foreplay was over."

"Foreplay *is* over." He leans forward to suck on my nipple, which feels very foreplay-like, but then he goes on. "Take control, Lina. It will be easier with you on top. You can work my cock inside you on your time. You set the pace. This is all you."

Okay, that's....incredibly nice.

Truly. I'm not knocking the gesture. It's thoughtful. Definitely thoughtful.

And maybe it is the best way to handle the first time, but…I'm not so sure.

I shift nervously in his lap, feeling incredibly self-conscious about being on top of him. He really wants me to be in charge? I've never been good at keeping a beat, even in something as simple as dancing. What if I'm awkward and can't find a rhythm? I'm sporadic as hell with my speed when I'm just fucking myself with my dildo. I'm not going to be any better with legit human cock.

And what if I'm too heavy for him?

What if I put all my weight on him and break his dick? Can that happen? If it can, it will happen to me. Like… that's a lot of pressure.

"Um…" My voice trembles slightly.

Reid stills underneath me. "We can stop. You don't have any obliga—"

"No, I want fuck you. Just…I don't know if I can do the actual fucking? I'm worried I'll… mess it up somehow. Have you seen me try to play *Just Dance*?"

He looks like he's biting back a smile. "You can't mess this up. Just follow your instincts."

His reassurance does nothing to calm me. "And I'm so heavy. My ass is as big as—"

"Shut up. I could carry you up to the house without batting an eye."

"Well, that says more about how strong you are than how not fat I am, but—"

"Don't ever call yourself fat again, Lina. Ever. You're perfect."

His attempts at comfort are working, though I'm ashamed of needing the comfort in the first place, and even still I can't stop fretting. "And I'm going to be so worried about how much my boobs are flopping and whether my fat is jiggling—"

He cuts me off with a kiss. "You're absolutely the most beautiful woman I've ever seen."

"But—"

He kisses me again. "The most beautiful. But if you would rather have me on top—"

I don't let him finish speaking. "Yes. Yes. Please? Can you take over?"

The words are barely out of my mouth, when he pushes me to my back and stretches over me, positioning himself between my legs. "You want me to fuck you like I'm in charge?"

His breathing is short and heavy, his cock presses eagerly against my pussy, and I realize suddenly how restrained he's been. How hard it's been for him to play "gentleman."

What a fool.

"Yes, Reid. Fuck me like you wanted to fuck me the night we met." I spread my legs wider. "Please."

He doesn't respond, but he reaches between us and lines up the tip of his cock at my entrance. As much as I want this, as eager as I am to have him inside me right the fuck now, I can't help but tense up slightly at the sensation.

"Relax, baby. Breathe." Slowly, he pushes inside me, one inch at a time.

I feel a slight twinge of pain as my body starts to adjust to his size. He notices my wince and pauses.

It makes me frustrated.

Both with him and my vagina. Him because he's being too careful with me. My vagina because I've had years of self-care. This shouldn't be an issue.

Mostly, though, I'm embarrassed. He didn't want a

virgin for a reason, and I don't want to prove that his instincts to avoid me were right. "You wouldn't go this slow with anyone else. Stop worrying. Just stick it in."

"You don't get to both have me in charge and try to tell me what to do." He pulls all the way out, and just as I'm about to cry in protest, he shoves back in. Not all the way yet, but he's further than he was, and not only does it take my breath away, but the pain is considerably less noticeable.

"God, you're so tight," he groans, his voice strained with effort. "I'm almost in. Just breathe, Lina. I promise it'll feel good soon."

This time, I listen to him. Really listen. I stop worrying about him or me and start thinking about *us*. Not in a sappy romantic way, but as two people with the same goal. Working toward the same ending. Trying to get one large phallic shaped object into a snug but expandable hole.

I take a deep breath, and this time when I do, Reid reaches down and rubs my clit, just like he did earlier when he was fucking me with the dildo. A shiver of pleasure works its way through me.

My muscles relax, and he sinks all the way in.

"Is that it? Are you inside me?" I'm ridiculously excited.

"Yep. I'm in." His teeth are gritted. He's still holding back. Slowly still, he circles his hips, which is…interesting…and then, oh.

Oh.

Wow.

"That feels…that feels really, really…" *Full.* But nice. Warm, too.

"You just got so wet." The way he says it, I think he's about to unravel.

It really is time for him to do this right.

I lift my knees and brace them around his hips. As a bonus, the position opens me up even more, and there's no longer any reason for him to hold back. "Reid…"

Either he understands exactly what I mean, or he just can't hold out any longer. "I got you." This time when he pulls out, he slams right back in. Then he does it again and again. He continues to pound into me over and over and over at a frenetic pace.

"Oh, fuck." I clutch onto his shoulders, my nails digging into his skin. "Oh, fuck. Oh, fuck." It's all I can say. The only words that have any meaning. Soon, the two syllables become mush, and then they're just a long string of erotic sound.

The more vocal I am, the more powerful Reid's thrusts become. Then he's grunting along with me. Our noises grow louder, and I'm not a musician, but I swear we're harmonizing with the crashing waves outside.

Or maybe that's just the hallucinogenic effects of euphoria, because his dick is some sort of drug. He feels so good. I'm not even close to a climax, as expected, and I'm still very much into it. Like, we could do this all night, and I still won't be tired of it.

And then Reid starts talking dirty.

"Your pussy is going to be my undoing." He rolls his hips and arousal spikes within me. "You are so, so tight."

I arch into him, wanting more. Needing more. "You like how…tight it is? My…pussy?" It's not natural for me to fling out sex talk, but I try to match his brazenness.

"Fuck, yes," he groans, seeming especially turned on when I use the P word. "Your pussy is so greedy."

I'm too shy to say it again. "Greedy for…uh… your…cock."

"You're made to take big cocks, aren't you? Tell me your pussy is made to take big cocks."

My face flushes with heat, but I don't hesitate. "I'm made to take big cocks."

"Your *pussy* is made to take big cocks."

"My…*pussy*…is made to take big cocks. Made for your big cock, Reid."

Only yours.

But I don't say that last part because even under the influence of Reid's Big Cock, I remember my plan to try to say less of what's on my mind.

As it is, I've already toed the line. This is not supposed to mean anything. I know that. I promised it wouldn't before I even understood whether it was a promise I had any business making.

So maybe I *was* naïve. Maybe I shouldn't have made those promises, because there is an intimacy with this act that I couldn't have possibly imagined, and I find myself feeling unexpectedly linked with Reid on a deeper level than before—not just physically, but soul-ly? It's not necessarily an emotions thing—though, maybe it's that too. It's something that I can't put words to. A clarity that I couldn't have expected. How could there not be a connection when he's literally *inside* me? Literally touching parts of my body that have never been touched with a part of his body that, well, I hope not that many people are familiar with.

It's confusing. How to feel. How to believe it will be possible to go back to being just two people who haven't shared something incredibly intimate.

Amidst that realization, Reid shifts his body so that his pelvis rubs just right against my clit, and suddenly, pressure begins to mount inside of me. So suddenly that it throws my thoughts into a tailspin.

It's too much. Too much thinking and feeling and profundity.

I gasp, my eyes finding Reid's once again.

He seems to sense the shift in me. His brow furrows with concern. "Are you okay?"

I nod, unable to speak as I grapple with the intensity of my emotions.

It's not convincing, and he starts to slow down and pull back, which is the last thing I want him to do. I force myself to find words. Sex words. Words that will prove I'm okay, even if I'm really not. "I'm just…your cock…it's…I'm going to come."

It's actually not a lie. The sensations continue to build, my clit throbbing as though it might burst. I can't even pinpoint where the pleasure is coming from anymore—every nerve ending seems to be on fire, my entire body alive with the energy of a newborn sun.

"Fuck, Lina." Reid growls and his movements become more urgent. "You're so fucking sexy when you come. I need you to come all over my dick. Right now. Do it for me. Show my cock how good it makes you feel."

Usually if someone expects me to perform, I immediately can't. Whatever kind of performance it is. I freeze up. It's practically science.

But I must be a natural at the sex stuff—or Reid's Super Cock is just that good—because as soon as he tells me to come, I do it, shattering into a million pieces beneath him with a cry that would definitely have not gone unnoticed if we'd been doing this in any room of the house.

As I come apart, my pussy spasms around Reid's cock. In response, his pace quickens, his thrusts grow wild and more passionate. My breasts jiggle with each movement, my thighs quiver—thank God I'm beneath him and not in a position where all of this is on display.

Though, strangely, I've never felt more beautiful. My body, which I'm reasonably self-conscious about—as self-conscious as most normal people, anyway, I think—feels incredibly capable and strong and worthy. Not only has it brought me enjoyment tonight, but it seems to also be doing good things for Reid.

As if to confirm my epiphany, he lets out a groan. "I can't hold out any longer."

Then suddenly, he's orgasming too, his body tensing as he releases deep inside me, and it's the most miraculously incredible thing I've ever experienced. The physical feeling of him pushed up inside of me along with the awareness that I made him do this—I made him lose control. I brought him to this edge. I broke through this wall…

It'll go to my head, if I let it.

It'll go to my heart, if I'm not careful.

I *have* to be careful. So careful. As careful as I am with contraception because falling for him is not on the table, not with our families. If only there were feeling control options. Like condoms for emotions. Slip one on before you do anything intimate, and it will catch any feelings before they spread.

Where would you wear it? Over your torso? Would you swallow it like a pill? Drill a port in your chest to get to your literal heart?

My thoughts are interrupted when Reid rolls off of me and immediately props himself up on his side so he can study me. "Are you…?" He considers for a moment and rephrases. "How are you?"

I think about it before answering. "Not a virgin?"

He laughs, but there's an edge to his expression that I

haven't seen all night. "You're okay? The pain is manageable?"

"Actually…I'm not really in pain at all." I sit up abruptly and examine the sheets between my thighs before lying back down. "Only a little blood. Told you I already broke my hymen."

His laugh is short, this time. "God, you're so…"

But he doesn't say what I am. Just wraps his arms around me and kisses my forehead.

We lay there like that for a long time. Silent in our thoughts. Each second that passes seems to create space between us, which is a weird way to feel when he's still physically right here, holding me. My face is nestled on his chest. His hand moves up and down my back in long, languid strokes. It's so hypnotic, I could fall asleep if I weren't so in my head.

Is he in his head, too?

More likely, he's wondering how long he has to hold me before he can make his escape. Isn't that how guys feel after sex?

Meanwhile, I feel…off-balance. Like I'm on the ocean, instead of just next to it. Like the waves are rising and the boat is rocking, and I'm about to go under.

And fuck—I still don't even know how to doggy paddle.

Didn't I know to stay away from the deep?

"We should probably get going," Reid says, after a while. Not too soon, but so much sooner than I thought he'd say it, that it feels abrupt.

Panic starts bubbling in my chest. Inexplicable panic. "We're not going to, you know. Do it again, or…?" He'd said he wanted to fuck me all night long that first night. Before he found out I was a virgin.

Was I not good enough for a repeat round?

He kisses my forehead again, which is starting to feel more patronizing than sweet. "It's not the best idea."

"It's not?"

"You'll be hurting as it is."

I go still.

The thing is, endearing as it is for him to consider the state of my vagina, I thought we were past the I-know-what's-better-for-Lina-than-Lina bit. Way past it.

The fact that we're not…

I don't want to be *that* girl and say that it hurts. But it hurts.

And maybe I'm hurting for other reasons too—a whole glob of them. Like because our situation is fucked up, and neither of us can completely ghost each other because of our family, and my mother would be disappointed if she ever found out I'd been with him, oh, and I did just lose my virginity.

So yeah. Lots of reasons to feel not quite emotionally stable.

But definitely, one of those reasons is him.

Coldly, I push away from him and slip off the bed. "Let's go then."

"Lina…"

That fucking condescending *Lina*.

I refuse to look at him. My body is sticky and sweaty, and I can feel my juices leaking down my leg. I'd really like to search that basket for a towel to clean up, but I'm afraid if I don't get out of here soon, I'll get emotional, and what I mean by that is that I'm already emotional, and I should probably leave before that becomes evident to him.

Swallowing back anger-tears, I work my nightgown over my head. Then I hesitate over his shoes. To wear them or go barefoot? On the one hand, I don't want his charity right now. On the other, he's the reason I didn't go get my own shoes.

Deciding his issues aren't worth sacrificing the soles of my feet, I shove his sandals on and stare out over the ocean while I wait for Reid to be ready.

Behind me, I hear him sigh. "This is only the beginning for you, Lina."

It's so unexpected, that I have to turn to look at him. "What is that supposed to mean?"

"Exactly what it sounds like." He stands up, still naked, and I'd be focused on the fact that his dick still looks hard—is that normal, or…?—if I wasn't so focused on the terrible words coming out of his mouth. "You have a lifetime of sexual encounters ahead of you. You can explore and discover what you like. Figure out what you're into. It's uphill from here."

I am not an idiot.

I have to say that a lot because so many people—Reid, actually. He's the people—treat me like I am an idiot so often that I'm sometimes afraid that maybe I am.

But I'm not. I know exactly what he's doing.

And now I'm not just hurt—I'm pissed.

"Don't do that," I snap. "Don't try to minimize this for me. Or for you. This is the only night we get. I know that. I get that. I'm not going to become a stage five clinger, but we can still let it be special. Can't you let it be special? I'm going to."

He looks at me again like I'm too foolish to know anything. "I really hope that's not true."

It's as if he's slapped me. "Why would you ever say that?"

"Because one day you're going to learn that it's just sex.

It's just fun. It's not special. It's not anything to hold onto or assign value to, until perhaps you find someone that means so much to you that the sex is just the cherry on top—not the actual sundae—and then you can say it's something more, but until then, it's just sex."

There are many things to analyze in his words. Too many. Enough to probably convince me someday that this is a him issue and not a me issue, but right now it all feels like one and the same.

"Fuck you." My voice is shaking. "Fuck you, Reid Sebastian. You're a hypocrite. Treating me like a whore one minute and a child the next. If you recognized I was adult enough to fuck, then you have to recognize I'm adult enough to accept the consequences of my actions. I'm adult enough to decide what they mean for myself, so you can forget this night if it makes you feel better. But don't you dare tell me what I get to do with the memory."

Even though I'm not a hundred percent sure I know where the pathway back to the house is, I can't be in his presence one second longer.

So I stomp off alone, my heart pounding in my chest, leaving him standing naked in the cabana.

CHAPTER TWENTY

LINA

I look up from my sketchbook when I hear Denny's key in the door.

A few seconds later, he's in the hall outside of the living room, stomping snow off his boots. He brought in a gust of cold December air with him as well, and I shiver despite the fireplace.

"I thought you were going to shovel the walks." My tone is terrible. I hear it as soon as it comes out of my mouth, but I hope it goes unnoticed. He's not the reason for my misery.

"I picked up an extra shift at the studio." He hangs his hat and scarf on the wall hooks before coming into the room and plopping down in the armchair.

My gaze goes directly to his boots. "You could have at least left your shoes at the door instead of tracking snow everywhere."

"You could have done the walks yourself, and then I wouldn't have tracked in snow at all."

"But I wasn't the one who said I'd do them."

"And I'll still do them. Give me a few to warm up first, will you?"

Whatever.

It's not like I'm going anywhere other than this couch. Not like I've been anywhere other than this couch since I got back from Pier Point five days ago. So why do I care about the walks?

I *don't* care about the walks.

I don't care about anything.

I turn back to my sketch, which is a montage of so many broken ideas that now it's just nothing burgers. It's a reflection of my mood rather than the source, but staring at the mess only adds to my grumpiness.

I close the book and let it fall to the floor and cross my arms over my chest. "I thought the studio was closed today."

Denny takes a break from blowing on his hands to answer. "Was supposed to be. Last minute booking. New Year's Eve is technically a holiday so I got time and a half."

"Would have been nice if you'd told me you weren't going to be here."

"Sorry, *Mom*." He's not even as snotty as I deserve. "To be honest, I didn't think you'd notice."

"What the hell is that supposed to mean?"

"It means that you've been so wrapped up in your self-pity that you aren't aware of anything or anyone else."

"That's not true. I knew the walks needed shoveling."

He ignores my poor attempt at proving him wrong. "Frankly, you've become hard to live with. I would have taken that shift today, even if it wasn't overtime, just to get a break from you."

Okay, that was exactly as snotty as I deserve.

A wake-up call, I suppose. Not that I needed any waking up to the fact that I've been a capital B bitch, but a wake up to the fact that eventually it's going to ruin my relationship with my best friend. If it hasn't already, that is.

Determined to fix us before we're permanently damaged, I crawl down to the other end of the couch to be closer to him, and prop my chin on the arm. "I've been the worst, haven't I?"

"Absolutely the worst."

"The most despicable human to have ever lived."

"Most despicable of any creatures. Why limit it to humans?"

"Have you already hired a hitman to take me out in my sleep?"

He makes a dismissive sound. "I'm not wasting money on a hitman. I'll do it myself." He leans back so the chair's footrest comes up, and I bite my tongue when he puts his dirty boots on top of it.

"How will you do it? Poison? An 'accidental' fall down the stairs? Push me in the Hudson and let me drown?"

He lifts his chin, spending real thought on the question. "Fallen bookshelf."

"I'm intrigued."

"You have so many books, you'd be crushed under the weight of them."

"Death by TBR. Seems appropriate."

He smiles, which makes me smile because I know we're good now.

Probably, we'd be better if I offered to do the walks, but if it's not necessary, I'm not going to put it out there. "I'm sorry I've been hard to live with."

He shrugs. "Yeah. It's all good. Remember this for one day when I'm hard to live with."

"As if it's never happened."

"Never." He stares at me. "Dare I ask—PMS?"

I reach behind me to grab a couch pillow and throw it at him. "No, you prick." We have the agreement that, even if I'm moody and temperamental because of my period, he is not allowed to blame my moods and temperaments on my period. Unless I tell him I'm PMSing first, anyway.

He catches the pillow then hugs it over his chest. "Then it was whatever happened on that island."

I let out a sigh. "Yeah."

It's not like I've kept him completely in the dark. I told him the basics. That I had sex. That we were safe. That it was a one-time thing, and we'd agreed to that beforehand. That it was fine, and I was glad to have it done with. That his family left before mine the next day, and that I haven't spoken to him since.

In other words, I did exactly what I told Reid I wouldn't do—I minimized the entire experience. For a myriad of reasons. Partly because I didn't think Denny would be interested, but that was such a small part that it hardly counts.

He props his elbow on the arm of the chair and leans his cheek on his hand. "Was it not what you expected?"

"Eh..." It's not that simple of a question to answer.

"Was he a jackass after?"

I lift one shoulder and let it drop.

"Did you decide you're not into men, and now you're contemplating the lesbian life?"

That gets me to chuckle. "Definitely like the dick."

"You going to tell me about it?"

"You really want to hear?"

"I asked, didn't I?"

"Then…sure. I'll tell you about it." Pulling my feet underneath me, I sit up, and try to decide what I want to say.

"He has a small dick, right? That's what the problem was. Unfulfilling."

"No. Not a small dick."

"Too big?"

"No. Well…" I can feel my cheeks heat. "Anyway. It was…nice. I had a good time. Really, I did. Reid was patient—too patient, at times—but exactly what I needed in the end. He didn't hurt me. He made sure I…was satisfied. He kept to the parameters we set, but I guess you said it right when you asked if it wasn't what I expected. Because it wasn't. In a good way. Like, I expected it to be this small thing that I could put on my shelf and never think about again. A good book, but you know. There's a lot of books. No need to keep rereading one over and over again.

"But then there are some books that are big. I don't mean in length necessarily—" I blush harder, because Reid had a nice length as well as girth.

Denny shakes his head. "Leave it to you to use books as a metaphor for dick…"

"—but like, big in the way that they just don't leave your head. The story is done, the book is on the shelf, and you can't…stop…thinking about it. So now I'm trying to figure out if he's an asshole for treating it like it's the small thing that we said it would be. Or if I'm a fool for letting it be…big."

I felt more clear about it when I stomped away that night. It was only in the overthinking about it afterward that I started to question whether I might have been the one who was off base.

"Both could be true. He could be an ass and you could be a fool."

"Thanks a lot." I throw my head back and groan. "So unhelpful. And mean."

"You said it first."

I raspberry at him. "So you really think I made too much of it?"

"It doesn't matter what I think."

"Oh my God, I hate it when you do that." I find the other throw pillow and toss it at him, missing so terribly it lands on the side table, almost knocking off the succulent that lives there.

"Nice," he says, sarcastically. He tosses it back toward me, and it lands perfectly in my lap. "But since you asked…"

He leans forward so the footrest comes down, then props his elbows on his knees. "I wasn't there. I don't know what happened. From what you've said, what I've gathered about the guy, he only wanted a small thing and so that's all it was for him. He's old. He's had experiences. He doesn't need this to be monumental. And there's nothing wrong with that. Then you—"

Having a feeling I know where this is going, I interrupt him. "I didn't *want* it to be a big thing."

"Okay. Sure. You didn't want it to be, but then it was. And there's nothing wrong with that either. In fact, I'd be really sad if anyone tried to make you feel bad about how you felt..."

He's fishing, trying to get me to throw Reid under the bus so that he can too. He's a loyal friend like that.

"I'm not sure he *meant* to make me feel bad. I think he thinks he was trying to help."

"Ah. Fine. Give him the benefit of the doubt if you want to."

"I don't really *want* to..." I just can't see how it helps to have terrible feelings about Reid when I was trying to preserve the memory as a special thing.

"What *do* you want?"

"It doesn't matter what I want. It was a one-night stand. Sort of. Like a two nights with four months in between. Three nights, if you count the kitchen…" I shake my head. Denny definitely doesn't need to know about the kitchen. "It's a thing that is over. That's the point."

Which means I should get it out of my head and move on.

Suddenly, I feel really stupid for brooding. "Look, I'm going to get over it soon. It's just this stupid week—not having work between Christmas and New Year's. Who came up with that? It's too much time off."

"Complain about a salaried job that gives you ample vacation time…sure."

"I'm saying…" I didn't mean to sound like a princess. "It's just too much time with nothing to distract me, so my brain is stuck on the last interesting thing that happened. That's all."

"That's fair." He lets a beat pass. "But what would you want if you thought you could want it? Would you want to say screw you to the family feud and keep seeing him?"

"No!" Do I? "No. We're not…relationshippy. There's not enough between us to throw a middle finger to our families. Even if we saw each other in secret. Too much risk for…what? Orgasms? He doesn't even want more from me, so like, that's not even an option anyway."

But now he's given me permission to think outside the boundaries, and suddenly, I think I understand my feelings a little better. "I guess I wish that I could spend more time with him. Just to see what happens. And I wish that he wanted that too, even though that's so much to ask, considering our situations, and I'm just sad that he doesn't."

I hug the pillow to my chest, and rub my cheek along the seam, letting it catch a stray tear. "Dumb, right?"

"Not dumb." He sits back. "And anyway, I think he does want that too. He's been too crazy over you not to want that. He's just being a realist. Self-preservation. He's trying to be smart."

I glare at him. "Is that supposed to help?"

"Would it make you feel better to know he's feeling tortured at least?" He has a glint in his eye that I should ignore. The same glint he had the time he tried to convince me to skip class so I could go with him to see a drummer doing a workshop in Boston back when we were in college. I spent the rest of that semester trying to make up the F I got on the pop quiz the next day.

"You only ever try to get me to do bad things when it's in your interest. What are you after?"

"Nothing." He doesn't play innocent well. I see right through him. "Just if you're going to be over it next week, then this week you should allow yourself to be petty. Test my theory out. Go to the club tonight—"

"Tonight? We'll miss New Year's Eve."

"Believe it or not, you can celebrate New Year's from other places besides this couch." He's so smug for someone who has been my companion for most of the holidays I've spent at home. "Go to Spice. You know he'll be there. Dress real...provocatively. Flirt with other guys. See if he gets jealous."

"First of all, he won't. Second of all, even if he did, he wouldn't let me know. Third of all, what if he has a girl of his own, and I'm the one who gets jealous?"

"While he's working? On a big holiday night?"

"Fourth of all, he basically banned me." Actually…that's a better reason to go than to try to make him jealous.

Denny must read my thoughts from my expression. "Who is he to tell you where you can and can't be?"

"He does deserve to see that I can take care of myself. I don't need him to tell me to go out and have experiences. I can do that all on my own." Not really sure the logic still flows with that one, but I feel better and better about the idea the more I let it settle. "Let me guess—there's a DJ you want to see playing tonight?"

Denny gives an innocent shrug. "Heard about them today from the band recording in the studio. They're supposed to be incredible."

"You could have just told me that from the beginning."

"You wouldn't have agreed to go." He's right. "Even though you do owe me for this week of hell you put me through."

"Oh, please."

"Shark week, but without the blood."

I throw the pillow again. This time it lands smack in his face. "Bullseye."

"Now you really owe me." He stands, and even though I haven't actually agreed, he walks over, takes my hand, and starts to tug. "Come on. You need to shower. We can Facetime Jade to help you pick out a Hot Girl outfit."

"Fine. I'll do it. But only for you."

It's a lie, of course. It's totally for me. To prove to myself, as much as to Reid, that I'm totally capable of moving on.

That's a good thing. A healthy thing. I get more excited the more I think about it.

Or I'm just excited about the possibility of seeing Reid again.

Whichever it is, I'm going to look so good, the guy will eat his heart out.

CHAPTER TWENTY-ONE

REID

I tap the button on my headset and bark into my microphone. "Who let her in?"

My heart rate was already elevated. New Year's Eve at the club is one of our biggest nights of the year. I schedule extra staff so that I don't have to worry about covering any positions. Kaya is officially the manager on duty, taking care of all the money drops and paperwork. Security is doubled. There are enough bartenders that I won't have to step behind the counter at all.

Which means I can spend my time doing what I do best—engaging with customers and managing fires. Up until now, I've bounced from group to group, giving out free rounds of shots, playing the host for a big ass, celebrity-packed party.

Then when I was moving from the gold star VIP room to the main floor, I spotted *her*—Lina Quinn. Here in *my* club, dancing her heart out in a sheer black dress that hugs every curve and completely exposes the black lace underwear set she's wearing underneath, and my already racing pulse went into overdrive.

It's a major problem.

She's a major problem. A huge distraction.

And I need to know right now…who the fuck let her in?

Over the noise, my head of security, Cyrus, spouts in my ear. "Going to need more specifics than that, boss. Who we talking about here?"

"Emmalina Quinn," I shout back.

"Is she on the No Fly list?"

"Positive." She's definitely on the list. I put her there the day after she charged up my hotel bill and never bothered to take her off. It's a stroke of luck on her part to even make it to the door on a night like tonight. There's a line around the block—crazy in this December cold, a testament to Spice's popularity—and almost everyone who has been let in is a regular, famous, or rich enough to slip a thousand dollars to the doorman.

"Do you want me to send someone to remove her?"

Booting her from the club means making a scene.

It might be worth it, because I cannot have her in this building and expect to stay on task. She's already been at the forefront of my mind since that night. The night I've been trying like hell not to think about. The most incredible night of my existence. The night that should have put an end to my Lina fascination instead of rooting her even deeper into my psyche.

Cyrus prompts when I don't answer. "Boss?"

Fuck.

I spin toward the balcony where I can keep a better eye on her. "Find out how the fuck she got in. Whoever it was, I want them fired immediately."

"Uh..." In all our years working together, Cyrus has never paused when I've given an order. "I'll look into it."

"Look into it and make it happen." It's overreacting. There isn't anyone on my staff who deserves to be let go for such a minor infraction. Mistakes happen. Especially on chaotic nights like this one. It's definitely not the time to be down a man.

But that's what I do where Lina's concerned—I overreact. Since the very beginning. I accused her of being too interested, then I chased her down the moment I reconnected with her at the wedding. I got warned to back off, then I got inappropriate with her with a shower nozzle in the women's locker room. I promised to respect her space, and then I took her virginity like I had a right to it.

Then I told her not to let it mean anything when it is the only thing that has brought meaning to my life since I opened this club.

I didn't need her to call me a hypocrite—I'm well aware.

But there aren't any other options for us. Not that make sense, which is why she needs to *not be at my fucking club*.

A solid hand claps on my back. "Here he is! The man behind the curtain, ladies. The one who makes all this magic happen. My brother, Reid."

I'm so preoccupied with watching Lina that I forgot the main floor balcony is Alex's domain.

He's entertaining a sextet of women tonight, it seems. All of them models, if I had to guess from their appearances and the familiarity of some of their faces. His effusive greeting and the tray of empty shots on the table in front of him suggest he's well on the way to being drunk if not there already.

"Reid, this is...everyone," he says, continuing his introduction. "Ah, you found Lina." He must not be too intoxicated if he's able to follow my line of sight and realize who I'm looking at.

Suddenly, he has my interest. "You knew she was here?"

"I passed her and her nerdy friend standing in line when I came in so I slipped them in with me. You're welcome." He turns to address his entourage. "He has a bit of a crush, ladies. He's truly one of us."

"No, I don't," I say too quickly. It's not a lie. Crush is too mild of a term for my Lina obsession. "Wait…you let her in? Christ, Alex. You can't just…" I run a hand through my hair, unsure how to end that sentence without sounding like a lunatic.

"Can't just what? Help out family members?" Again, he explains to his friends. "She's our cousin. Shh. Don't tell anyone."

"He *is* one of us," one of the women says. A brunette with long, straight hair and big lips.

Alex goes on, "She was freezing out there. Her coat barely came past her waist, and if you've seen what she's wearing…"

"Yes, I've seen what she's wearing. It's obscene." Truthfully, it's far more clothing than some patrons are wearing, but it feels somehow wrong to see her out in public like that. Showing off parts of her body that should only…

Should only what? Belong to me?

Because that's a shit thing to think, but it's exactly how I feel. And that asshole crowding up next to her. One step closer, and I'll have him removed. I don't care if she's the one who started dancing with him first.

"Ladies, we need to help him out." Alex's tone is full of pity. "He might have it worse than any of us."

"Not worse than you," says a purple-haired woman

who's so short she barely stands taller than my waist. "Your case is the worst by far."

"Shh." Alex brings his finger to his lips this time. "We're talking about Reid right now. My baby brother, Reid." He slaps my back again, just as a waiter brings a new tray of shots. "Thank you, thank you." Alex hands a wad of cash to the waiter, Chance—a new guy who is doing so well that Kaya thinks he should be fast-tracked to management.

Chance raises a brow in my direction before taking the money.

"Take it," I say. Then I seriously consider sending him to break up Lina and the fuckface dancing entirely too close to her, but am fortunately interrupted by Alex before I can suggest anything so outright stupid.

"Play with us, bro. We're starting another round."

The women all speak at once, echoing Alex's invitation.

I have no idea what they're going on about—*he deserves it* and *worst case* and *one of us*—and the last thing I want to do is play whatever drinking game they're playing, but a shot sounds like a really good idea at the moment.

Especially after letting Chance go without giving him any Lina orders, which I immediately regret since the fuck-face is now practically riding her ass.

Tell him to fuck off, Lina. Push him away.

"It's hard being in the unrequited club," one of the ladies says. I don't know who since all I'm seeing is red. "Close your eyes, and choose a shot."

Everyone does so except me.

The last shot is put in my hand.

On the count of three, I swig back with everyone else. My throat burns as the liquor goes down my throat. "Shit, Alex, Jägermeister? Really? Are we in college?"

"Who else had the Jäger?" Alex asks. "I had the tequila."

I hadn't realized there were different shots on the tray. Vaguely, I'm aware of someone saying she has a match.

I'm not really paying attention. My eyes are still glued to the nightmare happening on the dance floor. Fuckface is no longer dancing in front of her because Lina's turned her back to him, which means I now have a good view of her expression. I can see the grin on her face as she starts grinding her booty against him.

My chest tightens with the force of a vise grip.

At the same time, a woman steps up to me and tries to kiss me.

I shrink back. "What the—?"

"She has your match," Alex says.

"Whoever has the matching shots have to kiss," the woman explains.

This is the game? Whoever has the same shots, kiss? Are we fucking teenagers trying to get laid, or…?

It seems that's exactly the game. Someone's kissing Alex. Two other pairs of women are kissing. Makes me wonder what would have happened if Alex and I had both had the Jäger. Or I *would* wonder, if I actually cared about the game.

But I don't. Not in the least.

I'm about to say *no, thank you,* and go on my way. Except, just then, Lina's eyes find mine. Click onto my gaze like a magnet finding iron. Widen as she takes me in, registers my presence.

I expect her to react like she's been caught out. With an expression of horror or dismay. Expect her to acknowledge she's in the wrong by being here. Dancing lewd with a stranger like it hasn't been just five days since I was inside her.

Instead, she throws me a smug smile and grinds even harder.

So yeah, I fucking let the woman kiss me. Let her slip me the tongue. Let her press her breasts against me. I can't say what the woman even looks like since my gaze never leaves Lina's, but there is a fair amount of saliva exchanged.

But then the fuckface is grabbing Lina's ass, really groping it, and I don't care if she invited the groping or if it's completely consensual—that ass belongs to me.

I push the woman off of me, managing to deliver a short, "Excuse me," over my shoulder. Bypassing the short staircase, I hop the rail to the floor below and beeline for my girl.

"Boss?" Cyrus's voice streams into my ear. "Seems it was Alex who—"

I have no patience to hear news I've already worked out, especially when I'm about to need my head of security on the scene for other reasons. "Need you on the lower floor by screen B."

He knows better than to question. "Headed there now."

His voice cuts out just as I approach Lina and her assaulter. My fingers wrap around the material of his T-shirt, and she screams, "Reid, no!"

But it's too late to be stopped, and anyway, I don't want to be. I pull that motherfucker off her and slam my fist into his jaw so hard I hear it crack.

Chaos breaks out after that.

Patrons cheering on the fight. The jackass crying about his face, which isn't even bleeding. Lina alternating between asking him if he's all right, and screaming, "What is wrong with you?" in my direction.

I shake my hand out, swearing under my breath at the spike of pain running up my arm. *Worth it.*

Lina tries to rush toward him, but Cyrus shows up with two of his guys. One grabs the fucker and pulls his arms behind his back. The other restrains Lina. All without asking any questions.

The power of being a Sebastian.

"How do you want to handle this?" Cyrus asks me, quietly.

"Take him to the security room. Get him to sign papers." I don't need to say more. We've had incidents before—not usually where I've been involved, but where certain VIP patrons have gotten themselves involved in matters that need to be hushed up. Cyrus knows the drill.

"As for her…" I nod toward Lina. The angry adrenaline running through my body is her fault as much as his. "She goes to my office."

"Got it."

"Wait…what?" Lina struggles as she's being directed off the floor. "I did nothing wrong. *He* did nothing wrong. Reid!"

I ignore her attempts to get my attention. I'll deal with her soon enough. She'd want me to cool down first. At the current moment, I'm not sure I could speak to her without having my hands around her throat.

Security leads them off, and the crowd closes in after them.

I head toward the bar, but am stopped by Denny, who appears out of nowhere. "Hey, what the hell is going on? Where are they taking Lina?"

I snap at him. "What the hell is going on is that you left your friend to be assaulted on my fucking dance floor." For all his bold talk about protecting her—where the fuck has he been?

His face goes white. "Oh, my God. Is she…?"

"She's going to be fine, no thanks to you." I push past him, then impulsively whirl back on him. "What the fuck were you thinking? Letting her come here wearing something like that?"

He puts his hands up like he wants me to back off. "That's a whole lot of shit you're saying that I think you know is not fair to me or Lina."

I might agree with him when I'm thinking straight. Right now I'm so worked up I can't bother with a conversation this menial.

Shaking my head, I turn away and start again toward the bar.

"Wait! Where is she? Can I—?"

"I'll have her text you," I call over my shoulder. A dick thing to offer him since currently both of their phones are locked away at check-in, but I couldn't care less about comforting Denny.

Thankfully, he doesn't follow after me.

At the bar, I ask one of the guys to toss me a couple rags. Leaning over the counter, I fill both with ice and am wrapping one around my hand when Alex appears. "Do you realize you're unhinged?"

"You're playing on the pity of hot women with some tale of unrequited love." Somehow, my subconscious has put that together while the rest of this shitshow has gone down. "I'm not sure that you're any less pathetic."

He shrugs. "No argument there. You…good?"

No, I'm not fucking good.

But he cares enough to ask, and that will be worth something when I look back on this later. "The ball's dropping soon," I say, nodding to the image on the main screen. The countdown says it's at ten minutes. "Go find someone to kiss at midnight."

"Already planning on it. But it won't be who I want to be kissing." He shoots his fingers at me, gun style, a gesture he'd never make sober. "You should try and do better if you have the chance."

I'm not exactly sure what he's encouraging, or if he even knows himself. I'm also curious who he wants to be kissing, but not enough to ask questions. It's easiest to just say, "I'll do my best," grab the other ice wrap, and move on to where I need to be next—the security room.

But it does have me thinking of the night in the kitchen at Pier Point. When Lina told me to "do better" when we were talking about how badly I'd been behaving, and how I vowed in my head at that moment that I *would* do better.

And then absolutely fucked it all to pieces by taking advantage of her body over and over again after that.

I suppose the question should be asked, though—what exactly defines "doing better" when it comes to her? Avoiding this undeniable attraction altogether because it can't lead to anything more or facing it head-on and admitting it's got a chokehold on me?

Outside the security room, I hear the crowd shout out the countdown's in seven minutes. For no valid reason, it lights a fire under my ass. I throw open the door with the intention of getting out again quickly.

"...you or didn't you touch the woman in question without her express permission?" Cyrus is sitting behind the desk, drilling the guy who is cradling his jaw with his hand. A stack of papers sit between them with a pen. Another security guard stands close by for intimidation.

"If she hadn't wanted to have her ass touched, she shouldn't have had it out on display," the asshead says.

I swear I almost thwack him across the skull. Sure, I said something of the same sort to Denny and Alex, but hearing it come from this dick makes me want to tear him apart. However a woman decides to dress, it doesn't give a man permission to treat her like his slut. It's a lesson this shit-head would do well to learn.

But I have other places to be, and another altercation will only delay that.

"Say shit like that again, and your body will be in the river before morning," I say, throwing the man the extra ice wrap for his face, then lean on the edge of the desk and stare him down.

He recoils like I'm going to beat him up, yet doubles down with his defense. "I'm just stating a fact. And there isn't a judge in town who won't say the same."

Clearly, he doesn't know about the power of the Sebastian name.

"You want facts? Here's the facts—any retaliation on your part will get you nowhere. There isn't a police officer in the city who will take your complaint. There isn't a lawyer who will say you have a case. Cyrus here is going to go over this non-disclosure agreement with you, which if you sign, will come with a ten-thousand-dollar cash payment for any medical expenses you might have in relation to this injury. In return, you'll be expected to never mention this incident, never return to my club, and more importantly, never speak to or attempt to contact the woman you were dancing with again. There will not be further negotiation. There will not be any further payments. The matter ends here tonight, whether you accept it or not."

It's the kind of threat I've only made a few times in my life—often at my father's command and on his behalf, but also for similar incidents at the club that have required burying for the sake of Spice's reputation.

I'm not exactly proud of those moments, but I'm definitely not ashamed of them either.

Never before have I meant the threat as completely as I do now.

Without waiting for a response, I stand again and head toward the door, ignoring the man as he calls after me. Cyrus will take care of things from here on out. I'll no longer be connected to the situation. I won't even be apprised of anything that happens after this.

Let's just say he definitely earns the fat salary he takes home.

Once the door slams behind me, I take a deep breath.

The crowd from the club shouts, "Three minutes," in unison.

My office is just down the hall.

Another security guy waits in there with Lina, who is probably giving him a piece of her mind.

I need to get in there before the ball drops. I'm not sure she'll give me the chance, but if she does, I'm going to take Alex's advice and *do better*.

CHAPTER TWENTY-TWO

LINA

"You can't keep me in here, you asshole." I already know that the guard won't respond. It's been ten minutes since he dragged me in here at Reid's command, and the guy hasn't said one word to me. Just stands against the door, blocking my escape like I'm a prisoner.

Whatever Reid pays him, he must pay him well.

I cross my arms over my chest and huff. At least Reid's office furniture is comfortable. The leatherback chair is exactly what I expected his tastes to be, and under other circumstances, I might be exploring every inch of this place, trying to garner more information about the man who tries so hard to keep me at an arm's distance.

But right now I'm too pissed for that. And every second that passes with me trapped in here, I'm more and more mad.

I stare over at the guard. He's super tall, super buff, with a shiny black bald head and serious expression. Intimidating, for sure, mostly because he doesn't flinch, no matter what I say. When I said I was a Sebastian, he didn't blink. When I told him I'd give him double whatever he was making to sneak me out? Nothing.

Which was probably for the best, considering I probably don't have that kind of money, and explaining to my mother and Samuel why I need it would come with an awful lot of questions that I think are best left unanswered.

Outside, I can hear the crowd's cheers as the countdown to midnight nears. This is not how I wanted to spend the last minutes of this year. If I want to get out of here anytime soon, I'm going to have to try another tactic.

"Hey, Brutus," I say, hoping calm and friendly might be how to win him over. "Is it okay if I call you that?" It's a name I picked out of a hat since he hasn't offered one of his own.

He doesn't glance at me. As if I'm so insignificant that he can't be bothered.

"I'm Lina. Nice to meet you. Awesome sunglasses, might I say. Really adds to the whole domineering effect. Or is it, like, meant to be a nightclub vibe? Are you trying to hide bloodshot eyes? Have you been doing lines while on the clock? A little…" I inhale twice quickly.

Not a fucking peep.

"You know, I understand that you're just doing what you've been told, but there are laws about holding innocent people in captivity." Not sure the details of those laws, but surely holding someone hostage in a back office without a cell phone is not legal.

The phone!

My eyes find the landline on the other side of Reid's desk. God, I'm an idiot. Why didn't I think about looking for it before?

I stand and carefully watch Brutus as I cross to the other

side of the desk. It's not like I'm exactly afraid of him, but… no, I'm totally afraid of him.

Cautiously, I lift the receiver off the cradle. "I'm just going to make a phone call…" I even pause, giving Brutus a chance to stop me.

And he doesn't!

Unfortunately, there are very few numbers I have memorized. I know my mother's, obviously, but even if she has her cell on at this time of night—she's the kind of woman who rarely makes it past ten, even on New Year's Eve—I really don't want to drag her into this drama.

Denny had to check his phone at the front door like I did, but it's been long enough since I've been brought in here, maybe he has it now? I dial the number, only to be met with a blaring beep in my ear.

I try again. Same thing.

This time when I push the hang up button, I realize the tone doesn't sound right. "Does this thing need a fucking pass code?"

I try dialing nine first.

It doesn't work.

I try the asterisk.

Same beeping.

I try nine-one-one because I'm starting to feel desperate, and shouldn't all phones override any interoffice code requirements when it's an emergency?

Beep. Beep. Beep.

I slam the phone down hard and scream at the top of my lungs. "Someone get me the fuck out of here!"

As if I've said the magic words, the door flies open. Brutus steps aside, and my knees give way at the sight of Reid.

I saw him earlier—of course, I saw him earlier. First

from across the club when he was wearing that woman's lips like they were chapstick. Then again when he was standing there, shaking his hurt hand and shouting orders like he was in charge.

Which, I suppose he is.

But it's only now that I have the chance to really take in how good he looks in his black slacks and blue long-sleeve, fitted, button-down shirt with gold accents that somehow manage to make his appearance sharp rather than tacky. A plain black T peeks out where the buttons are undone at the top.

Then there's that purposely unruly hair of his… It's just begging for fingers to thread between the strands and pull.

Unf.

It's ridiculously irritating how I'm still attracted to him when I so badly want to cut up all his clothes with a pair of scissors.

Goddammit.

Why didn't I think of doing that before now? There's surely scissors in one of his desk drawers, and I bet money he has a coat hanging in the closet on the other side of the room.

Too late now, I suppose, but I'm tucking the idea away in case another opportunity for destruction arises.

Brutus grunts a greeting.

"She give you any trouble?" Reid asks, as though I'm a troublesome child instead of a full grown captive adult.

Brutus shrugs. "Kind of cute, actually."

I scowl.

"It's a problem," Reid says, and my scowl deepens.

"Hello, I'm right here."

Neither of them acknowledges me.

"I've got it now." Reid takes something out of his ear, a

comm device of some sort, and pockets it. "Tell Kaya I'll be offline for the night, will you?"

I hate how badly I want to know who Kaya is almost as much as I hate the way my stomach flips at the thought of being left alone with Reid.

In an attempt to pretend I'm not at all interested in the prospect, I run around the desk and call after the guard, "Don't leave me, Brutus! You don't know what he'll do to me. Can you live with my blood on your hands? Brutus!"

The door slams shut, and then it's just me and Reid.

Goosebumps crawl down my skin.

"You can't keep me in here." Strangely, I felt more sure about that fact when it was Brutus at the door. "I didn't do anything wrong, and I demand to see my lawyer."

I don't have a lawyer, but it sounds good.

Instead of replying, Reid crosses his arms and leans against the closed door behind him, pretty much mimicking the guard's stance a few minutes ago.

Despite how über intimidating Brutus was, Reid, it turns out, can hold his own.

It's really hot.

And it pisses me off.

And I was already pissed off before he came into the room. "You know what? You have some nerve, Reid Sebastian."

Just like Brutus, Reid doesn't say a word. But the guard didn't even look in my direction, while Reid's eyes are pinned to me. As if he's waiting for my defense, and fuck that shit. I'm not the one who needs to defend myself.

"How dare you?" I'm not quite brave enough to point a finger at him, but I pound my fist through the air like an imaginary gavel on an imaginary…gavel thingy… What do they even call the block the gavel hits?

Whatever it's called, I imaginary slam my imaginary gavel against it again. "That guy did nothing wrong." Actually, he did grope me without my consent. I wasn't exactly thrilled with that, and that qualifies as wrong, so I rephrase. "That guy didn't deserve to have his jaw broken for…what? Touching my ass? You know how many guys get handsy on the dance floor? All of them. That's who. You going to punch every one of them? For the rest of my life?"

Reid raises an eyebrow, as if considering the question, but no answer comes.

"It was wrong. *You* were wrong. Very, very wrong."

His stone-cold silence makes me feel a bit twitchy in my skin, because I'm not entirely innocent myself. Mostly innocent, yes. Definitely not to blame for the handsy dude getting his face punched, but I did come here tonight with the sole purpose of provoking Reid.

"Look, I know I'm not supposed to come here, and that I'm probably on some list to not be let in—though, you told me that after the first night, and I thought we were over all the drama from that night now, so I don't feel I should still be on a blacklist, if I am. But to be fair, I could see how you might have reinstated my blacklist status after Pier Point because you're a giant dick and need ginormous boundaries, and so having Alex bring me in might have been crossing your lines and may have been sneaky, and I did feel a little bad when I did it. Which is stupid since this is a public place, and if I am banned, you should make me aware of any rights I have to appeal because that's really the most considerate thing to do…"

Somehow I think I lost sight of my point.

"Oh!" I found it.

This time I do shake my finger. Not at him directly. Just in the air to enunciate my words. "Punching a guy for dancing with me is incredibly fucked up, even if I did sneak in, and you should have let me handle it myself, and you know if I tell Samuel, this will only add tension to the family feud." Maybe. I'm not sure, honestly. "So the best thing you can do is let me go right now, and then we can forget about all of this.

"After you make amends to that guy with the jaw, anyway.

"And tell him I'm sorry.

"But also not to touch women without permission."

Several seconds go by. Several long seconds.

Then, finally, he speaks. "You're free to leave, Lina. I'm not going to keep you here."

That should feel like a victory.

Except how is it a victory? He acts like an asshole, then I'm supposed to be happy about being allowed to go home and forget all this ever happened?

And also…I can't believe he just wants to let me leave. He doesn't even want to fight about it?

In the background, the crowd shouts, "One minute to midnight!"

I don't know if I should move. I don't know if I want to move.

"Go ahead." Reid takes a step to the side, so he's no longer blocking the door. "It's unlocked."

Maybe I'm missing something. "What's the catch?"

"No catch."

I take a tentative step toward him.

"But if you're still in my office at midnight, it means you're on board with whatever happens after that."

A shiver runs down my spine. "That's stupid. Why would I stay?"

He tilts his head, but doesn't answer.

My eyes narrow, trying to figure him out. What he's after. What he wants from me. "And what do you mean by 'whatever happens after that'? What would happen? What are you planning to do to me?"

On the one hand, I could be putting myself up for some sort of weird punishment—one I don't deserve—and I'm so not into pain.

On the other hand, there was that time he spanked me, and that was stupid hot.

But back to the first hand, why does he get to punish me for him being the biggest dick on the planet?

But yet on some other hand—I'm not sure if I'm still going back and forth between two points of view or if this is another view entirely—I know deep down in my soul why Reid punched that guy out. Wrong as it was, it's the sign of a jealous man.

I've read enough romance books to know what that looks like, though I'm floored that someone would behave like that over me. In real life.

But I'm nearly almost a hundred percent certain—ninety-nine point nine percent certain—that's exactly what happened.

Does that mean Reid is finally ready to face that this thing between us isn't going away?

I lift my chin, trying not to get too hopeful. "What will happen if I stay?"

He shrugs, but doesn't answer.

I start to doubt myself. I take a step toward the door.

I stop.

Another step. "You *want* me to leave. That's what you're trying to do. Get me to go. Just like when you kicked me out of your love nest. It's a pattern with you. Because if I leave, you don't have to face that there's something between us. You can go right back to hiding your head in the sand."

Reid doesn't react.

The crowd outside shouts, "Ten!"

I take another step toward the door. Then a step back toward the chair.

The countdown continues.

I'm breathless from his intense gaze. My chest pinches with hope, and I swear I'm going to cry from uncertainty. "Tell me what you want from me, Reid!"

"Five," he says, joining the chorus outside the door. "Four."

Panicking, I run to the chair and sit down. "I'm not afraid of you."

I'm kind of afraid.

Excited, too.

"Three," he says. He reaches out to lock the door.

My heart slams against my throat.

"Two." He prowls toward me. "One."

I bolt up out of my chair, needing to face him head on.

At the stroke of midnight, Reid's hand comes around the back of my neck, and he pulls me so close that there's only a breath between our lips. "You stayed."

His mouth crashes against mine. His kiss is desperate and greedy. Like he wants to devour me.

And it's mean.

The way his tongue pushes between my lips. Brutally warring with my own.

His hand remains firm at the back of my neck as he backs me up until my ass hits his desk. Then, breaking the kiss, he reaches down and tears my dress—actually tears through the material, which isn't the most outrageous accomplishment considering the fabric is sheer, but it's still incredibly sexy.

Especially when he slides the crotch panel of my panties to the side and slips his fingers between my wet pussy lips.

"You think you can come into *my* club, and flaunt your body for other men in front of me?"

Damn, those words.

I moan with pleasure. It helps that he finds my clit and rubs it with just the right pressure.

"You think you can wear clothes that invite other men to touch you and that I won't have a reaction to that?"

I consider answering, but just then, he moves the hand at the back of my neck to clasp around my throat. He exerts light pressure with his palm, so I can feel the restraint with each ragged breath. Any reply is lost to the exquisite thrill of being dominated.

"You think you can show up here and act like you're offering this pussy to other men?" He flicks my clit with his thumb and forefinger, and I jump as sensation jolts through my body. "This is my pussy. This pussy belongs to me."

It's a sentiment that I knew to be true long before now, but the claiming of my body does something to my insides that I can't explain. It's like all my cells have attuned themselves to him. Like he's named them, and in that naming, they bow down to his command.

It's crazy, really. Feeling like I belong to him. Because he took my virginity? Maybe. But I think it goes deeper than that. Some invisible part of me has spoken to some invisible part of him. We share a language that I can't verbalize on a conscious level, but I know it in my blood. In my soul. In the very marrow of my bones.

Right now, my body cries out in that language with the need for him to fill me.

He hears it, and brusquely, he clears his desk with a sweep of his arm. His computer falls to the floor along with his phone and the various papers and supplies that sat there a moment before.

With the space now empty, he lifts me up on the desk, pulls me to the edge, and spreads my knees wide with his hips, making room for himself in between my thighs. He claws at my underwear until the crotch panel is torn. Then he fumbles with his pants, undoing his belt and reaching in his boxer briefs to pull out his very erect cock.

I'm wet and panting and so turned on. I wriggle with anticipation, my pelvis bucking forward like a kid who can't help but reach for the cookie jar. Though my presence here alone is consent, invitations and permission fall from my lips. "Fuck me, Reid. I need you inside me. Please, please, fuck me with that big cock of yours."

He gives me no warning or warmup. Once his tip is lined up with my entrance, he shoves inside me and quickly adopts a jackhammer pace that makes my breasts jiggle despite the fact that I'm still wearing my bra.

"You want to be fucked? You think you deserve this cock?" His words bite with a harshness that is more filthy than cruel. "After you let this body be touched by someone else?"

"I only want you."

My declaration is met with a sharp smack on my upper right ass cheek. "This is my ass. You let that piece of shit grind his dick against my ass."

Am I a total disappointment to the women's movement if I love his possessive talk?

Because I love it as much as I love his cock knocking against that sensitive spot on my vaginal wall.

He smacks my ass again, letting it sting instead of

massaging the pain away. "Were you trying to get my attention?"

"It worked, didn't it?" I hitch my thighs around his waist, crossing my ankles so my heels dig into his backside.

"You tried to make me jealous."

"I did."

"You tried to give what's mine to someone who doesn't deserve it."

As much as I love each statement of ownership, the vulnerable truth bubbles up to my tongue. "You didn't want it. You pushed me away."

He shakes his head rapidly, as though vehemence can defy the facts. "I gave you the opportunity to be free. You turned that down the minute you showed up here looking like you were greedy for cock."

"That's slut shaming."

"Is it? Or is it just honest? Did you or did you not come here, wearing this farce of an outfit, hoping that I'd put my dick inside this cunt? No lies, Lina."

Is that the truth? When Denny had suggested the plan for the evening, when Jade chose the most scandalous dress from my closet for me to wear, I wanted to make Reid feel bad. I wanted him to have regrets. But did I wish for more? Did I for one minute think I could end the night with him so deep inside me that I could feel his balls slap vigorously against my ass cheeks?

"I hoped."

"So you taunted me. Pretended you might let someone else wet his dick in my pussy." Unexpectedly, he spreads my knees apart and tilts me back so that I'm supported on my elbows and my heels are propped on the desk. It opens me up, and suddenly, somehow, his cock hits deeper. His pelvis rocks against my clit, and out of nowhere, an orgasm rapidly builds. "Do you know what that did to me to see you with him?"

Actually, I do. "You kissed another woman."

"She kissed me."

"Seemed like you were into it from where I was standing."

"Don't know how you could accurately determine anything with that fuckhole fondling your ass." His thrusts accelerate. My pussy clenches around him. "What did you think would happen?"

"I just wanted you to want me," I squeak out, my climax so near I can taste it.

"You're the only thing I've wanted in so long that I can barely find a reason to breathe without you."

Is it true?

Or is it just lust and desire and carried-away-in-the-moment speech?

It doesn't matter. My heart believes it, and it rings true in my veins. My muscles tighten and ecstasy lights up all my nerve endings as the room dims and stars streak my vision. "Fuck," I sputter, all the syllables drawn out as I cry out my orgasm. "Fuuuuccck."

I'm still trembling with the force of a mini earthquake when Reid pulls out of me. He jerks his hand swiftly up and down his bare cock, and when he tenses up, his face screwed up with a sort of agony/pleasure, I watch with fascination as he comes all over my inner thigh.

It's barely a trickle of white he leaves behind, but in my head it's enough to spell out *mine.*

The fog of bliss starts clearing, and I'm on the precipice of worrying what he'll do next, if he'll shut down and push me away again, but before I can fall off that cliff, he pulls me into his arms and showers my lips and jaw with kisses.

"I didn't suit up," he says, his mouth now sweeping across my eyelids. "I'm sorry. That was...irresponsible."

It takes me a second to realize he's talking about not wearing a condom. "Do you think it's a problem? I'm on the pill."

Thank you irregular periods for requiring birth control to be regulated.

He shakes his head. "You felt really good. I've never fucked bare."

"Never?"

"Mm hm."

"I've never fucked bare either."

He laughs then captures my mouth for another kiss that leaves me dizzy.

When he finally breaks away, he leans his forehead against mine and takes a deep breath. "You don't know what you started by coming here tonight, baby girl."

"It was already started." Whatever this is. "You're the one who keeps pretending it has an end."

He pulls back to study me before nodding in agreement. His hand comes up to cradle my cheek. He wipes a tendril of hair off my face. "I'm not doing that anymore."

Dammit, I feel so warm and happy and hopeful when he says shit like that, but I'm not unaware of our situation. His acknowledgment of this thing between us has changed, but the obstacles surrounding us are still the same. "What does that mean for us now?"

With his hand braced on the back of my neck, he thinks before he answers. "I guess we need to figure that out."

"We? That's a word I'm surprised to hear you know."

"Smartass." He pinches the skin at my nape before letting me go so he can unbutton his shirt. Once it's off, he takes off his T-shirt, and I'm starting to get really excited about a round two when he uses it to clean the cum off my leg.

"Ah," I say, watching the evidence of his passion disappear.

"I like the look of you dressed in my cum, too." He tosses the shirt to the ground, kisses my nose, then puts the button up back on.

So not another round then.

But I'm not ready for this to be over, and there is so much we need to work out. "Should we talk about it now? Us, I mean?"

"Tomorrow."

A frown threatens on my lips. I know it's late and our emotions are high, and I shouldn't be disappointed because he's only pushing it out to tomorrow—morning-tomorrow, I'm guessing, since it's already technically tomorrow now—but this conversation is important, and I want it to mean as much to him as it does to me. I want it to be as urgent for him as it is for me. I don't want him to send me away and have time to think and change his mind.

But then he adds, "Over breakfast."

I grin and throw my arms around his neck. "Does that mean you want me to spend the night? Are you taking me to your fuckpad?"

"Tempting since it's so close, and I'm not sure how long I'm going to last not being inside you."

Oh. Wow.

Whatever the equivalent of a girl boner is, I have one. "So then…?"

"I'm taking you to my home."

Boom. Happy fucking New Year. Things are getting real.

CHAPTER
TWENTY-THREE
REID

I'm half awake but fully aware of Lina in the bed next to me. Of her single finger tapping a pattern I can't discern on my back. At first I think it's a random design. Then it seems the shapes resemble letters.

But I don't want to think too hard trying to figure it out because then I'll be all the way awake, and as emasculating as it is to admit it, I'm bone tired.

After several minutes of her tapping and me ignoring, she changes her tactic. "Reid." It's technically a whisper, but it's so close to my ear that it sounds louder than it is.

I respond with a growl.

The growl, I thought, would communicate that I desire to be undisturbed.

Instead, Lina takes it as an invitation to disturb me more. "Wake up."

"Mm."

"Come on, Reid. Wake up."

"Why?" I grumble.

"I'm hungry. Can I scavenge?"

I hesitate for a couple of reasons. First, the image of her scavenging through my empty kitchen is entertaining. Surely, she'd have much to say about the empty cupboards and expired Greek yogurt. The truth is, I'm just not here enough to keep it reasonably stocked.

Secondly, I've just now realized her bare breasts are pressing against me, and whether I have the energy or not, my cock is immediately interested.

Thirdly, I specifically remember dealing with this issue earlier. "I ordered breakfast." Keeping one eye closed, I peek at the time on the bedside clock. "It should be here soon."

"When did you order?"

"After last time." It might have been the time before. The night is a blur of fucking and dozing only long enough to regain the energy to fuck again. Somewhere in there, I had the forethought to realize that eventually we'd need food.

Even remembered to tell the doorman to go ahead and let them through so I don't have to buzz them in.

"How clever of you." The tapping resumes. "Wake up."

"Mn mm."

"But I'm bored."

"Mm."

"Why are you so tired?"

Is she kidding me?

I'm not sure if I want to strangle her or kiss her senseless, but I can no longer ignore her tenacity.

Rolling her over, I pin her to the bed and hover above her. "I worked hard. All night. Do you need a reminder?" I slide my dick up and down the length of her pussy. She's wet—possibly because she's as responsive to me now as I am to her.

Possibly still from the last time we fucked since we didn't bother to clean up before passing out.

Without needing the use of my hand to guide it, my cock finds its way to her entrance. I nudge the tip in, barely holding back from shoving into her like I want to. "Do you hurt?"

We fucked so much that I'd expect her to be sore, even if she wasn't still new to sex.

Her legs wrap around my hips in invitation. "If I say yes, you'll stop. So definitely not."

Ah, this woman.

She makes me feel like a caveman. Makes me need to own her and abuse her and indulge her too.

I slide a little further inside, and roll my hips. "You want me to hurt you a little more?"

Before she can answer, the doorbell rings.

"Goddammit." I tell myself to pull out, but she feels so good and tight.

"The door," she says, as though I'm not aware.

I push in further. "They can wait."

"I wasn't sure you heard. I know sometimes people lose their hearing as they age."

I'm torn between a laugh and a groan. Not the good kind of groan.

Then her stomach growls, and I force myself to accept that my baby girl needs to eat, and that my cock will have to wait.

Grumbling under my breath, I roll off her and climb off the bed. I throw on a pair of sweats, and realize my legs don't feel as steady under me as usual. Probably a good idea for me to refuel as well.

I pad out of my bedroom to the apartment door, grabbing a wad of bills from my wallet from the entryway table as I pass by. The delivery man has already given up on me and is setting the food on the floor when I open the door.

"Sorry for making you wait." I hand him a couple of twenties. Then a hundred because I'm in that good of a mood. "Happy New Year."

"Thank you. Happy New Year."

I gather the bags of food off the ground. There are several, and I remember now that I'd been too tired to decide what Lina might like, so I ordered a bit of everything. Considering that's what she ordered the last time she stayed in one of my beds, it seems appropriate.

At least this time I got to wake up in my bed with her, and I have every intention of returning there, but when I've shut the door and turned around, she's in my living room, carrying my bed covers, and wearing the shirt I wore last night.

"What on earth are you doing?"

"Picnic." She shakes the blanket out and spreads it on the ground. When she bends over I get a spectacular view of her pussy lips.

"Eat in bed," I say, incapable of complete sentences, it seems, in this new caveman mode of mine.

"Ew. I'm a messy eater."

I want to be a messy eater right now. Filthy my face up with her cum. My dick refuses to stop thinking about it.

But she beckons me with her playful grin, and before I can register what I'm doing, I'm on the floor next to her, unloading several styrofoam containers onto the blanket.

"Whoa. How hungry are you?" Her eyes widen when I pull more containers from a second bag. "How hungry do you think *I* am? It's like a clown car. It just keeps going."

"I didn't know what you wanted so I ordered all of it."

She inspects her choices, leaving the containers open

and letting the likely already cold food get colder, but somehow it doesn't bother me like it normally would.

"God bless you!" she says when she discovers the Belgian waffle. Then she rifles through the condiments. "Is there syrup and butter and whipped cream? Come on, come on…" She holds up all three like they're a grand prize. "Boom!"

My smile is slight, though my chest feels like there's a whole sun inside it, trying to burst out. I find my egg white omelet among the items, and close the lids, casually watching her retrieve plastic utensils from the bag and prepare her waffle to her liking.

It's mundane shit, and I'm thoroughly engrossed.

When she takes her first bite, her eyes light up like she's about to orgasm—after last night, I know exactly what that looks like—and she hums with satisfaction. "God, that's good."

"Glad to provide."

She leans against the sofa and pulls one leg underneath her. I settle myself at her side, more interested in watching her than eating my own food.

At some point, she seems to notice she has my attention, and her expression loses some of its candor.

"This is not why I'm a curvy girl, by the way. It's an often inaccurate stereotype that curvy girls eat poorly. I don't usually eat junk food like this. I'm good with veggies. Love myself a good…cucumber."

"Eggplant," I correct. Because if we're talking innuendo here, let's get the dimensions right.

She laughs. "Yeah, sure. No way an eggplant is fitting in this vagina, but you can have your fantasy. Anyway, it's a special occasion so I'm indulging."

It takes me a minute to spot the insecurity underneath her words. "Do you think I'm judging you?"

She toggles her head back and forth. "I'm judging myself, I guess. Someone my size should probably never indulge."

I'm irritated and concerned, all at once. She's the most beautiful creature that has ever stepped into my life, and if she thinks there is one thing that needs to be changed about herself… Shit, I'm ready to murder anyone and everyone who put that notion into her head.

But also, I can't believe she doesn't understand how wrong that notion is.

"Don't do that." My tone is sterner than I intend. "You're perfect. Every inch of your body turns me on. And what the fuck is that about? Someone your size should never indulge. Bullshit."

She gives me the *come on* look. "Nice sentiments, but society doesn't agree with you."

"I don't fucking care about society. I care about you not realizing how goddamn stunning you are, and if you can't decide that for yourself and need someone to listen to, stop listening to them, and listen to me."

"Oh, yeah. Because you can just tell a person not to think something, and that's all it takes to change a way of thinking. How many times did you tell yourself to stop thinking about me?"

She loses her surety. "That was just a joke. Not saying you actually think about me all that—"

I reach out and wrap my hand around her neck, then pull her toward me until our mouths are almost touching. "Told myself so many times, but you have rented a room in my head, Lina Quinn."

I feel her lips curve up just before I capture them in a

kiss that reminds my dick that it had other plans for breakfast.

"You really think I'm stunning?"

"Have you not noticed my obsession?"

"I don't know. You might just be fucked in the head."

"Maybe. But you're objectively stunning." I kiss her again, hoping she'll let me get carried away. "Mm. You taste good."

I start to go in for another taste of her lips, but she holds her plastic fork up, a portion of sugar-entrenched waffle on the end. "Want a bite?"

"Can I eat it off your pussy?"

She backs away, and I can feel her put up an imaginary boundary between us. "It's breakfast. We have stuff to figure out. Remember?"

Ah, right. The talk I promised we'd have about *us*.

There are only hard realities in that conversation, and I'm enjoying the light banter. "You don't know how inspiring your pussy can be."

"But I know how distracting Reidgasms are for me."

"Reidgasms?"

"It's not very clever, but it works. Try this." Again, she presents the fork.

Reluctantly, I open my mouth. It's incredibly rich. Sweeter than I even imagined. "I can feel diabetes coming on."

"That's not how diabetes works, and I thought you weren't going to judge."

"It wasn't a judgment. I'm just saying my particular makeup is not equipped to handle so much sugar at once." I can already feel the inevitable crash coming on, and that's only from one bite.

"Oh, you mean you're old and your body doesn't

rebound as easily as mine. I've heard about that." Her and that cheeky smirk.

"I'm *not* old."

"If you say so…"

"I'm just not that into sweets." She looks like she's about to make a quip about her being sweet and me being into her, so I say, "Except for you."

At the same time she says, "Except for me."

"Especially your pussy." I pull at the hem of her shirt —*my* shirt—wanting to get underneath with a hunger that trumps any other interest.

But she bats me away, then points her syrup-soaked fork at me. "We still aren't talking about what we're supposed to be talking about."

I groan.

Denied access to the honey pot between her thighs, I settle for drawing circles on her knee with my finger. She's soft—not just her skin, but every part of her. The way she thinks. The way she lives. So different from me and the hard edged individuals that I've been surrounded by my whole life.

It draws me to her. She's a soft place to land, and fuck, I've never wanted so badly to land.

"Do you want me to start this discussion?" she asks when I don't take the lead myself.

It's not fair to push this off. I owe her this conversation. The longer we wait to have it, the harder it will be. There might not be a way forward for us, and prolonging the inevitable is only going to make it hurt more. That's the reality of our situation.

Despite all that, I can't help the words that come out of my mouth. "Maybe I want to pretend we don't have to have this discussion at all."

She tilts her head, studying me. "Well." Her lips twist together as she thinks. "How long can we put this off?"

"What do you mean?"

"Like…I don't have to be back to work until the fourth."

"SNC admin offices are closed that long? Wow. Your boss is nicer than my boss."

"My boss, at the moment, is Adly. Who's your boss?"

"Me."

"Then yes. My boss is nicer than yours." When her grin fades, she looks down at her plate, as though she's feeling shy all of a sudden. "I'm just saying—you don't have to feel pressured at all by this—but I could, you know. I have no other obligations, in the meantime. So if you wanted to push off the serious conversation for a couple of days while we hang out... It's probably not… I don't know… That's dumb, isn't it?"

I turn to face her, my legs bending as I rest my shoulder against the couch instead of my back. "If you're suggesting that we run away from the world for a few days and hole ourselves up in my apartment here, fuck like bunnies, and figure out what's next at the end, I think that's a brilliant idea."

Her flush goes all the way down her neck. "Fuck like bunnies, but also spend time together not fucking like bunnies."

"Surprisingly, I'm not opposed to that at all." It's startling to acknowledge since I can't remember the last time that I wanted more than sex from a woman.

"You think your boss will give you the time off or will you leave me locked in your tower like Rapunzel while you go off to work every day?"

"My boss is a dick who doesn't accept last minute vacation requests, but I know for a fact that he has a full staff this week, and he's not going to fire me if I call in sick." I already texted Kaya that was the reason I left last night. A flu would keep me out a few days, no questions asked.

Not that I need to give anyone an excuse.

Lina puts the back of her hand to my forehead. "Ooo. You're feeling awfully warm. I think you might be getting a fever."

"You should take my temperature."

"Oh. Is that…like a euphemism for butt stuff? I'm not against that or anything, but I am a beginner, remember, who needs lots of instruction."

Fuck, yes. "And I'm here for the instructing…" I reach for her, thinking the instruction can start right this minute, and for a second, she lets me pull her in.

Then she suddenly pushes me away. "Except, wait, wait, wait."

"What?"

"I'm still eating breakfast, and you haven't touched yours. And if we're going to spend…how many days is that?"

"Three days." Like at Pier Point. Is that what our life will forever be broken down to? Stolen moments? Time spans that never amount to more than a few days?

I push the thought away. *We're not thinking about that right now.*

"If we're going to spend three whole days together, we will definitely need to take some breaks from the fucking." She picks up the container with the omelet that has sat neglected between us and hands it to me. "But you should eat these eggs. Lots of protein. You'll need that if you're going to keep up with someone half your age."

I take the container and grab a fork from the pile of plastic utensils. "You're not half my age."

"Close enough. Tell me something. All of Grandpa Irving's grandkids are expected to work for one of his companies—the news corp or the industrial corp, right?" The way she moves from one subject to the next without any break for a transition is adorable.

It also keeps me on my toes. "Until they're thirty-six and can access their trust fund, yes." I take a bite of the now room temperature omelet, and consider briefly getting up to nuke it.

I decide against it. Cold eggs are worth not missing a second of this moment with her.

"So how did you get to own a nightclub?"

That's a reasonable question. Pertinent too, since my lack of freedom in my life is directly related to this answer.

Which makes it a serious question, and I'm still in the avoidant mood. "Boring. Tell me about your art."

"I asked first, but hold on." There is whipped cream on the corner of her lip that I want to kiss off so badly that I can hardly think straight. "What do you know about my art?"

"In your room. Sketches, works in progress. They have to be yours."

She blushes. "Depends what you think about them."

Her tongue comes out to wipe away the whipped cream, and I sigh.

"Oh. That bad?"

"No, that wasn't—" God, how do I explain that everything she does is a turn-on? "I was sighing because my dick is fucking hard, and that means less blood in my brain, and I'm sure as hell not going to be able to express exactly how not bad your art is."

She grins like she's just discovered a superpower. And

she has. "Sounds terrible for you. Tell me more about my not bad art?"

"It's thoughtful and richly imaginative and…" I search for words, knowing I cannot possibly do her work justice. "Clever. It stirred me. Really. I wish I could say it better. Are you doing anything with it?"

"Like…career wise? No. Because I'm a Sebastian and am expected to work at SNC like all the other Sebastians, only without the promise of a hundred-million-dollar trust fund. Do you think I could qualify for like a thousand-dollar trust fund? I could house so many cats with that."

A thousand dollars? I'll hand her that right now. The simplicity of her wants is grounding, and I hope to God that doesn't ever change.

Considering how immersed she is now in the Sebastian world, I'm not sure that's a reasonable expectation. "I wouldn't be so sure you won't get that trust fund. If you're family, you're family."

"Then if I get it, I'll quit SNC and open up an art shop online. It's fiteen years away. We'll see." She shrugs like it's not a big deal one way or another. So much more patient with the process than I was. "But anyway…" Her glare is demanding. "Tell me how you got a nightclub right now 'k thanks."

I bite back a laugh.

Then sigh. Again.

Fine. She wins. "I started out at SIC, actually. Hated it. Alex and Hunter were there as well, and with Dad in charge, I was always compared to them. Always told to be more like my brothers. Do better. Be better."

I pause to take a breath, and Lina interjects. "That's really fucked up. I'm sorry that happened to you."

I shake my head. "That's what my life has always been.

It's not… I don't deserve pity for it. It's what's expected when you're born into a world like ours."

She gives me the same disapproving look I gave her when she was body shaming. "It's not normal, Reid. If you think it is, then you deserve even more *sympathy*. Not pity."

"It's not normal. But the kind of money we have isn't normal either."

"Well, ain't that the truth." Her eyes flash with stubbornness. "But I'm still sorry about it."

Her compassion does something to the insides of my chest—squeezes everything together and pulls it apart at the same time—and I have this strange feeling that if I think about it too much, it will fuck me up.

So I blaze past it and continue on. "The only reason I brought it up was to explain why I hated the job. I might have done better at SNC, but that would have caused a bunch of different issues with Dad."

"I bet he'd have loved that. You choosing Samuel over him."

"Yeah, you get it." I open one of the bottles of orange juice and take a swallow. "So I was almost twenty-nine, and it felt like it was going to be forever before I turned thirty-six—"

"Seven whole years. Sorry, go on."

"—and I couldn't do it. I couldn't imagine doing it. And one day when I felt particularly bitter about it, I went to Grandpa and told him I couldn't do it."

"So then what did he say?"

"He asked me what I wanted to do instead. And I hadn't thought it through that far so I said the first thing that came to mind, and told him I wanted to run a nightclub."

"You panic-decided your career?" She puts her mostly-eaten waffle down. "I'm so invested in this story. Please continue."

"He said that sounded like a great idea and asked how I expected to fund it, and I told him I'd like early access to my trust fund."

"And Grandpa Irving's awesome. So he said okay?"

She's the most interactive conversationalist I've ever known. She jumps in with her inferences and commentary, her mouth often half full, and while some people might think it's annoying, I think I never want to talk to anyone else again.

I don't know if I want to look at anyone else ever again either, for that matter.

"What?" she asks, when she catches me staring.

I shake my head and take another bite of eggs before pushing the rest of it away. "Grandpa Irving is…awesome, I guess. Probably the most decent man in the family. But he has his rules and he believes in being fair, and he said he couldn't make exceptions for me…et cetera, et cetera."

"Ah, bad Grandpa Irving!"

"But he said if I could find an investor outside the family who would fund the project, he'd give me a space at the Sebastian Center. Suggested I could buy them out when I inherit my money later."

"So you found an investor, and now here you are."

I nod.

Then without exactly deciding to, I tell her the rest, the brutal secret that no one knows except the parties involved. "Except, I couldn't find anyone to invest. Everyone I spoke to wanted the trust fund as collateral, but they aren't set up to be used like that, or they wanted to be able to make decisions about the way the club was run or they wouldn't agree to the buy-out option, which was very important to me. The bank loans I applied for wouldn't give me the amount I needed—I had big start-up costs for the kind of club I wanted."

She's rapt now, her elbow on her thigh, her head propped in her hand.

"So when my father offered to give me the money through a shell company so that Grandpa wouldn't know it came from family, I took him up on it." It shouldn't be so hard to admit this, but it's the worst mistake I ever made, and I care what Lina thinks of me.

I'm especially ashamed since this is the reason I'm so confined by my father's every wish.

"It was a terrible decision," I tell her, my eyes on her knees. "He owns that deed and he, uh, leverages that against me at every turn. Uses it to make me do his bidding. Laundered some money for him in the early days. Helped him cover up one of his affairs. Took my uncle's ex to his wedding to try to stir shit up."

I glance up at her. "Sorry about that."

She nods, her green eyes glossy.

Fuck. I can't look at her.

My gaze drifts to my hands. "He's chased away anyone who might become important in my life, Lina. In awful, hurtful ways. Because that's what he does. With everyone. He wants to own the full attention of all those around him, and he's good at making that happen. So I don't have relationships anymore. I don't have friends. I don't let people matter. I can't let myself matter to anyone else because he'll... I can't—"

All of a sudden, she's crawling onto my lap. Straddling me, she runs a hand through my hair. "It's three more years, right? Three years under his thumb, and then you can buy him out? Will he let you?"

There's a ball in my throat that I have to clear before speaking. "I think so." He's a terrible man, but he honors his deals. And if I sued him, his name would be exposed during litigation, which would not be in his best interest.

"Three years, then. That's all we have to get through. Just three years." She kisses my forehead. "That's nothing. We can make it."

We.

I tilt my face up to study her. The conversation of what's next between us is still to be had, and she's already planning a future. Already signing on to carry the burden that's, for so long, been only mine.

Can I let her do that?

"We aren't deciding anything about us now," she says, as if she understands exactly what I'm thinking. "All I'm saying is that it's three years. And if you decided that you wanted me to be with you through it, then I could do it."

I open my mouth to tell her…shit, I don't know. That it's not about wanting her. Not wanting her was never the issue.

But she puts her finger over my open lips. "Shh." She rolls her hips over mine, and as distracted as I am with the emotions warring inside me, my cock is immediately hard. "Can we fuck like bunnies now?"

I almost do something stupid and tell her we should keep talking.

But I quickly come to my senses and roll her over so she's underneath me. Reaching down, I pull my cock out of my sweats and line it up at her pussy.

Then I push into her and let the three years left of my sentence get forgotten in the three days we have together now.

CHAPTER
TWENTY-FOUR
LINA

"So this guy, Twilight—"

Immediately, Reid interrupts. "Twilight's the name of a guy?"

"It's his code name. Not his real name. Don't worry—he's still all butch and shit." We're cuddled up on his sofa in the middle of the afternoon, a heavy soft blanket on top of us, and I'm showing him one of my favorite shows of all time, which I realize can be a bit of a culture shock for someone unfamiliar with anime, but if you're going to know me, you're going to know *Spy X Family*.

Honestly, it's amazing I restrained myself this long. It isn't like this is the first time in our three days that we've stopped to do something besides sex. We watched a couple of HBO documentaries, played checkers—a few rounds without stripping involved, even—and in exchange for letting me prattle about my favorite books, I let Reid play me YouTube videos of his favorite Olympic swimming competitions.

And I'd thought I was a nerd.

"So Twilight's tasked with spying on the notorious Donovan Desmond, but the only way he can get close to him is through Donovan's kid's private school. So of course he decides he needs a kid to enroll in the school."

"Of course."

"And it's the kind of school where the parents have to be married, so he not only has to find an orphan to be his fake kid but he has to find someone to be his fake wife. He ends up picking this adorable little girl, Anya. Look." I pause the trailer to point out her irresistible big eyes. "Super cute. But little does he know, she's telepathic. And then the woman he hires to be his wife, well, he has no idea that she's an assassin. And the wife doesn't know that he's a spy, but Anya knows everything because of the telepathy. Oh, and the dog has precognition."

"The dog?"

It's not a complicated show, but there is a lot of nuance that I'd hate for him to miss. "Do you want me to show you the manga it's based on? I have an app…" I pat my thighs, as if I have pockets and haven't been half naked for the last few days. It's meant less carrying around of my phone, which has been a nice break, but also means I don't have my phone for reference when I want it.

To be clear, Reid hasn't had his phone on him either. Nor any more clothes than I do. It's funny how, between the two of us, we only manage to wear one complete outfit at a time. He, in a pair of sweats, me in one of his shirts, neither of us wearing anything else.

"Skip the manga. Let's get to the show."

I'm not sure if his enthusiasm is genuine, but if he's faking, he's putting enough energy into it to get lots of boyfriend credit.

If he were a boyfriend, that is, and if boyfriends got

credit for doing nice things for women who may or may not be their girlfriends.

"Okay, we just have to download Crunchyroll onto your Roku." I start to type the name into the applications store, but am suddenly distracted by what's happening outside. "Look, it's snowing!"

I throw off the blankets and run to the windows to watch. I've seen snow a million times, yes, but not from so high up. While I wasn't paying super close attention when we came up in the elevator that first night—there might have been a lot of I-can't-keep-my-hands-off-of-you going on—I do know that we're really high up. Thirty floors or so. You can see all of Manhattan out of his windows. They span the length of his apartment. Floor to ceiling in every room, and though all the glass means less places to display much needed art—this apartment could really use some personality—the view is next level spectacular.

"It's a wonderland below us." I press my head against the window and try to see the ground, but it's too foggy, and all I get is a cold face. "We should make a blanket fort."

"For the people in wonderland?"

For the most part, Reid seems to be getting used to my non sequiturs. He follows a quarter of the time now and only makes fun of fifty percent of my out-of-nowhere comments. I'd thought this one was obvious, but apparently not. "For us. In here."

He glances down as if he doesn't already know that hard wood makes up all the flooring in his apartment. "That sounds uncomfortable."

We'd drag the mattress out here too, of course, but I decide that's a fact better saved for after I've got him on board. "I'll let you fuck me against the windows."

"You'll let me anyway."

"But we could pretend I wouldn't." The real miracle is that I haven't banged him against the windows already.

We've banged in every room in the apartment now, which sounds impressive, but his place is so small that it's really not that big of a feat. There's only the main room, the guest room, the office, the living room/dining room/kitchen—all one big room, but we made sure to hit all three areas to get the most bang per square footage. The foyer isn't technically a room, but we did it (quietly) against the door after the neighbor came by to ask if Reid had brought home a feral cat. I guess I got a little bit too loud in one of our romping sessions.

We even banged in his laundry room, which he doesn't really use because he sends his clothes out, and of course the shower, and his walk-in closet because it turns out sex in front of a full length mirror is the kind of filthy I'm into. So yeah. I've had a tour of the house, so to say.

It gives my fort idea another selling point. "We could count it as an extra room."

"Are you still going on about how small my place is?"

I plop down on the nearby ottoman. "I'm just saying we wouldn't have gotten through all the rooms in my place yet."

"Do you know what two-thousand square feet costs in Tribeca?"

From the way he asks the question, I think I'm supposed to be more impressed with his space than I am. "A million dollars?"

"Try ten."

Riling him up shouldn't be this fun.

Sometimes I totally do it on purpose. Sometimes, though, I just don't get what the big deal is. This place, for example. It's very lux. The furniture looks like it came out of an episode of *Succession*. Every fixture is high end. The kitchen and bathroom counters are made of marble, and all the molding is ornate. All of that is nice, but my brownstone in Brooklyn has almost three times the space.

"For ten million dollars," I hold up my hand to count off what's missing, "you should have a library, a gym, at least three more bedrooms, a media room—"

"That's a lot of new rooms to fuck in."

"We can scope out places on Zillow later. And we're definitely doing a blanket fort." I've convinced him, even if he doesn't realize it yet.

But something I meant to ask him about earlier suddenly pops into my head. "Those awards in your office, are those all for Spice?"

He blinks at me like I've given him whiplash.

It's a look I know well. "It seems out of the blue, but I thought of it earlier, and I couldn't exactly ask then because it was when you had me bent over the desk, and I was facing the wall and saw all the plaques, and I was reading what they said, and some of them were really impressive, but I didn't want you to think I wasn't fully enjoying what you were doing behind me with your cock between my legs so it seemed maybe not the best time to mention it."

"Obviously, you weren't enjoying what I was doing enough not to have other thoughts come into your head."

"Oh, geez. Is that the definition of good sex? Because I hate to break this to you, but I have a lot of thoughts come into my head when we're banging. Now whether or not I have the capacity to voice them is something else entirely."

His expression doesn't ease, and I can't help giggling. "Are you…did I offend your manhood? Do I need to be better at boosting your male ego? I'm not used to what's expected. I've never been a girlfriend—"

I catch myself, and my smile fades.

We still have hours to go before we have to have that conversation. I'm not trying to jump the gun or make assumptions.

It's just so easy with him. Every minute is, and it's hard to imagine that later tonight, it could just…end.

Thankfully, he gracefully skips over my faux pas, as if I haven't brought an elephant into the room. "Yes, they're for Spice."

"That's a lot of awards."

"They aren't all very prestigious. My father would not consider any of them notable, but some of them mean a lot to people in the industry."

"They mean a lot to you, don't they? I was just thinking that you ended up in this career so impulsively, but you seem to have really taken to it."

"I guess I have." He considers it, and from how concentrated his expression appears, I have a feeling he's never really thought about it until now. "I think, at first, I felt like I had to succeed because of how much I had riding on it. I didn't want to let Grandpa Irving down, and even my father…I'm convinced he thought I'd fail.

"But somewhere along the line, I found it suited me. It's just enough business mixed with just enough play. Every night's a party, and at the end of it, I don't owe anyone a call or a text."

"You really aren't into commitment, are you." It's not a question. It's been my experience with him from day one.

I regret voicing it immediately. Why am I so eager to toe this line? It's only three-forty-three, which gives us plenty of time left to pretend that tomorrow won't be completely different for both of us. There are hours before my heart has to be ready to accept that Reid might not want to commit something to me.

Fuck, even thinking about it makes me break out in metaphorical hives. I rub my arms, scratching away the metaphorical itch.

"It's colder by the windows." He lifts the blanket, inviting me back to the space next to him. "Come here, and I'll warm you up."

It's sweet how he jumps to the conclusion that I'm cold. If the last couple of days have shown me anything, it's that he likes to take care of me. And that I like being taken care of.

But it's too late now. I've already taken the blinders off. There's a silent countdown going on in the back of my brain, and no matter how much we try to pretend it isn't there, I hear the tick, tick, tick, like a bomb waiting to go off.

No. I'm not going to waste the hours we have left.

I jump to my feet. "You know what we need? Hot chocolate. Please, please, please tell me you have hot chocolate. I know that's asking a lot since your cupboards are like Mother Hubbard's…"

"*Mother Hubbard's*." He laughs. "Actually, I think the gift basket the neighbor left at Christmas had hot chocolate packets."

"And we have the whipped cream we ordered for the pumpkin pie last night!"

"Yeah, that's why we ordered that."

"I'll start the water." I head to the kitchen, which means just crossing the big room to the counters that make up the kitchen area.

Reid crosses to his bar. "I'll grab the Maker's Mark."

"Oh, we're doing adult versions. Okay." Let's be drunk

while we discuss important decisions about our maybe/maybe not relationship. Totally fine. No big deal.

"Can you handle it, little girl?"

No. "Please. I can handle the liquor better than you can handle the sugar."

"I handled it just fine when I was licking it off your tits."

He passed out cold for four hours after, but I decide it's not necessary to point out.

Especially now that we're both in the kitchen. I fill the kettle with water. He reaches above my head for the stowed away cocoa packets. I set the kettle on the stove. He grabs two mugs from the cupboard. I pull out the whipped cream. He pours a shot of whiskey in each mug.

It's a domestic dance of sorts. It's comfortable, and yet I shiver each time he brushes past me. When all that's left is to wait for the water to boil, he leans against the island, and I lean against the counter across from him.

The distance feels too far.

"Alexa," I call out. Reid hasn't indicated he has the virtual assistant, but it's worth a try. "Play us some snow music."

There's no reply, and Reid's amused stare tells me I'm getting nowhere.

"Hey, Siri." Nothing.

"I have Alfred," he says, eventually.

"What's that?"

"Another virtual assistant. It's custom built."

Of course it is.

"Alfred? Like..." An assistant named Alfred feels pretty obvious. "Like Batman? Do you pretend you're a broken billionaire recluse like Bruce Wayne and ask Alfred to tell you stuff? You do, don't you! Oh my, God. You do!"

"I don't know what you're talking about."

"Alfred, play snow music." I'm so giddy, I'm surprised the technology picks up on my command, but sure enough a song starts. It's slow, something I've never heard before, about the snow softly flying and a winter night "with you" and so perfectly what I'd wanted.

I walk up to Reid, throw my arms around him, and rock back and forth.

"What are you doing?" He returns the embrace before I respond, his bare skin making me instantly hot.

"Dancing. Duh."

"Duh," he says, echoing my mocking tone.

But he starts dancing for real, spinning me barefoot around his kitchen.

I'd known he was a good dancer—a fact he proved at my mother's wedding—but I'd been so concerned with my own feet that night, my own words. I couldn't let myself be in the moment.

This time, it's easy.

I lean into him, feeling his rhythm instead of trying to anticipate it. His mouth brushes against my forehead, then at turns his chin rests at my temple. Our breathing is in sync, and something deep, deep inside me shifts and my entire body feels warm.

I'm so into him that I miss half the song, and when I finally try to listen more to the words, wanting to memorize every part of this moment, I realize it's a song about longing. That the winter's night spent together was in the past, not the present, and it feels so much like a foretelling that my eyes start to gather tears.

I tighten my grip around him.

Then the tea kettle begins whistling, quickly getting louder and impossible to ignore because of course it chooses to go off when I'm trying not to be emotional.

"I got it." I pull away quickly so I can beat him to turning off the stove. It gives me a chance to try to blink my eyes clear. Then when I'm pouring the water, the steam hits my face, and now I have something to blame for any lingering tears.

Grabbing a spoon, I top our drinks with a whopping spoonful of whipped cream. Then, knowing it will be too hot to drink, but feeling eager, I grab a couple of ice cubes from the fridge door and plop one in each of our mugs before handing one to Reid.

Even with the ice, I find I have to sip mine cautiously.

Reid seems more tolerant of the heat. "I haven't had hot chocolate since my mom was still around."

"Your mom?" I don't know why I haven't thought about her before. It's obvious Nelani isn't his mother, since she's very clearly around the same age as he is, but I didn't think to wonder what happened to his real mom, which is mind-blowing considering all the things I want to know about this guy. "You've never mentioned her before. What…?"

I'm not sure how to finish the sentence, wanting to be sensitive.

"She's not dead," he says, reading my mind. He resumes leaning against the island.

I once again take my spot across from him. "Oh, good. I mean, I have a dead parent, and I know it can be weird to talk about and yet, I went bluntly into asking about her without. You know. Thinking about it."

"Was it hard losing him?" he asks.

And I guess now we're talking about Dad, which was definitely not on my agenda for the evening, but as far as important subjects in my life go, his death should top the list.

"Yeah. Yeah. It was the worst thing imaginable. I can't

really remember anything from high school that isn't related to his illness or his actual death, and there's very little that happened in college that wasn't related to getting over said death. Kind of why I didn't have time to get to the sexing until, you know, recently."

His smile is cautious. "Is it inappropriate to say that I'm glad you got sidetracked?"

"If you're saying you're glad my dad died so you could be the first to bang me, then maybe a little inappropriate." I laugh, though, and when he tries to refute, I beat him to it. "But I get what you're saying, and I feel the same."

He grows serious, and for a second I worry I revealed too much somehow. Again. "But you and your father…you were close?"

Oh. "Yeah. I don't want to say I loved him more than my mother, because that's hard to compare, but…I don't know. We had something special. He was silly, where Mamma is serious, and he didn't mind listening to my ramblings, wherever they went. I think he was even somewhat entertained. I don't think I realized how much he took care of us, until he was gone. I'd thought my mom was stronger—and she's not weak, by any means. But I didn't get how much she needed…someone…to be with her all the time."

I'm feeling all mushy and vulnerable—for a variety of reasons—and it's weird so I try to lighten the mood. "You know what I loved? Telling dad jokes. Sometimes he even laughed."

"Was that…was that a dad joke?"

Laughing, I wave my hand in the air, as if I can erase the terrible wisecrack. "A bad one. Sorry."

Then something occurs to me. "Wait—do you think I have Daddy issues? Are you worried that's why I'm with you? Not that I'm *with* you, I'm just, you know. With you right now and have been for the last several days. Can alcohol hit that fast? Because I think my tongue feels incredibly loose all of a sudden. Or is this just me normally?"

"It's you normally."

"You're right. It is." I can't even take a real swallow yet since the drink is so hot. "Anyway. Can we talk about your mom now?"

"I didn't get out of that one?"

"You did not." I set my mug down and prop my elbows on the counter behind me. "I'm ready for it. Spill. Is she as terrible as your dad? She can't be, right?"

"I'm not sure. It's possible she's worse. She hasn't been around since I was five, when my parents got divorced, so I couldn't tell you."

"Hasn't been around since you were…" My stomach turns to lead. Whatever the possible reason for her being gone all that time, it can't be good, and while my empathy level is always pretty high, it's almost overwhelming around Reid. I can't ever remember feeling so heartbroken over someone else's wounds. It should make me want to run away from any trauma he might mention.

Instead, I find myself wanting to share it. Wanting to take it on.

"Dad wanted full custody," Reid explains, his tone steady. "But he couldn't bribe the judge into granting it—at least, that's what I've gathered. So instead, he bribed her."

"He *bribed* her." I'm a stupid parrot, repeating what he says, but only because I want to clearly process.

"Paid her off to never have contact with Alex or me again."

"You can't be serious. And she took that offer? What mother would take that offer?" I'm back to blinking a lot because the tears are threatening to come fast and hard. "You have to be wrong. How do you know that for sure?"

"I didn't know it for sure until about eight years ago, when I tried to track her down. Found her in Ibiza through a PI. She's well set up, it seems. Beautiful house. New husband. New kids. The PI gave me lots of pics. She looks happy as fuck, and I should have known…" He shakes his head, changing his mind about whatever conclusion he thinks he should have come to. "I called her. Told her who I was, and before I could even get to the part where I asked to see her, she told me she couldn't talk to me. *Wouldn't* talk to me. And that I needed to make it plain to my father that *I* reached out to *her*, and not the other way around, so that he wouldn't come after her for it.

"Then she hung up. And the pieces fell into place. I know what kind of person my father is. He buys everyone he can. Her financial records show she had more money deposited in her account than she had been awarded at the divorce. It doesn't take a genius to—"

I cross the short distance between us, unable to hold myself back anymore. The tears that I've been fighting waterfall down my cheeks, and I burrow my face against his neck. "I don't want to be another person who leaves you."

His arms come around me. "What?"

I know he heard me. I'm blubbering, but my words are distinct and my mouth is near his ear. "I don't want to be another person your father scares off. I don't want to be another person who doesn't commit to you."

"Shh, baby girl." He kisses my hair, and yeah, he's trying to shush me, but he hasn't pushed me away.

"No, I can't be quiet about this, Reid. I can't keep this in. I feel…" So much. So many emotions all at once. Too many to try to label or point out. "It's not fair. And I know that life isn't fair and all that bullshit, but this shouldn't be a thing that keeps people apart. I don't want us to be done."

His body stiffens underneath me. "So we're talking about this now?"

I shake my head against his collarbone. "Yes. I don't know. I just. I don't want to be done."

He pushes me back, gently, but only so far that he can lift my chin and meet my eyes. "Then okay. We won't be done."

I blink a few times, unsure what he means. "But we can't…you can't risk your nightclub." Reynard would take away Spice if Reid and I tried to be together. There's no way he'd stand for it.

Then there's what I'd lose—would my mother ever forgive me for having a relationship with the one person she said was off-limits? And what would Samuel do? Would he be so mad at me that he'd take it out on her?

I couldn't bear to be the cause of hurt after she's finally found a new life for herself.

"Fuck. There's no way for us, is there?" I'm a contradiction in wants, unable to see a right path.

Reid wipes tears from my face with his thumbs. "Did you mean it when you said you could make it three years?"

I hadn't thought it through as clearly as I should have when I said it, but I haven't stopped thinking about it since. "I could. I can."

He instantly corrects himself. "I'm not saying we're at a place where I expect that we know what's going to happen in three years. But we need time to figure out where this could go, and either we wait until then to try—"

"No," I say instantly, rejecting any plan that means I don't get to be with Reid now.

"Or we keep figuring it out. Like we have been. As best as we can. Without anyone else knowing."

"Like…you mean…?" I was the one who suggested it first, really, without saying it so bluntly, but it was what I meant. "We keep us secret?"

"I know that's not fair. And I don't *want* to keep you secret, Lina." The *but* hangs there in his subtext. "I know what it is to hide something like that from everyone, and I don't have any right to ask you—"

I cut him off. "You didn't ask. I offered."

He studies me, and I can see the battle happening in his head, the one where he tries to decide if I should be allowed to make this decision or if he should be the martyr who makes it for both of us.

"Don't." I raise my finger at him. "You can't take it back now. You said we won't be done. You said it." I turn my head and call to the air. "Alfred? I know you things are secretly recording everything that's going on—you heard him, right? He said we won't be done. Can you replay that for him?"

"I'm sorry, I'm unable to help you with—"

Reid interrupts the digital assistant. "Shut the fuck up, Alfred. I don't need to hear it replayed. I know what I said."

"Yeah, shut the fuck up, Alfred." I move my hands up Reid's torso and to the back of his neck. "So you mean it, right? Really mean it? God, I'm really pathetic right now. Begging you to give us a chance. I can't imagine how unattractive—"

"You've never been more beautiful."

He wipes more tears from my cheeks, and it hits me that he's still here. Still holding me. "That doesn't sound like a breakup line. Not that we can technically break up because we haven't been officially together, but the point is you don't sound done with me."

He leans his forehead against mine and sighs. "I'm not done with you. Nowhere near."

"Is that our official status? Can I put that on my social media? *Not done with Reid Sebastian*."

"You can't put anything on your social media status. That's the opposite of secret."

"Figuratively speaking. *Figuratively*. I'm not an idiot."

He stares at me again, and I'm snotty and tear-stained, and I don't need a mirror to know that I'm blotchy as fuck because my skin always does that when I get emotional, yet still, somehow, he really does look at me like he only sees beauty.

No shade against him either when he hands me a napkin to clean up said snot before he kisses me. There's a limit to how much DNA I'm comfortable sharing, and thankfully he feels the same, and not having to worry that my lips are covered in mucus makes it much easier to get into the kissing.

Then the kissing turns more into groping, and I'm familiar enough with how these makeout sessions of ours go to know that I'm about to have a dick inside me if I don't put a stop to it, and as much as I want to have his dick inside me at all times, we have some other things to address first.

Miraculously, I manage to untangle myself from him. Then I step back and put my hand out in front of me to stop him from following. Giving him a clear boundary. "So we're really going to do this."

"I was hoping we were about to do something else."

I hold my hand up higher. "I need…just tell me one more time."

He adjusts his cock first. "We're really attempting to do this."

I'm not even ruffled by his added caveat. I feel too good. Hopeful, for the first time in days. For the first time since I saw him at my mother's wedding. And I know that this isn't a declaration of anything permanent, just a chance to find out, but that's more than I ever thought possible between us.

And if it becomes more…

Well, we can deal with the consequences of that when we get there.

Of course, Reid can never let a nice moment linger. "It's not going to be easy. You get that, don't you? We're going to have to be so careful. We'll have to make rules. We'll have to avoid each other in family settings."

"Sounds hot." I'm aware it isn't going to feel like that all the time, but I'm a glass half full kind of a girl, and I'm not letting him ruin my mood.

"This isn't a joke, Lina. The stakes are—"

I put my finger to his lips. "You can lecture me all you want in our blanket fort."

I didn't mention it's a naked blanket fort, but he'll find out soon enough, and let's just say, I have a real good feeling this lecture won't last very long at all.

CHAPTER TWENTY-FIVE

LINA

My phone buzzes quietly in my lap. I wait until the team member turns back to his presentation before reading the text.

Westalis & Ostania aren't real, are they?

Well, now I know what Reid's currently doing. Not like I was wondering.

I was totally wondering.

It appears I've created another *Spy X Family* addict. The marketing department should put me on their payroll.

I bite my lip to keep from grinning as I type back a response.

They're E. & W. Germany

In an alt. world

What ep R U on?

I put my phone face down while I wait for his reply. Fortunately, the art department staff meeting is interesting and manages to keep my attention, even though part of me just wants to think about Reid every minute, all day long.

There's a lot of Reid I like to think about in particular. That new trick he showed me with his tongue is at the top of the list, but it's not just the sex that preoccupies my mind. I'm endlessly fascinated with what fascinates him, which is hard to get him to reveal. At first, I thought he might be boring. A guy with no real interests, especially after I discovered he panic-chose his career path.

After our three days together, though, I've started to think he just hasn't let himself love anything. Probably because he's afraid it will be taken away by his mean old ass of a father. No wonder Samuel hates his brother so much. Reynard deserves hating.

It's a miracle that Reid got brave enough to allow us to try for a relationship. He thinks I don't understand the risks, and maybe I don't understand them the way he does, but when we stayed up late last night, figuring it all out—in the most spectacular blanket fort that ever existed—we realized our lives are practically made for a secret affair. We both work at the Sebastian Center. I get off work at five. The club doesn't open until nine. His staff doesn't arrive until seven-thirty. That gives us two and a half hours every day to hang out in his club alone.

This morning was unusual because I came straight from his apartment to SNC. Denny, the only person who's been let in on our secret, was cool enough to bring me a change of clothes. (He did kind of owe me after all the times I've gone out to see DJs with him.) Even taking the subway from Reid's place, the trip was so much faster than the usual trip from Brooklyn, which is a bummer because we both decided that coming to his apartment is too risky. He's not one of the most paparazzi-chased Sebastians, but there are occasional reporters outside his doors.

Which is why we have chosen my brownstone as the spot for any sleepovers. I'm on no one's radar, so we think it's safe, but we'll have to keep that to a minimum to make sure it stays that way.

And of course I can always visit the club when it's open, too. Stare at him longingly from across the room while he does his suave bartender thing. Watch him flirt with the women who want to get in his pants and then not be able to rush over and claim him openly as mine…

Maybe there are a few downsides, but it's doable, and that's what matters.

Ep. 22

I think that's around when Anya discovers Fiona is a spy too. Reid is cruising through this. He'll be done with the season before we meet after work tonight. I start typing that out when I hear my name called in a sharp tone that sounds enough like I'm in trouble that I startle and drop my phone. "What? Yes. I'm paying attention."

Looking up, I see Samuel staring at me. Adly's right behind him, covering her mouth like she's trying not to laugh. Everyone else at the meeting is picking up their belongings, which suggests that I might have been more in my head than I realized.

And now not only have I been caught by my boss, but also by the man who runs the company.

"Hi, hi." I stand and straighten my skirt. "Sorry, I was, uh, marking those dates on my calendar." I'm not sure there were actually dates discussed, but deadlines are so often mentioned at these meetings, it feels like a safe enough bet.

Adly crosses over to stand behind me. "She's really on top of things, Dad. Fitting in well."

It's such a minor thing, but having her literally *behind me* emboldens me. Because, if I do say so myself, she's not wrong. I am really on top of things, and I do fit in well. Maybe at this particular moment I was distracted, but only because Reid's distracting, and the newness of this thing with him is distracting. Except for him, I'm so in tune with this latest job path Adly has me on that I can actually envision myself as a future leader of the department.

So I feel confident when I address my superior/stepfather. "Is there something I can do for you? Want to quiz me on relevant terms? I've memorized the whole glossary I was given. Made flashcards and everything."

Samuel's eyes squint, and he seems a little to be looking down his nose at me, but he's also really tall, and probably looks down his nose at everyone. "That's not necessary. I am interested in your thoughts about the design Alan presented today."

"Ah. That." I'm not used to people asking me my viewpoint about things like this, and considering how *not* well I was paying attention during today's meeting, this could be a landmine for me.

Fortunately, however, I only missed what Alan said in his presentation. Not only did I carefully study the graphics, but I also have opinions. Strong opinions.

Also, the main design is still projected on the screen behind Samuel, so it's an easy reference.

Avoiding the temptation to look behind me for Adly's support, I try to determine if Samuel wants my real opinion or if I'm supposed to suck up. "So…I think Alan has a clear understanding of what has worked for SNC in the past, which is why my thoughts are maybe not the most important here."

"If I didn't think they were important, I wouldn't have asked."

"Sure. Okay." I swallow. Fuck. *Here goes nothing.* "Well, the color choices are strong, and I see from the early testing data that there's a strong resonance with older demographics, but there's a reason we didn't get a lot of response from the twenty- to thirty-nine-year-old brackets."

"Because the youth aren't interested in news." He says it like it's a statement, but I think it's supposed to be a challenge.

It makes me feel challenged anyway. "They aren't tuning into news television, but believe me, a lot of us are interested in the news. We just don't think we prefer it from traditional sources, and no wonder, because when I look at these designs…"—I point at the screen—"No offense, Samuel, but that set looks like a grandma's living room. No one my age wants to hear about the state of the world from a Boomer. Sorry, uh, Baby Boomer, I think is the correct term.

"I mean—there are other barriers that I can't speak to. We like to digest in bits and pieces, and that usually means clips that show up in our social media feeds, and that's a whole other department that decides what's released where, and all that, but when that clip is released, the set behind the commentator had better have some youth to it, or we're not going to let it play through. Better yet, there even shouldn't be a set. The look should be less static. Utilize greenscreens. Talking heads over video clips always get me to stop scrolling. Make the logo less political looking. No reds and blues. Use muted greens and yellows. And add more round images. These hard edges are too…hard. The news is hard as it is. Can't there be some softness to the design around it? Seriously. I feel like I need to take a whole container of pot gummies just looking at that logo."

It's when I hear the words "pot gummies" come out of my mouth that I realize I may have said too much. "But of course, I'm the newbie here and don't know a lot yet, and also I would never know what a pot gummy even looked like or how it's dispensed, like, do they even have pot gummies?" I shrug. "Just guessing."

I suppose I'll know how much my mother and her husband tell each other if she starts sending me links to anti-drug campaigns after this.

Samuel stares at me for a long moment.

To be fair, every moment feels long when I'm being stared at. It's quite possible the moment is really not long at all and/or that the seconds that pass are not at all correlated with a reduction in how competent he thinks I am.

The point is that I have no sense of what he thinks and by the time he responds, my hands are clammy and my throat is dry and there's a literal bead of sweat on my brow.

"Have we done testing with this kind of art concept?" he asks.

This time I do glance behind me because there's no way he thinks I know the answer, but Adly looks strangely tightlipped—strange for Adly, not like her expression is actually strange—which leads me to the conclusion that it is me that is being asked. "I don't think so?"

At least, none of the concepts that I've been shown have incorporated elements meant to grab the attention of the youth.

"Mock up a reel, will you? I'll let Alan know you're on it."

"Uh…okay." I'm going to definitely need to Google how to mock up a reel later on since that wasn't in the glossary I was given for reference.

Then, to my shock and amazement, he adds, "Good work, kid."

And while I'm not necessarily fond of older men who call me *kid*—except Grandpa Irving because he calls people even twice my age *kid*—I do have a jittery feeling in my chest, a lot like the one I get after I've had a lot of coffee, and it feels…good. Like I've been seen. Like I have things that are interesting to say.

No wonder everyone's always jumping for Samuel's approval. Samuel's approval is an upper.

I'm vibrating from his compliment, and when he motions for Adly to come with him, and she tells him she'll catch up in a minute, I know she's going to congratulate me.

Except when Samuel has left, and I turn to face my stepsister, she does not have a congratulations smile on her face. "You're sleeping with Reid?"

"What! No." Then I spot my cell phone in her hand. The phone that I dropped on the ground when Samuel and Adly came in the room. "No!"

She hands it over, and sure enough, there's Reid's name on my lock screen—because I put his real name in my phone like an idiot—with a text that says something about what he wants to do to my pussy before the preview cuts off, because of course it does.

Of. Course. It. Does.

"No!" I say, again. It's a lament at this point. "It's only the first day." How could I fuck up on the very first day?

"The first day of what? I told him to leave you alone. Didn't he leave you alone? What's going on?"

Ignoring Adly's demand for answers, I close my eyes tight, as if that will make everything go away. When I open them, I glance at the message again, which is actually kind of hot, and try to see if there's any way I can convince her he's talking about a cat, but unless it's a regular thing to lick cats senseless, it's not going to fly.

"I suck at secret, is what's going on." I sink into a chair and bang my head on the conference table a few times before shooting her a desperate look. "You're not going to tell, are you?"

"Tell *what*?" Adly sits in the chair next to me. "I still don't know what's going on."

"Oh, good! So there's nothing to tell. Better if you don't know. Pretend you never saw this." It's only now that the idea occurs to me. "You know what—it's not even the same Reid."

She glares at me.

"I deserve that." Realizing she doesn't know what I'm referring to, I add, "That look you're giving me."

"I told him to leave you alone."

"You did! And he did. And then he didn't." Or I didn't. We couldn't leave each other alone, in the end, I suppose.

"He didn't..." She puts her hand over mine, suddenly very serious. "If he did anything inappropriate, Lina, you can tell me. I know it feels like these rich boys get away with everything, but I swear on my life, I'll make—"

"God, no!" I only let her go on so long because it takes me a second to realize what she means by inappropriate since pretty much everything I've done with Reid feels inappropriate. "All consensual. I swear."

"Well, that's good. I had to ask, considering most apples don't fall far from the trees."

"Yeah, Reynard is a fucktard—ha ha, that rhymes—but

no, Reid is…" He's the son of a man that Adly has been raised to hate. "He's not a bad guy, Adly. Reid's not. Whatever you think about him, he's not that."

"I don't really think…" She shakes her head. "Look, I like Reid. He's my cousin, so ew, but I've always gotten along with him. I don't know him as well as I could since our fathers are so insistent on making us enemies, but Grandpa wants us all to get along and both Dad and Reynard want Grandpa happy, so we've all learned how to play rival more than we actually mean it.

"But the point is that Dad does hate Reynard, and that extends to his children, and if he thought there was something between you two…"

She lets it trail off, but I'd kind of like to know the worst that could happen. "He'd…what?"

"I don't really know, I guess." Her laugh quickly dissipates. "But he doesn't let things go, Lina. He won't stand for it, and the ways that he might go about ending things can be awfully cruel."

Surely, not Reynard-level cruel.

I'm too afraid to ask. "It's not anything really," I say instead, deciding it's better to minimize the situation as much as I can. "Just fooling around. A fun secret thing."

"Those fun secret things…" She lets out a breath of air, and I swear she sounds like a woman with a secret of her own, but she doesn't give me a chance to ask. "You don't know how easily fun secrets can turn into serious problems."

"It won't. It's nothing. A fling."

"Really?"

God, I wish I was a better liar.

"No, not really." I drop my head to the table again. Facing the laminate surface, it's easier to admit the truth. "I really like him, Adly. Really like him, and I think he likes me. Or he likes me enough for us to keep seeing each other while we figure it out, and I know there's risks, but don't we deserve the chance to see if we could be something?"

I lift my head, suddenly feeling passionate about it. "And it's stupid. Who I like, who he likes—we aren't actually cousins. Samuel and Reynard hate each other? Why does that have to continue down the line? What age do we live in? *Romeo and Juliet* doesn't take place in a contemporary setting for a reason."

"Thank God because, spoiler, they both end up dead." She rubs her hand over mine some more. "You're right, though. All of it. It's stupid. And you should keep seeing him if that's what you want to do. I'm not going to 'tell.' I support you. Please, don't ask me to help, though, because I—"

"No, no! I wouldn't."

She runs her teeth over her bottom lip. "Okay, if you really need something, you can ask. I'm a fucking hopeless romantic at heart."

"Long live smut." I give a tentative grin.

Her smile is more sure. "Fucking change his name to something else in your phone."

"Oh, I know. Doing it now." I type in Twilight because it's the first thing that comes to mind.

She continues her speech. "Don't ever try to sneak him into SNC—too many security cameras. No using office computers or phones for communication. Probably best not to tell Reid I know. And do not—*do not*—ever try to defend him or Reynard to Dad. That goes even if you aren't seeing Reid. That's a losing argument, no matter what proof you think you may have on your side."

"That all sounds like really good sisterly advice." I

finger the bracelet she gave me at Mamma's wedding then hold it up for her to see. "I never take it off."

She pulls back the sleeve of her shirt to reveal the identical one on her wrist.

"Twins," I say.

"Well." She stands, and I follow. "Dad's going to be looking for me soon. Good luck." She hugs me. "Let me know if you need anything, okay? But don't need anything."

I laugh. "Okay."

She pulls away and starts toward the door.

"Oh, Adly. One more thing." When she turns around, I give her my most innocent eyelash bat. "Could you maybe tell me how to make a mock-up reel?"

At least she smiles. "I'll email you some info."

"And also, I'll probably end up telling…" I don't want to say his name when she's across the room, but she doesn't know his code name. "You know who…that you know. I'm not good at secrets."

"Lina!"

"I mean, I'm not good at face-to-face secrets. Sneaking around secrets are a whole other kind of secret, so it'll only be a problem if someone asks me directly."

The look she gives me now is another one I deserve—it says I better get my shit together, and quick.

CHAPTER TWENTY-SIX

LINA

I stretch out on the couch, planting my feet in Denny's lap.

"Hey," he says, with mock annoyance. Or maybe it's a little bit real annoyance. Either way, he sits back so he can still have room to move his controller.

"You want me to pretend like I'm interested in watching you play Zelda, then you have to sacrifice."

"I thought the sacrifice was listening to you catch me up on your life while I try to concentrate."

"What can I say? The cost of my company is expensive." Honestly, I was the one who suggested he play a game. It's the first time our schedules have lined up in a while, and I'm glad to just spend a Saturday together.

It helps ease my guilt, too, since most of my free time has gone to Reid the last couple of weeks. I don't feel a lot of guilt about it—I'm giddy and obnoxiously happy overall—but since Reid wasn't able to hang out before work today, I offered my afternoon to Denny. Even let him dominate the early part of our conversation with tales from awful bands he's worked with in the studio and a new DJ that he's discovered in the DC area.

After getting me to promise that I'll take the train with him sometime to check the new talent out, Denny turns the focus to me. "What's going on with that mock-up reel you were working on?"

"Bleh," I groan, tugging on my braid. The final product came out okay, but it took hours to put it together, mostly since I didn't know what I was doing, and as far as I know, Samuel hasn't seen it. I haven't seen or heard from him in the three-plus weeks since he gave me the assignment, anyway.

Alan didn't say much when I handed it in, either.

"They added it to the market testing samples. We'll start getting feedback soon. Whether I'll have access to that feedback remains to be seen."

"You don't sound as enthusiastic as you did when you first started working on it."

"Yeah, well. All the pride I'd felt at being tasked with the project sort of dissipated when I discovered a bunch of interns were working on the same thing. On the one hand, I'm learning from the ground up, just like everyone else. On the other hand, it's plain as day I'm a nepo baby because my paycheck is at least triple what they start the interns on."

Denny pauses his game to stare at me. "Are you complaining about making too much money?"

"Or I'm complaining that the interns don't make more."

My expression changes as I hear the sound of the front door open and close. Denny and I exchange glances.

"Your boyfriend," Denny says, because Reid is the only other person who has a key, but he's supposed to be doing inventory all day.

I stand up, ready to investigate, when Reid walks into the living room, his arm tucked inside his coat.

"What are you doing here? Why didn't you hang up your coat? Is this a short visit?" I cross the room to kiss him hello. Four weeks into our relationship, and he still takes my breath away every time I see him. In some ways, the effect he has on me has only gotten stronger.

His kiss is short and fairly chaste, probably since we aren't alone. "Denny," he says, acknowledging my friend.

"What's up?" Denny doesn't seem to expect a reply, immediately returning his focus to the TV screen.

"I didn't actually have inventory today. That was an excuse so that—"

I lose interest in what he's saying when his coat starts wriggling. I start pulling back the fabric to investigate. "What's in—oh, my God, it's a kitty!"

A black and white baby tabby, to be exact. With huge eyes and the cutest little nose and a fluffy body that I just want to squeeze.

I take the cat from Reid's hands and hug it to my chest. "Is it yours? Is it mine? Is it *ours*? Did we just adopt a baby together? Please, please, please say that's what we did because you're never prying this kitty out of my arms again, and I'm going to teach it to call you Daddy, whether you like it or not."

He laughs, but his expression seems to be as much adoration as it is amusement, which makes me grin like crazy, and then he's grinning like crazy. It's stupid annoying how into each other we can be, and I totally understand why Denny calls us obnoxious and prefers to be holed up in his basement rather than spend too much time around us.

"I got him for you." Reid glares over at my roommate. "Because when a woman wants a cat, you get her a cat."

Denny puts his hands up in surrender. "She was never actually my woman."

"You sure acted like it was your job to protect her like she was."

"Now, boys. None of that." They pretend they're always irritated by each other, but after I caught them talking club mixes for an hour while they thought I was asleep on the sofa the other night, I'm pretty sure it's all an act. "Did you say it's a him? What are we naming him? Do we need to get him food? Oh, and we need a litter box." I plop down on the floor with the cat in my lap since he's awfully squirmy.

Reid takes his coat off and hangs it up in the hallway as he answers. "I have some supplies out here. More is being delivered." When he returns, he gets down on the floor with me, never mind that he's already dressed for work in nice slacks and a long-sleeve blue gradient button-down. "For a name…Twilight?"

I haven't told him that's what I'm using for Reid's code name in my phone, but obviously, that means I can't use it for the cat.

Anyway, the kitty doesn't seem like a Twilight. "I don't think it fits. He has mischief in his eyes."

Reid meets my gaze, and in unison, we say, "Donovan Desmond."

"You're naming the cat after the bad guy in *Spy X Family*?" Denny shakes his head.

"Donovan's a great name," I say, defending our choice before burying my face in my new kitty's fur.

"*Donovan Desmond* is a great name," Reid corrects. "I think you need both parts to really nail it. Besides, we wouldn't want to get him mixed up with any other Donovans out there."

"Agreed." It seems I do a lot of beaming when Reid's around. My cheeks are always hurting because of the wide smiles he puts on my face, and right now is no exception.

When Donovan Desmond wriggles out of my hands and runs off to explore my non-kitten-proofed living room, I lean forward to give "Daddy" another kiss. One that shows a little more appreciation than the one we exchanged when he first arrived.

"You got me a cat. I love..." I almost say *you*, but change gears, last second, "him." I'm there, emotionally, I think. But I've never said anything like that to a boy I wasn't related to before, and even though I'm full of the feels, I don't expect Reid to be there anytime soon. He's too cautious and guarded, and for good reason, which doesn't make it any easier to accept, but I'm trying to be an adult about our very adult relationship.

Reid strokes a finger across my jaw. "Happy almost one month anniversary."

My belly bursts with butterflies. "This is an anniversary gift? Wow. I'm so impressed and turned on right now. Seriously."

His eyes darken. "A pussy for my pussy."

Denny tosses the game controller to the couch. "That's it. I'm out."

Laughing, I jump up to tackle-hug my best friend on his way to the basement. "Thanks for hanging out. Want to do pizza later?"

Denny looks past me at Reid. "You aren't stealing her for the rest of the night?"

I pinch Denny's chin and direct it back toward me. "Don't ask him. He's my boyfriend, not my boss." But then

I glance toward Reid. "You're not stealing me away for the rest of the night? No secret plans to take me to Paris later or anything?"

"Sadly, no." Reid moves from the floor to the more comfortable armchair. "Working tonight as usual."

Working tonight means a couple of hours before he has to leave Brooklyn to be at Spice for opening, though. His schedule is basically tattooed into my head, and I pretty much know down to the last minute how much time he needs to get from one place to another. Such is a life living in stolen moments.

I turn back to Denny. "So we'll do pizza. We can watch *Thousand Year Blood War* since it's on Hulu now."

We solidify the time, and as he departs, I mouth, *Thank you and don't come back upstairs for a while,* because it's only fair to give your roommate a warning when you're about to get nasty with your boyfriend in the shared living space.

I wait until I hear the basement door shut before I turn to face Reid and coyly pull at my braid. "You got me a cat." Appropriately, I'm practically purring.

"Am I on the best boyfriend list?" His smug expression says that he knows very well that he is.

And if he wasn't, he would be now because he referred to himself as my *boyfriend*. Though I call him that all the time when talking to Denny, Reid has only used the term a handful of times, and every time it makes me need to change my panties.

Hell, I should just take them off all together.

I lift my sweater dress to my waist and put on a show of wiggling free of my underwear. "You're about to be on the *happiest* boyfriend list," I say, then climb onto his lap and straddle him.

"I should lie to you about doing inventory more often."

"As long as the lie means I'm getting a gift, sure. I'm good with that." Especially when the gift proves he remembers an anniversary. I buck my hips, sliding myself over his cock, which is quickly stiffening up. "Four weeks. Four weeks with no other pussies but mine. That's big time committed for you. Are you freaking out? Can you believe it?"

He doesn't have the fuckpad suite at the hotel anymore, which I love to tease him about. The more stories he tells me, the more I realize my man was what they call a slut. He tries to hide it from me, thinking I'm going to look down on him for it, but all I see is benefits reaped. If it took sleeping with lots of random women to learn how to make my toes curl with just a swipe of his tongue, I think I came out the winner.

As for the commitment thing, from my perspective, he's a lot more relaxed than he used to be. Maybe that's just because he isn't always trying to fight our attraction anymore, but the way we fit together is so natural, it doesn't feel like there's an obligation at all.

Reid runs his hands underneath my dress and up my ribcage. "The hardest part to believe is that you've managed to make it four weeks with only telling Adly."

"Well, and Jade." And Joe and Amani, but I swore them all to secrecy, and they don't really count since they don't know anyone that matters, so who would they tell?

He squints his eyes and scrunches up his face, and it kind of looks like he just stubbed his toe. "I keep purposely forgetting you told your friends."

It's the one recurring argument of ours—not a serious one. No one yells or throws things. Just Reid thinks "secret" means no one on Earth should know, which does seem like the safest way to go, but on the other hand, my friends are much more likely to keep their mouths shut when they know what's going on with me versus when they don't know. That's when they start speculating and all sorts of rumors get started.

I'd remind him, but I'm not in the mood for that disagreement right now. "Totally understand," I say, working on his belt buckle. "Help me get your cock out."

It's like he was just waiting for me to ask, considering how quickly he gets his pants down, just far enough to release what I'm looking for. He circles his hand around the base and strokes up his length. "Are you good with being on top?"

It's the position he offered me our first night. Four weeks of steady fucking, and I still haven't ventured to try anything that put the reins in my hands. I'm under the impression that Reid is content being in control, but I also think he enjoys it when I try to get bold.

He gave me a freaking cat. He deserves some bold gratitude.

Or at least a bold attempt. "I guess we're going to find out here real soon."

I lift myself up on my knees and center myself over him. Reid helps, sliding down in the chair then holding his cock to guide his tip to my opening. Once his crown is tucked inside, though, he lets go. "It's all you, baby girl."

All I do is sit down, and he's inside me. "Oh. Whoa."

It takes me a minute to get really comfortable. My thighs are in the way, at first, and I'm not able to get his cock in all the way until I push my knees farther apart. Fortunately, my pelvis is flexible and I can stretch that far. Plus, the chair is oversized so there's room to spread.

"You're doing fucking amazing." He pulls my ass forward, and hisses when I'm finally fully seated.

"Oh, shit. You're so deep." I squeeze my pussy around him. He feels different in this position. His cock hits a new place inside me, and it's weird and wonderful all at the same time. Slowly, I experiment with movement. Tilting my hips forward and back rubs my clit in a delicious way, but it's when I start bobbing up and down that Reid's expression turns feral.

"Fuck. Lina." He tugs at my dress, gathered at my waist. "I'm taking this off."

I lift my arms above my head so he can pull it over my head, freeing my breasts. "You kill me when you don't wear a bra."

"In a good way or a bad way?"

"Is there a good way to be killed? Fuck." He palms my tits, kneading them roughly. "I love your fucking breasts."

I love when he manhandles me—when he tugs at my nipples and treats me like playdough—but I also love it when he removes his hands completely and lets them bounce with my movement. It's not exactly comfortable, but that somehow adds to the eroticism.

There's a little bit of discomfort to all of it, actually, as well as the pleasure. It takes work to keep bobbing up and down, and I'm certain my thighs are going to feel this for days. It's worth it, though, to hear our skin slap together.

But it's when Reid starts massaging my clit that I'm really sold on the position. When he doesn't have to concentrate on the fucking, it turns out he can put the effort into a skill I didn't know that he could perfect upon.

Apparently, he can, and soon my breaths are laced with moans, and I can feel my orgasm just at bay.

Until I hear Donovan Desmond slide across the floor and pounce on something behind me.

I slow down my bounce, which helps ease the cramp

that's starting to form in my thigh, and peer over my shoulder. "Is it bad for him to see us like this? Will he forever be traumatized by Mommy and Daddy getting it on?"

He pulls on my braid, directing my attention back to him. "We're modeling. Teaching him how to properly say thank you."

"We're such good parents."

"The best. Here." Reid brings his hands to my hips and manipulates my pelvis so that it tilts back and forth while rocking up and down. "Try moving like this."

"Like…this?" I attempt the pattern on my own and discover that not only does it give my thigh muscles a break, but it also rubs my pussy in a new way. "Oh, there we go. That's good, isn't it."

In answer, he brings a hand behind my neck and pulls my mouth to his. He's always a good kisser, but when he's really turned on, his kiss gets possessive and mean, and I'm complete mush. "You just got really wet all over my dick."

"What if I make a mess on your pants?" My voice is so high and squeaky, it doesn't sound like mine.

"Trying to warn off other women? Put your scent all over me and claim me as yours?"

"If that works, then…" It feels so good, I'm having a hard time thinking. "Oh, shit."

"Your cunt is so fucking tight."

"Because I'm about to come." My vision is darkening. My limbs are tingling. My breath feels stuck inside my belly, and all my muscles are locked.

"Don't lose the rhythm. Keep bouncing on my cock, baby girl." Reid returns his hands to my hips to try to help me.

"I can't…I can't…" Not only have I lost control of my movement, but my pussy keeps trying to push Reid out.

He grunts in frustration. "You did fucking beautifully, Lina. You're so good at riding cock. But now I need to..." He holds my hips in place and takes over, fucking up into me at a frenetic pace that draws my orgasm out and within seconds we're coming together.

As soon as I have possession of my body again, I cup his face and we kiss more. Slow kisses this time. Sweet kisses as our breathing normalizes and my heart calms down.

He's still pretty hard inside me, and I rock my hips sensually over him. "I'm going to need to start doing more squats." Or like squats in general, since I currently do none.

He chuckles, and the sound vibrates all through my body. "You were really amazing."

"I know."

He chuckles again, then caresses my jaw with his thumb as he studies my face. "I'm..." He takes a deep breath. "You overwhelm me, Lina."

I know what he's saying because I feel it too. It's hard to name. It's just big and total and consuming.

Scary, too, so I have to ask, "In a good way?"

"Oh, baby girl. In the best way." He leans up to kiss me again, but pauses when we hear the distinct sound of a door opening.

No way Denny's coming back upstairs after the warning I gave him, and besides, it sounds like the front door rather than the basement. But who the fuck else has a key?

The answer comes when a voice calls out, "Lina?"

Oh, right, there is someone else who has a key to this house—*her* house—my mother.

CHAPTER
TWENTY-SEVEN
LINA

"Fuck." I spring off of Reid at a speed I didn't know I'm capable of. While I'm pulling my dress back on, he's putting himself away. I spot my panties by the living room entry just as my mother appears in the doorway.

"Mamma." *Don't look down. Don't look down.* I will her not to look, but also will myself, because knowing me, I'd be the one to draw her attention to them by glancing at them first. "What are you doing here? Did you tell me you were stopping by? Is everything okay at home? Did you try to call?"

I get a little chaotic when I'm nervous. And when I'm not nervous, so hopefully she doesn't think anything of it.

She stares hard at me.

Then at Reid who is still in the chair, leaning forward with his elbows on his thighs, making me wonder if he didn't manage to finish doing up his belt.

Then at the kitten that just decided to try to eat my big

toe, and though only a few seconds have gone by without her responding, it's much too much silence for me.

I scoop the cat into my arms. "Reid remembered I wanted a kitten, from something I said at Christmas, or something someone said at Christmas, and look. His neighbor's cat had kittens—it was your neighbor, right?—and he brought me this one. His name is Donovan Desmond. From a show. Not one you watch. But one of my favorites. Congratulations! You're officially a grandma."

Mamma's eyes narrow. "Your dress is on backwards."

My face flushes completely, which is kind of shocking because I was already pretty flushed from the sex and then from the adrenaline of her entrance. I didn't know there was more blood left to color my skin, but hey, that's what I get for being so Irish girl.

Reid stays silent, but I know he wants me to protect our secret at all costs. If he weren't sitting right here—if I couldn't feel him pushing me to keep up the pretense—I'd probably cave right now. It's my mother, and we've been close these last few years. It's hard to keep secrets from her.

But I want to keep Reid more, and so that wins. "Oh, scrum," I say, looking down at the tag sticking out on my chest. "How embarrassing. Why didn't you say anything, Reid?"

"I…" He shrugs. Then stands up, and oh my God, his pants *are* done up, thank the Lord. "To be honest, I didn't notice."

"Thanks, Mamma, for pointing it out," I say, with heavy sarcasm. Because wouldn't it just be fantastic if I'd accidentally been wearing my dress backward all day and her mentioning it was the awkward part of this moment?

A girl can wish.

"I'm going to, uh—" Reid points toward the hallway

then looks at me. Or near me, because he's having a hard time meeting my eyes. "You should have everything you need for Donovan Desmond out there."

He waves as he heads toward the door.

"Thank you, Reid. Thank you." Except I can't stand him leaving without me talking to him. "Let me walk you out."

"It's not necessary."

I turn to my mom and point after Reid. "I'm going to just…" Then I hurry into the hall after him, and find he's already putting on his coat. "I'm freaking out!" I whisper-shout.

"I shouldn't have come."

"No, don't say that." We've made such progress. I can't stand it if this has him backing away from me again.

He finishes buttoning his coat and looks toward the living room before looking at me. "It'll be fine. She doesn't *know* anything. Call me, later. Okay? Tell me what happens."

He turns toward the front door, but I grab his arm to stop him. "But Reid. Don't leave like—"

Abruptly, he tugs me to him. "I didn't mean it. I'm *not* sorry I came. We're good." He kisses me to prove it. "Okay? We're good."

A kaleidoscope of butterflies takes flight in my belly, and when I lock the door behind him, I'm calmer than I was when I chased after him.

It doesn't make it any easier to go back into the living room and face my mother, though.

First, I fix my dress. It's beyond mattering, but at least it makes me feel a little more put together.

Well, until I enter the room, anyway. My mother's standing by the couch now, which is good because it means she probably couldn't hear what Reid and I said in the hall, but is bad because now she has a direct eyeline to what had previously been at her feet. "Your panties are on the floor, Lina."

"I'm using them as a cat toy?" So much for feeling like I had this handled.

I scoop them off the floor and wad them up in a ball, but then remember I don't have any pockets and have nowhere to stash them, and since it feels weird and wrong to just have my panties in my hand while my mother scolds me, I end up stuffing them inside a box of tissues on the coffee table and hope to God I don't forget about retrieving them later.

When I turn back to face her, she's wearing a mournful look. "I didn't realize you weren't a virgin anymore."

My hands fly to cover my face. "Oh, my God, I want to die."

"I always thought you'd tell me, Lina."

I drop my hands, surprised that this is where she started the conversation.

Maybe it shouldn't be surprising. I used to tell her everything. We were always very open about sex and my lack of experience. She even passed along some of her favorite books with spicy scenes to me. She knew I was ready to have it happen.

"I would have told you. But…" But she met Samuel, and it seemed like our relationship changed, and I couldn't tell her things like that anymore.

My mother picks up a different reason behind that *but*. "But it was *him*."

Him as in Reid, which is true too. I couldn't tell her about him.

She sits down on the sofa, and I immediately plop down at her side. "I'm sorry. I'm sorry. I'm so, so sorry."

Not sorry enough to stop seeing him, but sorry that it hurt her.

But she surprises me again when she puts her hand on my knee. "Why are you sorry? Do you think I'm mad?"

Uh..."You told me *not him*. At Christmas. Anyone but him."

She rolls her eyes, as though her meaning should have been obvious. "Well yes, because it's very inconvenient, and this makes things difficult on many different levels, and I really hoped you would think about that before starting anything with a man that could make your life—and mine—very complicated. I was trying to protect you." She reconsiders. "Protect *us*. If it was still possible."

"That's fair. Just..." I stare down at my lap, trying to explain how it happened. "It was already started. Before we even knew who the other was."

"Angela thought there might be something going on with you. Said she thought she caught you in a heated moment."

"Angela told you about...?" I really need to stop being surprised by things. "And you didn't say anything to me?"

"I told her she was crazy because you would have told me. So when I saw you together at Christmas, I thought there was a chance that it was all on his side."

A completely different perspective starts to emerge as I imagine my mother's point of view. "Oh. He probably seemed like a creepy predator to you, then."

"It crossed my mind." She glances down at her hand still on my knee, and her ginormous wedding ring. "I recognize the hypocrisy considering the fact that I'm married to a much older man, but I don't know Reid, personally. What I do know is what Samuel has said about Reynard, and honey, it's not good."

"Oh, Reynard is the devil, but that doesn't mean that Reid is the same." I shift to face her better, nudging her hand off me as I do, sort of on purpose because it rankles me that she would automatically blame Reid for his father's shit. Especially when Reid has had to deal with so much of that shit himself.

"You're right. It doesn't, necessarily. Though children learn from somewhere."

"Not Reid, Mamma." I take a deep breath before I get too worked up. "He's not like his dad. He's decent and good, and I wish I could tell you that what's between us is nothing and mean it because I know this is complicated, but..." There are paragraphs of things I could say, but none of it feels like enough.

My mother finds the short way to say it. "But you love him?"

"Yeah. I do." It's a relief to say it out loud. A bigger relief to get to say it to the person who knows me best in the world. "I don't know if he feels the same, but he feels *something*, and we like being together, and we can't stay apart when we try, even though we know that it causes problems, which is why we've kept it secret while we try to figure out what's going on between us."

"No one knows?"

"Adly." As soon as I admit it, I know I need to explain. "She found out. I didn't tell her on purpose. I wanted to tell you."

"Oh, baby. I'm sorry you didn't think you could." She opens her arms for me, and dammit. She's my mom.

I fall onto her shoulder, and of course I'm weepy because good moms make it easy to be vulnerable. "I'm a big baby. I don't know why I'm being like this. I'm actually really happy."

"I can tell."

I laugh, which helps shorten the cry. When I sit back up, I start to go for the box of tissues but remember my panties are in the box at the last minute so I just wipe my face with my sleeve like a four-year-old.

"It isn't that I didn't trust you," I tell her, realizing it needs to be said. "I didn't want to put a strain on your marriage."

"It's true, I can't tell Samuel. I won't tell him."

Immediately, I feel guilty. It's one thing for me to have to face backlash because of who I want to be with, but it's not fair for her to have to face it on my behalf. It's also not fair for her to have to keep my secrets from her husband. "You don't think you could help him see that Reid isn't like his father?"

"I don't think it's that easy. He looks at any of those kids, and all he sees is..." She trails off, her gaze off in the distance.

When she returns her attention to me, she seems to have made a decision. "Okay, I realize this is hearsay and doesn't take into account Reynard's version of events, but Samuel told me it goes back to Sonya."

"Samuel's first wife?" I force myself not to lean forward, but damn if I'm not eager to hear the tea.

She nods. "All three of them grew up together, but Samuel dated her a bit. It was casual for her, more serious for him, and then he went away for a few months to work with his father in Europe, and when he came back, Sonya was pregnant, and—this is where the story differs, depending who tells it—she told Samuel that Reynard had raped her. No proof to the fact, but—"

"You believe women. Yeah, me too." After everything

else Reid has told me about his father, it almost seems predictable.

Heartbreaking too.

"Poor Sonya never got over it. Reynard had good lawyers and good connections, and Sonya knew she couldn't press charges and win. She ended up spending some time in a mental health facility trying to deal with it, and that fucker used it as an excuse to get custody of her kid when he was born as well."

"Hunter? Oh." My stomach churns as the pieces fill in. "That's fucked up."

"It is. Samuel loved her, though, and he married her, and that meant he was constantly faced with what Reynard did because Sonya wasn't the same woman she'd once been. It didn't matter what Samuel did, he couldn't fix what his brother had done—of course he couldn't—and Sonya was very unhappy for the rest of her short life.

"And yes, Samuel's wrong to pass that burden of blame onto Reynard's offspring, but Samuel is human, and that is something he'll have to come to terms with in his own time."

It's the first moment I've really gotten the sense that my mother and Samuel have something special. I've tried not to think their relationship is all about sex and security—fine if that's what she wants, but I don't need to think it—so it's comforting to discover there is an intimacy as well.

For her sake, I try to grant her husband his humanity and see it from his perspective. "I suppose it doesn't help that Reid is always doing fuckey shit for his father. That can't have helped Samuel form any other opinion."

"Like when Reid brought Samuel's ex to our wedding as his date? No, it doesn't."

"Not of his own will. I promise."

She shrugs. "It worked out fine. To be honest, I enjoyed showing off my ring to someone who thinks she deserved it more."

"You were so nice to her!"

"Kill them with kindness, they say."

I had no idea my mother was such a petty badass. I'm impressed.

But then I'm back to thinking about the dilemma of me being with the man I love. "So what would happen if Reid and I ever wanted to be together…openly? Would you have to choose between me and Samuel? Would I be banned from family events? Would I ever get to see you?"

She looks like I've slapped her. "Yes, you'd see me. I'd never choose my husband over my own child. You are my world, Emmalina. Banned from family events? Not a chance. Not if he expects me to be there as well. Now there may be more difficulty getting Samuel to let Reid into his house, but we'll figure it out. We wouldn't be the first family that had to deal with tension over Thanksgiving dinner."

When she says it like that, I feel kind of foolish for ever thinking otherwise.

Then again, there are other aspects that don't seem quite as simple. Reynard, for example, does not have a history of making things easy for anyone. There's also my job. "Do you think Samuel would fire me from working at SNC?"

My mother considers before she answers. "I suppose he might. He doesn't like the idea of Reynard having any access to the company at all. But do you really care if you don't work at SNC?"

It's funny, because I hadn't really thought I had any other choice. Or maybe it just seemed like the easiest choice because it was in fact a choice, and without it, I have to figure out what to do with my life instead, and that feels so daunting.

Given encouragement to think broader, though, I mull it over. "It's really good money. But in all honesty, I don't need that much."

"You have a rich boyfriend now. Let him take care of you."

"Mamma! That's so anti-feminist."

"Please. Feminism means options. I choose to be taken care of by a man, and I'm very happy about it. If that's not your pathway, so be it." She reaches out and tugs on my braid. "You don't need his money anyway. This house is yours—it's why I was coming by. I finally got the title signed over for you. It's in my purse. Officially no mortgage payments. Denny offered to pay you rent—accept the offer. That should give you some income without SNC. You'd have to stop splurging on UberEats, but if you're good with your budget, you can take your time to decide whatever you want to do with your life."

She's giving me a gift. So why does it also feel like she's cutting the strings?

"But all Sebastians work for the company."

"You aren't a Sebastian. You're a Quinn." She bops me on the nose with her finger, and I've never felt so grown-up and little girl at the same time. "Unless Reid is planning on putting a ring on that finger of yours…"

"No way. Uh-uh. I'm not… Nope. And Reid's not anywhere close to…" My face is hot with denial. It feels crazy that she'd even say something like this. I know she got married in a whirlwind, but I'm only twenty-freaking-one years old.

Then I remember this is what she always does. "This is why I can't tell you things. You start planning grandbabies.

Remember how you used to imagine all the kids I'd have with Denny?"

She lifts one shoulder in a shrug. "I like babies."

I reach down for my new kitten, who I'm pretty sure just peed, if the puddle nearby is any indication. "Here. Donovan Desmond is yours for the doting. Get used to loving on him because I'm really good with my birth control."

She smiles as she takes him from my hands. "Donovan Desmond. You're too cute for words."

"Isn't he?" I just gave him away, and already I want him back. I haven't had a chance to properly smother him yet.

Mamma rubs her face in his fur, the same way I did, then gives me a sly grin. "He gave you a cat, Lina. I think the boy loves you."

Once again, I'm beaming. Reid's not even here, and he makes my cheeks hurt. It's embarrassing, and I try to divert her attention from the sun trying to break through my face.

"You know who *I* love?"

I hug her, in case the answer isn't obvious.

But my smile lingers because of Reid, and for once, I'm happy to admit that my mother usually tends to be right.

CHAPTER TWENTY-EIGHT

REID

Nothing sends my blood pressure up like walking into Spice on a Friday afternoon and discovering the alarm isn't on.

The security team that walks the building would have notified me if it had been off all night, but none of my staff is due in for another several hours.

I have my suspicions who it could be.

Cautiously, I make my way down the hall, my phone in hand, knowing that if I'm wrong, I might be about to be overtaken by a burglar. I'd almost prefer that to the alternative.

Sure enough, my office door is open, and my father is sitting behind my desk, reading last night's closing reports like he cares about the numbers.

Before making myself known, I shoot a quick text to Lina.

Don't come by. Dad's here.

She still has almost an hour before she's off work, so hopefully she checks her texts before showing up. We've been extra careful about our meet-ups since her mother caught us last weekend. We cut out sex in the living room and stopped our midday rendezvous in the women's locker room, which used to be how Lina spent many lunch hours.

In some ways, though, I've felt more relaxed than ever. Giulia's and Adly's support has made this secret easy. I've gotten comfortable. I forgot my father has access to almost every part of my life. What if he'd shown up here an hour later?

We're going to have to rethink meeting at the club.

Right now, there's my father to face. He never shows up without wanting something, and he never wants anything simple.

"Don't know how I feel about you in my chair, Dad." That's a lie. I know how I feel. I loathe it.

He doesn't acknowledge me with a greeting. Doesn't even look up from the report. "It's Kaya's name on most of these. You don't close the club yourself anymore?"

No, because I like to leave as soon as the rush is over so I can have a few hours in Lina's bed before she has to wake up for work.

"Paperwork and till-balancing aren't the best use of my time." He isn't going to give me my chair back, so I plant myself in the guest chair. The seat is lower than mine on purpose—so I can intimidate whoever is sitting there. It's the first time I've been able to see how well the tactic works. "There a reason you stopped by? Four o'clock on a Friday. I expect you on the golf course by now."

"Tee time is tomorrow." His smile is stiff, as though he doesn't use it enough to quite know how to pull it off.

Not that I've never seen him happy. Give the man a

victory, he grins like a wolf. That's a much different context, though. The kind of smiles meant to share humor or enjoyment with another person are rarely seen on his face.

"I might ask you the same thing," he says, without answering the question first. "It was my impression you don't need to open up until around seven."

The lie comes without having it prepared. "I've been coming in earlier. Easier to get ahold of vendors and other business partners during typical work hours."

"Mm." There's judgment in that single syllable, but his expression is stone. He wants to wait and dole his opinions out when he thinks they'll be the most impactful.

But I'm not interested in his games today. "So do you need something? Because if not, I should—"

Setting the report down, he cuts me off without apology. "Sam's wife."

He lets the statement hang, as if waiting for a reaction.

My stomach twists, but I practice matching my expression to his. "Giulia? What about her?"

"Our little wedding present didn't go as I'd hoped. Not your fault, I'm sure. Sam's clearly no longer interested in his Bunny. He's always practiced fidelity. I shouldn't be surprised he's continuing that with this new one." He leans back in my chair and steeples his hands together, a portrait of the perfect villain. "We'll have to start ripples some other way. We'll go directly to the wife."

I open my hands to the air, asking for more info. If he thinks I can guess the direction of his thoughts, he's wrong. My mind isn't that brutal.

"Get her attention," he says, clearly irritated that he has to spell it out. "Flirt with her. Fawn over her. Fuck her, if you have to. If you want to. Just make some waves."

I stare at him for a long, hard beat. I won't do it, of

course. Because of Lina. Because I'm *with* Lina, not just because Giulia's her mother. Turns out I'm a guy who practices fidelity, too.

The shit thing is that, if it weren't for Lina, I'm not sure I would have batted an eye. That's how this relationship has always worked, even before Spice. He gives me an order, and I jump. He raised us this way. He'll probably raise the next one this way, too. Another soldier in his army.

It makes me sick. Sick for all of us.

But having never said no to my father, I'm not sure how to even start.

So instead, I ask, "Why?"

"'*Why*?'" He throws the word back at me like it's a foreign language.

"Yeah. Why? Why do you need to create ripples in their marriage at all? Why not just let them be? Is Samuel fucking with your marriage? Did he send someone to try to get Nelani's attention? Are you retaliating against some move he made? Just…why?"

He squints at me, seemingly staggered that I have to ask the question, or maybe shocked that I dared question him at all. "Samuel took what's mine."

"Sonya?" Since Lina told me what she'd learned about Hunter's mother, I have new curiosity regarding my father's feud.

"No, not Sonya." He says her name like it's a bad taste in his mouth. "SNC. The news corp should have been mine. I'm the second eldest. Henry should have had the industrial division. I should have had the news corp. The other three should have been placed under us. It was going to be that way too, until Samuel fed Dad with bullshit and lies, and next thing I knew, I was seconding Henry while Sam took the helm at SNC in *my* place."

"You mean Grandpa didn't give you SNC because you raped a woman." Boldest I've ever been with him, but it occurs to me that Dad respects bold.

His jaw flexes. "You don't know what you're talking about."

"Then tell me."

"There's nothing to tell that you don't already know." He seems about to leave it there, then goes on. "That girl was fucked up before I ever touched her. She got herself knocked up, hoping that I'd marry her. When I didn't, she cried rape. You have to be careful with women, Reid. Nowadays, especially. A woman can change her mind and all of a sudden you're dragged all over social media. Anyway, Sonya came out okay. Bagged herself a rich man all the same. Not my fault that Samuel tied himself to that bag of bricks. He could never accept that he was a bad judge of character."

There's so much that he's said that is appalling, but perhaps the most horrific is his opinion that Sonya came out okay. The woman is dead, and if the rumors I've heard from my cousins are true, her death was at her own hand.

She very clearly needed help.

"She was the mother of your child, Dad. You should have done something for her."

"I did. I had her committed. I made sure she didn't have custody of Hunter."

"That's stuff you did *to* her. What did you do *for* her?"

Dad looks about to defend himself further, when he reconsiders. "Who's getting into your head about all this? Is it that woman's daughter?"

Panic floods through my veins like I've been administered the emotion through a fast-acting shot. There's no way he doesn't mean Lina. What other woman with a daughter would he be talking about?

I play dumb. "Who…?"

This time it's that wolf grin on his lips. The one that says he's triumphed. "You think I don't know what happens under my roof? You forget—the deed to this place belongs to me. You think I don't have my own system?" He points to the ceiling.

I don't truly understand his meaning, though, until he takes his phone out of his pocket and pulls something up on the screen before passing the device over to me.

There, in black and white, is an image of me and Lina. Caught in a very…*intimate*…moment.

The color drains from my face and the floor feels like it's disappeared from underneath me.

I scroll through his photos, seeing he has more than the one. More than a dozen. All taken at the club. All as scandalous as the first. I'm mortified on Lina's behalf. I'm outraged. These moments were private. These moments were ours.

As I keep flipping, I realize something else. The angles don't match the cameras I know about. The office security cam points at the door, not my desk. The one by the main bar is pointed at the register, not the counter.

Which means…he has his own surveillance system installed in my club?

Fuck.

And then the complete reality settles in—he knows.

He's known the whole time.

He knew, and he saved telling me until he could use it for manipulation.

I'd always thought my feelings for my father were indifferent, but I was wrong. I hate him. I hate him so much that I wish he were dead.

But he's not. He's right here, right in front of me, with images that could humiliate my girlfriend and an array of veiled threats.

"What is it you want from me?" I ask, trying not to let defeat sound in my tone.

"I want you to fuck Samuel's wife the way you fuck her daughter. She's closer to your age anyway, I think."

I taste bile in the back of my throat. "Or what?"

"I think you know."

The photos are embarrassing, but there isn't real leverage there. Neither of us are married. We're not really cousins. The age gap isn't that unusual. Lina's of age. He could release them, but they aren't interesting enough to the public to get the traction my father needs to blackmail me. We'd have to endure an initial tabloid scandal, but I could hire someone to scrub the internet, and they'd be gone in the blink of an eye.

The real threat he has is the same one he's always had—my club. He'll take Spice.

"Why?" I ask again. "For revenge? Fuck her and then what after that? You send Samuel the pics? And then what after that? You cause strain in their marriage. Maybe they get divorced. You won't get SNC. That ship has sailed."

He waves his hand dismissively. "Hunter will get SNC. Don't worry about that."

"Then what's this for? Just to be mean?"

Abruptly, he stands and pounds a fist on my desk. "I don't have to answer to a piece of shit deserter. You think you're so much better than everyone else that you should get to skip out on putting in the hours for the family business? The rules are the rules because then everyone gets the same deal. You want to build something else? Then you wait until you get your trust like your brothers and your cousins. You don't get to jump the line."

I'm familiar with his raised voice. I'm used to his demeaning remarks. I'm even well acquainted with his bitterness, though it hasn't ever been pointed so vehemently at me.

I've been numb to it, until this moment. Now it feels like an anvil bearing down on me, and I can't wait three years to be free of its burden. I won't.

One thing I have to know first. "If you felt that way, then why did you ever step in?" I never asked him to buy the club. He offered.

That wolf grin returns. "Because it was an opportunity. And what I learned from the time I put in at the business is how to tell the good opportunities from the bad."

I process his words. "I was a good opportunity because you knew you could use me however you want and hold that deed above my head the whole time."

"Looks like you learned something now, too."

I look around the office, taking in the space with the eyes of someone about to lose it. So many memories. I grew up in this office. Figured out how to be an adult. Did the work, despite my father suggesting the job was cake because it was one I'd chosen. I made something here.

It's funny because I'd never realized how much I loved it until this moment.

Because it's *mine*.

Whether the deed said so or not. Spice was born from my tears, sweat, and blood. My soul is in this club, and I didn't know how much losing it would gut me. It *will* gut me.

But the alternative is...what? Lose Lina? Lose who I am?

Spice was all I was before her, but she's helped me see I could be more. She makes me want to be more.

There's no contest.

I get to my feet and pull my wallet from my back pants pocket. "Actually, I learned more than you realize, Dad. You own this place. I've only ever been the face of it." I take my key card from my wallet and throw it down on the desk. Then my Spice AmEx and Mastercards. Then my stack of business cards that falsely say *owner*. "That means Spice is your responsibility."

For the first time ever, my father looks scared. He doesn't know shit about how to run this place. Kaya and the other managers can handle things for a while, but eventually Dad will have to step in. He'll hire someone, in the end, but it's fun to think about him scrambling in the meantime. Especially when he has to try to explain what happened to me, the supposed owner.

He doesn't seem to be as amused. "Don't be so fucking impulsive."

"You've held it over my head so long, I've actually had a lot of time to think about it. I've realized that, if you'd loaned me the money outright like I wanted instead of insisting everything be through your shell company, it would be my name on all the credit reports. Thanks to you, I can truly wash my hands of it. It's all yours, Dad. I quit."

Then I walk away from the one thing I ever loved and head toward the woman that I love far more.

CHAPTER TWENTY-NINE

LINA

I walk into my tiny cubby of an office from a department meeting at twenty minutes before five, only to be met at the door by Adly.

"I didn't tell him anything," she says, before I can offer a greeting. "Swear to God. He just called me and asked if I knew anything about you and Reid, and I said, 'No, what about them?' like I was totally in the dark, and then he said he was on his way down to talk to you, and he asked me to join him."

I don't need to ask who she's talking about. The only He that matters around here is Samuel Sebastian.

There are a lot of other questions on the tip of my tongue, though. It's a lot to process, and fast. Thoughts of seeing Reid after work were all that kept me going through the last-minute staff meeting, which was tedious as hell, since all we talked about was the same static image for an hour and nine minutes straight. Worse, I left my phone behind so I couldn't stealthily scroll during the bore-athon either. I practically skipped back to my office when it was done.

Now, I'm in full-blown panic. "He's coming *here*? To *my* office? Now? And he knows? How does he know? He's going to fire me. That's why he sent you, isn't it? Unless he knows you know. Does he know you know? What am I supposed to do?"

Adly rubs a calm circle on my back. "First, you're going to take a second and breathe."

While I do, she stacks the magazines, reports, sticky notes, and doodles that litter my desk into an orderly pile. Then she directs me to my chair, and fluffs up my hair and uses a tissue to wipe at the corner of my lip.

"Yogurt?" she asks.

"Are you kidding me? That's been there since lunch. No one bothered to tell me?" I'm about ready to dig into my purse and find my phone so I can use my camera as a mirror, but I hear Samuel's voice asking where to find me.

"I'll go meet him," Adly says. "In the meantime, keep breathing."

She leaves, and despite her instruction, I stand and almost follow. My office is too small. There are two chairs besides mine, but it's cramped, and not suited for meeting anyone important. Perhaps it would be better to move down the hall to one of the meeting rooms.

Except, those all have glass walls. I can imagine the whole art department lining up outside to watch us, not that that's something they usually do, but they absolutely could. Especially if they thought something gossip-worthy was happening, and Samuel venturing down to our offices is gossip-worthy even when he isn't here to fire his only stepdaughter.

I sit back down.

At the last second, I remember Reid. I pull out my phone from my purse in the bottom desk drawer, planning to tell him I'm going to be late, but see a text from Twilight across my screen.

Don't come by. Dad's here.

I don't have time to wonder if it could be a coincidence because when I look up, Samuel's in my doorway with Adly right behind him.

"Oh. Hi. Um. Hi." I throw my phone back into my purse, stand up, and shut the drawer with my foot. "I was just…ordering a Lyft. The streets were icy coming in, and I slid a bunch on the way in, even in my sneakers—I wear those for coming and going and change into my heels when I get here since they aren't the most professional. Though, I do have to say, they look pretty cute with this particular outfit. Tennies with skirts is kind of in right now, but anyway, I thought I'd splurge and take a car instead of mass transit. So that's why I had my phone out during the workday. Because it's only like, ten minutes before it's time to go. If you think I should wait until exactly five o'clock—"

Behind her father, Adly makes a cutting motion with her hand at the level of her neck, which I think means I'm babbling.

But then I don't know how to wrap up or even what I was saying anymore so I just leave it there, in the middle of a sentence.

Samuel stares at me for a second. Then, as if I haven't said anything at all, he says, "I apologize for catching you at the end of the day on a Friday, but I have something urgent to discuss with you."

My stomach drops. I'm surprised it could still sink since it pretty much hit the floor after Adly told me what was up.

"Sure." My voice sounds too high. "Do you want to…?" I scoot out from behind my desk to offer the nicest chair to him.

He glances around my office and spots the nook with the extra chairs, which isn't immediately visible from the doorway because of the cramped layout. "No, stay. Please. Adly and I can take these."

"Uh. Oh. Okay."

He shuts the door, then I watch as one of the most powerful men in the world perches on a cheap, barely padded stackable office chair. He looks surprisingly graceful and not as out-of-place as I'd expected. With Adly at his side like this, it's the first time I've really noticed how much she resembles her father. Not in her appearance so much as in her countenance. She learned how to carry herself from him, or she inherited a gene. Or maybe she just grew into herself, and I'll be just as poised as she is one day.

Or I might have been. After this meeting is over, it's possible I'll be too humiliated to ever recover.

Once we're all seated, Samuel doesn't waste any time before jumping in. "I just received an interesting call from my brother, Reynard."

Reynard called Samuel? All my hair stands on end.

"He wanted to inform me about a potentially scandalous situation involving you and his youngest son, Reid. Are you aware—?"

The door swings open, interrupting Samuel's speech, and speak of the devil, it's Reid. Reid who has never once come to the SNC offices to see me. Reid who diligently makes sure that we are never seen together in public. Reid who looks breathless, his cheeks full of color, as if he ran all the way up several flights of stairs to get here.

"Lina, I'm in love with you."

I open my mouth, but nothing comes.

"I am," he continues from the doorway, as though he didn't expect me to say anything anyway. "I'm fucking in love with you, and my father? Fuck him. Fuck him for everything he's ever done. Everything he's ever made me do. He threatened to take Spice again, but you know what? I quit. I handed him my key card and my credit cards, and I walked out, and I love my job, Lina, but I don't fucking care about losing it because I love you. *I love you.*

"And it will be hard—for me, mostly, since I've only ever lived this lifestyle, and I haven't had a chance to dream of any future besides this one—but I swear it will be worth it. If you're by my side, I don't need anything else, and I don't even know if you feel the same way, but I'm praying you do. Because you are what matters, Lina Quinn. Nothing else. I don't need anything from the life I had before. I only need you."

Is there such a thing as blissful chaos? Because that's what's going on inside my head and heart and, damn, every part of me. A whole bunch of emotions and concerns but all of them doused in this simple declaration. It feels a lot like rainbows on a stormy day.

It's also shocking, to say the least. His appearance here, his announcement. His rambling that sounds more like a speech I'd deliver than one I'd expect from him. And I'm like a thousand percent sure he has yet to notice I'm not alone, but too stunned to point it out.

And then he's going down on one knee—

Immediately, I jump from my seat and find my voice

"Oh my God, get up!" I tug him to his feet. "I'm only twenty-one. Only twenty-one!"

I'm beaming, though.

And clutching onto his button-down shirt like he's the only thing in the universe.

"I don't even have a ring," he admits. "It was impulsive. I just…I want you with me, Lina. Whatever that looks like. If you're not ready to talk about marriage, I'll wait. I don't need a label. I pretty much wrecked my whole world, and the only person I want to rebuild it with is you. I don't want to keep secrets anymore. I only want to keep you."

I have to blink a million times because I'm definitely tearing up. "I want to keep you, too."

"You do?" His relief is palpable.

"Yeah. I do. I've loved you for a while now. Wasn't it stupid obvious?"

"I guess I didn't know what it looked like."

I cup his face and would be three seconds from going full make out with him if I didn't remember that this very intimate scene has taken place in front of witnesses.

Also, Samuel chooses this moment to clear his throat.

Reid turns his head toward the sound, and when he registers his uncle's presence, his face goes white. "I didn't realize…"

Adly quietly grabs a tissue off my desk and dabs at her eyes.

"We were just wrapping up a meeting," I explain.

Samuel had been trying to say something, and I know I should apologize for the interruption and let him resume the floor, but the thing is, I'm generally more impulsive than Reid. I usually consider it one of my messiest character traits, but after seeing how romantic and swoony impulsivity can be—or maybe because his bravery is just contagious—I'm suddenly moved to make my own rash decision.

"Actually, Samuel." I lace my hand in Reid's as I turn to face my stepfather boss. "I'm so grateful that you embraced me into your family and gave me this job and a wonderful opportunity that I would never have had without you. And maybe it's impertinent to jump to this when I'm pretty sure you're in the middle of firing me, but I don't think this place is the right place for me. And I know that you said that Sebastians work for the company, and I might be losing a place in this family because of my choices today—a place in your family. Not my mother's, because she'll always love me—but I'm not a Sebastian." I look at Reid. "Not yet, anyway. I'm a Quinn. And I'm still figuring out what it means to be a Quinn, but I don't think I can do that in a space that doesn't have my heart."

I turn to address Reid. "I'm sorry. Maybe we should have talked about that first? I suppose it isn't the best idea for us to both be jobless at the same time, but—"

He squeezes my hand. "We'll figure it out," we say in unison.

"My God, they're perfect for each other." Adly grabs another tissue from my desk.

Samuel's expression remains stoic as he stands. "I'm sure you're planning to turn in a resignation to Adly with appropriate notice given."

"Yeah, yeah. Of course." Since this was all spontaneous, I was planning no such thing, but I can take a hint.

"My children are required to work for the company in order to be eligible for their trust fund. As you have stated, you are not officially a Sebastian, and whether or not my father would have made the same generous gift to you, I can't say. That's not my business.

"As for why I came down here today, it seems my question has been answered. My brother's call had me concerned that there was impropriety on Reid's part, but it seems this relationship is consensual. On a more urgent note, he mentioned there might be compromising photos?"

"Photos?" My eyebrows crease as I glance up at Reid.

Reid turns to me, his face animated, and I've never seen him rush so fast to speak. "I didn't know anything about it, Lina. He had cams installed. Throughout the club. He saw…"

He trails off, but I can fill in the blank. I was there.

I feel the color drain from my face. "Oh. Wow."

I put my hands on my thighs and bend over, trying to breathe. A slideshow of memories plays in my mind. Images of all the things we've done in that club. All the things that Reynard has seen.

I'm officially a porn star.

For my stepuncle.

It's not breathing I'm having trouble with—it's my stomach. I might puke.

Reid squats so he's eye level with me, a firm hand resting on my back. "He suggested he'll release them if I didn't do more of his shit, but I promise that what he wanted was even worse than those pictures. It was the last straw, Lina. I had to walk out. But I swear on Grandma Adeline's grave, I'll do whatever it takes to get those pictures taken down. Whatever he does with them. I'll get lawyers. I'll hire web scrubbers. Whatever it takes."

"Okay. I trust you." I mean it, too.

And honestly, what's a little skin on the internet anyway? Maybe home porn can be a backup method of income. Just kidding, but also, I'm open to being open-minded.

"Actually, this is where I come in," Samuel interrupts.

"How so?" Reid stands, and I follow suit, leaning on him for support since I'm still a tad unsteady.

"I'd hoped that was a ruse on Reynard's part. It was, in part. He'd suggested you were behind them, surely trying to put a wedge between the two of you."

Get in line, Reynard. You aren't the first to try and you aren't the first to fail.

Samuel turns to his daughter. "Adly, can you get them in touch with Scott?"

She nods, understanding. "Scott is in charge of cleaning up PR crises. He'll be able to direct you through this. I'll reach out immediately. If we're on top of it, they may never be seen at all."

It's astounding how contagious her reassurance is. I'm immediately relieved.

"Make sure they aren't. I'd hate for Giulia to have to see those." Samuel buttons his suit jacket. "That takes care of my agenda. I'll let you get to your weekend."

I exchange glances with Reid and Adly. *That's it?*

He's still in the doorway when I call after him. "Wait a minute, Samuel?"

He swivels his head back toward me, and I can't tell if his expression is irritated or bored, but I'm not sure if I have anything to lose by pissing him off or not because he's barely shown any reaction to all of this, and I kind of need to know. "So you were only here about…the pictures?"

"It would cause trouble at home as well as for my image in the media. We try to run a wholesome network here."

"Then were you planning to fire me?"

"For the pictures? No. We've had plenty of employees involved in these kinds of scandals. We wouldn't have half our employees left if termination was our standard practice."

"No…for…" I glance at the man next to me. "For loving Reid."

Reid wraps his arm around my waist, tugging me close.

Samuel glances at his watch, impatient to leave. "I hadn't known about this…*affair* of yours. So of course I had no plans regarding news that I've just learned."

Is he being purposefully obtuse? He sure seems to be avoiding the question. "I am trying to find out if this means you're okay with the two of us being together. Even though he's Reynard's son."

Samuel frowns. "It was my impression you didn't accept a proposal. I'm optimistic that this will run its course before it gets that serious. In the meantime, I'm confident that Reid won't cause any trouble that will upset your mother." He peers down his nose at his nephew. "Will you, Reid?"

"No, of course not." His teeth are gritted when he smiles.

"If there's nothing else…?" When no one says anything, Samuel leaves.

"He said not to upset my mother," I say when I'm sure he's out of earshot. "He didn't say anything about not upsetting him."

"You read my mind," Reid says.

"He's kind of a prick, isn't he? Sorry, Adly. Not as big of a prick as Reynard, but still."

"Most all of them are assholes," she says. "Our generation is trying our best not to follow in their footsteps, aren't we, cuz? Fantastic grand gesture, by the way. Chef's kiss." She kisses her fingertips and then opens her hands to the air. "I've got to get to calling Scott, but I'm definitely calling you later so you can fill me in on a whole bunch that I seem to have missed."

"Thanks, Adly." I wave after her then turn to Reid. "Actually, I think there's a lot I need to be filled in on, too."

He circles his hands around my waist. "And we kind of need to make a plan for what's next."

"We should probably both say I love you a bunch more times too, because I think I really like both saying it and hearing it."

"We should definitely be fucking some of those times that we say it."

"Does it count when you say it during sex? I'm still new to all of this."

"It doesn't count if you've never said it. But if you have said it, and you mean it, I hear it counts double during penetration."

"Wow. So much to learn." I throw my arms around his neck. "Should we bang one more time at the Sebastian Center since it seems we might not have this luxury in the future?"

He considers. "I think I'd rather fuck you in a bed. Besides, Donovan Desmond is likely missing his parents."

We kiss though, and say I love you a few times, and when we finally leave the office, we walk out proudly together, our fingers laced for the whole world to see.

CHAPTER THIRTY

REID

The door to Lina's room swings open, and she appears with Donovan Desmond following, carrying a glass of milk and a single plate stacked high with carbs and sugar. "Pancakes for dinner!"

So it's not my usual meal choice, but she's so fucking adorable with batter on her neck and syrup on her shirt sleeve, already trying to reduce our spending by cooking herself instead of ordering in. I wouldn't dare complain.

I am curious about the button-down she's wearing, however. It's oversized and sexy, but it's not mine, which makes me wonder who the fuck is giving her shirts to lounge in?

It's definitely on my agenda to find out.

Right now, though, I finish up my text to Kaya and hit Send. While Lina cooked, I filled Kaya in on some basics of the situation, not because I'm still worrying about the club but because she's a good woman who doesn't deserve to have a bunch of shit piled on her with no explanation. Hopefully, she'll get a raise out of all this, though if she decides to walk out, I wouldn't blame her, and might even cheer her on.

Now I'm officially and forever off the Spice clock.

It's a wound that's going to hurt for a while, but I'm starting to be able to see past it.

I toss my phone to the nightstand and make room for Lina to climb in bed with me. "You want me fat and happy, don't you? Spoiled too. I thought you said it was gross to eat in bed."

"Gross to eat in *your* bed. I didn't know what yours had seen. I'm comfortable with the DNA on mine." She curls a leg up under her and hands me the milk before she sits in the spot I made for her. "And don't get all judgey about my pancakes. Not only are they whole grain and full of fiber, but I also added protein powder because I knew you'd say something about the carbs. We can't afford meat at every meal if we're living on a budget.

"Actually…" She bites her lip and gives a guilty smile. "Protein powder is super expensive—all supplements are. Good health is for the privileged. It's a fact—but I stole this container from the family locker room at the Sebastian Center. We aren't getting kicked out of there, are we?"

"Pretty sure my last name is still Sebastian."

"Then the gym is going to subsidize your protein needs. And you don't have to give up your fitness routine, because gyms are expensive too. Look at us. Adapting already." She piles her fork with pancake and lifts it toward my mouth. "The syrup is low sugar and made from natural maple, too. So fuck off about being fat and happy. You can be happy and still keep your ten percent body fat, if that's what you want."

I swallow before answering. "That's really good." A little sweeter than I'm used to, but I take a sip of milk—

which turns out to be almond, thankfully—and the taste combination is perfect. "Really good. You're amazing, did you know?"

"Mm." She takes a bite of her own. "Like, would you say you love me for my pancake making skills?"

"I love you for your pancake making skills. I love you for thinking about my fitness routine. I love you for finding ways to max our budget."

"I love you for saying that." Her grin is infectious. Like how sunshine spreads across the sky as it rises for the day.

She holds out another bite of pancake, but she's the one I want to eat up.

"Uh-uh," she says. Either she can read my mind or my expression gave away my wanton desires. "We have things to work out. And you need fuel. I need fuel, anyway. Brains run on carbs, you know. They aren't as evil as you think they are."

"I'll let you explain that to my trainer." I take the plate from her hand and pass over the milk. "Oh, shit. I don't get to keep my trainer anymore, do I?"

"Add it to the spreadsheet. I'm guessing it has to go, but we'll see."

We shuffle things again—she sets the milk on the nightstand and takes back the plate so I can grab her laptop off the floor. Since we were working on it earlier, the screen opens to the Google sheet she started on her phone on the ride home from the Sebastian Center. There had been a short debate about whether or not we should spend the funds on ordering a car considering we were now both without jobs, but she allowed it when I told her my driver was salaried and had already been paid for the week.

Hearing that, she suggested we should give him at least two weeks' notice and use him as much as possible during that time. Not that either of us have anywhere to be now, but I'm sure she's already started a list somewhere with all the places we can take a car until his last day.

Lina sidles up next to me as I enter the cost of my trainer onto the budget sheet. She feeds me another bite of dinner and then—after pausing to coo over Donovan Desmond destroying a roll of paper towels that is mysteriously just sitting on the floor—Lina frowns at our new expense total. "Yikes."

"I could sell my condo." After losing Spice, every other loss feels minor. I was barely at the condo anyway. My best memories there had been the ones shared with her.

"We don't necessarily need it, but…are you sure? What's the mortgage payment?"

I add it to the expenses, and her eyes practically pop. "Yeah, maybe you should sell it. Will you make anything? You said it was a ten-million-dollar condo."

"I've only owned it a couple of years and with the recent market downturn, I'm pretty sure we'll come out about even."

"But at least we won't have that mortgage payment." She slips another bite into my mouth. "I love you because you keep saying *we*, by the way."

"I love you for trying to keep my condo that I really don't care about." I wipe out the mortgage payment from our expense column, and the total goes back to a much less scary—though still scary—number.

She points to another digit on the screen. "What's that?"

"What I currently have in my bank accounts."

She stares at me, then at the screen. Then back at me. "Jesus, Reid. We're rich. This will get us through years. Decades."

"Are you kidding me? This is…this won't last more than a couple of months. At most."

"Oh my God. We're fine." She shuts the laptop and returns it to the floor on her side of the bed this time.

This time I'm the one staring at *her*. "You clearly are out of touch with the cost of living."

"You clearly are out of touch with what's essential and what isn't."

"This house is old. What about repairs? The utilities will go up with another adult living here, as well as groceries, clothing, and healthcare now that we don't have insurance."

"Oh, right. I forget people your age have to see the doctor more." She smirks and sets the pancake plate on the nightstand.

I pretend she isn't delightfully amusing. "Not to mention saving for future expenses. Weddings aren't cheap. Honeymoons. If we start a family, we won't have room for Denny, so there goes rental income."

"The bride's mother pays for the wedding—which will be years away—and you might not know this, but my mother married into money so that's taken care of. Grandpa Irving will let us honeymoon at Pier Point, I bet. The other room on this floor is a perfect nursery. But I'm not going to be ready to have kids for at least a decade, maybe longer. Can you even still make babies when you're that old?"

I reach over and tickle her since I know it drives her crazy. "Men can make babies well into old age, so trust me. As soon as you say I can knock you up—" I snap my fingers. "Instant baby."

"Okay, Mr. Super Sperm." She laughs. "Never mind that it's only some men who can have babies in old age and that research shows most guys also have a biological clock ticking, but I'm sure we'll be fine."

"I am not *some men*. We'll be fine." If my Dad is still able to have babies in his late sixties, I'm not going to worry about my forties.

Then she turns serious. "You're not really worried, are you? You're going to get a job. We'll have more income. You know most people live paycheck to paycheck, right? We're way ahead of that. You still might have your trust fund, too."

"You're right. You're right." It's just a lot of unknowns. The kinds of unknowns I've never had to worry about.

Grandpa is the biggest unknown of all. I'll have to tell him the truth soon about Spice, which I'm dreading. I know it will be better if I explain before Dad does, but I want to do it face-to-face, and Grandpa's currently at his Florida house until next week. It will give me some time to prepare what to say, at least. I've already accepted that my inheritance will be taken away since I broke all the trust rules.

As for a job…"I know this is an opportunity to clean the slate and maybe change my career, but I already know what I want to do."

She turns toward me and props her head up with her elbow. "What?"

"Own my own nightclub."

"Yeah? I love it."

It's a lot of money, whether I start one myself or buy one, and maybe that's why I'm so anxious about our bank account balance. Because I know that's a long way down the line, possibly never, with our current situation.

But I have some ideas. "I can start out managing. I was thinking about Hudson Pierce—he has a great nightclub that his wife runs with another woman. They both have young kids. Maybe they're ready to turn the place over to someone else."

"Right, because women can't still have careers when they start families."

"That's not what I..." I trail off. She keeps me on my toes, this one. Definitely makes sure I treat women fairly. "Well, not that then. But I have a great resumé now. Awards under my belt. Maybe Pierce would want to open another location. If not him, another investor might see my value, especially if I'm not as stubborn about what I expect from a business relationship."

She runs her fingernails across my stubble. "I think it's a great idea."

"Do you love me for my great ideas?"

"I love you so much for your great ideas."

Fuck, I love this woman. "What about you? Any thoughts about what you want to do?"

"Oh, I was going to take care of Donovan Desmond. Be a stay-at-home cat-mom." She stretches and rolls to her back. "No, seriously. I was thinking I can finish cleaning out my old room upstairs and turn it into an art studio of some sort. I don't know exactly what I want to sell. Maybe a patchwork of things. Decorated book edges. Fan art. Original sketches. I'm not very fast at creating so I'll probably have to supplement my income with a quote unquote real job. Part time, at least."

She swivels her head toward me. "Do you think we have a future in porn?"

"Fuck, no."

"No?"

"No one sees my baby girl come but me." I'm kind of eager to see her come right now. I roll over so I'm on top of her, supporting my weight on my hands by her head.

"No one but you and your dad, it seems."

"No, no, no." I shake my head vehemently. "I'm going to pretend you didn't put that thought in my head." It's already there, though, and I rest my forehead against hers, heavy with regret. "I'm sorry I didn't protect you from that."

"I appreciate it, but I'm fine. He's a creepy old man and that icks me out, but I'm happy with how everything's turned out, and like I said...if this is the start of a new career..."

I reach under her shirt and pinch her bottom. "Uh-uh. Not a chance." I undo her top button, half expecting she'll stop me for some other thing we haven't worked out, but she doesn't. So I unbutton the next. "Whose shirt is this?"

"Mine."

"It's a man's dress shirt." I continue to undress her.

"It looks like a man's dress shirt. It's a nightgown for women who want to pretend they have boyfriends or something. At least, that's why I bought it."

"I'll give you one of mine." *I love you wearing my clothes.* I don't bother saying it because now her shirt is open, and I'm too busy loving her naked. "You were downstairs making pancakes with no panties?"

"It's a long shirt. Denny had no idea." She unbuttons my cuffs before working the button at my collar. After she gets a couple undone, I pull my shirt overhead and toss it to the floor.

"Careful of Donovan Desmond."

"He's fine," I say, without looking. Spotting the pancake plate, I reach over and drag the tip of my finger in syrup so I can drip it onto her nipple. Then I suck her pointed tip into my mouth. "It's really good syrup."

"Fresh from a bottle," she says, but her voice is sultry

and her breath catches when I follow suit with the other nipple.

Part of me wants to go downstairs and find that bottle so I can drip it all over her body and lap it all up.

But my cock is a fucking steel rod in my pants and it's aching for her warmth with an urgency that supersedes creative foreplay.

Lina appears just as eager. She claws at my belt then pulls her nightshirt off her arms when I work on getting my pants off.

When we're both completely naked, I suck my thumb and reach down to rub her clit. "I love you for being on birth control," I tell her. "Because I love getting to feel you with nothing around my dick."

"I love you for putting your dick inside me without being a total tease."

I'd laugh, but my mouth is preoccupied with kissing her while I continue to taunt her with my thumb. My cock joins the action, sliding up and down along her wet slit. "I love you for being mine. For waiting for me—even though you didn't know you were waiting for me. For giving me this pussy. Letting me own it."

"I mean, I did have to practically beg for you to take it. Some things never change." She bucks her hips up underneath me. "Come on. I'm dying here."

She grinds against me, and this time, I move a hand to her hip to keep her still. I line myself up at her entrance and shove into her abruptly.

She cries out at the sudden intrusion.

"Shh." I brush my thumb across her lips and then move my hand to her throat. Under my palm, I can faintly feel her heartbeat. It's an anchoring pulse. A steady ba dum, ba dum, ba dum.

The feel of her around my cock is overwhelming—every goddamned time—and I have to breathe so I don't come too early. All the women I've fucked, it never felt this good once. With Lina, it just gets better and better and more consuming every time.

When I have a hold of myself, I rock in and out of her following the rhythm of her pulse. Slow at first. Speeding up with her excitement until I'm too distracted by the intensity of her gaze.

"What are you thinking?" I ask, wanting her every thought to belong to me. It's fucked up how I stopped things with her that first night because I thought she'd try to turn us into something special, and I'm the one who is now addicted to every single part of her. I'm the one who thinks she's the most incredible person to walk the planet. I'm the one secretly afraid she can't possibly feel the same way about me as I feel about her.

"I'm thinking you're right," she says.

"Of course I am." In. Out. She clenches around me. "About what?"

"It counts double when we're fucking."

I have to think for a second before remembering that's what I said earlier about saying *I love you* during sex. "But I haven't said it."

"I can feel it, though. Can't you feel it, too?" She wraps her legs around my waist, drawing me closer. Deeper.

"Does it feel like your chest is expanding and being crushed all at once?"

She nods. "Like nothing matters but what's between us. Like this is the only thing that's easy, even when it's hard. Like no one could ever understand, but you do, and I do, and it's the best secret, and it's only ours."

Yeah. Yes.

My spine tingles at the base, and I take another breath, not ready to come yet.

I move my hand from her throat, lace it with hers and do the same with the other. Stretching them over her head, I kiss her softly, and then really say it. "I love you."

When she says it back, I know we're going to be just fine.

CHAPTER THIRTY-ONE

REID

"Wow," Lina says, as we step into the lobby of Grandpa Irving's Park Avenue apartment building. "This place is incredible."

"You should see it in the daytime."

"I can imagine. All the light coming through those windows…I'd want this place too. If I had a billion dollars."

"Several billion dollars," I correct. It's literally Grandpa's building. He owns the entire thing, not just the penthouse, and like everything he owns, it's pure luxury from top to bottom.

Though he has houses all over the world, this Manhattan space is the one I've been to most over the course of my lifetime. I can almost smell Grandma Adeline's perfume the second we walk inside, even though she's been dead now for years. It's a place that gives me the immediate feeling of home.

Usually.

Today, my stomach is too knotted to feel anything but dread.

It's been almost two weeks since I was forced to quit the club, and I'm finally facing the man I'm most scared to face. I've been dragging my feet, but Lina insists I can't stall any longer because there is no good subway stop around here, and we only have a hired car for another day.

How a person can be so practical and so quirky at the same time is beyond me, but I love her for both.

After checking in with the doorman, we head to the penthouse elevator. I hesitate before pushing the call button. A vivid flashback of the time I came here to ask Grandpa for permission to open Spice fills my mind. I thought I'd been nervous then, but today my anxiety is tenfold.

Back then, the worst thing that could happen was that I'd be told no. Today, the worst thing has already happened —I let my grandfather down. No matter how he reacts, I can't take that back, which means the worst thing has already happened, and I have never felt like such a piece of shit in my life.

Needing her strength, I reach for Lina's hand, but it's only in my grasp for a few seconds before her phone rings, and she pulls away.

"Adly," she says, when she sees the caller ID.

"Call her back later." There's a good chance she's calling to make sure I haven't backed out of coming clean to Grandpa. She's been on my case along with Alex.

The day after everything went down, I called and told him everything. He'd already left a handful of texts asking why I wasn't at the club on a Friday night. He hangs out at Spice so often, I couldn't get away with keeping him in the dark. Telling him wasn't as hard as I know it will be to tell Grandpa, but Alex definitely hasn't made it easy. Not because he's been exactly mean about it, but because he hasn't stopped laughing.

"What kind of a fool makes a deal with Reynard Sebastian?"

It's a fair question. One that I haven't been able to answer, which is probably why I've put off seeing my grandfather for as long as I have. If Alex wants to know, Grandpa Irving will certainly demand to know, and I'm still not sure what I'll say when he does.

Disregarding my appeal—and despite the fact that we're already five minutes late—Lina answers Adly's call.

"Hey, we're at Grandpa's now," she says.

I roll my eyes and point to my watch, but she ignores me, and I spend the next few minutes listening to Lina's side of the conversation, which mostly consists of acknowledgments of whatever Adly is saying.

Strange, considering how Lina can often dominate a conversation with her rambling thoughts, and the longer it goes on without much from Lina's side, the more curious I get.

By the time she hangs up, I'm itching for information. "Well?"

"Get this." Her expression is animated and her eyes bright. "She called to tell me that Alan—Alan is the Art Department manager. Well, assistant manager, technically, but I rarely worked with the other guy, so Alan's the one I think of as being in charge. No shade to the other person. What was his name? I can't remember, but anyway. Alan told Adly that the market reel that I developed had been through several test groups now. Remember how I spent forever working on that and then it didn't go anywhere? Well, it only felt like it went nowhere because they were doing all the testing, which I guess is a really long process sometimes, and—"

"Lina. Get to the point, baby." I'm very much aware of how long we're making Grandpa wait, but even more, her excitement has me dying to find out where this is going.

"Oh. Sorry. Um, it performed well! Like really well. Alan said it got reactions from a demographic they've previously been unable to target, and the feedback they got was super useful.

"But that's not the best part! The best part is that Adly told Holt and Holt reached out to this guy he knows who runs a marketing firm—Donovan something. I only remember his first name because it's like Donovan Desmond—"

"Kincaid," I say, biting back a laugh. Who the heck doesn't know Donovan Kincaid?

"That's it! And his wife, Sabrina, runs the marketing department there, and Adly sent over my reel to her because Sabrina said she was looking for someone to work on stuff like that, targeted at Gen Z, and long story short—"

"Too late."

She gives me an adorable sexy scowl. Not sure she means the adorable or the sexy part, but everything she does is adorable and sexy. "She wants to hire me!"

"You got a job?" I'm not surprised. I'm fucking proud as hell.

"It's only part-time, but it has benefits, and it's working in a real corporate office, and it's not a nepotism job—I mean, it's kind of a nepotism job, since it was Adly who reached out to people she knew, and I probably wouldn't have been considered if she wasn't my stepsister. So that's a total nepotism job, isn't?"

I put my arms around her waist. "You got it on merit. You deserve it. I'm so—"

"Wait, that's not all, Reid." She leans back and slams her

palms on my chest, dramatically. "Adly also showed some of my artwork to a friend of hers who wants to hire me to design the edges of one of her favorite books, *The Secret History*. She's going to pay me for it. And I haven't read that book, so I'll have to read it first, and that means I'm basically getting paid to read a book, Reid, it's the dream job, there is no other dreamier dream job."

"You got *two* jobs?"

"Two jobs!" She's glowing and, fuck, I think I might be glowing too with how infectious her excitement is.

I'm jealous, too. I'm not going to lie. She's joked that I need to find employment soon because she thought she'd be jobless forever. Now here she is, ruling the world, and I've barely put together a resumé.

"You're next, old man," she tells me, as though she knows exactly what I'm thinking.

"Thank you, and I love you for reading my mind." I kiss her, quickly. "But before I can move forward, we have to..." I point up.

"Have to go see Grandpa. Yep." She pushes the call button, then takes my hand and the second her fingers are threaded through mine, it's like all her confidence and energy is transferred through osmosis, and I'm a much stronger person when I step into the elevator.

The ride is smooth, and short. Before I know it, the doors are opening into Grandpa's foyer. His assistant, Elias, greets us quickly, as though he's been waiting for us, and considering how late we are now, he definitely was.

"Thought you got lost," Elias says, with the familiarity of family, since he's worked for Grandpa so long, he's practically one of us. "Doorman called up to say you arrived almost fifteen minutes ago."

Lina raises her hand. "Hi, that's me. I'm the problem.

Got a phone call in the lobby that I had to take. Well, I didn't have to take it, but I'm glad I took it. I got two jobs! Also, I'm Lina. I don't think we've met yet. Unless you were at my mom's wedding, and I never saw you or I don't remember you, in which case, I'm super sorry, and I'm really embarrassed, and I promise I won't forget you this time. Also, this place is amazing, and we're only in the foyer."

Elias grins—it's impossible not to around Lina, I swear. "I was there briefly, but we never had the pleasure, unfortunately. I'm happy to make your acquaintance now, and any other time, I would offer a tour, but you're expected in the library at the moment."

"Library?" Lina's eyes are as bright as a kid going to Disneyland.

"Not that kind of library." There are a fair amount of books on shelves that will likely catch Lina's attention, but *library* is really code for *Grandpa's Gambling Room*. "Thanks, Elias. We'll see ourselves in."

The nerves are back now. Lina finds my hand, and together we walk through the living room to the library, where sure enough, the large TV is playing a NASCAR race and Grandpa Irving is seated in an oversized leather chair, yelling at the screen. "The outside! Run the outside, you mother fucker. Ah, goddammit, caution flag already? Elias, what did I have the odds on—"

He cuts short when he sees us. "You're not Elias. Where's my remote?" He finds it immediately in his lap and hits the mute button. "Reid. You were supposed to be here an hour ago."

I check my watch. "We'd said seven, didn't we?"

"It's twenty minutes past, and if you're on time you're late, so I assumed you'd be here at six-thirty." He doesn't sound angry or annoyed. Just regular old Grandpa, who is crotchety but full of heart. "Well, you don't expect me to stand up, do you? Come in. Sit down. This accident is going to take a minute to clean up anyway."

We start toward the couch, and that's when Grandpa seems to notice I'm not alone. "Ah, Lina's with you."

Instinctually, I let go of her hand. Too much time keeping secrets, I suppose, and as soon as I let go, I immediately wish I had it back.

At ninety-six, the man still has the eyes of an eagle. "Don't need to let go of her hand on my account. You two a thing now?"

I start to answer but then he addresses Lina. "A bit old for you, isn't he?"

"Is he?" She squints at me as though she's never considered our age difference. "I actually hear age gap is on trend right now."

"Wouldn't know. Can't keep up with the trends like I used to." He shifts in his chair so he's angled toward us. "Is it serious? Are we planning another wedding soon? Reynard has to be right pissed about this." He chuckles. "I like it."

"No wedding," Lina says.

"Yet," I add.

"I'm only twenty-one. Too soon, but I assure you we are as serious about each other as you can get without an engagement ring—we have a cat together."

I lower my head so she can't see me laughing.

"And Reynard is *right pissed,*" she continues. "If that means really pissed, anyway. I've never heard that term before, but he's definitely not happy is my point."

"Good enough." Grandpa points to the couch. "Sit down. I don't like talking up to people. Reid, you have something you wanted to say to me? Make it quick, before the race starts back up."

As if I wasn't feeling the pressure already. "Okay. Uh. Yeah. So." I lean forward and brace my hands on my thighs. "I want you to know that I am so appreciative of the opportunities you have given me. I recognize that you believe in fairness and rules and tradition, and allowing me to—"

"Ya da, ya da, ya da. This is boring." He makes a circular motion in the air saying to hurry it up. "Where's this going?"

Fuck. I had a monologue prepared. "Well…" I look to Lina who gives me an encouraging thumbs-up.

"Don't thumbs him up. He's dragging this out." After chiding Lina, he stares at me. "You're here about Spice, right? You want to tell me your father's held the deed all this time, and you walked out. Does that about sum it up?"

How the hell does he know?

I exchange another glance with Lina. "Alex," we both say in unison.

"Yeah, Alex. He filled me in on the recent shit. Your dad being a dick and pushing you to quit. Honestly, I'm surprised it took this long. But I knew it was Reynard who invested pretty much from the beginning."

"From the beginning?" I'm dumbfounded. That was years ago.

"You were renting space on my property. The money came in from some LLC I didn't recognize. Of course I did the research on the owner." Grandpa places his hands on the arms of the chair and stands up. "Rey probably thought he covered his name, but he forgets I taught him how to do that."

I stand too, because when Grandpa stands, that's what I

was taught to do. "I don't understand. You knew all this time. Why didn't you say anything?"

It feels familiar. Like how Dad knew I was with Lina and decided to wait until he could use the information against me before he told me.

But Grandpa isn't like Dad. Not the Grandpa I know, anyway, though stories go that he was a different man when he was younger. Brutal. Hard. Cutthroat. A man who succeeded at all costs. That's supposedly the kind of person he was when he was raising his kids, which explains why my father and my uncles are not the nicest people in the world.

Maybe Grandpa's really still that man underneath, and I just haven't seen it.

I brace myself for the consequences that type of man will inflict.

Instead, he shrugs. "Why did it matter?"

"Because I broke the rules. Because I lied to you."

"Rules, shmules." He waves his hand dismissively. "Look, kid. You know why I set up the trust funds the way I did? Because I realized too late in life that I'd raised a pack of greedy, entitled, narcissistic pricks. Adeline and I decided things needed to be different for your generation. I was the boys' example growing up. How could I expect them to do any better with their own kids when they had everything handed to them? It was me who fucked them up. I needed to be the one to make sure you guys weren't just as fucked.

"So I require you to work for my companies, where I can watch what you're doing and see how you perform. That way I'm sure you learn ethics and responsibility and hard work before you get your inheritance handed to you on a platter. Sure you got your money from your father, and yeah, you twisted the rules, but you still learned. On my turf, too. The way I like it. Made good money from your rent as a bonus. What else mattered?"

I run my hand through my hair, wiping sweat off my brow as I do. "I just…I don't know what to say, Grandpa. I thought…"

"You thought I was going to be pissed? What…" He chuckles. "Did you think I was going to take away your trust? Come on, Reid. That place is a high-end success. You proved yourself just fine."

He crosses to a round table with papers and miscellaneous items—his betting station, as he calls it—and starts rifling through the stacks. "Your father, though… He's a problem. He'd run Spice to the ground if we gave him the chance. For spite. Which would be a shame."

I don't know if I should agree or explain my reasons for quitting or ask for his advice.

While I'm thinking about which route to take, Lina jumps in. "It would be, Grandpa. But not to be a tattle—"

"Go ahead, tattle," Grandpa says, then immediately changes his mind. "Actually, I don't want to know. I don't *need* to know. He probably threatened you. It probably had to do with Samuel. Whatever. It's not going to be an issue. I've already taken care of it. Ah. Here it is."

With a manila envelope in hand, he walks toward me. "Rey agreed to sell me the place. At a bargain, by the way. Already started the paperwork. The deed should be in my hands in a couple of weeks. You and I can negotiate a decent sell price in a few years when you get your trust."

It's a lot of information, and I've barely processed any of it when he hands me the envelope. "This is yours. If you want it."

Lina sidles next to me to watch as I open it. Inside is my

key card to the club along with all the other items I dropped on my desk when I officially quit.

There's a golf ball sized lump in my throat. Even if I had words, I couldn't speak.

"He wants it," Lina says, eagerly. "I mean, maybe he changed his mind, but I think he wants it."

I clear my throat. "I want it." It's so generous, and I don't deserve it, but I want it with every part of my soul.

"Of course you want it. It's already yours." Grandpa claps me on the back with surprising strength for a man his age. "Do me a favor and freshen those business cards up. They're not up to Sebastian quality."

"Oh! I can help with the design," Lina offers. "Wait. I didn't mean to assume. Or put pressure on you. I can apply like every—"

I wrap an arm around her, pull her close, and burrow my face in her hair. "You're hired." Forever and always, as far as I'm concerned.

"Three jobs!" She would probably do a full on cheer if I wasn't holding her so tightly. "Hold on—I am getting paid for this, right?"

God, I love her.

"Because I know I teased about it, but I really do want to be a girl who carries her own weight financially. Does it count as me carrying my weight if you're the one paying me?"

"It counts," Grandpa and I say at the same time.

"Don't forget you have your own trust to look forward to," Grandpa continues.

"Uh, I'm. Wait. What?" She looks at me then back at Grandpa.

"You're a Sebastian. I take care of my grandkids."

"But I'm not working at SNC anymore. I'm not sure if you knew that, so I want to be clear."

"You come from good stock, Lina," he tells her. "I'm not worried about your work ethic. I'm definitely not worried about your entitlement."

"Oh, wow. I don't know what to say." She wipes a stray tear off her cheek. "Everything I've read about you said you had a reputation for being ruthless back in the day, but all I've seen from you is the most generous heart, and it really is true not to believe what you read on the internet."

Abruptly, she pulls away from me and tackles Grandpa in a hug. "Thank you for everything. And for what you've done for Reid. I'm so lucky to be part of your family."

In all my life, Grandpa's generosity has never extended to being touched. Even Grandma Adeline loved with a hands-off approach.

Yet after a stunned few seconds, he returns Lina's embrace. Awkwardly and briefly, but it's going down in the family history book all the same.

"Thank you, Grandpa," I say when their moment is over. "I can't tell you how much I appreciate this."

"Good. Don't. I can't stand that mushy bullshit anyway." He turns his back on us, returns to his chair, and picks up the remote control, a not-so-subtle cue that he's ready for this encounter to be done.

I can take a hint, but there's something I need to know. "Grandpa, how did you get Dad to sell?"

He gives me a look that says, *Are you kidding?* "I'm not dead yet, kid. My son knows very well I could still change my will."

"He's gotta be so pissed," Lina says, grinning.

I make more of an effort to hide my smile. "It's going to be awkward at family events."

"He'll act like none of this ever happened." Grandpa points his remote control at me. "Because that's what I told him to do, and he does what I say."

There's a glimpse of the man who raised my father. No wonder Dad thinks the way to parent is by keeping his kids under his thumb. I can't decide if I should appreciate Grandpa's methods or not, but I am grateful for how this situation has worked out.

He moves the remote back toward the TV. "Track's cleared." He turns up the volume, and I know from experience, we're already gone, as far as he's concerned.

Still, I offer a goodbye. "We'll let you go, Grandpa."

Taking Lina's hand in mine, we turn to go, and I'm surprised when he calls after us. "Don't tell your cousins you got away with this. Let them discover for themselves whether they're brave enough to break the rules."

"Got it, Grandpa," I call back.

"Hope your car wins," Lina adds.

By the time we're back in the foyer, she's fretting. "Was that the right thing to say or is it bad luck to say nice things like in theater when you say break a leg instead of good luck? Should I have said something like get a flat tire, or—"

I tug her into my arms, and cut her off with a kiss.

And not one of those chaste kisses either. The kind that might make Elias uncomfortable if he's lurking around the corner somewhere.

"I'm not sure what that's for," she says, when I let her breathe. "I'm not the one who bought Spice for you."

Fuck, does she not get it? "I'd still be my father's subordinate if it weren't for you. Would still be carrying the burden of that secret. Would still be just getting by, putting everything into the club but never really getting to love it because of all the fear and guilt surrounding that arrangement. You changed everything."

"Well, when you put it that way…I am kind of awesome. You should probably reward me somehow. Take me to a bookstore or get me another cat or—"

"Fuck you in the elevator?"

"Reid! Grandpa is just in the other room." She blushes, but she also pushes the elevator button. "You know, everything's changed now. We have so much to figure out. Do we keep the condo? Do we sell it? It might be nice to have it since we both have jobs in the city. I have so much better space for my art in the brownstone, though. But we get to keep our car service."

All my hopes for an inappropriate quickie on the way down are dashed. "You're going to insist we discuss it all before you let me in your pussy, aren't you?"

The elevator doors open, and when we step inside, she throws her arms around my neck. "I love you for knowing me so well."

"Yeah, that's what I thought." Bad news for the semi happening in my pants.

"But also, didn't Grandpa Irving just encourage us to break the rules?" She reaches over to the panel, her eyes wide with anxiety and mischief, and when I nod, encouragingly, she pulls the emergency button. "Oh my God. I did it. I can't believe I did it. I mean, we've already banged for the camera so I guess this is nothing. Hurry, hurry. Before we're caught."

She lifts her dress and pulls down her panties as she talks, and I reangle the security cam and get my cock out faster than I ever have in my life. With her leg hitched around my hip, I thrust inside of her silky cunt.

Then I hammer into her over and over like a man with a mission.

It's hot and off-limits, pretty much like our whole relationship has been. We ignore the blaring alarm bell, as well as the voice that comes over the intercom asking if we're okay, too focused on each other.

"I love you," she whispers between giggles and moans.

I throw in a few dirty words, and an, "I love you more," and we both come in record time, just in time for the elevator to start again.

The doorman is there when we walk out of the elevator into the lobby, me sweaty, her glowing, the scent of sex clinging to us like cheap cologne. Lina rambles an unnecessary explanation, and in no time at all, we're out on the street waiting for our car.

"You think the doorman knows?" she asks, straightening her dress. "I don't think he does."

She's the most incredible person I know, the most beautiful woman I've met. Funny and charming and smart, but she's as transparent as a newly cleaned glass window. It's a wonder we ever thought we could keep our relationship discreet. Especially considering how much I want everyone to know how I feel about her. I'll shout it from the rooftops. Put a ring on it, when she lets me. Slap her with the burden of the Sebastian name, just so the world sees that she's mine.

But she looks so sure that we pulled our quick tryst off, and I don't have the heart to tell her.

"Not a chance," I say, and wrap myself around her, protecting her from the brutal February cold. "It'll be our little secret."

EPILOGUE

LINA

Five years later

"Come on." I tug at Reid's arm, pulling him away from the crowd that has gathered at Spice to celebrate his thirty-eighth birthday party.

It's maybe not the nicest girlfriend move since he rarely lets himself take a night off to just hang out with friends and family. Usually, he's on the clock, no matter what the occasion. Especially since he opened Spice BK in Brooklyn, only a few blocks from our brownstone home—both locations paid for free and clear with his trust fund money.

We're downtown tonight, but he usually works most of his shifts at BK. He says he wants to be closer so he can be a *present father,* though we're still not married—or engaged for that matter—and the only babies we have at this point for him to father are Donovan Desmond and his sister kitty, Anya. I think it's his way of hinting that his biological clock is ticking. He'd have knocked me up by now if it was all up to him, but he's not the only one with a career/home life to balance. Not only does my part-time job at Reach demand a lot of time, but my online art store has more orders than I can handle, and I'm going to have to quit something or hire someone or hire two someones—it's all good problems, and I'm still young. I have time to figure things out.

But I have figured one thing out.

A big thing, and I'm so eager to tell Reid that I can't wait any longer, which is why I'm stealing him from his own party.

Trying, anyway. "Reid? Are you coming?" I tug again at his sleeve.

Finally, he extracts himself from Holt's conversation. To be fair, the news network he co-runs is booming and so fascinating to hear about, and on any other day, I'd be begging him for stories myself if I didn't have another pressing agenda.

"Where are we going, anyway?" Reid asks, now that I finally have his attention.

"The courtyard. I want to give you your birthday present."

"I'm all for sneaking out for a quick fuck. Do I get to choose where I stick it in?"

Of course he assumes that my gift is going to be sex, because…well, it often is. And if it was what my gift was this time, then yes. I'd let him choose where to put it. We've been together now for five years, and in that time, the man has stripped me of every last speck of virginity.

If you ask me, we really could have a career as porn stars, but I'm just as happy to keep what we do between us. And the occasional stray security cam.

"I'm not giving you a quick fuck this time," I say,

pushing through the employee-only door to the outside courtyard where we first met on my twenty-first birthday. I laugh every time I think about that night now, how he was so dead set on keeping us string-free and anonymous.

Silly old man.

"It's going to be a long fuck? Maybe I should say goodbye to some people first."

"No, you sex addict." Laughing, I pull him to the bench where we first kissed. "I actually have a present. Like, in a box and everything."

He looks down at my empty hands—well, empty except that one is laced with his. "Lina, is my birthday present stuffed in your bra?"

"It wasn't there all night." Thank goodness, because it would have been awfully uncomfortable, and I wouldn't have been able to keep it hidden for that long because it sticks out and Reid can't go too long without a casual glance at my breasts.

Suddenly, I'm feeling nervous as I stick my hand inside my dress top and pull out the small square jewelry box. With clammy palms, I hand it over to Reid. "It's not wrapped, obviously, but that would have been weird. And scratchy, I think. There wasn't much room in my bra as it was."

His brows knit as he takes the box from me, and I can practically read his mind. Cufflinks. He thinks I got him stupid cufflinks. Or a tie pin. What other types of gifts do men get that come in a box this size?

That's what makes it such a great present. It's totally unexpected.

At least, I hope it's a great present.

My heart's a woodpecker in my chest, rat-a-tat-tat-tat-tat-tat-tat, as he lifts the lid and looks inside.

He stares for far too long, and when he looks up at me, his gaze is intense. "Lina, did you buy yourself a ring for my birthday?"

Doubt and insecurity overtake me, and I'm suddenly the awkward girl I was five years ago—as if I'm not still that same girl every day. "Ah, fuck. It's dumb, isn't it? I thought it might be cute, you know? Because you keep asking me, and I keep putting you off, and I know you know what kind of rings I like, so it wasn't about that, but I thought if I just went ahead and bought it—it's on your credit card, by the way—then it would be a kind of adorable way to say I'm ready, but you're right. It's not really a gift for you. It's a gift for me, and I thought, I thought it—"

In a blink, I'm in his arms, pressed against him, my words cut off with his kiss. "It's the best birthday present I've ever gotten. There's nothing I want more. Nothing."

"Really?"

"Yes, really. Yes. Yes."

"I think that's what I'm supposed to say," I joke, but he's not paying attention because now he's on one knee, and dammit, why am I crying? I'm the one who planned this. "You don't have to do this now," I tell him. "You can keep it for when—"

"Shut up, Lina. I've been waiting for this moment for years. Fucking years." He takes my hand, and I'm embarrassed to find it's shaking. "Baby, I love you so much. From the minute I first saw you, I think. And I know I thank you all the time for waiting for me, but it was really me who was waiting for you. All my life. Waiting for you to bring light into the dark shell of a life that I lived before you. Everything has been brighter since I walked out into this courtyard and found you talking to yourself like an adorable lunatic. Every day has been sunshine and dad jokes and weird animé and pussy cats." He smirks. "Lots of pussy."

My laugh puts a momentary pause in the tears streaming down my face.

"I've wanted to put this ring on your finger and make you mine for so long. Since that day I walked away from this place. You might have needed time to belong to me, but I have belonged to you ever since. You have my heart. Please, please, do me the honor…" He maneuvers the ring out of the box one-handed, without letting go of me because he's fucking amazing like that, and he slides the jewel onto my finger. "Of taking my name, becoming my bride, bearing my children, sharing my life. I will commit every day to doing my best for you. Emmalina Alessia Quinn, will you marry me?"

"I'm already yours, Reid Sebastian. But yes. I will so marry you."

He's on his feet in an instant. His hands cradling my face, he kisses me like I'm precious and new and everything, and gosh, I love him. More than I ever thought possible.

"I need to look at it again," he says, pulling away. "The ring. Is it what you wanted?" He takes my hand to study it. It's a two carat round cut diamond held by four prongs on a platinum band with a pavé setting, and it's stunning.

"If you're asking if I bought on a budget, I promise you, I did not. Do you like it?"

"I love it. You've never looked more beautiful." He brings my hand to his mouth and kisses it. Then, with the biggest grin I've ever seen him wear, he picks me up and spins me around. "She's going to marry me!"

I'm not sure who he's telling since no one's out here

with us, and the club's too loud for anyone to overhear, even with him yelling at full volume. But it makes my chest feel like it's going to burst with how happy he is.

"Do you want to go inside and tell everyone?" I ask.

"Yes." He sets me down and pulls me toward the door, then abruptly changes his mind. "No, actually. I do, but are you sure you don't want a quick celebratory bang first?"

I giggle. "Well, I mean, it is your birthday. But I should tell you—I've never had sex while engaged."

"Oh, so I'll be your first."

"Yep. And fair warning—I'll probably think it's special, and I'll remember it for the rest of my life. Do you think you can handle it?"

He kisses me again, a kiss that feels like a whole new beginning. "You know, Emmalina, I think this is going to work out just fine."

Want a bonus scene from Brutal Secret? Sign up for my new release newsletter and you'll receive a link to all my bonus material.

Reid's story is over, but you may be wondering about Alex and his unrequited love woes. His story is up next with **Brutal Arrangement**.

You can also find a Sebastian family tree on my website to clear up those pesky relatives and how they're connected.

Meanwhile, if you haven't met the other Sebastian men, there are plenty of stories to catch up on in this world. Turn the page to learn more.

WANT MORE SEBASTIANS?

Meet the Sebastians in a world of power, sex, secrets, and brutal billionaires

Check out the Sebastian family tree at www.laurelinpaige.com/sebastian-family-tree

Man in Charge - Scott Sebastian office romance, boss/employee romance, alpha billionaire, arrogant playboy heir, public spice,

Man for Me - Brett Sebastian billionaire romance, friends to lovers, office romance, he fell first, short read/novella

Brutal Billionaire - Holt Sebastian billionaire romance, imagined love triangle, boss/employee, forbidden, morally grey, alphahole, "good girl"

Dirty Filthy Billionaire - Steele Sebastian billionaire

romance, kinky, class differences, "you owe me", short read/novella

Brutal Secret - Reid Sebastian billionaire romance, forbidden, age-gap, curvy girl, forced proximity, first time, awkward heroine, obsessed hero, new adult, no third act breakup

Brutal Arrangement - Alex Sebastian coming soon

Brutal Bargain - Adly Sebastian coming soon

Brutal Bastard - Hunter Sebastian coming soon

ALSO BY LAURELIN PAIGE

WONDERING WHAT TO READ NEXT? I CAN HELP!

Visit www.laurelinpaige.com for content warnings and a more detailed reading order.

Brutal Billionaires

Brutal Billionaire - a standalone (Holt Sebastian)

Dirty Filthy Billionaire - a novella (Steele Sebastian)

Brutal Secret - a standalone (Reid Sebastian)

The Dirty Universe

Dirty Duet (Donovan Kincaid)

Dirty Filthy Rich Men | Dirty Filthy Rich Love

Kincaid

Dirty Games Duet (Weston King)

Dirty Sexy Player | Dirty Sexy Games

Dirty Sweet Duet (Dylan Locke)

Sweet Liar | Sweet Fate

(Nate Sinclair) Dirty Filthy Fix (a spinoff novella)

Dirty Wild Trilogy (Cade Warren)

Wild Rebel | Wild War | Wild Heart

Man in Charge Duet

Man in Charge

Man in Love

Man for Me (a spinoff novella)

The Fixed Universe

Fixed Series (Hudson & Alayna)

Fixed on You | Found in You | Forever with You | Hudson | Fixed Forever

Found Duet (Gwen & JC) Free Me | Find Me

(Chandler & Genevieve) Chandler (a spinoff novel)

(Norma & Boyd) Falling Under You (a spinoff novella)

(Nate & Trish) Dirty Filthy Fix (a spinoff novella)

Slay Series (Celia & Edward)

Rivalry | Ruin | Revenge | Rising

(Gwen & JC) The Open Door (a spinoff novella)

(Camilla & Hendrix) Slash (a spinoff novella)

First and Last

First Touch | Last Kiss

Hollywood Standalones

One More Time

Close

Sex Symbol

Star Struck

Dating Season

Spring Fling | Summer Rebound | Fall Hard

Winter Bloom | Spring Fever | Summer Lovin

Also written with Kayti McGee under the name Laurelin McGee

Miss Match | Love Struck | MisTaken | Holiday for Hire

Written with Sierra Simone

Porn Star | Hot Cop

ABOUT LAURELIN PAIGE

With millions of books sold, Laurelin Paige is the NY Times, Wall Street Journal, and USA Today Bestselling Author of the Fixed Trilogy. She's a sucker for a good romance and gets giddy anytime there's kissing, much to the embarrassment of her three daughters. Her husband doesn't seem to complain, however. When she isn't reading or writing sexy stories, she's probably singing, watching shows like Billions and HGTV design competitions or dreaming of Michael Fassbender. She's also a proud member of Mensa International though she doesn't do anything with the organization except use it as material for her bio.

www.laurelinpaige.com
laurelinpaigeauthor@gmail.com

Made in United States
North Haven, CT
01 May 2024